An Unwilling Accomplice

An Unwilling Accomplice

Charles Todd

HARPER **LUXE**

An Imprint of HarperCollins*Publishers*

AN UNWILLING ACCOMPLICE. Copyright © 2014 by Charles Todd. All rights reserved. Printed in the United States of America. No part of this book may be used or reproduced in any manner whatsoever without written permission except in the case of brief quotations embodied in critical articles and reviews. For information address HarperCollins Publishers, 195 Broadway, New York, NY 10007.

HarperCollins books may be purchased for educational, business, or sales promotional use. For information, please e-mail the Special Markets Department at SPsales@harpercollins.com.

FIRST HARPERLUXE EDITION

HarperLuxe™ is a trademark of HarperCollins Publishers

Library of Congress Cataloging-in-Publication Data is available upon request.

ISBN: 978-0-06-232644-7

14   ID/RRD 10 9 8 7 6 5 4 3 2 1

Again . . .
For John
With so much love
Now and always . . .

Chapter One

I'd just brought a convoy of wounded back to England, and as I walked into Mrs. Hennessey's house in the cool of early morning, I thought what a haven of tranquillity it was. Here I could put the war behind me for a few brief hours and perhaps sleep peacefully. We'd been too close to the heavy guns for weeks, turning even the pleasantest dreams into nightmares. My ears still ached from the incessant pounding.

I moved quietly toward the stairs so as not to disturb Mrs. Hennessey, but she popped her head out the door of her downstairs rooms to say, "Bess? My dear, welcome home! Will you be staying?"

Smiling, I said, "Only for three days. Too brief to think of going to Somerset. But long enough to catch my breath. It was a rough crossing, and my patients were seasick. As were three of the orderlies. Are any of my flatmates here?"

"Mary came in last week. I haven't seen Diana in a bit. She spends as much time as she can in Dover."

Her fiancé had been posted to Dover Castle, much to his chagrin, but Diana was very happy that he was needed there and not in France. I wasn't quite sure what it was he was doing, something in Intelligence, although I had a feeling that her amusing, offhand comments about his standing guard on the castle ramparts were designed to conceal just how hush-hush his real duties were.

Several of us had taken the first-floor flat in Mrs. Hennessey's house in the autumn of 1914 when we began our training as Sisters, for it was not thought to be proper for unattended women to stay in an hotel. It had become a second home for all of us, and Mrs. Hennessey spoiled us when she could.

"There's hot water for a bath," she was saying now, "and I'll bring up a fresh pot of tea after you've had a rest."

"That would be lovely," I said gratefully, and went on up the stairs.

Half an hour later, I'd no more than touched my head to my pillow when Mrs. Hennessey was at my door. I struggled up and went to help her, wishing she'd waited an hour or so before bringing up my tea.

But it wasn't a tea tray in her hands. It was a letter.

"This just came by special messenger, Bess, dear. I didn't like to disturb you, but it appears to be official."

It was from the War Office. But why would the War Office be writing to me?

I thanked her, and she waited anxiously while I opened the envelope and took out the single sheet inside.

I scanned the letter and then, dismayed, I read it again.

Looking up, I said, "Good gracious! I've been asked to attend a wounded man who is to receive a medal from the King. Buckingham Palace . . ."

"My dear, what an honor," she said, pleased for me.

"But there must be some mistake. I don't believe I've nursed this man. The name isn't familiar. Sergeant Jason Wilkins."

"Perhaps the Sister he wanted to ask is presently in France, while you're available."

It was possible. "Well, this is a surprise. I expect it means they'll extend my leave. The King's Audience isn't until early next week. I could have a weekend in Somerset, with my family."

"How nice," she said, but I sensed her disappointment. While she was pleased for me, it meant I wouldn't be here for several days after all. And she was lonely, a widow, with only a handful of old friends. The comings and goings of her young tenants was something she looked forward to, and she'd grown comfortable with us in the weeks and months that had become years.

I smiled. "Never mind. We'll have today and tomorrow. And then I must come back to London on Monday."

Her face brightened. "That would be lovely, Bess. I must admit, it's been dull with all of you in France."

The war had kept us busy for four bloody years. And now, when rumors of an end were spreading both in France and in England, the killing was still going on. Wounded and dying men were being carried into the forward aid stations without respite. And even when the fighting was finished, the guns silent, even then there would still be wounded to care for.

"Do you need to respond?" Mrs. Hennessey asked. "I could post a letter for you."

"It's official. They expect me to appear," I said. I tried to suppress a yawn. "It means having a fresh uniform," I added. "Those I brought home are not good enough."

"I'll be happy to launder them for you," she offered. "You must rest, if you're to look your best." Something else occurred to her. "What sort of wound does this young man have?"

"He's probably going to be in an invalid chair. I'll be asked to push it forward when he's summoned to the King to have the decoration pinned on his uniform, and then back to resume our place in the row."

"I've never seen the King," she said wistfully. "But I did see his late father, King Edward. And I saw Queen Victoria as well, on her Diamond Jubilee."

"Did you indeed?"

"Oh, yes, it was the most exciting thing. Mr. Hennessey took me to see the procession, and I remarked how small she was. Empress of India, and hardly up to my shoulder. I saw King Edward on his way to his coronation. Such a fine figure of a man for his age."

"Well, I shall tell you all about it," I promised. "Thank you, Mrs. Hennessey."

Before I could close the door, she added quickly, "Shall I send a telegram to your parents?"

"Yes, that would be nice." It wasn't necessary, but she was so eager to help that I couldn't say no.

Pleased, she nodded and then hurried toward the stairs. I shut the door and went back to bed.

It *was* an honor. The sergeant must have asked for me particularly. Usually an orderly attended the patient. But what mattered even more were a few days at home. As I sank back against my pillows, I smiled sleepily. Whatever the reason for my being chosen for this ceremony, it had extended my leave. And that was an unexpected joy.

Chapter Two

It was Simon who came into London to fetch me. He had a bruise along his jawline, still a dark shade of purple and blue. I glanced at it but said nothing. It wouldn't be the first time an overeager recruit had put more enthusiasm than ability into showing his mettle. Or some assignment in France had resulted in unexpected action.

He'd been a part of my life as long as I could remember. First as a young recruit who made his own life and my father's miserable for reasons I'd never been told. My father had, in his usual fashion of keeping his enemies close, promoted the rebellious youngster to the position of batman—an officer's personal servant. Out of that simple solution had grown a friendship that had endured much over the years, and resulted in Simon becoming one of the youngest Sergeant-Majors in the British Army. An honorary position usually won after years of service, I might add.

He now lived in the cottage just through the wood at the bottom of our garden. That is, when he was not off somewhere at the behest of the War Office.

As he set my kit in the rear seat, then opened the door for me, Simon commented, "Your mother has already seen to a fresh uniform. I was to tell you that before you asked to be taken round the shops today."

"Of course she has. I should have guessed. Will they be coming to London as well? My mother and the Colonel Sahib?"

"The Colonel is away. Your mother was making noises that sounded to me very much like decisions on what hat would look best."

I laughed. Rested, eager to see my parents, I was glad to be in Simon's motorcar, the bonnet pointed toward Somerset.

Simon glanced at me. "You look much better than the last time I saw you."

"Amazing what a little sleep will do."

He laughed in his turn, that deep chuckle that meant he was truly amused.

It was a long but easy journey to Somerset, and my mother was there on the steps to greet me as the motorcar pulled up. It was only for two nights—but I was at home.

I left Somerset very early on Monday morning, my new uniform packed in tissue paper in the rear seat of Simon's motorcar, to prevent it from being crushed. My mother, much to her disappointment, couldn't come. There was a new widow to call on, the wife of a young Lieutenant in the regiment that had once been my father's. The present Colonel's lady was at the bedside of her very ill sister, and Mother had volunteered to take her place.

According to the letter I'd received, I would have an opportunity to meet my patient, Sergeant Wilkins, in the early evening when he arrived in London, and then tomorrow I would escort him to his engagement at the Palace. His bandages would be seen to before he came down from the hospital in Shrewsbury, and my role was a ceremonial one, unless of course he had an unexpected setback.

King George was popular—a family man himself, he had guided us through the trying years of war, a quiet strength that had given all of us courage.

Simon escorted me to the hotel to call on Sergeant Wilkins. He knocked on the door, and we heard the patient call, "Come!"

We walked in to find him lying propped up in bed, his well-padded left leg a long hump under the coverlet, his right arm in a sling. A third bandage encircled his head. I couldn't see the color of his hair, but I thought it might be fair, judging from his eyebrows. His blue eyes were—for lack of a better word—troubled. I thought perhaps he was in more pain than he cared to admit, or perhaps the journey down from Shrewsbury had been harder than he'd expected.

"Hullo," he said, surveying us. "It's good to see you again, Sister Crawford."

"Sergeant Wilkins," I said in acknowledgment, trying to place what I could see of his face. "How are you this evening?"

"I'm well enough, thank you. The orderly who brought me down from Shrewsbury has gone to fetch our dinners. He left me as comfortable as possible."

We sat down in the only two chairs in the room, and I presented Simon.

"Sergeant-Major," my patient said, nodding. "A lot of fuss over nothing," he went on. "But it's good for morale, they tell me."

"Machine-gun nest, was it?" Simon asked.

"Yes. I tossed in a grenade, but they were still firing, and that was unexpected. I discovered later that the grenade was a dud. There was nothing left but to finish the task myself."

Small wonder he was being decorated for valor. Then I realized that Simon must have looked up the sergeant's record.

They talked about the war, and then an orderly, an older man by the name of Thompson, came in with a covered tray, and we took our leave.

Walking down the hotel passage to the stairs, I said, "I've dealt with so many wounded. It isn't surprising I should forget some of their names. But not their wounds."

"It's more than likely he was misinformed about the Sister who sent him back to the Field Hospital."

"Yes, that's true."

Many men were grateful to us for saving life and—sometimes more important to them—limbs. The only angry tirades I'd endured were when someone came out of surgery without a limb and blamed me for letting it happen. The men knew, of course, that I'd had nothing to do with the decision to amputate, but I was *there*, and their fear and shock were very real.

I'd taken a room of my own at The Monarch to be available if Sergeant Wilkins needed care, even though Thompson was staying in his room. But when I looked in on them before going to bed, he was quietly sleeping. And the orderly was sitting by the lamp, reading. He nodded to me, and I left without speaking.

The next afternoon, at the time appointed, I went down the passage to collect my patient.

He was ready, the parts of his uniform that had had to be cut away to accommodate his bandages skillfully pinned out of sight by the orderly.

I said after greeting Thompson, "I'm to bring him back here after the ceremony?"

"If you would, please, Sister. And he'll be in your care until tomorrow morning when the hospital sends someone to collect him. I'm to return to France tonight."

"Fair enough. His treatment schedule and list of medicines are all in order?"

"Yes, Sister. I've set them on the table there at the window. There are powders to help him sleep, as well. Shouldn't be any trouble. The Sister in charge at Shrewsbury asked me not to change the dressings, just to refresh the bandaging. But he'll need them replaced before he takes the train again. The orderly they're sending to bring him back will see to that as well."

We settled Sergeant Wilkins in his invalid chair, covering his legs with a blanket. Thompson helped me wheel him out to the lift and down to Reception.

A motorcar was waiting for us, and after we had stowed the sergeant safely in the rear seat, I wished Thompson well in France, then joined my patient. In no time we were arriving at the gates of Buckingham Palace, our papers carefully checked by the policeman on duty.

Wilkins gave me a wry, nervous grin. "The machine-gun nest wasn't this bad. I wonder if anyone has ever fainted from sheer anticipation."

"Not in my charge," I said briskly, with a smile.

We were through the gates and arriving at the portico where we were to alight.

There, red carpeted stairs loomed before us, and Wilkins said, "Oh dear."

But footmen in uniform were there to help him out of the motorcar, into his chair again, and to carry him up the short flight of stairs to the main reception hall.

Another, far more formidable, staircase met us there. Again, the Palace was well prepared. Unhappily they had had four years of practice. I followed the two tall footmen bearing the invalid chair and the sergeant, his face grim, to the landing and then to the top of the steps. Above us was a glorious painted ceiling, and enormous paintings surrounded us. But I didn't think Sergeant Wilkins saw them.

He hadn't expected this awkwardness, that was clear enough, but there was no way around it. One of the footmen leaned over and said something I couldn't catch as they set down the invalid chair.

The sergeant's face cleared, and he smiled.

Another man in dress uniform met us there, taking over from the footmen, giving us the instructions we needed before proceeding to an antechamber where we were to wait until all of the recipients had arrived. Around us were men on crutches, others using canes, and quite a few in invalid chairs like Sergeant Wilkins's. Most of them were accompanied by family members, and I wondered if any of the sergeant's family planned to attend. So far no one had come up to us.

I also saw a number of men and women in sober black, standing apart, a mixture of pride and grief in their drawn faces. They were to receive medals given posthumously to husbands, brothers, and sons. I felt a wave of sadness.

Wilkins was less nervous now, in spite of the grandeur of this room, and I cast a quick glance over his uniform and his bandages, making certain that everything was as it should be after the short journey.

Watching me, the sergeant said, "Do I pass muster?"

"Indeed you do. Quite handsomely."

The doors at the far end of the antechamber opened, and we were led into the Audience Chamber, where the ceremony would take place. It was a regal crimson and gold, intended to impress those who were to be honored, to show how they were valued by their King and Country. At a little distance from the throne, rows of chairs had been set out for the men who would be decorated, and a second section was set aside for family members. I found there was a space waiting for the sergeant's invalid chair, with a seat next to it for me. All the rows were soon filled.

We were given final instructions. I saw that I was the only Sister present, and I sat there quietly, waiting to stand behind my charge when the King entered. Sergeant Wilkins was trying to look around him without appearing to stare, and I hoped he was savoring the moment. Or was he looking for someone?

"Is your family here?" I quietly asked him. If they were coming, they were very nearly going to be late.

"Alas, no," he said briefly.

And then behind us the great doors we'd come through were closed, and in a few moments, the King walked into the room from another door.

He was in full uniform, his beard carefully trimmed, but nothing could disguise the circles beneath his eyes or the lines in his face. Instead of ascending his throne, as I'd expected him to, he stood before us with only his equerries and a handful of officers in attendance.

The ceremony moved forward with dignity, the announcements of name and award and a brief summary of the act of heroism were made clearly, the men stepping forward one at a time, spending a brief moment in private conversation with their grateful sovereign, and then moving back to the rows of seats.

When our turn came, I gently pushed the chair forward so that the sergeant was directly in front of the King. An equerry removed the decoration from its polished wooden box and passed it to the King.

He stepped forward, bent down without in any way embarrassing a man who could not rise and bow, and pinned the medal to the pocket of his blouse. Straightening again, the King spoke to Sergeant Wilkins.

"We hope your wounds are healing well? Are you in any pain?"

"They are healing, Your Majesty, and the pain is bearable. I look forward to rejoining my regiment as soon as possible."

The King nodded. "Your country is grateful for your courage and your fortitude. The Queen and I have visited so many hospitals, and we know the cost of this war. We wish you well, Sergeant. And a speedy recovery."

"Thank you, Sir."

The King turned to me. I wasn't expecting to be noticed.

"Sister Crawford. Remember me to your father. I have known the Colonel for some time, and he has served his country well in this war."

"Thank you, Sir. I shall be happy to tell him."

The King nodded, and I moved the wheeled chair back to its original place as the next recipient was summoned to be decorated.

Sergeant Wilkins cast me an interested glance, then turned back to the ceremony. Some twenty minutes later, the audience was over. The King was escorted from the room, and then the men turned to meet their families and be congratulated, touched tearfully by wives and mothers, hands heartily shaken by their proud fathers.

There was no family to congratulate Sergeant Wilkins, and so I said the words for them.

He seemed surprised, then thanked me. I thought he was tiring, sitting for so long in his chair, cushions notwithstanding, and as I began to push him toward the tall double doors, they opened as if at a signal, and someone was there to see to it that we were guided to the portico and our motorcar summoned from the queue.

It was not until he was settled in the rear seat and we were moving sedately toward the opening Palace gates that Sergeant Wilkins said, "I didn't know your father was a Colonel."

"He's retired from active service," I said evasively.

"But he's in uniform, he still serves his country. According to the King." He turned to look at me as we passed through the gates.

Everyone was in uniform. Even the wounded had special ones to wear while recuperating to show the world they had done their duty.

Still, even though my father—and Simon—had left the regiment, because of their vast experience both of them had been recalled to duty in 1914, ostensibly to help in the training of badly needed new recruits with no military experience. Of course it went far beyond that, although not even my mother knew precisely what either of them did. More than once I'd encountered Simon in France, when he was on some mission or other.

"Yes, he was very happy when the Army found a use for him, although I daresay he'd have been much happier if they'd sent him back to the regiment," I answered lightly. "I think he misses that."

Whatever my father—and Simon—were doing to help King and Country, it was kept quiet. They appeared and disappeared without warning, and I knew it was not something to be talked about.

But Sergeant Wilkins didn't say anything more.

We drove in silence to The Monarch Hotel, and there he was lifted once more into his chair and I wheeled him across Reception to the lift. Several people noticed us and there was a smattering of applause as we passed, an account of our afternoon having made the rounds.

The sergeant nodded his thanks, but I thought he would have preferred not to be such a center of attention. I'd found this to be true of many decorated men. They had done what they had done for their comrades, not for public acclaim.

The lift doors closed on us and he sighed with relief. "That was unexpected."

"I'm sure the hotel was pleased to have you staying here."

"I'm no hero," he said sharply. "What I did had to be done. And there was an end to it."

I didn't answer him. The lift doors opened, and we moved down the passage to his room.

When I got him there, he said, "Don't fuss. Please."

"Your bandages are fresh. There's a list of medications on the table. I'll see what you ought to be taking just now."

"Sister Crawford."

I turned toward him.

"Please. I have a few friends who would like to step in tonight. Nothing more than a brief word. If I take my powders now, and rest awhile, will you allow me to speak to them? I'm returning to hospital tomorrow, early. It will be my only chance."

"There's your dinner," I pointed out.

"I'm not hungry. I ate a very good breakfast and had an excellent lunch. Thompson saw to that. I'd rather just—these men were—I haven't seen them since I was wounded and left France." His voice cracked. "They recovered faster than I did, and they're sailing themselves in a matter of days. Surely you understand?"

I wasn't happy about this. Still, his wounds had healed well enough for him to make the journey to London. And there had been no one at the ceremony from his family. Perhaps seeing men he'd served with would be just the thing. Sometimes healing the body also meant healing the mind. *Something* was troubling him. It was in his eyes, in the lines about his mouth. And not just the grim lines of pain.

"There will be no drinking, no carousing."

He smiled wryly. "I give you my word. Besides . . ." He shrugged. "It's not a time for that, is it?"

With reluctance, I let him have his way. "I'll come back at nine o'clock, shall I, to see if you need anything. And to give you your last powder. I'll expect your friends to be gone by that time. You've a long day ahead of you tomorrow, traveling."

"Better still, leave the next powder by my cup. I'll take it after my friends go. You can trust me to do it right. God knows, I've been taking them long enough."

I had the briefest frisson of fear. He wasn't planning on doing himself harm, was he? The powders could kill, in the wrong amount.

As if he understood what I was thinking, he added, "I have every reason to live, Sister. I just have to heal first."

It was against the rules to let him take his own powders. And I said as much.

"There's your duty. I understand. All right, come in at nine o'clock if you must. I don't mind." There was resignation in his voice.

He'd been cooped up in hospital for months. And sometimes a little relaxation of the rules could give a patient a fresh start, renewing his belief in his recovery and his eventual return to duty. It was what so many of them wanted.

I warned, "If you're foolish tonight, you could set back your recovery by weeks. Months even. You've come too far to take that risk."

He said, his voice level and yet forceful, "A medal doesn't buy me a place on a transport ship. Only the doctor can do that."

It was reassuring. I took a deep breath. I was responsible for his welfare—but I was not his jailer.

I put the powder by his cup. Then I got him into bed, gave him his afternoon medicines, and handed him the book he'd been reading. "I'll leave the lamp on beside your bed. When the last friend says good night, he can see to it for you, if you like. If he's sober enough to find the door in the dark."

Sergeant Wilkins laughed. "They're not much for drinking. My friends. We've been through too much. Besides, it doesn't help. Terry will probably be the last to leave. And he can find his way anywhere in the dark."

"Good enough," I replied, and then, with one last glance around, I started for the door.

"Could you move the water jug closer to hand? Several of those powders leave me thirsty."

I moved the jug to where he could easily reach it, and he lifted his good hand in a friendly wave, settling back against his pillows as I walked to the door.

I closed it behind me, and went on down the passage to my own room.

Simon was waiting there for me.

"Did it go well? The ceremony?"

"Very well." I told him what had transpired, and then added what the King had had to say about the Colonel Sahib.

Simon smiled. "He'll be pleased. Shall I tell him, or will you?"

"I don't think I'll see him before I sail. I leave very early Thursday morning."

"And what about your patient? Are you having his dinner sent up to him?"

I explained what we, Sergeant Wilkins and I, had decided.

"A little unusual, isn't it?"

"Very. On the other hand, his injuries aren't critical just now, or the Palace would have waited to summon him for the ceremony. This is just that slow, wearing time when there appears to be no progress. And then suddenly your exercises begin, and you wish yourself *back* in this limbo."

"As I know very well," Simon replied wryly. He'd been severely wounded not all that long ago. "If you have no other plans, I'll take you to dinner."

"I'd rather stay close to the hotel," I said. "There's a dining room downstairs."

Simon rose from his chair. "Then I'll give you a little time to rest, and return around six. A little early perhaps, but if you're to look in on the sergeant later this evening, we shan't have to dash upstairs at the last minute."

I was grateful for his understanding.

He left, and kicking off my shoes, removing my apron and cap, I sat down in the chair that Simon had just vacated and sighed.

This brief interlude had brought me a little more time in England, but by Thursday I'd be eager to return to my duties in France. It was where my years of training and experience counted in the endless struggle to save lives. It had been difficult, exhausting, and stressful work often enough, and all of us in Queen Alexandra's Imperial Military Nursing Service had had bad dreams from time to time, dreams we tried not to remember in the light of morning. But knowing we'd made a difference kept us going.

I must have drifted into a light sleep. And then my internal clock woke me at a little before five thirty. I was dressed and ready when Simon knocked on my door just at six.

He smiled and said, "I expected to find you asleep."

I returned the smile. "After visiting Buckingham Palace? How could I sleep?" I replied, stepping out into the passage. It was quiet. I glanced down toward the sergeant's door, but all was quiet in that direction as well. If his friends were coming, they'd been thoughtful enough to give him time to rest before descending on him. That was reassuring.

We went down to the hotel's dining room, where Simon had already booked a table, and it was a pleasant dinner. I wished my mother could have been there—she would have enjoyed the outing—but Simon and I were always comfortable together.

We were still sitting there, talking over our after-dinner cup of tea, when Simon glanced at his watch and said, "It's nearly nine o'clock. Go on up and look in on your patient. I'll see to the account and then escort you safely to your room."

I did just that, taking the lift and walking down to Sergeant Wilkins's door. It was quiet, and I knocked softly.

There was no answer. And I couldn't see a light under the door. His friends had come and gone, he was asleep.

I tried the door, found it locked. Frowning, I tried it again. This time it opened, as if it had been jammed, and I stepped into the doorway, listening.

I could just see the outline of Sergeant Wilkins's body under the coverlet, but his breathing was so quiet and deep that I could hardly be sure I heard it.

Had he taken his powder, as he'd promised? After his friends had left?

On the floor next to the table by the bed, a crumpled bit of white paper lay, as if he'd accidently brushed it off as he put down his cup. Yes, all was well.

I listened a few seconds longer, then, satisfied, I closed the door again quite gently and walked on toward my own room. Simon was just stepping out of the lift.

"All well?"

"Yes, he's asleep. I didn't disturb him. He's taken his evening powder, as he'd promised he would."

"Good. All right, go inside and lock your door. I'll come by tomorrow after you've seen the patient off to Shrewsbury. I'll even take you to lunch."

"Done. Thank you for dinner," I said, and went into my room. I'd brought a book with me from Somerset and tried to read for a while, but I was in bed by ten thirty. The deep fatigue of France hadn't quite left me, or perhaps it was the excitement of the ceremony at the Palace. At any rate, I was asleep before the hands on my little clock reached eleven.

Chapter Three

When I opened my eyes, I met my first bad news of the day. The sunny weather had broken, and rain was coming down hard, barely letting in the early morning light.

Oh, dear, I thought, wishing I could turn over and sleep for another hour. But I had duties to perform. I threw back the coverlet, and got out of bed.

By eight o'clock, I had gone down to my breakfast. Simon and I had arranged last night for tea and toast to be taken up to Sergeant Wilkins at seven thirty, just as the orderly, Thompson, had done for the previous morning.

It was there, in the hotel dining room, that I received my second bit of bad news.

The desk clerk walked in, looked around, found my table, and came over to me with an envelope in his hands.

"A messenger brought this just now, Sister Crawford. For you."

"Thank you," I said, taking it from him, smiling. But the smile quickly faded as I opened the envelope, drew out the single sheet, and read it.

Simon's handwriting.

My dear girl, I'm deserting you after all. The call was waiting for me when I arrived at my club. I'll be away for several days. Safe journey back to France. And I promise that lunch on your next leave.

It wasn't signed.

Disappointed, I sat there staring at the lines on the page. I had looked forward to spending the afternoon with Simon. Now as soon as my patient was on his way back to Shrewsbury, I would be returning to Mrs. Hennessey to spend my last evening alone. Or not alone—Mrs. Hennessey would be sure to come upstairs and ask me to dine with her, happy to have me there to join her.

With a sigh, I put the letter away and finished my breakfast. It was time now to wake up the good sergeant and have him freshly bandaged, dressed, and ready for his escort back to Shrewsbury. I didn't envy him the journey in this rain.

I went into my own room, picked up my kit, and walked down the passage to Sergeant Wilkins's door.

I tapped first, then reached for the knob and turned it, expecting to find my patient resting again after his light breakfast.

"Good morning," I said cheerfully and crossed the room to the windows to open the curtains and let in the watery morning light. "Although it's actually quite dreary, I'm sorry to say. Did you enjoy seeing your—"

I broke off as I turned around. In the dim light from the windows, such as it was, I could see the mound in the bed more clearly. Sergeant Wilkins hadn't stirred.

My first thought was that he'd taken a fall in the night and injured himself. Or had he drunk too much on top of his evening powder? He lay too still for normal sleep, and that meant something was wrong.

"Sergeant Wilkins?" I crossed the room and put out a hand to touch the shoulder of the sleeping man.

And instead of flesh and bone, my fingers touched something—soft.

Without really thinking, I flipped back the covers.

And there in the place of Sergeant Wilkins lay a mass of crumpled bandaging, splints, and extra pillows that had been used to give his wounded leg the support it needed.

I stared at the shocking tangle.

Where was Sergeant Wilkins? And what had hap-pened here?

He'd been asleep when I looked in last night. I was certain of it.

But was I?

The room was dark, the man's breathing had sounded relaxed, as if he were sleeping quietly. There had been no sign of his friends, nor of any party.

Had they left, against all rules, and gone out drinking? Had he collapsed somewhere and his friends had been too frightened to summon me? Or had they simply taken him to the nearest casualty ward?

I searched the room. There was only the wardrobe and the bed where he could hide. And the sergeant was in neither. Nor was he under the bed. Ridiculous to look, but then his friends could have put him up to tricking the Sister who expected to find him rested and sober this morning. I'd had to deal with the high spirits of healthy soldiers and wounded ones alike for a very long time. Someone might have thought it quite funny to hide him.

What was more worrying now was that the sergeant's belongings and his kit had disappeared as well. But the invalid chair was still behind the door.

Turning, I spotted the key to the room lying on the desk by the window. I caught it up, put it in the lock as soon as I'd closed the door, and turned it.

No one could come in—or get out.

I took my kit back to my room, then went down on the lift. I crossed to Reception to ask them to let me telephone the London hospitals until I located my missing patient. If he came wandering in, drunk and disorderly, I'd have him taken up by the Military Foot Police. He had been invited to London to appear before the King, not carouse. Wherever he was, I was angry with him now—and more than a little worried.

The man in uniform ahead of me in the queue had just finished his business with the clerk behind the desk. I was about to take my turn when what the clerk was saying to him as he passed him a key stopped me in my tracks.

He'd just been given the spare key to room 212. Sergeant Wilkins's room.

And in the same instant, I realized that this man was an orderly. My heart sank.

"Are you from Shrewsbury?" I asked.

He turned, his lined face tired from traveling all night on the train.

"Yes, Sister?"

"Have you come down from Shrewsbury to fetch Sergeant Wilkins?" I asked him again.

"Sergeant Wilkins? Yes, Sister. Are you Sister Crawford?" He yawned prodigiously, then said, "Sorry,

Sister. It was a troop train, and no one slept all the way to London."

I could sympathize. But there was no time. I had to think quickly.

"Have you had breakfast?" I asked hastily, before he could turn toward the lift. "If not, I suggest you go through to the dining room and have something. Before you—er—before we disturb the sergeant."

"Very kind of you, Sister. Kind indeed. I could use a little something. Mostly tea that doesn't taste as if it were strained through a stocking."

Despite my worry, I had to smile. The tea on troop trains was usually strong enough to march into battle on its own.

"I'll be in to join you directly," I promised and turned back to the clerk. I waited until the orderly was out of hearing to make my request. Then I was escorted into an inner room where the manager must work, for the desk was cluttered with papers and accounts and what appeared to be Official Orders regarding military guests.

The operator was sympathetic when I told her I needed to find my poor brother, who had gone out the night before with friends from the Army and not returned. "He's not accustomed to drinking so much," I added for good measure. "And I'm afraid he may have been taken ill." Commiserating with me, she connected me with each of the long list of hospitals turn by turn, and none of them recognized the name of the sergeant or a description of his wounds.

It was clear there was no patient anywhere within the city of London who was my mislaid "brother." Then where *was* the man and what had become of him?

He could very well still be out celebrating with his erstwhile friends.

I was beginning to feel something was very wrong.

After putting in a call to the police stations closest to the hotel, I gave up and reluctantly allowed the manager to return to his office. Then I turned and walked through to the dining room for the second time that morning.

The orderly—I discovered that his name was Grimsley—had just finished his breakfast, as hearty as the hotel had been able to provide, and charged it to the sergeant's room.

I sat down across from him and asked the server if I could have another pot of tea.

Grimsley was saying, "I didn't intend to take so long, Sister, but they were very busy and I had to wait to be served."

Judging from his accent, he'd grown up in Lancashire.

"We have a small problem, and I'd hoped I could work it out before telling you about it. But I can't."

"I'll help in any way I can, Sister," he offered. "Don't tell me he smuggled strong drink into his room and is drunk as a lord?"

"Would it were that simple," I said. Taking a deep breath, I added, "When I went into Sergeant Wilkins's room to help him dress and to change the outer bandages, I found he was gone. There's nothing in his bed but the bandages he'd removed and his extra pillows. I don't know where he is."

"You've lost him?" Grimsley asked, staring at me incredulously.

"It appears that I have," I said as my tea arrived.

Grimsley sat back in his chair. "Miss—Sister. Are you telling me that a man who was just decorated for gallantry under fire has *deserted*?"

To hear it put into words was as shocking to me as it was to the orderly.

But what else could it be but desertion? I didn't want to believe it.

"I don't know. I wouldn't have said—but then he lied to me, didn't he? He lied about his *friends*."

He must have done. They weren't hanging about when I left to dine with Simon, and they weren't there when I opened the door at nine o'clock to look in.

Had I heard the soft breathing? Or had I simply *expected* to hear it, and thought I had? Suddenly I couldn't be sure.

I sat there, trying to think. I poured my cup of tea, and then stared into its depths, as if to find the answer floating in the golden liquid.

"Tell me what happened, Sister," Grimsley was saying.

I began with our return from Buckingham Palace. I didn't spare myself. I told him that I'd felt rather sorry for the sergeant, no family there to support him. That was no excuse for what came next, allowing him to spend the evening with friends. Or to pretend to. But I'd checked his room *twice*.

The question now was how long had he been gone? How long had he planned for this moment? Because if he'd left behind his bandages and his splints, then he'd been closer to recovering and returning to France than I'd been led to believe.

Had he been standing behind the door when I'd thought it was locked? Was that the soft breathing I'd heard? Or had he left while I was dining with Simon?

And that brought me back to the horrifying possibility that the man had *deserted* while he had the chance, knowing he'd have a night's head start.

But he wasn't that well, surely! He must have had some help.

Grimsley was saying, "He's been slow to heal. I can't think how he'd taken off his bandages."

I'd been accustomed to men trying to convince me of a faster recovery than was humanly possible, in order for them to be cleared for a return to France and their men. As well, there had been a handful who had tried to make their recovery seem slower than the general run of wounds, in order to delay their inevitable return. I couldn't call them cowards, I'd never reported them as malingerers. I knew all too well what it was like in France. And so I'd said nothing, hoping that when the time came, when they could put it off no longer, they would step up and do their duty. And most of them had.

Sergeant Wilkins might have lied to the doctors. Talked about pain that wasn't there, showed a weakness that had already strengthened. As a rule, clinic doctors had more patients than they could manage. It was the Sisters who took up the slack, leaving the doctors free to deal with the more severely wounded, those who were still in danger.

If anyone knew what was going on with the sergeant, it would be his nurse in Shrewsbury.

But she would have to wait.

Like it or not, I had to report Sergeant Wilkins as missing. There was nothing else I could do. To the Nursing Service, and to the Army.

"Give him another hour to show up," Grimsley was saying. "He might have a change of heart in the cold light of morning."

I finished my tea. "All right. We'll wait in his room, shall we?"

I paid for my tea and we took the lift back up the stairs. As we went I told Grimsley that I'd called hospitals and even two police stations, and he shook his head.

He was a small man, his dark hair already liberally sprinkled with gray, and his kind face was lined, as if the war had aged him. He looked at me with sadness. "It won't go well with him. Not after receiving yon medal. They'll come down hard on him."

"We aren't sure he's deserted," I reminded the orderly.

"If he's not drunk somewhere, Sister, and he's not been run down by a cabbie, then where is he? And why haven't his friends arrived, shamefaced, trying to explain how it was they lost him? After all his promises?"

He was right. And I couldn't quite convince myself that the worst had happened. It seemed so appallingly awful.

Grimsley waited while I unlocked the door, and we went into the room. He regarded the bandages in the bed, looked in the wardrobe and at the abandoned invalid chair, and then sighed.

"What about you, Sister? What will they do to you, if he doesn't show his face in the next hour?"

"I don't know. I hadn't considered that," I said slowly. "I was too busy worrying about Sergeant Wilkins."

"Yes, well, I think you should start worrying about yourself."

I sat down in one of the two chairs, and Grimsley went to the window to stand looking out at the gray day. We waited in silence. I could almost hear the ticking of my little watch, pinned to my apron.

Time seemed to drag at first. And then it seemed to fly, and the hour was up.

Sergeant Wilkins hadn't come back.

I wished with all my heart that Simon was here, but he was not.

The train to Shrewsbury would be leaving in forty-five minutes. We had no choice, Grimsley and I, but to make an official report. To tell the Army Medical Service and the Army itself that I had misplaced their patient.

And then I would have to report my own negligence.

Was it negligence? It would most certainly be seen that way.

But even if I hadn't given him permission to celebrate with a few friends, he could have left at any time during the night, and I'd not have been any the wiser.

Still. I'd given him a very good head start. And that meant that Sergeant Wilkins could be anywhere by now. The longer we waited, the longer it would take to find him.

"Do you think he's planning to meet us at the station—the train?" I asked.

Grimsley shook his head. "If he was planning that, he'd have left you a note. For fear you'd be hasty in reporting him missing."

There was nothing for it. I rose. "We must make—I must make my report. Will you accompany me to confirm my statements? Or you could wait here. In case."

Grimsley shook his head. "To what purpose? He's gone, Sister. And we've got to make the best of it."

We. It was kind of him.

Chapter Four

The next two days were very unpleasant. I'd known they would be.

The Army was furious. What's more, they would have to tell the Palace what had transpired, and that was beyond belief in their view. Men weren't given decorations like his lightly.

Soldiers did desert. Sad to say. But I'd been responsible for the welfare of this man and for his safe return to Shrewsbury in the company of Grimsley.

I sat through meeting after meeting with increasingly senior officers of the Medical Service and then the Army itself.

I didn't bring my father's name into the proceedings. It would have been unfair. He had nothing to do with the sergeant. This was my problem and mine alone. And so I listened to the anger and the accusations and the disbelief.

Someone went round to the hotel to look at room 212. I had left instructions for it to be held for one more night, and so whoever it was examined the bandages and the splints, then I was asked if I had aided the sergeant's escape in any way. If I had been a party to it.

Someone had canceled the sergeant's breakfast order. Was it me? To delay discovery? For that matter, why hadn't I summoned the Military Foot Police at once? Why had I wasted time telephoning hospitals and police stations? Having a second pot of tea? Continuing to wait in room 212 for another hour? Had Wilkins left his bandages behind because he knew I'd meet him later to replace them?

I explained as calmly as I could that I'd never met Sergeant Wilkins before I accompanied him to Buckingham Palace, and therefore I had no reason to help him desert.

But the Army couldn't quite believe that a man so wounded had simply walked out of his hotel room. Besides, he'd asked for me, I hadn't been selected at random.

The staff had been questioned—but no one had seen the sergeant leaving. Officers and men were as common as flies, many of them had been wounded. No one took any notice of them. When asked if anyone had walked out using a cane, the answer was disbelief.

As the staff put it, canes were even commoner than flies.

"You couldn't turn around twice without seeing a dozen," one of the maids said. "Not to mention crutches and invalid chairs. How were we to know to look out for one in particular?"

I had been seen at dinner with Simon. And that was the nail in my coffin, so to speak. After all, I'd been on duty. I shouldn't have been dining with anyone, even an old family friend. I was forced to give his name, dragging Simon into the picture. I was asked if he'd helped smuggle Sergeant Wilkins out of the hotel.

In the end, unable to prove that I'd had any part in the man's disappearance, the Army considered my fate and turned me over to the Queen Alexandra's Imperial Military Nursing Service on a charge of dereliction of duty.

The Matron who interviewed me had no sympathy for me, suggesting that I had succumbed to the blandishments of a family friend rather than strictly attend to my duty. It didn't matter that I'd looked in on Sergeant Wilkins. I had brought disgrace on the Service I'd served so long, and with the potential of scandal breaking over the desertion of a hero, there was no pity for me.

"You will return to your lodgings and remain there until we have made a decision about the disposition of your case," Matron said. "It can be argued that your record thus far has been impeccable and that you have served your country well. We will of course take that into account. But I warn you not to hold out any hope. If I have my way, you will be made an Example, Sister Crawford. This man was in your sole charge. If you had done your duty, he would be back in Shrewsbury now, and none of this would have occurred. Your negligence gave him his opportunity. And that is the heart of the matter."

I listened in dismay. Sergeant Wilkins could have left at any time of the night. Short of sleeping in the chair in his room, there was no way I could have foreseen what was to happen. Or stopped it.

But that didn't matter.

"It isn't the fault of Sergeant-Major Brandon," I said. "He wasn't told what my orders were. I made the decision to dine with him. He simply asked if I were free. And I said that I was, as long as we didn't leave the hotel."

"You are at least honest, Sister Crawford. I will make a note of your confession."

It wasn't a confession. It was a statement of fact. But I said nothing. The Service had been embarrassed. And it was my fault.

It was important for the Service to be seen as above reproach. Women alone attending strange men on a battlefield or in hospital wards must be above reproach. We were nursing Sisters, and we had Standards.

I accepted my fate without argument. For one thing it wouldn't have done a bit of good to argue. Matron had decided this case as soon as it had come before her. Nothing I could say would move her from that. All she wanted right now was to prevent any hint of scandal. And if that meant dismissing me, she was prepared to go that far.

My heart sank. It *was* my fault. I'd been the person responsible for Sergeant Wilkins. There was no getting around that. I was responsible.

I left Matron's office and walked down the corridor, blindly finding my way to the main door and out into the street. Those I passed studiously ignored me. They wouldn't know what I'd done, but they would already have a very good idea that I was in trouble, and no one wanted to look at me or offer any signs of sympathy. I couldn't fault them.

In the street, I took a deep breath to hold back the tears that were burning my eyes and making them water. I walked for a while, aimlessly, taking this street and then that. After a time I came to the river, staring down into the gray water. It was still raining, had been for days now, as if to lower my spirits even further. Raindrops dimpled the swelling tide below where I stood, and I could feel the shoulders of my coat now, damp and heavy.

Turning, I found a cabbie, and went to Mrs. Hennessey's house. I wanted more than anything to go to Somerset, to lick my wounds safely at home. But I'd been told to stay in London, and I would do as I'd been told. This time. For the last time?

Slipping into the house, I made my way upstairs, opened the door to our flat—and walked straight into Diana, who was just taking off her own coat and hanging it up.

"Bess! What luck! I didn't know you'd be on leave at the same time. How good it is to see you."

She came to me and hugged me, and that simple gesture of friendship nearly broke my heart.

There had been no kindness for the past few days.

But Diana was bubbling with news, and I listened, hiding my own feelings as best I could. I really didn't want to have to tell her what had happened. It was too soon and my feelings were too close to the surface, too raw.

She asked if I'd go out to dine with her. She was famished, she said, and even the food that was available was better than what she'd been eating. So she claimed, but I knew she was simply restless this first night of leave. I'd felt that way too many times myself not to understand.

I told her I was too tired, and of course she thought I'd also just come in from France. Disappointed, she nodded, then said, "Tomorrow night. Promise?"

I was saved from answering by Mrs. Hennessey. Happy to have two of her young lodgers home at one time, she'd come up to ask us to have dinner with her.

"Such as it is," she confided apologetically. "But there are eggs and a little bread, and I have the last of the jam dear Mrs. Crawford gave me in the spring. We must use it while it's still good."

Neither of us could say no to that, and so we followed her downstairs.

By the time I came up again to go to bed, I was feeling as if the past few days were a burden on my back pressing me straight down into my pillows.

I didn't expect to sleep, but I was too tired not to.

The next morning the sun was shining, but I didn't feel any brighter.

Simon was waiting for me downstairs. It was Mrs. Hennessey who came to fetch me.

"He's looking terribly grim, Bess. I do hope there's nothing wrong in Somerset."

"He's probably taking time away from whatever he's been asked to do to look in on me," I said. "Could I borrow your sitting room for a few minutes? I don't like to keep him standing in the entry, if he's tired."

Simon Brandon had once saved Mrs. Hennessey's life. At least that was her version of what had happened, and she treated him like a favored nephew now. But he still wasn't allowed up the sacrosanct stairs to my own parlor. Such as it was.

"But of course, my dear. I have a short errand to attend to. You'll have a chance to visit."

True to her word, she fetched her purse and her shawl, showed us into her sitting room, and was on her way with a happy smile.

Simon, looking after her, said, "She doesn't know." It wasn't a question

"I haven't told anyone. Diana is here. I didn't want her to know either."

"This is the very devil," he said, beginning to pace. I thought the room must feel too confining for him, but I said nothing. I didn't want to go outside to his motorcar for this conversation.

"I am to blame, Simon. Officially, he was my responsibility. Sergeant Wilkins."

"Damn the man," he said between his teeth. "If he was intending to desert, why did he drag you into this business?"

I hadn't considered it from that point of view.

"Perhaps he thought I'd be easier to deceive than an orderly. Besides, I couldn't stay in his room. An orderly would have. He did ask for me specifically."

Simon stopped his pacing. "There's that. I wonder why."

"I told you, I didn't think I'd ever nursed him. He must have got the names confused. Or he just needed a Sister's name. Anyone would have done. I was in London, after all."

"But who knew that?"

"That I was in London? Mrs. Hennessey, of course. You. Mother."

"Someone who might have seen you at the station or on the street? Even on the transport from France? And passed the word."

"That's silly. Who could be watching me? And why me?"

"I don't have an answer to that. But in the end, I shall. Be sure of it."

"Simon, I think it was happenstance. I think he must have asked for me, and when the Army looked, I was already in London. Handy. I might have been in Rouen or Ypres or even Calais. It just happened that I was not in France."

"Yes, all right, until I know more, I'll accept that."

"How did you find out about this? I haven't even written to my mother."

"I was called on the carpet to explain why I had taken you away from your duties. I told the officer in charge that I had brought you to London for the ceremony and that I'd been asked by your mother to see you safely on the train for France the next evening."

"I wish you hadn't brought Mother into it. They'll ask her if that's true."

"No, they won't. I assured them that I had merely been asked to take your father's place, since he was away, and I had not thought it suitable for you to dine in a public hotel dining room alone. I had been with you when twice you checked your patient's room, and all had been quiet and unremarkable. That short of sleeping in that room with him, you had done all that was possible to assure his safety and well-being."

Simon. It had been said in India that he feared neither man nor devil. He'd certainly dealt often enough with superior officers not to be intimidated in their presence. I felt the sudden urge to laugh, and I wasn't sure whether it was relief or fright.

"You shouldn't have—"

He stopped me in midsentence. "I told the absolute truth, Bess. The Colonel would have expected no less."

Simon was right.

"Yes, I understand. I just didn't want this problem to spill over into the family. Not for a while at least, not until I know what they will do with me."

"I expect by last Tuesday evening, being shot at dawn in the Tower would have been an attractive choice for your sentence." Simon grinned. It was to make me feel better. And it did.

As the grin faded, he added, "I doubt they can show that you did anything to aid and abet Wilkins's desertion. You reported the disappearance as soon as you were certain you weren't raising false alarms. And that man Grimsley was with you. He clearly believed in your innocence."

"Did they question him?"

"Thoroughly. He stood by his belief that you had been taken advantage of by an unscrupulous man who hadn't had the courage to return to France and who had felt no sense of shame at involving you."

"But Grimsley had just met me. How could he have known any such thing? For certain, that is. And how did you know?"

"I asked to read his statement."

"And they let you?" I was astounded.

"Not officially," Simon answered slowly. "A friend left it lying where I could see it."

I took a deep breath. Grimsley had believed me. That was something. After he'd been taken away for questioning, I wasn't sure what he'd say. But why should he lie? He himself was not involved. He'd arrived at The Monarch long after the sergeant had left.

"Simon, someone in Shrewsbury had to know how badly—or how well—Sergeant Wilkins was mending. Whether his wounds were still draining or had closed. If he could walk out without sticks or a chair. Surely the Sister in charge of his case would have been aware of all that."

"What about the man who brought him down from the clinic?"

"Thompson told me he was leaving for France. Besides, if he'd been ordered only to change the outer bandaging, not the dressing itself, he'd have followed instructions. As I did, when I was told that the next orderly would see to them before taking the train north."

"I'll make certain he was telling the truth about leaving."

The question still was, what had become of the sergeant? Had he left the country? Disappeared into the vastnesses of Wales or Scotland, where he wouldn't be found for some time? Or had he got to Ireland and safety? Such as it was.

As if he'd heard my thoughts, Simon began to pace again. "I'll find that man Grimsley and see what I can learn about the Shrewsbury hospital. Stay here, as you were told. I don't want it to appear that you've met Wilkins at any point. The Army may even have set a watch in the event Wilkins turned up."

"Why should he come here?"

"To apologize. To rid himself of you, now that he's finished using you. Who knows what's in his head by now? Just be very careful."

"But I don't want to sit helplessly here and do nothing. I want to find this man or whoever it was who helped him."

"Not now. Not yet. Follow orders. Then we'll take the next step."

Simon's cooler head prevailed. I knew he was right, of course, but it was maddening to sit here idle, and wait for whatever was to come. Not when I felt I could do something to help myself.

He smiled whimsically. "I know. But tell me, even if you were free to find this man Wilkins, just how would you go about it?"

That gave me pause. I knew nothing about the man, where he was from or where he might go. Or why.

"I'd start in Shrewsbury," I said after a moment. "This had to begin in Shrewsbury. Concealing just how far he'd come in his recovery. Someone there lied for him, Simon, made him seem weaker than he was. If he could leave the hotel under his own power, then he didn't need Thompson, the first orderly. Or me. Or Grimsley, the one who came to fetch him. He could have traveled alone by train, with someone to see him off there and someone to meet him here in London. So why the charade?"

"A very good point," he agreed.

"And I suspect it must have been the Sister assigned to care for him."

"You're probably right there as well. I'd offer to go and speak to whoever she is myself, but I think she might talk more freely to you."

I sighed. "And here we sit, in London."

"She won't vanish into thin air," he told me. "She'll still be there when you're free to go."

"Will she? Or has she already left the clinic, intending to meet him somewhere? That would make sense too," I said.

"If that's the case, then the Army and the Nursing Service will quickly see that *she* was involved and that this was a carefully planned disappearance. But I doubt it very much. He's used her just as he's used you."

It was galling to think I'd been so trusting. But then I'd gone against my better judgment, hadn't I, in allowing the sergeant an evening with his friends when I should have sat with him until he slept. If nothing else, my presence would have delayed his escape.

But only by a matter of hours.

Where was the harm in a few friends coming to wish him well . . .

"Simon. What if instead of several men in his unit, there had been only one. The one who came to help him leave the hotel?"

He considered that possibility. Then he shook his head. "It would be too much of a risk, involving someone else."

"But we can't depend on that, can we? Usually my instincts are so sound," I added. "How did he manage to trick me so easily?"

"He didn't. You looked in on him twice. And you refused to leave the hotel to dine with me."

"Yes, well, you see it from my point of view," I said glumly. "Not from that of the Army, with a missing hero on its hands, or the Nursing Service, with what appears to be callous dereliction of duty."

And then a thought occurred to me.

"Diana is here. I could ask her to travel to Shrewsbury and speak to the Sister in the clinic."

Simon shook his head. "Patience, Bess. Don't drag Diana into this. It will turn out all right."

I wasn't so sure.

Chapter Five

Over the next three days I pretended to feel a slight chill coming on. It was the only way I could refuse Diana's repeated invitations to go out to dine without explaining that I was confined to quarters. And Mrs. Hennessey had asked me if I'd care to go with her to market, to see what we might find for the evening meal.

"You must eat, Bess. It will do you good, appetite or not. I shouldn't have to tell a Sister such things," she ended with a smile on the third day.

But it wasn't my slight chill that had spoiled my appetite, it was the waiting. I'd thought surely I'd hear something before this. And the longer I waited, the worse my punishment would be. Or so I'd nearly convinced myself.

The morning of the fifth day Mrs. Hennessey came up the stairs and knocked on my door. When I answered it, she stared at me with large, worried eyes.

"Bess, my dear," she said in a whisper, "there's a man in my sitting room who insists he must speak to you privately. He won't give me his name. Shall I fetch Constable Williams? I really don't like the look of him."

My heart sank. "Is he in uniform?" What did the Army want with me now?

"Uniform? No, not at all."

"Young?" Surely it wasn't Sergeant Wilkins having second thoughts about his desertion? And the damage was done. Now there would be no need to kill me to keep me from telling the Army what I knew. Still, I felt a twinge of concern.

"No. Closer to your father's age, I should think."

"Did you tell him I was here in the flat?"

"I think he knows you are. I only said I'd come and see if you were in."

I couldn't think who this man might be. Certainly not someone from the Nursing Service. Nor from the Army. Had someone sent a solicitor to interview me? That would mean serious charges were being brought against me.

I said with more assurance than I felt, "Tell him I shall be down directly. Then put on your hat and shawl, take up your market basket, and leave. Bring back Constable Williams if you can find him."

"Yes, that's the very best plan," she said hurriedly, and turned to go.

I gave her five minutes, and then I took my time descending the stairs in her wake. The door to her sitting room stood open, but as I walked toward it, I couldn't see anyone waiting inside. I hesitated, then briskly stepped over the threshold.

There was a man standing with his back to me staring out the window. He turned, frowning, and said, "Is that silly woman fetching the *constable*?"

I said, "Mrs. Hennessey? I have no idea."

"Sister Crawford?" He strode across the room and held out his hand. "My name is Stephens. Inspector Stephens, Scotland Yard."

My mind was in a whirl. If he'd told me he was the King of Siam, I couldn't have been more astonished.

"May I see your identification?" I asked.

Annoyed, he dropped his extended hand to his pocket and brought out his identification.

I examined it carefully. I'd dealt with Scotland Yard before, I knew what I was looking at. And he was indeed an Inspector.

Gesturing toward the rosewood chairs in front of Mrs. Hennessey's hearth, I said, "Please."

He put away his identification and took one of the chairs after I'd sat down in the other.

"I am sorry I didn't identify myself to Mrs. Hennessey, but I didn't wish to make my visit generally known."

"I see," I answered him, for lack of anything else to say. I couldn't imagine why he was here. Losing Sergeant Wilkins wasn't a police matter, it was Army business.

The front door opened, and I could hear Mrs. Hennessey and Constable Williams coming toward us.

Rising again, I went to the sitting room door and said, "I'm so sorry, Mrs. Hennessey, Constable. I didn't know it was Mr. Stephens waiting for me. It's all right. I'd like a—a few minutes in private with him."

The constable looked my visitor up and down, decided he was fairly respectable and I was under no duress. He said, "Very well, Sister Crawford. I wish you a good day."

He turned to leave, and Mrs. Hennessey, still uncertain, dithered for a moment. I smiled at her. "It's all right. Truly it is."

She nodded finally and hurried to catch up with the constable. We could hear the outer door close behind them.

Returning to my chair, I sat down. I didn't think I owed the Inspector any apology for my protectors, and indeed, he smiled for the first time.

"The constable was quite right to see that I offered no threat."

"I have a reputation to protect," I said simply. "As a nursing Sister."

"Yes, well, that's what has brought me here."

I felt a surge of unease.

"Then perhaps you should tell me."

"I understand you were the last person to see a Sergeant Wilkins, before he disappeared from The Monarch Hotel on Tuesday last."

"Yes, that's true. I looked in on him at nine o'clock, and all appeared to be as it should be. I left him to sleep, and when I came to wake him up the next morning, his bed and his room were empty."

"What did you make of him? Before this disappearance?"

"He received a medal for gallantry under fire." I went on to explain my actions and the result, all the while wondering where this was leading.

Surely Sergeant Wilkins wasn't a spy—or associated with spies? But it was the only reason I could think of for Scotland Yard to take an interest in the man.

"And he seemed normal to you? Calm, collected, as far as anyone could be after an audience at the Palace?"

"Yes. Most of the men who have done brave things appear to think it's nothing out of the ordinary."

"An interesting observation. What can you tell me about the sergeant's friends?"

"I never met them. I couldn't even say with any certainty that they came to call on him. Only that he claimed he was expecting them to come."

"And the orderly, Thompson?"

"He did what he was ordered to do, and then left for France. So I was informed."

"Yes, we've checked. He was on that train, all right, and on the transport to which he was assigned."

"Is anything wrong, Inspector? I really don't know why you're asking me questions about Sergeant Wilkins. I've already reported all I know to the Army and to Matron at the Nursing Service."

"We are aware of that. Your report was concise and to the point. And you've given me no reason to doubt it now."

"Which still doesn't tell me why you've come to interview me?"

Stephens looked down for a moment before answering me. "We have been informed by the Inspector in a town in the north that two days after he disappeared from London, Sergeant Wilkins was seen there by a witness whose identification is trustworthy."

"Then you've located him?" I said, surprised and uncertain whether I was pleased or not. From my own point of view, it was good news. But deserters got short shrift from the Army. He would be tried and executed. Hero or not.

"Not to say located him," Inspector Stephens said brusquely.

Which meant, surely, that he'd been seen and then got away before he could be caught.

I waited.

After a moment, Inspector Stephens added, "The charges against this man Wilkins now include murder."

It was a shock. I'd never considered Sergeant Wilkins a candidate for desertion. Much less murder.

"I can see this is unexpected."

"I—yes, it is. May I ask who he killed?" All I could think of was his accomplice, or even the Sister who had lied about his wounds for him.

"A man by the name of Lessup. Sergeant Henry Lessup. He was at home on extended leave."

"Had he helped in Sergeant Wilkins's escape?"

"He was never in London on the dates in question."

I could think of a number of explanations why one soldier might kill another. But the most likely reason in this case must have to do with that medal Sergeant Wilkins earned. Perhaps there was more to the account of his bravery than we knew.

When I said as much, Inspector Stephens shook his head.

"Lessup wasn't in France when Wilkins was there. In fact he's spent most of his war in England."

Surprised, I said, "Then it was something that happened before the war."

"Frankly we can't find any connection between the two men at all. That's why I've come to speak to you. To see if he'd mentioned anyone by that name."

"But how could the witnesses know that the murderer was Sergeant Wilkins?"

"According to the Inspector in Ironbridge, a man who fits our description of Wilkins was seen in the town two days before, and he asked several people where he could find Lessup. The next morning, Lessup was discovered hanging from the iron bridge. And Wilkins was gone. The description is quite clear, and the man had apparently been wounded, for he had a limp and carried one arm with care."

"But that could describe many wounded men."

"I understand. Which is precisely why we're looking for this man Wilkins. First to hear what he has to say, and then to bring him face-to-face with his accusers in Ironbridge."

"What does the Army have to say about the sergeant?"

"They are as eager to find him as we are at the Yard."

"I can't help you. I spent less than twenty-four hours in the man's company, and most of that time he was in his room or with me at the Palace."

Inspector Stephens studied me for a moment and then took out a card. "I'll leave this with you. If you remember anything, or think of anything that might be useful to us, please contact me at the Yard."

I couldn't have said, if my life had depended on it, whether the Inspector believed me or thought I was concealing information from him.

"Thank you, I will most certainly do all I can to help you." I took the card, and he rose to leave.

"I appreciate that, Sister." He walked to the door, then turned. "Would you aid this man if he came to you for help?"

"I was kind once. And it has cost me dearly. I would do what I could, if he were hurt, it's what I'm trained to do. But I would have no hesitation in turning him over to you or the nearest policeman I could find."

Inspector Stephens smiled. "I very much hope you mean that."

And he was gone, closing the outer door behind him.

What on earth had Sergeant Wilkins dragged me into?

It was the question foremost in my mind as I sat there, staring at nothing. I wouldn't have said, if I'd been asked a few days ago, that Sergeant Wilkins was capable of desertion, much less murder. But then I'd accepted him at face value. As had the Palace and the King and even the hotel staff.

But he'd killed all those German soldiers manning the machine gun. Hadn't he?

That was war. Not a quiet town in the north, not too far from Shrewsbury.

Still, I now had to wonder how this would affect my own circumstances.

Had Inspector Stephens believed I was a party to whatever Sergeant Wilkins had done? Even if I could prove I hadn't left London, I'd been involved in his escape.

I rather thought he'd given me the benefit of the doubt. And the more I considered that, the more I believed it must have been because of Constable Williams.

The Inspector had accepted the judgment of one of London's experienced policemen that I was a young woman of good family and here was a stranger asking to see her privately, something that Mrs. Hennessey had felt was not quite proper. Constable Williams had stepped in to assure two women that all was as it should be. Or else he would have escorted the stranger out to the street and seen him off.

It might have been enough, that encounter, to assure Inspector Stephens that I wasn't harboring a fugitive in our flat, and that I wasn't the sort of young person who had a reputation with young men.

I heard the outer door open again, and Mrs. Hennessey's footsteps hurrying across to her door, eager to hear what this visit had been about.

And what was I to tell her?

She came bustling in, smiling. "Wasn't it fortunate that I met Constable Williams just at the corner? And he told me afterward that we had done the right thing, summoning him. I didn't care for that man at all. And if he's someone you know, I'm sorry for it, but I think it was a wise precaution."

"Yes, indeed, it was very fortunate," I agreed. "He was from the police, as it happened. The caller. About one of the wounded I've treated. He appears to have got himself into some sort of trouble," I added evasively.

"But why turn to you, Bess?"

"I expect, to see if I could give the man a good character."

"Ah, yes, of course. Then I won't ask any more. It's just as well I went on to the butcher's while I was out. He's kept back a bit of ham for us. Do you think Diana will care to join us for dinner? There's barely enough, I'm afraid."

As it happened Diana had other plans, and that left me to spend the evening with Mrs. Hennessey. I'd been wondering how to let Simon know what was happening, but I didn't like writing it down and mailing the letter. Better to explain face-to-face.

And so I tried to be lighthearted and listened to the gossip Mrs. Hennessey had gleaned while visiting the butcher's shop. The evening seemed endless, but after our second cup of tea, dear Mrs. Hennessey began to nod, and I covered her with a shawl before slipping away to the flat.

Diana came in just then, wanting to tell me all about her evening, and so it was nearly eleven o'clock before I could shut my own door and lie down.

But not to sleep, most certainly. What had Sergeant Wilkins done? Killed a man, Inspector Stephens had said. Murdered him by hanging him from the iron bridge. It was a terrible thing to have done, and I had no idea whether he had gone north to find this man and kill him or if it had happened after an argument. Unpremeditated and perhaps a little more excusable. Not because I sympathized with the sergeant, or wanted to believe that he wasn't as bad as the police and the witnesses suggested. It was more that he had behaved with such gallantry on the battlefield, and I couldn't quite balance that with murder.

I tossed and turned, restless and unsettled, then finally got up and made myself a cup of tea from our precious store. Sipping that by candlelight, I decided that as soon as I knew what the Nursing Service intended to do with me, I'd go north and learn more about Sergeant Wilkins.

I didn't have long to wait.

The second day after Scotland Yard's visit, a very official-looking envelope was handed to Mrs. Hennessey with the rest of the post.

Excited, she hurried upstairs, calling as soon as she came through the open door—London was suffering from a belated heat spell and the flat was terribly stuffy—"Bess, dear? I believe your new orders have just arrived."

I flew out of the bedroom and took the envelope she was holding out.

Mrs. Hennessey, eager to hear where I'd be sent next, watched me take out the single sheet inside and unfold it.

Scanning it quickly, I realized that it was a far more generous fate than I had been expecting.

Sister Elizabeth Crawford, it seemed, was to be given two weeks' official leave as her punishment for neglecting a patient.

I wondered if the decision had been tempered by what the Yard had learned about the sergeant. After all, there was now a small matter of murder, and I couldn't be held responsible for that. Could I?

With a sigh of relief, I folded the single sheet and shoved it back into the envelope. "I'm to have two weeks' leave," I told the waiting Mrs. Hennessey. "I expect I ought to go home."

Her smile faded. She'd wanted to keep me in London, having enjoyed the time I'd been in the flat, but she also knew that I would like to see my parents. Putting as good a face on it as possible, she said brightly, "How lovely for you."

But I was already thinking about Shrewsbury. I needed to borrow my own motorcar. And that would mean going home and then having to explain to my parents why I was on leave, when they knew Sisters were still in great demand in France.

On the other hand, I could take the train to Shrewsbury, stop at the hospital, and then find other transportation over to Ironbridge. And finally take another train for the return journey to London. That would put me back at Mrs. Hennessey's in a matter of days, and I could still travel on to Somerset.

I couldn't just walk into a hospital and ask for the Sister who looked after Sergeant Wilkins. I couldn't

think of any way around that, and in the end I asked
Diana if she knew anyone in Shrewsbury's Lovering
Hall.

Frowning, she said, "I once did. Sister Murray. I
think she's back in France. Who else? There's an absolutely delicious young doctor there. Dr. Meadowes. All
the Sisters were agog over him. I don't know if he's still
in charge or not. And then there's Matron, who is an
absolute tyrant, I'm told. You can hardly claim friendship with *her*. But what's in Lovering Hall? Don't tell
me you've found someone new? And what does our
handsome Simon have to say about that?"

Diana, the flirt. Even happily engaged, she still
remembered a handsome face.

"Actually, I'm more interested in a patient there. A
former patient, in fact—he left some days ago. But I
wasn't convinced he was ready to return to France." It
was a lame excuse. It was the best I could do.

Surprisingly enough, Diana nodded in understanding. "Yes, a few hospitals have a reputation for that. I
didn't know that Shrewsbury was one. I'll bear it in
mind. But if they are rushing patients out the door and
back into the trenches, you need to get to the bottom of
it before you register a formal complaint. Ask for Sister
Murray. That should get you in the door, and your own
ability to talk your way into Matron's good graces ought

to give you a fairly general idea about what's happening there."

She was right.

"Thank you, Diana, you're a sweetheart," I told her, grateful.

The next morning, I set out on the omnibus for the railway station, a timetable in my hand and only my kit with me.

There was a long wait. A troop train had come through heading to Folkestone, and all the other trains were delayed. I went into the busy station café and had a cup of tea with a small bun. It was stale, but I didn't mind.

The stationmaster came through, announcing the arrival of my train, and I paid my account, went out, and found an empty seat next to a young officer on his way home.

"New baby," he said, his face wreathed in smiles. "A boy. I don't know how the Major wangled leave for me, but I'm terribly grateful."

He talked about his wife and the child all the way north. I felt I knew the family intimately by the time we arrived—very late—in Shrewsbury.

The Captain—his name was Jackson—insisted that I come home with him.

"At this time of night, you can't go to an hotel," he said, taking my arm. "It's a bit of a walk, out to my house, but you'll be safe there, and in the morning you can go on about your business."

"Your wife—"

"Polly won't mind. She'd read me the riot act if she thought I'd abandoned you. Here, let me have your kit. We'll make better time." He was eager to reach his house, and I saw as we made our way up the winding drive that it was a handsome old manor.

There were lamps lit in the parlor and by the door—I could see the glow through the fan light—and he had no more than reached the front steps when the door was flung open and a woman who appeared to be his mother threw herself laughing into his arms and welcomed him home. "We tried to convince Polly to rest, but she insisted she must be awake when you arrived."

She was touching his face, holding his arm, assuring herself that her boy was indeed here and safe. And then she saw me standing below the steps in the shadows.

"Oh, how thoughtless—Sister?"

"Sister Crawford," I said, holding out my hand. "I'm afraid your son was insistent that I not find an hotel at this hour."

"And he's absolutely right. Do come in. Francis, you know the way. Polly is waiting. I'll see to Sister Crawford and come up later."

Captain Jackson all but bounded up the stairs, and Mrs. Jackson smiled fondly. "It was a love match," she said, watching him. "She's counted the days. And there's the child. Such happiness . . ."

"All the way from London, he talked of nothing else but his wife and son."

"I expect he did. Now, you've had no dinner, have you? No, don't give me a polite answer. You must be starved. Francis will discover he's hungry too, in a bit. I put a roast chicken, potatoes, and a dish of carrots aside for him, and there's more than enough for two." She retrieved my kit from where her son had dropped it in his eagerness to greet his mother and then go up to his wife. "Tell me what brings you to Shrewsbury?"

"I'm going to a hospital on the outskirts of town. I know very little about it, but I'm looking for a Sister Murray. I have a message for her from a friend."

"Ah, that's surely Lovering Hall. Extremities? Yes, that's where you want to go. They do marvelous work with leg wounds."

"You know the Hall?"

"I knew the Loverings. When their son was killed, they turned the Hall over to the Army and moved to their town house. I've gone out there a time or two with Mrs. Lovering. She keeps an eye on her gardens." She led me down to the kitchen, apologized for not opening the dining room tonight—"We seldom entertain these days. Food is scarce, people have their own sorrows to occupy them."—and set out a lovely meal.

I was very hungry, although I ate politely and listened as Mrs. Jackson went on about her son and his Polly, obviously terribly fond of her daughter-in-law, and then gave me a little history of the house.

"It's very old. Sixteenth century, and added to several times. My husband's grandfather made it habitable for generations to come, and I have always been grateful for his foresight."

By the time I'd finished my own dinner, we could hear Captain Jackson clattering down the stairs.

"Warm milk, and she promises to sleep. That looks delectable. Any chance there's more?"

After his mother took the warm milk up to Polly, she showed me to a guest bedroom just down the passage from her own room. "It's comfortable," she said, "and the sheets are clean, the bed well aired."

It was all of that, and I was grateful. I fell asleep at once and didn't stir until tea was brought to me at seven, and then I came down to breakfast at eight.

The Jacksons insisted I couldn't be allowed to walk to Lovering Hall, and so Mrs. Jackson drove me there after the meal.

She said, taking her place behind the wheel, "I've had to learn to drive, you know. My husband, God rest his soul, would have been shocked, but what were we to do when the chauffeur was called up, and there was no one else?"

I nodded in understanding, adding that my mother had also learned to drive with the start of the war.

"Yes, well, we've done many things since August of '14 that we never expected to do. Or see. I don't need to tell you that after four years in France."

It was a pleasant drive, and then we were turning into the gates at Lovering Hall. The house was larger than the Jacksons' home but had seen greater changes over the generations. It was ideally suited as a convalescent clinic, as far as I could see, with its wings and extensions.

Mrs. Jackson was reluctant to leave me on my own. I assured her that I would be fine, that I could easily find a way into Shrewsbury with one of the staff, and at length she let me go. I waved as she reversed the motorcar and drove back the way we'd come.

Then, squaring my shoulders, I walked into the hospital, a smile pinned to my face, and asked to speak to Matron.

Chapter Six

I'd given some thought to my approach here at Lovering Hall. And I'd decided the best way to begin was to speak to Matron. I wasn't sure how she would receive me, and I wasn't sure what access I'd have to the house and staff. But it was the only open way I could think of.

Two minutes in her company, and I was certain I'd made the wrong decision.

She'd been affable enough when I came in and introduced myself. And then I mentioned Sergeant Wilkins, and the fact that I had accompanied him to the Palace.

Her face changed, her manner as well.

"I should like to know what you have to say for yourself, Sister," she demanded coldly.

I found myself wishing I'd brought Mrs. Jackson in with me.

One didn't argue with Matron. Or contradict her. But she was asking me to explain myself, and I'd have only one chance to do that. Concisely and to the point, if possible.

"What I have to say is this: Sergeant Wilkins tricked me just as he tricked Medical Orderly Thompson and Medical Orderly Grimsley. He had intended from the start to leave the hotel without our knowledge or consent, and he did just that. What I'd like very much to know is, how severe were his wounds at the time he was given leave to travel to London? Did he require help in his escape? And if so where did he find it? Or was he able to leave the hotel under his own power?"

She stared at me. It wasn't at all what she'd expected to hear.

"You deserted your post," she said tartly.

"Did I? I looked in on him before I went downstairs to dinner and again before I returned to my room. Short of staying the night in his room with him, I had no other way of making certain he was all right. I believe that's precisely why he requested a Sister—an orderly would have shared his room. I couldn't."

"The Army said—" she began.

It was rude to interrupt, but I had no choice. "The Army, when his disappearance was first discovered, was as shocked as we were, Grimsley and I. They interviewed me at length, believing I must have been involved. They've searched everywhere and even enlisted the help of Scotland Yard to find Sergeant Wilkins, hoping to apprehend him before news of his desertion reaches the newspapers. But now it's a police matter, because it appears the sergeant committed a crime while he was at large. A serious one."

She hadn't heard that. I didn't think she had.

"And so my reputation—and the reputation of this hospital—rests on just how capable the sergeant was to leave his room and disappear."

She stared at me. "Are you suggesting that we allowed the sergeant to malinger?"

"Matron, no. What I've come to believe is this. The sergeant began planning his escape as soon as he knew he was to be awarded that medal by the King himself. It would mean traveling to London, away from watchful eyes here. He truly wasn't well enough to be allowed to make the journey alone. And so he decided he must have two things—an invalid chair and a nursing Sister to push it. That meant trying to seem slower than most to recover. No one would mistake that for malingering, not from a hero. But it *would* require a sympathetic ear."

Taking that in, she said nothing. After a moment, she asked, "And why do you feel that it's your responsibility to ask these questions?"

"I've had a long and respected relationship with the Nursing Service, and I don't believe it's fair that one man's scheming should change that. It hurts to be accused of something you didn't do. Even you took it for granted that I was involved in what the sergeant has done."

She began to see, finally, that I might be innocent. *And* that the hospital might soon come under fire for not realizing that Sergeant Wilkins was farther along in his recovery than anyone knew. I'd worked in such a hospital. I knew how meticulously records were kept to prevent malingering. When a man was well enough to return to duty, the Army must be informed.

"I remember when Sergeant Wilkins requested a Sister Crawford to attend him during the ceremony," Matron began slowly. "I asked him if there was anything personal between you. He replied that you'd tended his wounds at the forward aid station and saved his leg. He felt it was fitting for you to be there when he received his medal."

"I was told the same thing. But when I met Sergeant Wilkins, I couldn't place his name, his wounds, or his face. I put that down to someone guessing who was on duty at the forward aid station that day. And he took the guess as fact."

"Or he believed that whether you remembered him or not, you would have no knowledge of his present condition. Whereas a Sister from Lovering Hall would know such details and take a different view of his abilities."

"Thompson was the MO who brought him to London."

"Yes, a good man. He'd just received his orders to go to France. We asked him to accompany the sergeant because we'd have been shorthanded if we'd had to send someone else. But now that I think about it . . ." She paused. Looking into the past, she said, "Thompson was assigned to the shoulder cases. Not the limbs. He knew Wilkins by sight of course, but he didn't work with him daily on exercises and the like. He didn't change his bandages, for instance."

"I believe he did a cursory job on the morning before the audience with the King."

"Yes, we had decided that the outer layer should be changed, but the dressings closest to the wound shouldn't be removed. They were clean when the sergeant was driven to the station, and we felt that by not touching them they would be a barrier against new infection in an hotel room or on a train."

It was good thinking on her part, especially if the wound was draining. But it shouldn't be, surely, if he was allowed to leave Lovering Hall in the first place?

"Who was his nurse?"

"Sister Hammond. She's young, but she came here from another hospital and was well recommended."

I'd never encountered her. "Is Sister Murray still here?"

"She left five weeks ago. And Sister Hammond took over the sergeant's care."

I'd done the right thing after all, speaking first to Matron.

She was rising, on her way to the door. "I'll summon Sister Hammond."

"Don't you think—" I began, and she stopped, her face set.

"If you call her in here, she'll know something is wrong, that something has happened, perhaps even concerning the sergeant. Would it be better if I talked to her quietly to see what we could learn?"

"How do I know I can trust you?"

Stung, I said, "You don't. And if you don't, then perhaps you should summon her."

Debating with herself, she said finally, "For your sake as well as my own, I think it best."

She opened the door and asked someone passing by to find Sister Hammond and send her to Matron's office.

We waited in a stiff silence for that someone to locate her.

After a time, there was a light tap on the door. Matron went back to her desk, sat down, then said, "Come."

Sister Hammond stepped into the room. "You wished to see me, Matron?"

I could tell at once that she had never served in France. I never really understood what it was that set Sisters who had served in aid stations near the front lines apart from those who had not. But I could read that difference in Sister Hammond's face. The wounds she had seen had already been treated, or were surgical cases that were addressing infection or stubborn problems with incisions and healing. She had never plunged her hands into a torn leg looking for the artery that was bleeding, or probed a chest wound for a shell fragment that was perilously near the heart, or cleaned a head where part of the skull was missing.

I wondered what she could read in mine.

"Sit down, Sister. This is Sister Crawford. She's come from London to ask you about Sergeant Wilkins's wounds."

Sister Hammond blinked. "His wounds?"

"Yes," I said pleasantly. "I was concerned about the head wound, for instance."

Her face cleared. "That was his little joke," she said, smiling. "He never talked about what he'd done. In France, I mean. He said it could have been any one of half a dozen men named in that dispatch. That he was no braver than they were, and he really felt it would be difficult for him to stand there—or in his case, to sit—and listen to his name being called and hear the Palace praise him."

He'd said something along those lines to me.

"And so you wrapped his *head*, even though he had no head wound?" Matron asked, striving to keep her reaction out of her voice.

"He said it wouldn't matter, that it would just make it easier for him to seem like one of many wounded men. Anonymous. 'The King won't be affronted, and I won't have to face the photographers and the other guests.' I didn't think it was wrong to help him."

After a moment, Matron said, "He also told me that the award should have gone to braver men than he. I thought perhaps he'd refuse to accept it. But later, when he was told he was invited to come to London, he seemed quite pleased."

"Yes, that's right," Sister Hammond replied, happy that Matron was agreeing with her.

"And you told MO Thompson that he should completely remove only the sergeant's outer bandages?" Matron went on.

"For fear he might see there was no head wound. It would do no *harm* to leave them—the leg wound is healing well, although the scar is still quite tender and the muscles aren't very strong yet. That's why we decided that splints and bandaging would help support the leg and protect the scar from being rubbed by his uniform. We were trying to be practical, you see."

And Thompson had followed instructions. It must have seemed quite logical to him not to take risks.

But I knew—and so must Matron—that judging how tender a scar might be or how strong the leg muscles had grown was dependent on the patient's responses.

"And his arm," I said. "How badly was that draining?"

She blushed. "Well, actually, it wasn't draining at all. In fact, he didn't need bandaging or a sling. Still, it wasn't strong enough to allow him to use crutches. That morning—when he was about to leave for London—he told me his arm was aching again. He thought the exercises might have been too much and he was worried about it. And so I wrapped it and gave him a sling. I saw no problem with that. If it made him feel uncomfortable, it could come off again. He was planning to remove the sling anyway, for the ceremony, so that he could salute the King."

But he hadn't removed the sling. Nor had he saluted the King. He had given everyone to believe that he was an invalid.

I was stunned at how easily Sister Hammond had been manipulated. And yet that was hindsight. At the time she must have believed she was trying to do her best for her patient. Goodness knows, I was in no position to cast the first stone.

"What worries me," she went on earnestly, "is that he can't be taking care of himself now. He could do serious damage to his leg if he doesn't rest it often. He's not used to long walks or standing about. And if he should reopen the incision from his surgery, anything could happen. The same could be said of his arm. He mustn't overuse it. Please, Matron, this is the truth."

Matron, listening to her without interrupting, glanced at me before saying, "Yes, I must agree with you, Sister. He will need to be very careful. He ought to be using a cane. But I must ask if you had any inkling of what he was planning to do? If you think he might have been farther along in his treatment than we thought?"

"No, Matron. I was as shocked as anyone else. And I don't see how he could have concealed his progress from us." She was upset now, close to tears as it began to sink in that she may have been led down the garden path.

I said, "Sister. What sort of man is Sergeant Wilkins? I must admit I saw him very briefly, when all was said and done. We couldn't converse during the audience with the King, and he was very tired when we returned to the hotel several hours later."

She glanced quickly at Matron, as if afraid to say too much.

"He wasn't what you might call *charming*," she said after a moment. "We have patients could sing a bird out of a tree. They're very difficult to deal with because they're always pushing the rules." She turned to me, as if for support in this. "They think because they're charming, they can be forgiven for staying up half an hour longer or sitting on a bench in the garden just a little longer, or spending a bit more time with their families when they're visiting, even though they've overtired themselves. You must know how it is."

I did. Many of the handsome ones, the charming ones, generally didn't feel that rules could possibly apply to them. But it wasn't what I wanted to know. I raised my eyebrows, as if waiting for her to go on.

"He was never any trouble. He didn't ask for favors. He just got on with what he had to do. Even when he was in pain, he tried not to make a fuss. But I enjoyed talking to him, he was always interesting."

"What did you talk about?" Matron asked.

"I—nothing in particular. Just . . . conversation."

I gave up. "Did no one notice his extra bandages? Mr. Thompson, for one, the orderly who traveled up to London with him?"

"Everyone knew it was going to be a difficult few days. That we didn't want anything untoward to happen. If Mr. Thompson wondered about anything, he didn't speak to me about it."

His mind was on his return to France. Or perhaps the sergeant had already had a word with him.

It was becoming clear even to Matron that Sergeant Wilkins had planned his escape with great care, alarming no one, sending up no flares. I felt vindicated, but it didn't make me any happier. I could see the worry in Sister Hammond's face, and the growing hurt as she realized how she had been used, just for being kind.

I could see that Matron was about to arrive at the same conclusion. She was looking at me, and then she turned to Sister Hammond.

"And he said nothing to you, Sister, about not coming back?"

Sister Hammond came close to tears. "Only that he would ask permission for us to go into Shrewsbury for my birthday next week. For taking such good care of him."

Interpreted in hindsight as gratitude for making a patient look far more vulnerable and in need of help than he really was. But then he had also maneuvered me into allowing him an entire evening in which to manage his escape.

Sister Hammond said urgently, "Matron. I didn't think I was doing anything wrong. No one stopped Sergeant Wilkins at the door. No one spoke to me."

Nor would they have, with a nursing Sister and a medical orderly supervising his departure. Whatever anyone might have thought, it would all have appeared to be under control. After all, the patient, an acknowledged hero, was on his way to Buckingham Palace.

How had so many people been drawn into this man's plot?

Matron answered that, saying thoughtfully, "We thought we knew this man."

A hero. A man of honor. The last person anyone could imagine deserting. What no one had said, what must have been in Matron's mind—or the Army's—or even my own Nursing Service's—was the fact that this man was not an officer. He'd been expected to set an example for the ranks.

Whatever had made Sergeant Wilkins decide to desert, it must surely have been personal. Or it wouldn't have ended in murder.

Matron was saying, "I shall have to draw up regulations to make certain that this sort of thing never happens again. In my hospital or any other."

She dismissed Sister Hammond, then turned to me. "I have misjudged you, Sister Crawford. It appears that the problem began in my own hospital. I would have said that that was impossible, before you walked through my door."

"None of us was prepared."

"Orderly Grimsley had already told me that you'd been misjudged. I refused to believe it. An apology is in order. And I shall be writing to the Nursing Service on your behalf."

"Thank you, Matron. That means a great deal to me under the circumstances."

Her eyes strayed to the file she'd set aside when I was announced. "Is there anything else you need, Sister Crawford?"

"I should like to speak to Grimsley before I leave. I'm still trying to make sense of any of this. I wondered if he might have learned something more about the sergeant and his plans, after he returned here to Shrewsbury."

"If he had, I'm sure he'd have said something to me. But I see no reason why you shouldn't see Grimsley."

Ten minutes later, Grimsley and I were walking under the trees in the park. He hadn't wanted to talk to me indoors.

I told him what I knew—including the visit from Inspector Stephens, which I had mentioned to Matron only in passing.

Grimsley looked up at me, whistling under his breath.

"Murder."

"So I've been told. The police are searching for the sergeant. I don't know anything about the man he is said to have killed. The name Henry Lessup doesn't mean anything to me. Does it to you?"

He walked at my side without speaking for several minutes. Then he said, "Ironbridge? I don't recall that he ever received any letters from Ironbridge. For that matter, I don't think anyone else has. It was one of my duties, delivering the post."

"What about his belongings here?"

"The Army came for them. But you've been in a convalescent hospital. There's not much a man brings with him, when he comes in from France. Whatever is in his kit. Whatever they have time to collect or send on, from where he was posted."

"Did he have any family?"

"At a guess, his parents are dead. They've never come to see him, and the only letters he got—they were few enough—came from his men in France. The company he'd left behind when he was wounded."

I sighed. The sergeant had told me he had no family. And no one was in attendance at the ceremony. But that could mean anything, that they were dead, that he was the black sheep long since cut off from them, that they were not well enough to travel or to write.

"How did he come to have my name, Grimsley? I still can't remember ever treating him."

"We've had a few you did attend, Sister. I will say that Sister Hammond was that disappointed when she wasn't asked to accompany him to London. I expect she thought he might choose her."

"She knew him too well," I said pensively. "I was more easily tricked."

"Look at it this way, Sister. Any name would have done. Yours was just one he'd heard and could use. But what are we to do about this business? It leaves a bad taste, not seeing it finished."

"Scotland Yard will attend to that. I'd thought about going on to Ironbridge, while I'm in the north.

Inspector Stephens didn't give me very much information about the man the sergeant is alleged to have
killed. Perhaps if I learn something there, it might help
explain the man. He was terribly clever, Grimsley.
He let everyone believe he was a deserter, and all the
while, he must have been planning on going directly to
Ironbridge. To find that man. The question is, where
is he now? A few days ago, he was fewer than twenty
miles from here!"

"Licking his wounds, wherever he is. Or already
out of the country. He could be in Ireland as we speak.
I don't see much hope of going to France. He'd run
straight into the Germans. They'd know who he was. It
would be quite a coup to capture him."

The Army had kept the story out of the newspapers,
when Sergeant Wilkins went missing. There had been
nothing about it. Nor anything about his being suspected of murder since then.

"You aren't going to Ironbridge alone," Grimsley
asked me as we turned back through the gardens
toward the house. "I don't like that very much."

Neither would my parents or Simon, I thought
wryly. But I couldn't see that it would do much harm at
this stage. Sergeant Wilkins wasn't there, surely.

"I'm not due leave, I can't offer to go with you,"
Grimsley went on. "Take my advice and go back to

London. I'll find someone to carry you back to the railway station in Shrewsbury."

Before I could answer him, I saw Sister Hammond
come out the main door and stand there, looking
around. I realized she must have just come off duty.

"I think she's searching for me," I said.

"Talk to her, Sister. I'll wager she didn't tell Matron
everything. She'd be too ashamed. I'll find someone
traveling back to Shrewsbury. You won't mind riding
in the butcher's van?" he ended anxiously.

"I don't mind."

I stood where I was as he hurried back toward the
house. Sister Hammond spotted me then and walked
out to meet me.

"I was getting ready to leave," I said, smiling. "Did
you think of something more that we ought to know?"

She looked as if she were ill, pale and very tentative.

"I feel wretched," she said at once. "You don't
know—it's not as if he'd *said* anything to me. It was
just—when I first came here, he couldn't sleep for the
pain. I'd read to him sometimes. And there wasn't
much more we could do to ease him. He'd sit there,
staring into whatever darkness was in his mind, and
then after a bit, he'd slowly relax. The arm healed, but
the leg was stubborn. It must have been very trying for
him. Several times the Army doctors debated whether

he was able to return to light duties. I tried to protect him, because I knew it was too soon. You'd have done the same. You *have* probably done the same. When the time came to travel to London, I really was afraid the Army would seize on the improvement. When he asked if I'd help him with the head bandage and then the sling, I thought it was for the best. I thought, they won't know how weak that leg is still. They'd see him smartly turned out, and they'd order him up before the board while he's in London. You'd been in France. Light duties—that's what they offer, but you know and I know he'd have been back in the line within a fortnight."

She'd been used just like the rest of us. But in a way I could see her point. The boards did push men back into the trenches too soon. I'd seen it happen, and in the end the man was too slow, he couldn't quite make it back to the trench in time, and he'd wind up caught in the wire, a target for the snipers. I couldn't fault her. But I also thought that, forbidden or not to have personal feelings about a patient in our care, Sister Hammond very likely had begun to fall in love with Sergeant Wilkins. And I had a feeling that he had callously used that. Possibly even encouraged it.

"But surely someone noticed the differences in his bandages. I can't believe they didn't."

"Didn't you know? He and Thompson left here before first light. They had to be driven into Shrewsbury, then meet the early train. Who was there to notice, except Thompson, the orderly? And if he said anything, it wasn't in my hearing. If he asked questions later, then Sergeant Wilkins was able to divert any suspicion. To tell you the truth, I think there was a send-off for Thompson. He was heading back to France, you see, and even the night porter appeared to be a little the worse for wear." She smiled wryly. "They're not supposed to get drunk, but who can blame them? I went back to my own bed and said nothing."

I wondered if Sergeant Wilkins had contributed a little something to the farewell party. Enough to ensure that the porter and Thompson were not at their best in the early hours.

The more I learned, the more I could appreciate how thoroughly the sergeant had laid his plans.

"Did he ever mention Ironbridge to you? Or anyone he knew there?"

"I don't think Ironbridge ever came up. I mean to say, it's an iron bridge, isn't it? And the village on both banks of the river? And not too far from here. I don't think anyone else spoke of it while I was with the sergeant."

"Where are the letters he received from his company in France?"

"They must have been with his things. In the cupboard. When the Army came."

Or perhaps they hadn't been, if there was anything in them the sergeant didn't want the Army to find.

I shook my head. "No one could have foreseen what he was planning."

"But I *should* have. I was his nurse, I should have been aware of any change in him, any suspicious change. Like wanting those extra bandages. Looking back at it now, I see how very foolish I was. At the time—I thought how brave he'd been and how wonderful it was that the King himself would decorate him. In my wildest dreams, I couldn't have imagined anything like this."

She looked back toward the hospital. "I shouldn't have come out to speak to you. They'll wonder what I had to say, if there was anything I hadn't told Matron."

"Was there?" I asked after a moment.

"No. Not really. Only that sometimes he cried out in the night. The sergeant. I'd hear him, when I was on duty. Something was tormenting him. And I never knew what it was, because in the morning, he couldn't remember anything about it. Or so he said."

I had dealt with men who cried out in the night. Some of them lay awake into the small hours, afraid to shut their eyes and dream.

What had haunted the sergeant?

I realized Sister Hammond was studying me. I said, "What is it?"

"You've served in France. Fresh wounds, men dying. Nothing tidy and at one's fingertips, the way it is in a surgical theater. How do you bear it? I don't think I could. It took me weeks to learn to look at the stump of a limb or an arm, without being sick."

She had volunteered, knowing she would be looking at terrible things. But here in the hospital, they had become ordinary. What had happened to these men, her patients, in France she hadn't wanted to learn.

Small wonder Sergeant Wilkins had found it easy to play on her openness and sympathy for the wounded in her care.

"I try not to think about it," I answered her. "Someone must be there for the men, and I've come to understand how important early care can be."

"You must be very brave," she said, then rousing herself, she added, "I must go. But truly, Sister Crawford, I never dreamed what he was up to. The last man who disappeared was trying to return to France and his company. Perhaps Sergeant Wilkins has done the same by now. I'd like to think so."

With that she turned and hurried back toward the house, slipping inside as quietly as she could.

I stood there, watching her go, then went to find the butcher. He was waiting for me near the kitchens, and his face lighted as I came round the corner of the house.

"I was about to come looking for you. It's time we're off."

I nodded and followed him to his van. It had seen better days, but when the motor turned over, it ran smoothly. Settling myself into the seat beside him, I asked, "I should like to go to Ironbridge. While I'm in the north. Can you tell me how to get there?"

"It won't be easy, Sister. But I'll ask around and see if I can find someone needing to make a delivery in that direction. You never know."

It brought home to me how much I missed having my own motorcar. With a sigh, I let Mr. Barker do most of the talking all the way back to Shrewsbury.

I took a room in an hotel not far from the castle, and Mr. Barker agreed to leave a message for me at the desk if he was successful in finding transportation for me. There was, I learned at the hotel, a train that would take me as far as Coalport, but I decided to trust Mr. Barker.

The bed was comfortable, but I spent a restless night, trying to put everything I knew about Sergeant Wilkins into some sort of order.

The next morning, very early, a lorry driver was at Reception, asking for me, and I found myself accompanying a vast number of cabbages to market in Wolverhampton—by way of Ironbridge.

My companion was a middle-aged man by the name of Frank. He had a wife in Shrewsbury and a daughter in Wolverhampton, and by the time we'd covered the fourteen or so miles to Ironbridge, I'd heard all about his new granddaughter. The apple of his eye, he told me unabashedly.

Frank set me down by the bridge itself, the first bridge ever built of iron, and that only because a Coalport man had in 1779 learned how to smelt iron with coke, making it far cheaper than it had ever been before, and far more useful to the budding Industrial Revolution that was coming. Frank's many times great-grandfather had worked on it.

I walked to the water's edge and looked up the Gorge, this narrowing of the riverbed that made the bridge across the Severn possible. It was quite spectacular, and as I looked up at the bridge itself, I tried not to think about the man dangling from a noose thrown over the tall iron railing. All the while, the water ran wildly, noisily between its banks.

I went back to the road and considered crossing the bridge.

A voice behind me said, "Visitor, are you?"

I turned to find a man standing there, hat in hand. The words had sounded friendly enough, but his eyes were cold.

"I've never seen the bridge before," I said brightly.

"How did you arrive in Ironbridge?"

In a lorry filled with cabbages? I could imagine what my inquisitor would make of that. I said, "A lorry driver gave me a lift." I turned toward the bridge, intending to cross it, but the man stayed with me, and I was beginning to feel a little frisson of concern.

"What brings you here?"

"I'm on leave," I informed him. "And this is a pleasant change from the rigors of my duties in France." I began to walk on.

"You wouldn't by any chance be one Sister Elizabeth Crawford, would you?"

Stopping short, I said, "I'm sorry. I don't know who you are, or why you're questioning me."

"My name is Jester. Inspector Jester. Local police."

Uncertain and determined to take no chances, I said, "I should like to see your identification, if you please."

Chapter Seven

I really didn't think the Inspector was going to show it to me. He stood there glaring at me, his eyes even colder, if that was possible.

And then finally, his mouth a tight line of disapproval, he reached into his pocket and brought out his identification, holding it out for me to see.

It appeared to be real enough. But I studied it longer than was needful while I swiftly prepared myself for the interrogation that was sure to follow.

"I don't think you wish to cross the bridge," he said, snapping the folder closed. "There's still a toll required to go from this side to the other. The booth is just there, on the far side."

"Indeed," I said, and deliberately walked out to the middle of the bridge, looking up the Gorge. It was quite beautiful, and I could hear the sound of the water clearly. The Inspector followed me.

"Look. The Yard told me about you. That you were with Wilkins when he was in London. He's killed a man on my patch, and I'd like very much to find out more about him than the file included."

"I don't know much more than you do," I said.

"I haven't had my breakfast. There's a small shop just there, along the road. I'll buy you a cup of tea, if you like."

I hadn't had my breakfast either. Frank and his lorry had appeared before the hotel dining room had opened.

"Very well."

He turned, and I followed him back across the bridge and toward a shop right along the road. A sign above the door read ROSE'S, and I could smell food almost before he'd opened the door and ushered me inside.

We found a table near the back, set apart, and I couldn't help but wonder if this was where Inspector Jester conducted his interviews.

A woman of perhaps thirty, with pink cheeks and dark hair, came to take our order. She looked me up and down, then turned to the Inspector.

"What will you have, luv?"

"Breakfast for me, Rosie. The usual. Sister?"

"I shall have the same," I said.

Without apparently heeding me, she said, "We've only the brown eggs this morning."

"Brown eggs it is, then," Jester answered with a sigh. She went away, and he set his hat in the third chair, then observed me for a moment. "You aren't what I expected."

"In what way?" I asked, warily.

"The Army gave me to understand that you might have been in collusion with Wilkins, aiding and abetting his escape."

"Indeed? I'm afraid he tricked me just the way he'd tricked everyone else. I believed he was what he was supposed to be, a wounded soldier summoned to London to receive a medal. Recovered enough to be included in that week's ceremony. After all, it's what I was told. We did go to the Palace, he was given it by the King himself. Which only makes matters worse, of course."

Inspector Jester considered me, as if weighing me up.

I was going to stop there, but during the night, I'd tried to put myself in Sergeant Wilkins's shoes. And here was an opportunity to discover if the police knew more now than I'd been told in London. "The question is, was this man intending to kill someone, was that why he deserted? Which I find very strange, since he was in hospital in Shrewsbury, not so very far from here. Easier to explain wandering off for a day, surely, than to desert. Or did his victim recognize him and threaten to turn him in? It would have been clever to come north, while everyone else searched in other directions."

"If this is true, if you weren't a party to any of this, what are you doing in Ironbridge?"

"If I don't clear my good name, who will?" I replied bluntly. "What's more, I was punished by my superiors for what this man has done, and I've still received no orders to return to France. If he isn't found, if I can't prove he deceived me, I'll be discharged from my duties. And so I traveled first to Lovering Hall, where the sergeant was being treated, and afterward I came to Ironbridge to see if there was anything more I could learn."

"And where are you intending to meet Sergeant Wilkins when you leave here? Or has he deserted you as well? Perhaps that's why you've come here, to find him."

It was my turn to stare at him. "You must be joking," I said roundly.

"It was my first thought, when I realized who you must be. We don't have a military hospital here in Ironbridge. Three of our young women have trained as nurses, but I know them by sight."

Rose brought a tray with our tea and cups, setting the pot in the middle of the table.

I waited until she was out of hearing and said, "If he'd planned everything else so meticulously, don't you think he'd have arranged to meet me somewhere far less conspicuous than the bridge where he committed his crime? There are dozens of towns and villages between here and London."

"Unless, of course, he intended to be rid of you, and thought that coming here might see you arrested as an accomplice."

Exasperated, I said, "Really, Inspector Jester, do you seriously believe what you've just suggested?"

He didn't answer. Instead he changed course. "What did you learn at the Hall?"

"That the sergeant hadn't just taken an opportunity when it came his way. He *planned* for London, as soon as he knew he'd eventually be sent there for the audience. And it succeeded because no one expected him to do such a thing."

"Why should I believe you?"

"For starters," I said as Rose brought a second tray, this one laden with our breakfast, "you might contact Inspector Stephens at Scotland Yard. He's already interviewed me, and I think he believed me."

"Because your father is an important man in Army circles?"

I should have stood up and walked out, but I was hungry and Rose's breakfast was tantalizing. I said, "You must indeed be very short of clues if you're reduced to insulting me."

He blinked at that.

"Wouldn't it be more useful," I suggested, helping myself to my share of the eggs and toast, "if you told me what had happened here? I know only that Sergeant Wilkins is accused of murder, that no one knows why he chose this particular man to kill, or what connection he may have had with Ironbridge before this."

Inspector Jester took his share of the meal and then busied himself buttering his toast. I couldn't help but think that the longer he took to answer me, the more of the food I'd have eaten before I was forced to decide what to do.

Finally he looked across the table at me and said, "All right. A truce. When I saw you walking down by the bridge, I was angry. Wilkins killed a man we all knew well. And I thought you'd been sent here to see what we'd discovered. Or not."

"Why should it matter what you had learned—or not? He got away, no one knows where he is or what he's doing now."

"Yes, I see that."

"I also don't understand how you knew that it was Sergeant Wilkins who had committed this murder?"

"There was one witness to the confrontation. She didn't see the murder, but she was crossing the bridge on her way home when Wilkins passed her and stopped the man walking along some paces behind her. They went together to the middle of the bridge, just as you did this morning. Where they couldn't be overheard. Traffic on the bridge was light at that time, for it was coming on to dusk. No one knows where the two men went from there. It was well after midnight when someone noticed the body dangling from the bridge. Apparently much earlier Mrs. Heatherton had seen a photograph in her father-in-law's newspapers—she reads them to him regularly. It was of some of those who would be honored at a ceremony the next week. Wilkins's photograph was there. That troubled her, and she came to me of her own accord to tell me. She thought it might be useful in helping us find the man and question him."

"But—" I hesitated. "Are you sure of that identification? I didn't see the photograph in the newspapers, I can't judge how much it looks like him. Whether it was an earlier one when he joined the Army, or one taken after he was wounded. It can matter; suffering changes people. Particularly since Mrs. Heatherton must have had only a glimpse of Sergeant Wilkins's face." I had no reason to doubt her evidence, but if the murderer wasn't the sergeant, then everyone was looking for him in the wrong place.

"He was limping, using a cane, and one arm was bandaged, in a sling."

I didn't know where he'd found a cane—they were everywhere, he could have stolen one. As for the bandage and the sling, I tried to remember if the sling had been among the bandaging left in the bed at The Monarch Hotel.

"There's a problem. I've been to the bridge. I don't see how he managed to hang a man over the railing, if one arm was damaged and he needed a cane."

"And you're defending him, aren't you?"

"No. I've been a nurse for four years. I know something about wounds. Unless his victim was much smaller than he was, how did Sergeant Wilkins manage it?"

"We don't really have an answer to that," he said tersely.

"I'm sorry. I didn't mean to disparage your witness or the events on the bridge. I'm just trying to be practical."

"Yes, well, I could do without that, thank you very much!"

"Had he hit his victim over the head? Perhaps that's how he managed to subdue him?"

"It's possible. The doctor couldn't say with any certainty whether the blow on the back of the head came as he was lowered on the rope, or if it occurred before the rope was put around the victim's neck."

"If both men were in the Army, the connection between them could lie anywhere. France, a transport, a troop train. It means looking deeper into the victim's background."

"The victim was in the Army, but he'd never served in France."

"I see. Does the victim have a name?" I didn't want him to know that the Inspector in London had told me.

"Lessup," the Inspector told me grudgingly. "Sergeant Henry Lessup."

"If he was in the Army, why was he in Ironbridge? Was he on leave?"

"Yes, that's right. He told his sister he'd been ordered to shut down the site where he had been posted, and as soon as that had been done, he would be on indefinite leave."

Indefinite leave? I had heard all the rumors about the war ending soon, but it was unusual to be given indefinite leave while hostilities continued. This man could have been sent to France to join a depleted regiment, transferred to a recruit training site, or seconded to an officer in transport or general stores, any number of postings where he could free another man to fight.

"Was he in charge of some aspect of testing? Or even some sort of training?" I asked. If he'd been working on something that was secret, he might not be reassigned. It was the only reason I could think of for indefinite leave.

Inspector Jester shrugged. "I don't think he ever said. I'm not sure he even told his sister."

We were always being warned that enemy ears might be listening.

"We're straying from the point," he went on. "He's dead. It's likely that the man you escorted to Buckingham Palace was his murderer. And I still haven't heard the full story of how Wilkins eluded everyone and disappeared."

"Hardly *eluded*," I said. "He removed his bandages and walked out of the hotel, one of dozens of officers and other ranks passing through Reception at that time. As he went striding out the door, who would have taken him for that pathetic creature in the invalid chair, upstairs resting? I myself looked in on him twice. But he'd requested a Sister, you see, and so there was no orderly to stay in his room. Only the man who had brought him down to London and then was on his way to France, and later the man who came to escort the sergeant back to Shrewsbury."

"He was getting a medal, you say. Did he earn it?"

"Actually, I'm told he had. One can be quite brave under fire and still be a murderer."

"But we don't expect that to be the case, do we?" He put his napkin on the table. "If you've finished . . ."

"Yes, thank you, I am," I replied, and gathered my belongings.

Rose came over to the table. I had a feeling she resented my presence, that she was accustomed to having the Inspector to herself when he came in for a meal.

He settled our account with a smile for her and a joking word about the brown eggs.

"If the war lasts much longer, you'll be grateful for them," she scolded him, but it was lightly said and with an answering smile. "There's eel for lunch," she added. "I've put some by for you."

The Inspector thanked her, and we left. I followed him out of the small shop and we walked back toward the bridge. The sky, so clear and bright when I arrived, was now grayer, and the river was dull, a pewter in the pale light.

"Rain," he said, glancing up at the sky. "Very well, Sister Crawford, tell me what it is you intend to accomplish by coming here? I won't have you disturbing Lessup's sister, or allow you to speak to a witness. It's just as well they don't know what role you played in this business. For your own sake, mind you. Lessup was well liked, and I don't think you'd be happy caught up in the backlash of his murder."

"You're saying I'm not safe here, if I go about asking questions?"

"I'm saying nothing of the sort. But I don't have the time to follow you about. Nor the inclination, come to that. Just tell me what it is you want and respect the limits I've set. And I'd take it as a kindness if you don't add to the trouble I already have. I don't want Scotland Yard sending someone up to sort out my patch. I have every intention of doing it myself. However long it takes," he ended grimly.

"But that's the point. I don't want to upset anyone or quarrel with you over duty. I simply want to understand why this man did what he did. Are you still searching for him?"

"We've been searching since we found Lessup's body. I'd already questioned half the village before we learned who the killer might be. I don't have the manpower, nor do my colleagues in Coalport, to go too far afield. Still, I've alerted every constable in a twenty-mile radius. He's got to show his face sometime. In a shop, buying food, in a coach stop or railway station looking to move on. Raiding a henhouse, if it comes to that. Any stranger seen anywhere will be reported to me."

In my opinion, Sergeant Wilkins had long since left the circle where Inspector Jester was casting his net. He'd have been a fool not to. Cornwall, Northumberland, Kent, he could be anywhere, and attracting little or no attention to himself.

We had reached the middle of the bridge again. I looked down at the dark water hurrying through the narrow gap that was the Gorge.

I could see why, if a ferry had been the only way to cross this river, a bridge had been a godsend, for mills and forges and farms alike. Arched and high above the water, it was a stately bridge, a thing of beauty as well as utilitarian. But why hang a man from it? Why not simply kill him and toss his body down into the water below, and let it carry the corpse away? By the time it was found, the killer could have covered many miles in any direction.

"A personal killing?" I asked. "Do you think?"

"I expect the sergeant wanted Lessup to suffer. To know he was dying and helpless to save himself." He leaned over the railing and looked down. "If that's what you mean by personal, then yes." Looking back the way we'd come, he went on. "Do I trust you, Sister Crawford?"

"I have no reason to cause any trouble. You've answered most of my questions. Except one." I was watching a young man peddling by along the road. "Has anyone reported a bicycle missing?"

"A bicycle? Do you think that's how he escaped? Or do you know it?"

"I don't even know how he got here. But if I'd just done murder, I'd want to move away quickly. A bicycle would be a fairly easy thing to hide, if he brought it with him. If he walked from Coalport or elsewhere, then it would be something he'd look for, I should think. To take him as far as possible as fast as possible." Even walking would depend on the state of his leg, according to Sister Hammond. A bicycle might be beyond him as well.

"We've sent out word. So far no one has reported a bicycle missing."

"Then perhaps he arrived on one he'd stolen elsewhere." I gestured to the edges of the river. "There are enough trees down along the water, he could have hidden it there."

"Don't leave Ironbridge without saying good-bye," Inspector Jester told me, touching the brim of his hat in a rather sardonic gesture of courtesy. "I should hate to have to bring you in as an accomplice. But I will. Your superiors won't be best pleased."

With a nod he was gone. I stayed on the bridge, watching him walk up into the village. It was not really a village by Somerset standards, more a place that had grown up around industry and its ever-pressing need for water. I was surprised that it ran to an Inspector. On the other hand, at one time, with all the mills and foundries and whatever other industry had thrived here since the bridge was built, there would have been a need for someone to keep the peace.

The land rose precipitously on either side of the Gorge, houses perched where they could find space. Industry would have kept to the riverbanks—again, for the precious water and water power. And the village was small enough for everyone to know everyone else, as well as the denizens of the farms beyond.

Sergeant Wilkins had taken quite a risk to walk into this place and do murder. He could have been caught in the act. But perhaps he had such a deep hatred for the man he'd killed that it wouldn't have mattered to him.

Assuming, of course, that the witness was right and Sergeant Wilkins was the man she'd seen.

I found a pub—The Ironmaster—with a few rooms above, and took one of them. The woman who was behind the bar looked askance when I inquired about a room. For how long, she wanted to know.

"For tonight. I've only stopped to see the marvelous bridge. I'll be going back to Shrewsbury." I wasn't certain how I was to get there, but she was not to know that. When she still looked uncertain about letting me have a room, I added, "I've come from a hospital on the outskirts of that town. Lovering Hall. I don't have enough leave to travel all the way to London."

That seemed to satisfy her. If I belonged in Shrewsbury, I wasn't quite the stranger I'd appeared to be in the beginning.

And I could understand her concern. The war had brought about many changes, people moving about the country under orders from the Army or the Royal Navy, nursing Sisters appearing to staff a country house turned clinic, that had been a private residence not many weeks before, then the influx of wounded, strangers most of them, attended by doctors and orderlies and visited by staff officers and London specialists. It was unsettling, and no one seemed to know what to do about it. Even Ironbridge had very likely seen more unfamiliar faces in the last four years than in the past fifty.

The room, when she showed me up the stairs and down the passage, looked out on the bridge and the river. Comfortable but not grand, it would do nicely, and I thanked her.

She handed me an iron key that appeared to be as old as the bridge outside, and then walked away. It wasn't until much later that I realized she and her family lived in rooms down the passage in the other direction. Small wonder she was careful about guests.

Mrs. Hennessey had turned her own home into lodgings for strangers. It must have been very difficult for her at first. I wondered how many times we'd been a trial to her before she got to know us better.

That reminded me of one of my earliest flatmates, a Scottish noblewoman who had surprised all of us by becoming a very fine Sister. She had told me later how appallingly small her bedroom had seemed the first day she arrived at Mrs. Hennessey's, and how hard she'd found it, sharing such a tiny space with others.

I put my kit down on the bed, then stood by the window, wondering what to do now.

It was clear I'd already learned everything I could here. Who the victim was, how he'd died, and what the evidence was against Sergeant Wilkins. And any contact with Sergeant Lessup's grieving sister or the only witness was forbidden.

I wished I could talk this over with Simon, but I had no idea where he was. More to the point, he didn't know where I was.

Standing here was no solution. But as I turned to go, the rain was upon us, blowing down the Gorge in sheets. I was glad to have a roof over my head. It was late afternoon before it finally moved on. I went out then, not bothering to lock my door. For the next hour or so, I walked around the village, and then crossed the bridge to the tollbooth on the far side. I paid my fee, then walked up the road into some trees, looking about at this side of the river. I had paused, trying to decide just how far to explore when the young woman coming toward me stopped.

"Are you looking for someone?" she asked, smiling. There was a wooden basket over her arm filled with cut flowers still damp from the rain. She was also expecting a child. I thought she must be six months into her pregnancy.

"I'm—exploring," I said with a smile. "Do you live in Ironbridge?"

"Yes, my mother has the milliner's shop." She gestured to the flowers in the basket. "She also makes silk flowers. I thought she might like a few real ones."

"They're very pretty."

"My father-in-law owns Ashe Farm. I walk up there every afternoon to see if he's all right. He works too hard, all his tenants joined the Army, and now most of them are dead." Blushing a little, she added, "I do apologize. I was asking you if you were looking for someone."

"I've had a few days of leave," I said, repeating the story I'd given to Inspector Jester. "And so I came to see the bridge."

"You live in Wolverhampton?"

"No, I came from Shrewsbury."

She nodded. "I've been there two or three times." We turned and walked together down the slope toward the tollbooth and the bridge. "There's a tea shop there where we'd always stop. Do you know it?" She described it for me.

Of course I didn't, but she went on talking about Shrewsbury. We had paid our toll and were halfway across the bridge when she began to walk faster, not looking down at the water or up at the view ahead of us. I realized what must be disturbing her—the murder. But I said nothing about it, just keeping pace as she went on breathlessly. "I must hurry, Mother will be wondering where I am."

"I hope she enjoys the flowers," I said, just as she stumbled. I caught her arm, saving her from a nasty fall. That rattled her as well, and she nearly dropped her basket of flowers.

"Here, let me carry that." But I couldn't convince her to slow down until we were off the bridge, and by that time she had recovered her composure.

"Silly of me," she said, clutching the basket. And then she added, "Something happened on the bridge not long ago. I've not got over it."

"I'm so sorry," I answered, guessing that she must mean Sergeant Lessup's death, and not knowing what else to say, thinking she wouldn't wish to talk about it.

But I was wrong.

"It—someone was *murdered*. I'd never known anyone who was murdered."

"A friend?" I asked, wondering if she had some connection with the victim.

She shook her head. "I knew him by sight. He'd worked in one of the foundries before the war." She hesitated. "What's worse is that I saw the face of the man Inspector Jester believes *killed* him."

The witness? And yet—she was coming across the bridge in late afternoon. She'd just told me she walked this way every day.

"How trying for you," I said, and meant it, all the while wishing she might tell me more. It was something that obviously preyed on her mind.

"I was walking home from the farm—I shouldn't have stayed so late that day, but my father-in-law asked me to help him take down the curtains for washing. I rested afterward, which made me even later. I'd paid the toll and the man was walking toward me. I saw he was a soldier. But I didn't know him. As he came even with me, he spoke to someone just behind me. He said, 'Well, well, there you are. I've come about Who.'"

"Who?" I repeated, uncertain what she meant.

"Yes, I'm sure I heard him right. And the other man, the one behind me, asked, 'What's that to do with you?' His voice was rather surly. I hurried on, not thinking any more about them. And the next morning, I learned that someone had been killed on the bridge. It wasn't until later in the day that I discovered it was murder. Inspector Jester was asking everyone who'd been on the bridge what time they'd been there and who they'd seen. That afternoon, while I was reading the newspaper to my father-in-law, I remembered where I'd seen the man's face before. There were photographs, you see, of several of the men being given medals. That newspaper hadn't gone into the fire yet, and so I went through the bin to find it and be sure. I went back to the police, everyone said I must. But I didn't like giving such evidence. I mean, what if that man *wasn't* the killer? Someone else could have come along afterward, couldn't they have? And I didn't see the man behind me. I couldn't swear it was Sergeant Lessup. Yet it must have been. The timing was right. The police told me I'd been a witness." She shivered, uncomfortable with the role that an unexpected encounter had thrust upon her. "I don't know why I've told you. You won't repeat it?"

I smiled. "I won't be staying here long. And I don't know anyone to tell." I glanced back at the bridge. "What about the man in the tollbooth? Surely he saw something?"

"Unfortunately he'd just gone home to his dinner. It's been worrying me so," she went on. "I shouldn't have burdened you with my troubles. But they tell me it's best not to brood, in my condition." She bit her lip. "And yet I can't stop thinking about it."

"Try not to," I said. "You must take good care of yourself."

We talked about her pregnancy for a bit and about her husband, still in France. And then she said, "Oh, just look at the time. Mother will be worried about me. I must go. It was a pleasure talking to you, all the same. I hope you'll come back to Ironbridge soon."

"I'll try, if my duties allow it," I said, not wanting to make a promise I couldn't keep. And with a nod and a smile, she was gone.

The soldier she had encountered on the bridge might not be Sergeant Wilkins. And she was right, there might well have been someone else who spoke to the murdered man after the soldier—whoever he was—had moved on.

But the timing had been perfect. Close to the dinner hour when even the man in the tollbooth had gone home. The days were shorter, it would have been dark early, just as it was now.

It was damning evidence and would require a court of law to untangle it. But what on earth had brought Sergeant Wilkins to *this* place? He was in fact a stranger here, since no one had recognized him. Was it the other man on the bridge he'd come to see? How had he learned he was here? Or had he known all along? Had some casual remark been made one morning or after-noon in the hospital in Shrewsbury that set this whole affair in motion? *Remember Sergeant Lessup? You'll never guess. He's home on extended leave. Lucky devil.*

And Sergeant Wilkins need only ask, *Where's home, then?*

Less than twenty miles or so from here. A village called Ironbridge.

I'd have liked to ask the grieving members of Sergeant Lessup's family if the sergeant had known anyone in Shrewsbury's hospital. But there was no excuse I could make for disobeying the Inspector's direct order, and I couldn't risk being reported to my superiors for inter-fering in the inquiry into Sergeant Wilkins's affairs.

I looked down at the racing waters of the Severn, then up the Gorge. Such a lovely place, so wrong for a vicious murder.

Leaving the bridge, I turned toward The Ironmaster pub. Halfway there, I met Inspector Jester just coming out of a shop.

"I hope you've come to say good-bye. That you're leaving Ironbridge."

"I was. I am. The problem is, I don't quite know how to go about it. There isn't a train from Coalport until morning, and as I don't know anyone here, I can hardly ask for a lift to Shrewsbury."

"There's a very early train. I'll drive you over to Coalport myself in time to take it."

"That's very kind of you," I replied, wanting to add that I would be as happy to go as he would be to see the last of me.

"Seven o'clock then." He touched his hat to me and walked on.

As I went the rest of the way to The Ironmaster pub, my thoughts busy, I wondered why it was that the Inspector had taken such a dislike to me. Did it mean that by coming here to ask questions, I had made him doubt his own conclusions about the evidence?

Stepping through the pub door, I looked up to see Simon Brandon standing in the small parlor off the main bar, obviously fuming at being kept waiting.

Chapter Eight

"Your mother," Simon remarked, turning to see who had come through the door and realizing it was me, "thought you were in London. Mrs. Hennessey thought you had gone on to Somerset."

"I traveled to Shrewsbury," I answered, "to speak to people at Lovering Hall. Yes," I went on, to forestall what he was about to say, "I shouldn't have. But, Simon, I learned a great deal about the sergeant. And I could see he'd planned very carefully for what he did. If nothing else, it made me feel a little less guilty. There's no excuse for my part in this business, I know that, but it has helped me come to better terms with what's happened."

"And then you traveled to Ironbridge after Shrewsbury."

"As you see."

"Bess," he began in exasperation.

"I know. But, Simon, what else was I to do? I couldn't sit idly, waiting for what was to come. And I *needed* to *understand* . . ."

Glancing around at the busy pub beyond the stairs, he said, "We can't talk here. Walk with me as far as the bridge."

We turned to leave, passing a young officer just coming in.

We didn't speak until we were at the foot of the bridge. Simon, studying it with the eye of a soldier, said, "Impressive, isn't it? And there's the water power of the river, passing through that narrow gorge."

"It's amazing." We moved down the sloping side of the hill to where we could watch the water pulsing under the bridge, dark now and secretive. Behind us the town rose steeply. "I don't know if the fall broke the victim's neck or if he dangled there until he choked to death," I went on. "It's rather a nasty way to die, however you look at it."

"The killer took a risk." He turned. "How many windows look down on the bridge? Surely someone was standing in one of them, and saw what happened."

"Apparently not." I listened to the rushing water for a moment, then told Simon about the young woman

I'd met on the bridge earlier. "She was certain the soldier she saw and the man in the photograph were the same. I think, if he's brought in, she might still recognize him. Although she's almost convinced herself that he wasn't the murderer, that he, whoever he is, came later."

"He's an attractive man—Wilkins. His bearing, what one could see of his face, and he's well spoken. Not what you'd expect in a cold-blooded murderer. It makes it harder for her to accept."

"True."

"Are you ready to go home, Bess?" Simon turned back to look at me, speculation in his dark eyes.

"I don't know what else to do."

We stood there for a little longer. Then, just as we turned to walk back to The Ironmaster pub, someone came trotting down the street on a large dark horse, calling for Inspector Jester.

"I'm here," Jester shouted from the street above the main road into town. "Stebbins, is that you? What the hell's happened?"

"The bay horse has come home," the man shouted back.

"Wait there, I'm coming down."

We watched the Inspector make his way down a side lane toward where Mr. Stebbins and his mount stood waiting. In the dark, I could just make out faces. Simon pulled me back into the shadow of the bridge.

"The horse has come home," Mr. Stebbins repeated, as if Inspector Jester hadn't heard him the first time. "See for yourself."

"What condition is he in?"

"Muddy. Hasn't been groomed at all. But all right. Legs not savaged."

"Where did he come from?"

"You'll have to ask the horse that," Mr. Stebbins said with a bark of laughter.

"I mean to say," Jester demanded sharply, "any idea where he might have been?"

"None. I went down by the meadow this morning, and it was empty. I came back not a quarter of an hour ago, and there the bay was, big as life. I took him in, brushed him down, and looked him over."

"Damn," I heard Jester say.

"He was raised here, this bay. And he came home again. I'd never have guessed it. I thought he were gone for good."

"Yes, well, we still don't know if the killer took him. But my guess is that he must have done. And the horse came back on his own, as soon as he had the chance. It could mean that the killer hasn't got very far. Could you backtrack the bay?"

"There were muddy prints coming up from the south. But a mile on, he was on grass, and I lost him. Did you put out that query about the bay?" Stebbins asked. "I'm still of a mind to see that bastard in a cell."

"Of course I did. No one has seen it. At least if they have, they don't know we've been looking." He reached up and gently slapped the bay's neck. "All right then. I'll make a report. You can come in tomorrow and sign it."

"I'll be pleased to." Mr. Stebbins wheeled his mount. "I'm that glad he's back. A good horse. I hated losing him." He trotted back the way he'd come, throwing up a hand in farewell.

Inspector Jester watched him go. When it was too dark to see horse or rider, he turned back the way he'd come.

I started to go after him, but Simon held me back.

"But I want to question him," I said quietly, so that my voice didn't carry above the sound of the river. Why hadn't Inspector Jester told me about the missing horse, when I'd asked about bicycles?

"You don't need to, Bess. The killer must have found that horse in the meadow, unattended, and used him to put as much distance between this place and wherever he was heading as he could. What else can Jester tell you?"

More to the point, what else had the Inspector *not* told me?

As if he sensed that we were there, Inspector Jester turned, scanning the bridge and then the slope where we were standing. I thought for a moment that he was going to come down to see who was there. But he must have decided that there was no one after all, for he turned again and continued on his way up the lane. We could watch him as far as the next street above, Church Street, I thought it must be, and then he rounded a corner and disappeared.

"He had promised to take me to the train at Coalport, tomorrow morning," I said. "I don't think he cared for me being here."

"You'll be gone long before morning. My motorcar is behind the pub. We'll leave as soon as you can pack your things. Bess, it's not wise to be here. Or anywhere that Sergeant Wilkins has been. You don't want the connection between the two of you to continue being observed. Here or in Shrewsbury."

I could see his point. The words *guilt by association* passed through my mind.

It had been foolish to come here. Or to the hospital outside Shrewsbury. And yet, and yet, I was glad I had. Just as I'd told Simon.

Deciding it was safe enough, Simon led me back to The Ironmaster, and while I packed my belongings, he settled my account.

As I came down again and he took my kit from me, the owner's wife smiled. I had the oddest impression that she thought we were young lovers eloping, for she said, "I hope you'll be safe. You and your young man."

I answered that with a smile, neither agreeing nor denying the impression. If that was the tale she told about my being here in Ironbridge, so much the better.

Simon went out the rear of the pub to fetch his motorcar, and the owner's wife leaned forward to say softly, "I was young once."

I remembered the Inspector, then, and said, "I nearly forgot. Inspector Jester is coming in the morning to drive me to Coalport to take the train back to Shrewsbury. Could you tell him, please, that my family sent someone to bring me home? I shouldn't want him to think I'd gone away with any stranger."

"Of course not. I'll see he's told."

But precisely what she would tell him I couldn't be sure. As long as he didn't take it into his head that Simon was the Sergeant Wilkins the police were searching for.

We drove in silence until we'd left Ironbridge well behind us. Simon was heading south, I could tell that. Soon we came to the meadow where the bay was quietly grazing now. It was too dark to get down and look for the tracks Mr. Stebbins had mentioned, but I was willing to believe they were there.

"Are you going after Sergeant Wilkins?" I asked hopefully.

"Not exactly. By horseback he could go in any direction, he needn't follow the road. But it will do no harm to drive on and see what happens. What did he do, after he lost the horse? Or set it free? He's in no condition to walk very far, is he? There could be some fresh news that hasn't reached Jester's ears. Yet."

"A good point," I agreed

"You'll need your dinner."

"I'm not particularly hungry. And I'd rather not go back to Shrewsbury."

He said nothing, watching the headlamps picking out the road ahead. Eyes gleamed at us from the grassy verge, where spring's bountiful wildflowers had gone to seed.

"He lied to the Sister tending him at the hospital," I said after a time. "Sergeant Wilkins. She thought he was ashamed of having to sit in the presence of the King. But he wasn't fit for crutches yet, much less a cane. The more bandages, the more people understood why he didn't rise. That was what she believed. But what he was really doing was making it impossible for anyone in London to imagine he could walk away from the hotel with impunity. He wanted everyone to think he was helpless."

"Do you think he killed this man in Ironbridge?"

"I don't know. It could be convenient to blame a man already missing and in trouble with the Army. On the other hand, the woman I spoke to brought the photograph she'd seen to the police. That must have satisfied everyone that it was the sergeant."

"Is her testimony trustworthy?"

"Inspector Jester couldn't have found a finer witness. I do wish I knew more about Sergeant Wilkins. Whether he only planned as far as killing Henry Lessup, or if he knows what he'll have to do next to survive."

Simon was silent.

Finally I asked, "You met him. You're a good judge of men. Is he a deserter? A murderer?"

Simon answered slowly. "The man whose record I looked up doesn't appear to be either. In France he acted with bravery and without considering the danger he himself was in. He could well have died. Given his wounds, he probably should have died. It's possible that since he didn't, he felt the time had come to deal with whatever was on his mind. Or perhaps this is the first time he could actually reach his victim."

"Do you know anything about a Sergeant Henry Lessup? The dead man? You've been involved in all sorts of Army matters. Have you ever come across him? If he never went to France there must be a reason. Clerical work? Supply? Logistics? Training?"

I could see, in the glow of the headlamps, that Simon was frowning. "I've never run into him. The Colonel might have done."

"He was on extended leave."

"Odder still. Are you sure?"

"It's what the Inspector told me."

I could tell this was troubling Simon. After a time, he shook his head. "Never mind. I'll find him."

"I wish I could have spoken to his sister. She must know more."

Now we had to concentrate on where the sergeant and the bay horse had parted company.

Easier said than done. We couldn't ask outright. And so we concocted a story, Simon and I, that we hoped wouldn't travel back to Inspector Jester's ears. It had taken us half an hour to work out the details so that we wouldn't be caught out in an obvious lie.

We stopped at the fourth village south of Ironbridge. It was an arbitrary choice, but it was outside the twenty-mile radius that the Inspector had set. I was window dressing. My role was to sit in the motorcar, staring straight ahead, while Simon spoke to the local constable.

He was searching for his brother, who had stepped off a train heading to Worchester and disappeared.

"A head wound," I heard Simon tell the constable. "Sometimes he doesn't know where he is. Or even who he is." He went on to describe this imaginary brother, his height, coloring, and rank.

"Why do you think he might have come this way?" It was invariably the next question. "It's a long way from Worcester."

"We've been scouring the countryside for days," Simon answered. "My brothers and I. I'm taking our sister back to London. It's unlikely he came this direction. On the other hand . . ." He shrugged. "We're nearly out of hope."

But in each village, the constable shook his head. No sign of a stranger, no sign of our "brother." Which told us that either Sergeant Wilkins had never come this way, or that if he had, he'd left no trace. No strangers, no stolen food, no stolen horse or bicycle or any unsolved robberies. Nothing that would draw the attention of the police.

We varied the story a little, as needs must. But the answer was always the same.

It was a little after ten o'clock when Simon said, "I don't think we should wake up the constable in this next village. At this hour he just might become suspicious."

But we didn't have to. The constable was walking his rounds as we came down the High Street, and he nodded to us as Simon slowed the motorcar.

"Odd that you should ask," the man said, lifting his helmet to scratch his balding head. "One of the farmers spotted a bay horse out on the road one morning as he was going to market. This was ten days ago, I should think. No bridle, no saddle. It looked as if it had run off. He tried to coax it close enough to catch, but the bay was shying away. Finally it just took off across the fields, and as the farmer was driving a cart, there was no way he could follow. No one has said anything about seeing it since. But you said your brother stepped off a train."

Simon smiled. "I'm afraid so. Much as I'd like to think . . . but I doubt he could remember how to ride."

"Sad. Sorry I can't help you. But there it is."

Thanking him, Simon let in the clutch as he took off the brake, and we drove sedately away.

"What do you think?" he asked when we were out of hearing and around the bend in the road.

"We've found the bay." I'd been feeling the tension of the search, tired and more than a little depressed. Now my fatigue had vanished. I was revived, excited. "Simon, he got this far—and farther. He must have been near his wits' end, weary and hungry and in pain.

He could very easily have fallen off the bay, too tired to stay awake. But where is he now? What's become of him?"

"He could be dead somewhere. In a copse of trees, in a hedgerow, an unharvested field."

"Then we'll never know if it's Sergeant Wilkins—or if the murderer is someone who had a grudge against the victim in Ironbridge and just caught up with him finally." I could feel my spirits plummeting again. "And I can't clear my name and reputation."

Still, against all odds we'd found a trace of the bay horse. I ought to be grateful for even such a small triumph.

But the next question was—where had this triumph led us, if we couldn't find the man we were after and determine once and for all if it was Sergeant Wilkins or a complete stranger?

We weren't as lucky in the next village. It was silent, windows dark and no one about, not even a dog following a scent. I smiled, thinking that he would have been better off than we, because he could sniff the ground and know where to go.

Driving on, we found the next village just as dark.

By now it was well after eleven, and we'd been at this for hours.

We found a small inn where there were rooms to be had, just a short distance from the local constabulary. A sleepy clerk came out of the unlit nether regions and greeted us with surprise.

"We're accustomed to lorry drivers and commercial travelers," he said apologetically. "Still. The rooms are clean—the sheets as well."

It was all that mattered. He led us up stairs that creaked with every step and down a dark, stuffy passage. The first door he came to opened into a fairly narrow room, and Simon shook his head. The next was wider, the high ceiling making it seem even larger. The bed was Victorian, massive and ornate, the washstand and chairs much simpler. A window looked out on the street, and the clerk walked across to draw the curtains while I tested the bed. Simon glanced at me, and I nodded. He put my kit on one of the chairs and the clerk shut the door, wishing me a good night as he handed me the heavy key.

I could hear them across the passage, and then the door shut. Simon was satisfied as well.

I had slept in worse places, cots beneath dripping canvas, the ruins of a convent, and even under a sky filled with stars. I bathed my face and hands in the cold water on the washstand, found my nightdress, and climbed up into the high bed. The mattress was lumpy but comfortable enough. When I closed my eyes, I could still feel the motion of the motorcar as we'd traveled over the rough roads between villages. But that was all I remembered.

Simon insisted that I have breakfast in my room the next morning, because the common room was busy with commercial travelers. We set out shortly afterward, but we hadn't gone more than two miles when I saw a man standing by the side of the road with a pair of hens in a coop and a basket of cabbages at his feet.

"He's waiting for someone to take him to market," I said, having seen this many times at home in Somerset. Then a thought occurred to me. "Simon? If Sergeant Wilkins is without a horse now, he can't expect to get very far on foot. He must be searching for someone, a farmer or a lorry driver or the like, to take him wherever he's heading. Or as near to it as he can manage."

"A very good idea."

We went back to the inn where we'd stayed the night, and while I waited in the motorcar, Simon went inside to ask those at breakfast if any of them had given a lift to a soldier heading for London.

I could hear the voices inside but not the words. After a few minutes, Simon came out again and joined me in the motorcar.

"No one has seen anyone answering Sergeant Wilkins's description. Do you suppose he's changed clothes?"

"Short of stealing them, where would he find them?"

"He's been clever enough so far."

We were reversing to continue on our way when I touched Simon's arm. "Look, the police station. It's only a stone's throw from this inn."

"He'd be a fool to draw attention to himself here. It's one of the reasons Scotland Yard hasn't found him. He's canny enough to realize that if the local constable is contacted, he'll report what he knows or has been told."

And so began a very different sort of search. We bypassed any village with a police station, but stopped in those too small to have a constable. Of course there would be a constable in a nearby village or town who oversaw any problems that might arise, but who would think to mention a soldier looking for help?

Ten miles farther on, we had a bit of success when we stopped for petrol at a place simply called BURT'S.

The talkative man in the converted smithy, who proudly introduced himself as Burt, asked where we were heading, and Simon gave him the name of a village farther down the road, thinking it safe enough.

"Aye, my brother lives there. Do you know him?" He told us the name of his brother and the location of his cottage—"second lane past the church, Buttercup it's called, although why that's so nobody quite knows." He wiped his hands on an oily rag. I thought he must be close to forty, his hair heavy with gray, his face lined.

Simon answered, "Actually the Sister and I are searching for my brother. He went missing on leave from a clinic in Ludlow, and it's feared his wound may have reopened. He can't have had much money with him. He wasn't going far."

"Can you describe him?" Burt asked, suddenly interested. "I was in the Wiltshire's until I lost a kidney outside Ypres."

Simon did the best he could, this time without embellishments, although we knew precious little about what our quarry really looked like now. What's more, we were far enough from Ironbridge that we needn't worry as much about word getting back to Inspector Jester.

"Limping, you say? And in the Duke's Own? Here, now, I saw him not a week past. He was set down by a farmer on his way home from looking to buy a bull. And late that afternoon, a lorry coming through took him on. The lorry was heading for Oxford, though the lad said he was from Kenilworth."

Kenilworth? What associations did Sergeant Wilkins have with Warwickshire?

But we couldn't ignore it, for Burt described his limp very well.

"Felt sorry for him. He looked tired, as if he'd been living rough. I asked about that, and he said he was set on and robbed. They knocked him down, and he said his leg was hurting something fierce. I asked why he didn't go back to the clinic, and he said it was his only chance to see his mother. She wasn't well, she couldn't travel. I had a little beer in the back and I shared it with him."

"And the driver was on his way to Oxford?" Simon queried.

"Aye, so he said."

"Do you remember the firm that owned the lorry?" I asked.

"I do. As it happens, I see Danny from time to time, passing through. He'll stop for a pint, if he can spare a few minutes. General Hauling is the firm."

And how many lorries by that name plied the roads of England? It was a more or less common name for long-distance firms. But it was a start.

"Have you seen Danny since he offered the Sergeant-Major's brother a lift?" I asked.

"He hasn't come back this way since then. Is your brother in trouble with the Army for disappearing?"

The man turned to Simon, and it was too close to the mark for comfort.

"Sadly, I don't think he'll be going back to France anytime in the near future. We offered to help the clinic search for him. They believed we might have better luck than they'd had. But then they don't have the people or the time to go far afield."

"Well, Danny will see him right. You'll find him at your mother's, waiting."

I didn't think we'd have a ghost of a chance finding the sergeant in Kenilworth—he could disappear in a town that size or from there go in any direction he chose.

"He was looking to reach Kenilworth? Are you sure?" I asked

"Well, just outside it. He said that was close enough, he could find his way to his village from there." Burt glanced from one to the other of us. He was beginning to wonder, since Simon must know where his own mother lived, why we were still asking directions.

"Yes, yes, of course," I said hastily. "I couldn't think why he wouldn't go directly home. Of course there was a girl in Kenilworth . . ."

Burt nodded. "I doubt he had the strength left to go courting."

I smiled. We were becoming very good at making up stories about Sergeant Wilkins, Simon and I. If the Yard ever traced us, they would begin to wonder about our own role in this search. It was something to consider.

"Did the soldier tell you his name, while you were sharing a beer?" It was Simon's question. "My brother has had some trouble with his memory. There was a head wound, I'm told."

That elicited another nugget of information.

"If you ask me, it must have reopened when he was set upon. He went out back and cleaned it up a bit. Fearsome great knot, it was. I thought it must be hurting like the very devil. He called himself Wheeler. Jack Wheeler."

"Then he's all right," I said, giving every appearance of relief. "If he still knows who he is, he can most certainly find his way home."

All the while, I was thinking that the name he'd given was remarkably close to *Jason Wilkins*. And yet that was hardly proof of his identity. No doubt the Army records could produce several dozen soldiers by the name of Wheeler and Wilkins. We could actually be chasing a will-o'-the-wisp.

Simon, concluding the questions before Burt began to wonder why we were asking about a man Simon at least should know well, thanked him for his help and paid him for the petrol.

Driving away, I said, "Do you think the sergeant was heading for Kenilworth?"

"Who knows? He was wise enough not to travel as far as Oxford. Warwickshire is a large enough county. By the time Scotland Yard or the Army MFP could search it, Wilkins could be anywhere. Oxford however is too close to London. If that's where he's heading, he wouldn't want to show his hand quite so obviously."

"He must be going *somewhere*," I said with a sigh. "But where?"

"Assuming Wheeler and Wilkins are the same man."

"Yes, I'd already considered that possibility."

"Wilkins has no real roots. I looked at his record, remember? He has no family. He isn't married—" Simon broke off, frowning. "Hold on. Let me think."

We drove another mile or two before Simon spoke again. "By God, I believe I'm right. Jason Richard Albright Wilkins. As the elder son he was named for his two grandfathers and given his mother's maiden name. His brother was Jeremy Arthur Wheeler Wilkins. Wheeler was his father's mother's maiden name."

"You not only looked in the Army records, you went to Somerset House," I said, surprised. "Where is this brother? Did you look him up as well?"

Simon shrugged off the comment. "I had time on my hands," he replied. "As for the brother, he was killed earlier in the war. What matters is that Wheeler is a family name."

I wasn't sure I believed him about time on his hands. "Then you know where his family came from."

"Lincoln," he told me.

"Warwick is hardly the shortest way to Lincoln. What should we do now?"

"We can't catch the lorry up. It could be anywhere in England by this time. The best we can do is to make our way to Warwickshire and see what we can learn. Assuming he stays with the lorry that far. We'll cut across Worcestershire, I think."

It was a large assumption.

"And we must hurry. He could have found another lorry or farmer or the like to take him the next leg. I don't see why he didn't head for Scotland. Or Ireland for that matter."

"That's assuming he wanted to leave England."

"Wouldn't you, in his place?"

"It would depend, wouldn't it, on whether or not he'd finished what he set out to do. He's killed one man. It's possible he had it in mind to kill another."

I'd suggested just that earlier, but it was something I didn't want to think about, that if we were too late, another person might die. "All the more reason to find him. I wish Scotland Yard had been more successful. I could have stayed in Somerset all this while, with my parents. But he's been so clever—Wilkins. He never panicked, he kept his head and stayed out of sight. He probably couldn't help the horse getting away from him. Even then he was lucky—it went straight home, and no one could begin to guess how far it had been ridden. And we've learned something else, that he's been hurt. Do you think that could have happened when the horse got away?"

"Scotland Yard is shorthanded. They haven't got the men to scour Shropshire and now Warwickshire, as we've been doing. They're depending on a constable spotting Wilkins somewhere and reporting the fact to London."

We drove in silence for the next twenty miles. I said, as we passed through another village, "What if Wilkins told the man in the smithy one thing—and asked the lorry driver to drop him in Worcestershire?"

"That's a possibility. The question is, how do we find out?"

"We act on what we know. Warwickshire."

A heavy rain caught us an hour later, turning the dry roads into a morass of ruts and puddles. Simon suggested stopping, but I shook my head.

"The sooner we're out of this weather, the better time we can make. I'll spell you if you like."

"I'm all right."

But it was another two hours before we ran out of the rain, and soon afterward we were in country neither Simon nor I knew. We kept going, our sense of direction guiding us, and after a while, as early autumn darkness fell, we began to consider where to stop for the night. We found ourselves rejecting most of the possibilities. Several of the pubs had no rooms, while the small roadside inns had none to spare, or occasionally only one. We were well off the main roads now, and there was little call for accommodations for travelers. It was after nine, and then after ten, and finally going on for midnight.

Simon turned to me, his face set in the reflected light from the headlamps. "I'm tired. I think we ought to call it a night."

The question was, where could we stop?

We were in rather hilly country just then, and we hadn't passed a sizable town or village in some time. While there was bound to be one ahead, it could be another hour—two—before we found what we were after.

"If you can find a suitable place to stop, I'm for it," I agreed. I'd just caught myself dozing in my seat, and if I was tired, then Simon most certainly must be.

We drove on, the hills higher and closer together, the road a thread winding around the base of one and then following on around the base of the next.

"A string of lighted windows," I said, a few minutes later, pointing ahead. "It must be a village."

But it was no more than a widening in the road, the land flat enough to allow for a hamlet to grow up.

It wasn't large enough to boast an inn, nor even a pub of any size.

The next hamlet was a bit larger but still crowded into a long, narrow pocket of land. I saw the name, MIDDLE DYSOE, on a signpost at the curve in the road. But it offered little more than the first hamlet had done. There were a dozen or so cottages strung out along the road, one lane that disappeared behind several small shops, and a smithy at the far end.

"Would you like me to drive?" I asked once more.

"I'm all right. For now—" He broke off as the next turning revealed a half dozen or so sheep blocking the road. Swearing under his breath, Simon pulled up the brake, as we gave ourselves and the poor ewes quite a fright. After casting terrified glances over their shoulders at the monster that had so suddenly come upon them, they darted into a farm lane, their white backs milling and pushing to be the first out of danger. And then they were gone, out of range of our headlamps and quickly disappearing from sight behind a straggling clump of lilacs.

Simon sat there for a moment, then he said, "I don't relish having to pay a distraught farmer for his ewes."

I laughed, but he was right, we might have injured one of them.

In the distance, over the ticking of the motor, I could hear a dog bark once or twice, and then right across our headlamps an owl swooped low, landing in the grassy verge, before taking off again. I thought we must have spoiled his aim, for he appeared to have missed his prey.

Simon released the brake and moved on, this time even slower than the narrow and winding road demanded.

I had no idea where we were. Somewhere well out of Worcestershire, surely, and heading a little east, I thought, for this winding road had taken us slightly off course.

Ahead was another small sign at the outskirts of the next village, and as we approached, I could make out UPPER DYSOE.

It too had nothing to offer us.

I remembered seeing a barn just where the sheep had disappeared from view. Before I'd read the village's name on the little sign. The roof half fallen in but the stone walls still in fair condition.

Hardly satisfactory lodging for the night. But certainly safe enough to rest for a little while. The next time we might not see the flock of sheep in time.

Simon had noticed the barn as well, but at first he refused to consider it.

"You can rest for a bit before we move on again. Long enough to take the edge off our fatigue."

"Bess."

"There has to be a town nearby. Before we find it, we could round another hill and find ourselves in a ditch."

"All right. We'll take a look." He turned back, and when we reached the barn, he pulled off the road, judged the rutted lane that led up to the gaping space that had once held broad doors, and then moved forward into the shelter of the walls.

As our headlamps picked out the spacious interior, I realized that this barn must have been derelict for some time, not just through the war years. Twenty years? Thirty?

It appeared that anything that was still useful had been removed long ago. There was only the debris from the roof and fallen stone left. A good bit of that stone had also been carted away for building byres or walls in a field.

Simon helped me into the rear seat, handed me the rug he carried in the boot, and then settled himself into the seat I had vacated, stretching his long legs out toward the driver's side.

"Twenty minutes?" Simon asked.

"Yes, that seems about right. Half an hour at the most."

I fell asleep to the rustling of something in what was left of the roof.

Chapter Nine

I don't know how long we slept there. A faint glow of dawn was just etching its way across the eastern horizon when I opened my eyes again, and I could see through a gap in the roof that there were pink, fluffy clouds drifting across the sky. My neck was stiff, as if I'd slept with it in an awkward position, and as I moved to ease it a little, I woke Simon.

"It's almost light," he said. "Are you still asleep, Bess?"

"Not really. It's a very good thing it didn't rain!"

He chuckled. "There was nothing to fear short of a deluge."

"It reminds me of nights I've spent in ruined villages in France."

"Yes, it does that." He got out and stretched his shoulders. "I'm afraid there's nothing to offer you for breakfast. I don't think our accommodations run to morning tea or anything else."

But I was looking in the other direction, and I could see that on a makeshift shelf under the lee of the fallen roof, someone had collected a small mound of fruit from somewhere—pears and apples and berries. Beside them was a rusty, dented cup, and what appeared to be an old tin next to it.

"Simon. I don't think we're the only ones who've sought shelter here," I said in a low voice.

"A shepherd, most likely," he replied after walking over to look at the small hoard. "These are drying up—the berries turning gray with mold. Whoever it is, he hasn't been back in a while."

I wasn't so sure it was a shepherd. The barn was too close to the road.

Our very safe, comfortable camp was taking on a very different aspect. I looked around us, peering into shadows and crannies where the roof had fallen in.

Simon went outside, and I could hear him as he circled the barn, looking for any sign of recent occupation.

I had the uneasy feeling that we might be under observation. Simon must have felt it as well, for he said, "Stay where you are for now. I'll drive on."

He bent to turn the crank, just as a bit of the roof slipped down some ten feet ahead of us, landing with a thud on the dusty floor of the barn, and a pair of doves took off, startling me as they flapped through the opening and soared out of sight.

Simon got in, carefully reversed the motorcar, and drove out of the gaping hole where once doors had hung. We made it through the high grass and ruts in the lane back to the road without incident. I could see the doves sitting on the ruins of the roof now, settling back as we no longer threatened them.

I felt better at once. What if whoever was using the barn had come there and found us asleep?

Just then I saw a goat grazing on the far side of the road, nearly hidden by the summer's growth of briars. Sunlight caught her yellow eyes, and at the same moment, I realized that she was tethered. That bore out Simon's suggestion that a shepherd used the barn from time to time.

We stopped in another ten yards, and I moved to the seat next to Simon. My cap was crushed and wrinkled, my apron the same. I tucked loose strands of hair back out of sight and smoothed my skirts. "I believe I saw a pub in the village just ahead. Where we turned around last night?"

"I don't think either of us is presentable enough to approach the police and ask directions," he said with a wry smile. "The pub it is."

"I expect you're right." And then I asked a question I'd been putting off since Simon had found me.

"Has the Colonel Sahib had anything to say about my problem with the Army?" I told myself I hadn't wanted him to know, because I hadn't wanted to drag him into what had happened over Sergeant Wilkins's disappearance. But this morning I suddenly found myself thinking about him.

"I haven't spoken to him," Simon answered. "I've been out of touch."

Which probably meant he'd been in France. Or my father had. Not the happiest thought. I worried about them more than they knew.

Just then we came to the outskirts of the village, and down the street I could see the pub sign. THE SHEPHERD'S CROOK.

I could feel my stomach growling at the thought of breakfast.

"What do you say? We can stop here, freshen up, and bespeak breakfast before deciding where we are and whether to go back or continue."

"A very good idea."

Ahead of us a young woman with a market basket over her arm started to cross the street, a small liver-and-white spaniel on a lead trotting beside her. The little dog darted away, dragging his lead, and charged the motorcar, barking furiously.

The young woman cried out in alarm, calling the dog's name, and if Simon's reflexes hadn't been swift enough, the spaniel would have ended up under our wheels. Sounding the horn and veering away, he barely missed the little dog.

I breathed again, knowing just how close a call it was.

The spaniel must have realized that as well, for it fell back on its haunches as Simon sounded the horn once more, then it turned tail and ran back to its mistress, cowering beneath her skirts. She fervently thanked us, then bent to scold the dog.

We carried on and pulled into the pub's yard behind several carts and a horse-drawn milk wagon.

Apparently we weren't the only ones to decide to stop here for breakfast. Inside there were half a dozen farmers. The man from the milk van was talking to them and to the cart owners, comparing prices on goods. I gathered there had been a market in one of the neighboring towns the day before, and those who hadn't gone were discussing the cost of oats and barley and even beer, with those who had. They barely looked up as we crossed the room. I heard one of the farmers boast that he'd bought a bonnet for his daughter in Biddington, and the eager questions about prices turned into good-natured teasing. I saw the man flush with a mixture of embarrassment and pride.

The pub was old, dark, low beamed—Simon's head all but brushed the rafters as we walked toward the bar—and the air was rather smoky from the fire.

There appeared to be no separate dining room, although Simon inquired, and he turned to me to ask if I wished to drive on. But I shook my head. The smells issuing from the kitchen were heavenly, and what did it matter if we stayed? Four years ago, before the war began, I might have been more reluctant. Now, having lived in very difficult conditions in France, sharing my breakfast with farmers was the least of my worries.

"I think it's best to stay. But are there rooms available to wash my face and hands?" I asked him in Urdu, and he turned back to the man behind the bar.

It seems there were two rooms upstairs, although the man couldn't answer as to whether we would be satisfied with them.

We followed him up the narrow, creaking stairs to a dark passage lit only by a single window at the far end.

Simon had a look at both rooms before nodding to the man.

Mine was clean, but the furniture was heavy—the wardrobe took up most of the space—with a single cot, a washstand, and a chair. Someone tapped at my door, and when I opened it, a man well into his sixties brought in a pitcher of hot water and a pair of fresh towels.

It was heaven to bathe my face and hands, brush out my hair and settle my cap properly, then brush my clothes as best I could.

I was ready to go down when Simon came to collect me.

After we'd given our order to the man who came to our table—the same one who had brought my water and towels—Simon grimaced. "Your mother will have my head for this," he said, keeping his voice low enough for my ears only. "I shall have to do penance for a—" He broke off as the outer door opened and a woman in riding dress strode in.

"My horse has gone lame, Tulley," she said briskly to the man behind the bar, who had been washing glasses. She was quite attractive, slender and tall, fair hair tucked up under her riding hat. But her expression was imperious, as if she expected to be obeyed instantly.

Wiping his hands on a towel hanging from his belt, Tulley replied, "Jim's not here. But I can let you have the mare for now. Jim'll bring the gray to the house as soon as he's back."

She shook her head impatiently. "That won't do. He must take the gray to Maddie to look her over, then come and tell me what has to be done. Maddie will know."

She took it for granted that he would do as she asked, turning to us now and frowning. "And who are you?"

She included me in her glance but addressed her question to Simon.

He rose. "Travelers," he said briefly. "On our way home from calling on friends."

It wasn't like Simon to be so unforthcoming. His expression was civil but cold.

"And where is 'home'?"

"London."

"Indeed." She considered him for a moment. Then she turned on her heel and went out the door.

Simon stood where he was until the door had closed behind her, then resumed his place across the table from me.

The man behind the bar said morosely to Simon, "She's a right piece of work, but she owns the pub, she does, and there's naught we can do about it, Jim and me."

"Who is she?" I asked, curious.

"The late Mr. Neville's daughter. More money than God. Her brother was killed on the Somme, and her father's heart gave out from the shock. She was always one to want her own way. Even as a child. But now she can make life wretched for anyone stands up to her. Her brother, now, he was never one to cause trouble for anyone. A true gentleman, that one. He—" Breaking off he looked nervously toward the door as it began to open. But it was only a man roughly dressed like a workman, one eye covered by a makeshift patch, bony shoulders showing through the thin stuff of his shirt.

Relieved, the man behind the bar said testily, "And where have *you* been? Her ladyship left the gray in the yard. You're to take it to Maddie, and whatever Maddie says to do, you'll tell Miss Neville, then bring my mare back home."

"Not me. I'm afraid of that damned fool shooting at everything that moves."

"You'll do as you're told, or know the reason why," the man behind the bar said gruffly.

"Easy for you to say, you was never in France."

The older man, who could very well be Jim's father—they looked enough alike—came in with our food, but he'd heard enough to say, "Jim," in a tone of voice that brooked no argument.

Mumbling to himself, Jim turned and went out the door, slamming it hard.

The platters of eggs, cheese, and thick slices of toasted bread were set before us, and then he turned back to the man behind the bar.

"You can't push Jim too far. He can't bear the shooting. The sound rips at him, bringing everything back. Besides, that man's daft, and will kill someone yet. Mark my words."

"She'll put a stop to it if it gets out of hand. She's besotted, if you want my opinion. That business of the goat, for one. Did no harm until he wandered off and she had to bring him back."

My gaze met Simon's, and he smiled.

Who had wandered off, the goat or the man? Or both?

Amused by this conversation we went on with our breakfast, in a hurry to finish and be on our way.

"With any luck," Jim's father said finally, "she'll marry and that will be an end to it."

It was true. Unless the woman's father had managed to tie up the estate in his daughter's name, everything she owned would become her husband's property on the day of their marriage. And if her father had died suddenly, as it appeared from what the man Tulley was saying, there might have been no time to set out provisions to protect his daughter.

It was one of the inequities of life. Even my mother's inheritance had become my father's property, but the Colonel Sahib loved his lady very much, and he had never treated her like chattel. For that matter, I couldn't imagine my independent-minded mother allowing herself to become anyone's chattel.

The man trudged back to the kitchen and we finished our meal in peace. Simon went to settle our account and I prepared to leave.

We had just stepped outside when Jim came running toward us, chest heaving from his exertions. We moved out of his way, but he was already speaking to Simon, putting out a hand to stop us.

"Please, Sart-Major, does the Sister know how to take out a bit of lead?"

"Who needs this help?" Simon asked as he shot a swift glance in my direction.

"It's Warren—he owns the flour mill. He's been shot, Maddie says, and it can't be left in, Maddie says. But his sight isn't what it was."

"Is Maddie a doctor?"

"We don't run to doctors here, Sart-Major. Not here, not nowhere near. By the time Maddie gets Mr. Warren to Biddington, he'll be dead."

"I have my kit," I said to Simon. "But I don't know what else I shall need. Surely it's better to risk taking him to the nearest town. Perhaps we could drive him? That would be faster than a cart."

"Come and tell Maddie that. Maddie's bent on taking it out."

We hurried to the motorcar, taking Jim up with us, and followed his directions to a small cottage on the far side of the village. I could see why there was no doctor here, tiny as Upper Dysoe was. And in such cases, a woman with a healing touch was often part midwife and part doctor and part witch, with herb remedies and the like to cure fevers, heal wounds, and sometimes save the very ill.

The cottage was stone, settled into the earth as if it had grown out of it. Thatch beetled down to overhang the porch that shielded the door, and it had a rank smell. *Not very reassuring,* I thought as Simon ducked to step forward and lift the latch.

Expecting to find an aged woman inside, with poor Mr. Warren lying on her bed, however clean it might be, I was quite surprised when I walked through the door Simon was holding open for me.

The cottage was low-beamed inside, and there were only two rooms that I could see. Simon was forced to duck again. But there my image of what I'd find ended. Mr. Warren was lying on a low table set to one side of the main room, a clean sheet beneath him and one over him. A man nearly as old as Jim's father was bending over him, speaking to him in a comforting tone of voice.

He looked up as we entered, greeting us with a nod. "I'm sorry to trouble you," he said in an educated voice. "But I can't do this alone. There's too much risk."

Mr. Warren was trying to see who had come in, twisting his head to look in our direction, his mouth tight with pain. But that tiny movement was enough to set off an agony of reaction, and he quickly closed his eyes, groaning through clenched teeth.

Maddie pulled aside the sheet to show me the wound, far too close to the patient's lung for my liking. I crossed the room for a closer look. Maddie was watching my face, watching to see if I thought this was beyond my skills.

"He should be taken to the nearest doctor," I said, straightening up.

Maddie shook his head. "A doctor will ask questions about how he was shot, and the constable will want to know by whom. And that will be a problem."

I turned to Simon, who held my gaze for a moment, then shook his head.

"Who did shoot him?"

"Mr. Warren refuses to say."

I was studying the patient now. There was no bloody froth on his lips. But this wasn't proof that the lung hadn't been nicked by the bullet. I asked that he be turned slightly, but there was no exit wound. The bullet was still inside, possibly lodged in the bone. And the other problem was infection. Even if I successfully removed the bullet, I could do more damage than I knew. In several days this man might be dying, fever ravaged.

It was a task for one of the American X-ray machines, so efficient at finding shrapnel and saving the patient the suffering of blind digging.

Yet I had done this sort of thing time and again at the Front. Why was I hesitating to do it now?

This was England, not the trenches of France. There *would* be a doctor in the next village or the next who could do such work with the proper tools and septic powder, giving the patient a far greater chance of survival.

I shook my head again. "I don't think it's wise."

"Then I'll do it," Maddie said decisively. "With or without your help, it doesn't matter."

He walked to the door and held it wide for us to go. Mr. Warren had opened his eyes again. They were frightened, staring at me, then at Maddie. Pleading for one of us to do something for his pain.

I turned away and moved toward the door. But before I crossed the threshold, I stopped. I could see well, I could probe carefully. Would that make a difference in Mr. Warren's survival?

"All right," I said, coming back into the room. "But what shall I use? Can we light a fire and boil enough water? Are there clean bandages for the wound?"

Maddie pointed to the hearth. Kindling and wood lay ready for a match. Next he opened a cabinet standing in one corner. Inside was a tray of instruments, clean as any I'd ever seen, and well cared for. Below, on a shelf, were bandages, every shape and description, neatly folded and covered with a length of linen.

I stared at the cabinet, then looked up at Maddie's lined face. It gave nothing away.

Who was he? Had he been a doctor once? How had he come by these things, otherwise? A simple healer in a tiny village without a real physician?

And yet the very imperious Miss Neville had sent her horse to him.

Without a word he handed me a large apron, and Simon helped me put it on after I'd removed my own.

Maddie knew what instrument to hand me, and he stood at my side, intent on what I was doing, mopping the blood as it welled up in the wound while Simon and Jim held Mr. Warren steady.

To give the miller credit, he tried not to cry out, his eyes closed, his teeth clenched, and then mercifully, he lost consciousness.

I had to be very careful. Not to enlarge the wound, not to tear the edge of the lung or clip a major vessel. I realized suddenly that I could see better, and glanced up to find that Maddie was holding a lamp high to help me.

And then I felt something move against the probe. In another minute I had fished the bullet out of the wound, grasping it with forceps as it came nearer the surface. I blessed Mr. Warren for being a muscular man without much fatty tissue on his frame as I dropped the small piece of metal into the pan Maddie was holding for me.

It clinked loudly in the silence, and then I was putting antiseptic powder into the wound, using it liberally and waiting for the bleeding to clot.

Straightening my back, I looked at the men on the other side of Mr. Warren's inert figure.

Jim was nearly green, and I thought he might be close to fainting. I doubt he'd had to assist at surgery before this. He grinned ruefully at me, saying, "I've seen 'em shot and blown apart, but I couldn't watch the doctors at their work. A bloody shambles it was." And he turned to stumble out of the cottage. I heard him being sick outside.

Simon's face was grim, but he returned my glance and smiled encouragingly. I stood watching the wound for a time. Maddie had taken over now, frowning as he attended his patient.

Finally he turned to me. "Well done, Sister," he said. "Leave the apron by the door. I'll see to it later."

"That's from a revolver," I said, gesturing to the lump of lead in the tin. "It's not bird shot."

"I never said it was."

"No. But who shot Mr. Warren? And why shouldn't the nearest constable be summoned? It's attempted murder."

"It isn't likely to be that," Maddie said, distracted by his attention to his patient, who was beginning to come around. "I've a drop or two of laudanum. Mixed with a little water, and he'll be quite comfortable for most of the day."

"He was shot," I persisted. "And at fairly close range. Hardly mistaken identity, that, and I don't think Mr. Warren indulged in stealing chickens."

Maddie looked at me. "Hardly. It's rather complicated. A soldier. Home from the war and not quite right in his head. I shouldn't think the poor man would be helped by throwing him in a cell. He's not a killer. I assure you."

Shell shock? It wasn't talked about. Lack of moral fiber, cowardice, whatever derogatory term people used, it was considered shameful, something to hide.

As if he'd read my mind, Maddie shook his head. "An infection. Delirium. He got out, you see, and it was a while before we could find him again. He thought he was back in France. But of course he wasn't."

My first thought was that I'd found Sergeant Wilkins. But the sergeant hadn't been armed. And the revolver was an officer's weapon . . .

Maybe it was the man and not the goat after all that had gone astray.

Chapter Ten

S atisfied that my patient—our patient—was stable, I was ready to leave, but we hadn't reached Simon's motorcar when Miss Neville came galloping up on what must have been the pub owner's horse.

"What's happened?" she demanded, staring at me and at Simon as if we were responsible for whatever she suspected. Because it was clear that she knew something.

Maddie came out the door. "He's all right, Miss Neville. The miller. A wound in the shoulder, nothing more." His voice was quietly soothing.

But it had been much more than that.

"Dear God. I shall want to see him." She dismounted without help and went toward the cottage door. "What are these people doing here?"

"The Sister helped me. My eyesight. I've told you."

"Yes, yes. Where is Warren? Inside?"

Maddie stepped out of the way. Miss Neville went inside, and I could hear her clearly from where we were standing.

"Warren? Can you hear me?"

The miller mumbled something, for the laudanum was taking hold.

"I shall see you right, I promise you. The Major is not himself, or this would never have happened. Meanwhile, I shall see that there is someone to help at the mill while you recover. My estate manager will arrange it. Your family will be all right. Do you understand, Warren?"

I doubt that he did, for after a moment she came back out of the cottage, her expression impatient, a mixture of worry and frustration.

"Have you spoken to his family?" she asked Maddie.

"He was only just brought in," the old man explained. "Really, you must do something about that revolver. He will kill someone, next time."

"I *have* taken it away from him. Several times. Do you think I find this at all amusing?" she snapped. "Now I shall have to speak to Mrs. Warren. It really is too much."

She walked back to her horse, and said to Simon, "Give me a boost up, if you please."

He crossed to where she was waiting and lifted her into her saddle, then stepped back.

"I shall count on your discretion," she said. "This is a very delicate matter, and I should not like to find it the talk of the parish. I'll not have people clamoring for the poor man to be clapped up in an asylum. He's not dangerous, he's simply ill."

"Beyond Maddie's skills to cure?" Simon asked, keeping his voice level, although he was very angry. No one ordered Simon Brandon about.

"Beyond anyone's, sad to say. But not yet gangrene. I am thankful for that blessing." She cast a measuring glance at me, then turned her horse away and set out for the village.

I hadn't noticed a mill as we had come through earlier. But then I'd seen no stream to turn the great wheel, which meant that the mill must be down one of the side lanes of the village.

Maddie watched her go, his face unreadable.

I said, "Who is the Major?"

Jim said, his voice low, "The man she's to marry." As if that explained everything.

Simon was holding the door of the motorcar for me to step in, and I nodded to Jim as I turned to go with him.

As he walked toward the front of the bonnet to attend to the crank, Simon glanced up at me. I knew he was asking which way to turn.

"Let's finish what we started," I said as he joined me in the motorcar. But I could see that he thought it hopeless, and while I was inclined to agree, I wanted to be sure.

We looped back to where we'd crossed into Warwickshire last night. And in the daylight we gained a clearer picture of where we were as we worked our way back to Upper Dysoe.

Coming into the county, we'd made our way in the general direction of Kenilworth, slightly to the north. But of course English roads seldom ran straight, despite the head start the Romans had given us. We'd wandered off the main road in the dark and had been taking country lanes leading us more or less toward Stratford.

Still, in the villages where there was no resident constable, we stopped to ask if anyone recalled seeing a lorry pass through, leaving behind a soldier with a bad limp and a recent head wound.

It was possible that the lorry had made other stops before Kenilworth—general hauling meant just that— taking it across Warwickshire by a roundabout route. And indeed, eventually we discovered where one had crossed the border and delivered a new plow to a farmer. He thought someone, possibly the driver's helper, had been asleep in the front of the lorry. But he hadn't actually seen the man.

It was depressing news, because we couldn't be sure this was Sergeant Wilkins. Of course if it was, we'd been right to follow this lead.

Simon, driving down the road after the last encounter with a villager in what was little more than a hamlet, said, "We've assumed that the farmer back in Shropshire had indeed spotted the bay horse. But depending on the time of day—or evening—he saw it, he might have taken a guess at the color. We could very well be looking for one man and actually be tracking two or three."

"That's true," I answered reluctantly. "And yet, there's enough circumstantial evidence that I find myself hoping."

"Yes, I know. Shall we move on to Kenilworth, or turn toward Somerset?"

Of two minds, still I said, "Yes, Kenilworth. We've come this far. But first I wonder if we could have another look at our patient in Upper Dysoe."

"It's not that far out of our way." There was a silence. Then, "What would you have done if you'd found the man?" Simon asked, glancing across at me.

"I don't think he was afraid of returning to France. I can usually tell if that's what is troubling a patient. And considering the nature of his wounds, he'd have been invalided out of the Army before very long anyway. Why didn't he wait? What was so pressing about killing Henry Lessup that he couldn't have waited another few weeks? It makes no sense."

"You told me you thought there was something on his mind. Was it this murder? Or was he feeling guilt about what was about to happen?"

"Sister Hammond told me he'd had nightmares. Perhaps that was what spurred him to act now. In the hope that doing something about them might stop them."

"Neither Inspector Stephens nor Inspector Jester mentioned the bay horse to you. If you hadn't met that young woman on the bridge, you wouldn't have known how Wilkins was recognized at the scene of the murder. We've learned of both quite by accident. The Yard might already know what his motive was for murder."

"That's a very good point."

We'd reached that odd formation of rounded hills where the three hamlets called Dysoe were located. The hills looked so much like giant grassy thimbles piled so close together that there was barely room for the road that threaded through them, and in the daylight we could see they appeared to be mostly uninhabited, save for the houses huddled in the only places where the land between them widened slightly.

Lower Dysoe was only a scattering of houses, one tiny pub, and a shop or two in the lee of what appeared to be another ruined barn. Only a sizable wall was left standing. A tithe barn, once, perhaps, placed by the road like this? Last night it had been nearly invisible. Middle Dysoe, a bit larger, boasted a general merchandise store, a greengrocer's, and a bakery as well as a pub. Cosmopolitan by the standards of its neighbor.

On our way to Upper Dysoe we passed the massive and elegant iron gates to an estate nestled in a natural hollow. We could see the house, and I suddenly had a vision of Miss Neville riding down to the door. Was this where she lived?

Between the gates and the next village was the tumbledown barn where Simon and I had stayed the night. And then we were driving into Upper Dysoe, the largest of the three hamlets, with a pub, shops, and somewhere, the mill owned by Maddie's patient, Mr. Warren.

This time when we rounded the bend and came upon a flock of sheep spilling down the hillside opposite and already blocking the road, we could see them in time to stop. Looking very much like the sheep we'd met with last night, they milled around us, curious and seemingly unconcerned even when Simon sounded the horn.

Simon was about to get down and move them himself, when someone up on the hill to our left shouted, "They've as much right to be there as you do. It's their land, after all."

We looked up to see a middle-aged woman in dark brown walking clothes, standing near the crest of the hill just beside us. She had a long walking stick in her left hand, almost as tall as a crook. I might have mistaken her for a shepherd, at first glance.

"Their land?" Simon called.

"In truth it belongs to my stepdaughter, but the sheep use it, not she."

By now the sheep had lost interest in us, moving on to graze at the verge of the road or to disappear down the lane past the barn. Simon closed his door and began to weave slowly through the thinning flock.

The woman was marching down toward us, and I wasn't sure whether she meant to speak to us or just to walk on.

"Are you lost?" she called as she came nearer.

"We know our way. Thank you," Simon replied, but she was peering at me.

"Are you the Sister who assisted Maddie with that fool Warren?"

"I did help him. Yes." I didn't know where this conversation was going, but I was curious.

"Will he live?"

"Mr. Warren? Yes, I believe so, if infection doesn't set in."

She had reached the motorcar now, a straight-backed, graying woman of perhaps fifty, her mouth set in a severe, disapproving line.

"Can you do anything for my stepdaughter's fiancé?"

"I—don't know precisely what's wrong with him."

"Maddie can do nothing. He says time is the proper healer with head wounds. The leg he can treat. I am not particularly fond of the Major, but I would like to see a change for the better before the wedding."

I thought at first that she meant this would make the occasion a happier one, and then I saw that her intent was the opposite. That she wanted the Major well sooner for reasons of her own.

"He has no sense of the land, you see," she went on. "And land matters. It's not simply the acreage that surrounds a large house, it's the sustaining force in all our lives. Tenants, landowners, even the village."

This was very much a Labour position, that industry was wrong, it tore people from the land and made them vulnerable to the wealthy who cared little or nothing for their welfare. That a simpler world would be a happier world. Before the war, several books had been written on that subject. As if we could turn back the tide and return to an England before the rise of industry. Materialism was wicked, Agriculture the savior of mankind.

It was a very odd view for a woman of the wealthier class to take. And from her accent, she clearly belonged to it.

"Never mind," she went on, "we were discussing the Major." She placed a gloved hand on the door of the motorcar, where I had let the window down earlier. "What must we do about him?"

"It would be best," I said, "to send him somewhere for treatment. There are several very good hospitals that deal with head wounds. Dorset, most certainly. Or Surrey."

She shook her head. "That's not likely to happen. They'd only clap him up. And I'd say she was besotted with him, if I didn't know better. He seems docile enough one minute, and angry, withdrawn the next. Hardly the qualities of a lover."

"What was his regiment?" Simon asked.

"He wears the uniform of a Yorkshire regiment, but he's not a Yorkshireman. Who *are* his people? I looked him up in *Debrett's*, but he's not there. What's more, he didn't know Nadine's brother. And he should have, if they were officers in the same regiment. I really can't think what possessed Barbara to accept his proposal. It must have been pity. And pity is a poor beginning for a happy marriage."

"He could well be Yorkshire," Simon told her. "The Army is taking men from elsewhere and putting them in the old line regiments to bring up numbers. And if he *were* in a different battalion, it isn't unheard of not to know all the new men." He didn't add that at the rate officers were dying, there might be little opportunity to know a man before he was killed or wounded and removed from the active duty roster.

"I hadn't considered that," she answered, looking at him straightly. "A very good point." She had been peering in at Simon. Stepping back now, she added, "At least he doesn't appear to be a fortune hunter like the last two or three. But I'd feel better if he had any sense of the *land*. It would be all right then."

With an abrupt nod, she walked on.

We watched her go, striding down the road with determination. Just then she spotted the tethered goat we had seen only that morning, and stopped short.

"What's this?" she said, and then she went whipping up the embankment, disappearing into the undergrowth, reappearing shortly leading the reluctant goat down to the road again.

By this time we had drawn nearly level with her, for Simon had driven at a slow pace, some distance behind her. She raised a hand to halt us.

"I must take this creature back to where she belongs," she said. "Will you give me a lift back to the house?"

Beside me, Simon swore under his breath.

"I'm not sure we can persuade the goat to climb inside," I said quickly.

She stared at me. "Are you being difficult?" she asked. "Of course not. We'll tie her lead to the motorcar."

Easier said than done.

The first problem was reversing on this narrow road. And that upset the goat no end.

Next, it had other ideas about approaching closer than ten feet to the motorcar, taking an instant dislike to Simon's uniform. It was several minutes before we could persuade it to move near enough to the rear of the motorcar to attach the lead. When she was satisfied that the goat was in no danger, Mrs. Neville took my place, as if by right, beside the driver, and I got into the rear seat.

"Drive slowly. I'll direct you," she told Simon, and settled back.

I was looking out the small rear window at the goat as Simon put in the clutch and took off the brake. It dug in for a moment, and then as the motorcar took up the slack in the lead, it seemed to accept the inevitable and began to trot behind us as we drove slowly back the way we'd just come.

"Why was she tethered out here?" I asked our unexpected guest.

"Why? How should I know? You'll have to ask the Major. Nothing of this sort happened before *he* came to Windward. But she *would* have him stay here, wouldn't she? Duty and all that. Well, where was duty when she was asked to turn Windward into a hospital? I ask you."

It was rather apparent that Mrs. Neville had little patience with her stepdaughter.

She turned to give Simon directions, and very soon we were passing through the rather ornate gates that we'd just driven by.

The gateposts were brick, and crowned with a griffon. Close to, the gates themselves were lovely examples of wrought iron, tall, graceful, and intended to keep visitors out. The name *Windward* was engraved on a bronze plaque.

As a rule such approaches led to a looping drive that debouched before the main front. Here it led straight to one of the most beautiful early Tudor brick houses I'd ever seen. Crowned by chimneys and peaked roofs, it was a lovely rose color, windows set off by stone facings, and a large studded door in an arched frame that could have welcomed a King. And probably had.

Mrs. Neville must have heard my gasp of pleasure, for she said over her shoulder, "This doesn't hold a candle to the house that went with the title. The Nevilles are a cadet branch."

I stepped out of the motorcar to open the gates and then shut them after we and the goat had passed through. Continuing down the drive on foot gave me time to consider the house and the landscaping that set it off. I almost missed the wooden bench under the specimen maple tree. A man was sitting there, and at first glance my heart lurched. I thought it must be Sergeant Wilkins. Bandages were visible beneath the officer's cap he was wearing, and there was the bulge of other bandaging just above the knee on his left thigh. Such leg wounds were very common—German machine guns were often set to scythe through the charging line of enemy just at knee height. It stopped a man in his tracks, and made it difficult for him to crawl back to his own lines. This man wasn't using a sling.

On closer inspection, I realized he wore the smart mustache of an officer. And he was sitting there with the unmistakable air of a man who felt quite at home in these elegant surroundings. It was indefinable, but it was very real.

Could Wilkins pass himself off as a gentleman so easily? I didn't know him well enough to say. He'd been well spoken, his voice that of an educated man. That didn't necessarily mean he could cope with the complexities of a grand house like this one.

As the motorcar pulled up before the steps, Mrs. Neville waited for Simon to come around and open her door, then she called to the officer.

"Really, Major, this is too much. Take the goat back where she belongs."

He got unsteadily to his feet, starting toward us. I was watching his face, but he seemed not to recognize either Simon or me.

But before he reached us, a housekeeper came to the door and called over her shoulder to a middle-aged footman. Without blinking, the footman walked over and untied the goat's tether, as if he was doing nothing more than preparing to take our luggage out of the boot. His expression was bland, as if this was nothing out of the ordinary. He disappeared around the corner with the reluctant goat following him, balking every third step.

Meanwhile the Major had stopped. After a moment he returned to the bench and sat down heavily, careful of that leg, as Mrs. Neville said, "And where is your cane? You know you aren't supposed to go anywhere without it."

"I don't know," he said in a low voice. "I can't remember where I left it."

She made a noise of disbelief but said nothing more to him.

Turning to Simon and me, she thanked us for bringing her home, and walked on toward the open door.

It was dismissal. Simon had left the motorcar running, and he helped me into the front seat before coming around to take his place behind the wheel.

"I expect," I said quietly as the door closed behind Mrs. Neville, "we aren't presentable enough to be invited in to tea."

But he didn't laugh. Unsmilingly letting in the clutch, he went round the small circle and started back to the gates.

"Does that man—the Major—remind you of Sergeant Wilkins?" he asked.

"At first, yes, I thought surely it must be. But he isn't the sergeant. Is he?"

"I don't know the answer to that."

"There's the officer's mustache."

"A man can grow a mustache rather quickly, if he has a strong beard. A matter of days."

"Yes, that's true. But he didn't recognize us, did he?"

"That's the odd thing. Either he didn't know us or he's a damned fine actor."

I got out to open the gates for us. I looked back at the house, and the Major was standing there beneath the tree, staring after us.

I'd never seen Sergeant Wilkins on his feet. Nor had I seen his coloring, except for the fair eyebrows and blue eyes. Not to mention the shape of his ears, the definition of his chin.

Removing bandaging he'd insisted upon having before he came down to London had made it possible to leave the hotel without being recognized as the man who'd been given a medal. That too Sergeant Wilkins had foreseen.

And I hadn't been close enough to the Major to look directly into his eyes. But I had a feeling his eyebrows were also fair.

Getting into the motorcar once more, I said again, "Do *you* think it's Wilkins? If you do, we ought to tell someone."

"I saw less of Wilkins than you did. There's a resemblance. Height, weight. But I should think Miss Neville will have something to say about our sending Scotland Yard here on such slim evidence."

"It's just possible that he rode the horse as far as he could, fell off or was thrown, I don't suppose we'll ever know—and reached the Dysoes on foot. But how on earth could he have persuaded Miss Neville that he's someone else?"

"A very good question. I'd give much to know the Major's name. I could look him up, back in London."

"We could ask Maddie. It wouldn't be all that strange for me to look in on Mr. Warren before we go on."

Mr. Warren was still in a drugged sleep, snoring slightly when we got to the cottage after retrieving Simon's valise. I was pleased to find that his skin was cool, no sign of fever developing. Maddie had taken as natural my comment about wanting to see the patient a last time. But I had the feeling he wished we hadn't come back.

"We encountered Mrs. Neville on the road," I said, covering Mr. Warren's shoulder again with the clean sheet Maddie had spread over him. "She was telling us her views on Agriculture when we spotted one of the Windward goats tethered by the road. She insisted we take it back to the house."

"The goats have got loose a time or two," he agreed. "Clever beasts."

Clever or not, they hadn't learned to tether themselves.

"The Major was there. He seemed ill. Was he badly wounded?"

"He was. Miss Neville has insisted on nursing him. I'm told she knew him in London. Before the war, I believe."

"London? Perhaps I know him—he reminds me so much of Diana's brother, Major Havers. There were several cousins as well, if I remember. But I didn't like to ask if he were related because he seemed to be in such pain."

Diana's brother was at the Admiralty and his name wasn't Havers.

Maddie shook his head. "She hasn't favored me with his name," he said dryly. "He's just 'the Major.'"

I believed him. Miss Neville wouldn't bother to introduce her fiancé to the likes of Maddie. But I'd thought the Major himself might have, as a courtesy to the man trying to heal him.

And yet there was something in the way he answered me that was interesting. As if the oversight had been deliberate.

He stood there, quietly waiting for us to take our leave.

I couldn't think of another way of getting at what we wanted. And so we thanked him and went out to the motorcar.

Simon saw to the crank, then stood there for a moment, looking back down the road at the village of Upper Dysoe.

When he got into the motorcar, he said, "Kenilworth?"

"Do you suppose Tulley at the pub knows the Major's name?"

We drove back to the pub, but there were more than a dozen patrons being served their lunch, and Tulley was morose, unwilling to talk.

We walked away and set out for Kenilworth.

But when we tracked down the lorry we were seeking, it had long since moved on to Oxford, and the shop owner who taken delivery of a pair of horsehair chairs told us that the lorry driver had been alone.

"In fact," he told us sourly, "I had to help take out the chairs myself, which did no favors to my sciatica."

Where had he lost his elusive passenger?

We had nearly run out of time. We couldn't search every village, every hamlet. For that matter, the other man in the lorry could have stepped down in Kenilworth before the delivery of those chairs.

Reluctantly, I agreed that we'd done all we could. It went against the grain to give up, because we'd had some successes. Or thought we had. But they were so small that we couldn't take them to Scotland Yard.

We'd be accused of meddling. Inspector Stephens hadn't interviewed me with the object of setting me off on my own inquiry.

"Cheer up," Simon told me. "If he's out there, he'll be found. If not by you, then by the Army or the Yard. Or even your Inspector Jester."

Which was true. Only I wouldn't be allowed to see the sergeant, much less question him about what he'd done. To set my own mind at ease if nothing else.

The problem was, Sergeant Wilkins still traveled with us, for he was in both our thoughts as we headed south.

I smiled wryly as we reached the outskirts of Oxford. "We wouldn't have got as far as we did if it hadn't been for the bay horse, which had the good sense to come home on his own."

But for all I knew, Sergeant Wilkins was Miss Neville's Major, who seemed to have no qualms about shooting at people. Perhaps a side of our quarry I'd never seen. From the medical point of view, I wondered if either the sergeant or the Major was actually physically capable of hanging a man off Iron Bridge.

It would require a great deal of strength. Or a great deal of hatred.

Chapter Eleven

When I reached Mrs. Hennessey's, tired and dispirited, I found orders waiting for me. Apparently in my absence it had been decided that I bore no responsibility for Sergeant Wilkins's disappearance or his subsequent actions in Ironbridge. That was such good news.

I wondered if my parents were behind this return to duty. But I was grateful for it, however it had come about. All the same, that early suspicion was now a part of my record, and through no fault of my own.

I had less than twenty-four hours to meet my transport back to France.

I was ten minutes from leaving to take my train to Dover when Mrs. Hennessey came up the stairs to tell me I had a caller.

"It's that same man from Scotland Yard," she told me, her face set with a mixture of exasperation at the interruption and gloom at my departure.

I went down to meet Inspector Stephens, and he rose as I came into Mrs. Hennessey's sitting room.

"I understand you're on your way back to France," he said. "I'm glad."

Surprised, I said, "I'm glad as well. Is that why you came to see me?"

"There was a question I needed to put to you. Do you think Sergeant Wilkins was physically capable of hanging that man on the iron bridge?"

It was the question I'd pondered as well, but I said nothing about that. "I don't know," I told him truthfully. "You would have to ask his doctor at Lovering Hall. Or perhaps find out why he had done such a thing."

"We have spoken to his doctor. And he can't give us a straight answer. He said that it is possible, in the heat of the moment, to do something one isn't able to do ordinarily. I myself have heard of instances in France where a caisson fell on a man, and the rest of his company lifted it off him without thinking about their strength or their own wounds. They just got on with it. But the doctor also felt that the journey from London to Ironbridge could have taken a toll on healing wounds, depending on how the sergeant got there."

"I never examined him," I said. "You must remember that."

"You are an experienced nursing Sister. I'd like your opinion."

"Are you rethinking his guilt in the Ironbridge death?" I asked, intrigued.

"No," he said, with a heavy sigh. "Just attempting to shed any light we can on the matter."

They must be desperate, I thought to myself, if they are here asking me questions.

Should I mention the Major and Miss Neville? I thought about that and decided against it. There was nothing I knew that could actually connect the Major with anything that had to do with the murder or Sergeant Wilkins.

"If I do think of something that will help," I told Inspector Stephens carefully, "I'll be in touch. That's all I can promise."

He was clearly disappointed. But he said, "Thank you, Sister. I appreciate your willingness to help."

But had I been willing?

"Do you know why Sergeant Wilkins committed murder?" I asked.

"So far we're still pursuing our inquiries."

Which meant he didn't know—or wasn't free to tell me.

As we walked to the door, he added, "I understand the sergeant had a brother. He never spoke of him, but the Sister in Shrewsbury told me he dreamed about him sometimes. Nightmares might be a better word. Army records indicate that his brother died earlier in the war."

"I asked him, at the audience with the King, if he had any family members present, but he gave me to understand that he didn't. I found that rather sad. Most everyone had someone there. A wife or parents or sisters, all of them watching proudly."

Inspector Stephens grimaced at mention of the ceremony. But he said, "Yes, very sad. They might have been able to give us something useful to be going on with. We've been to the town where the sergeant grew up, but they can add very little to what we know at present."

It wasn't quite what I'd meant, but from Scotland Yard's perspective, information was more important than any sentiment.

He was just stepping out into the street when he turned and said, "The Sister at the Shrewsbury hospital tells me you came north to ask questions about the sergeant. Is that true?"

"Of course it is," I told him frankly. "This man has dragged me into his troubles, and I wanted to know just how wrong I'd been, trusting him. But I think, if you want my opinion, that he used the Sister at Lovering

Hall, just as he used me. Only in her case, he preyed on her feelings for him. In mine, he depended on my following instructions. But you see, that's what I've been trained to do. I was told not to disturb his dressings, and I accepted that. As far as I could judge, the leg wound was not weeping or in any way indicating that something was amiss after his travels."

"Thank you for your honesty."

He nodded to me, settled his hat firmly on his head, and walked on.

Mrs. Hennessey had brought my kit down, and she said, watching him go, "How inconsiderate of that man. Coming at the last minute to trouble you, when you've hardly had time to collect fresh uniforms. And the Sergeant-Major will be here any moment."

Simon arrived just then, my mother in the motorcar with him. I said nothing about the visit from Inspector Stephens. I didn't want to bring up the past few days just as I was leaving for France.

The Front had advanced a little, I saw that at once when I reached the forward aid station to which I'd been assigned.

The Americans were making a difference, just as Simon and my father had claimed they would, if they could be persuaded to enter the war.

Not everyone was happy about that. More than one soldier I was treating told me that the British and the French had faced the worst of the fighting, and here the Americans were, taking all the glory. Not that they weren't grateful—

I didn't care about glory as long as the killing stopped.

And the maiming. I worked with one torn body after another, and each time prayed that my patient would live to see war's end.

An American Marine was brought in late one afternoon. I didn't know how we'd come to have him—it was a long way from his sector—but as I tended his arm, he kept up a conversation that I thought must be his way of dealing with the painful probing for the rest of the shrapnel embedded in the muscle.

He was from Virginia, a soft-spoken man who would still have been considered a boy under different circumstances. Now he was a seasoned soldier, a corporal, and the line of his jaw was hard, his eyes harder.

He had been at Belleau Wood, he told me. And that was enough.

When the Russians had surrendered, German forces had been pulled from the Eastern Front and sent to France. The French and British had tried to hold the line, but these troops were very good, and the tired

Allies were getting the worst of it. I'd heard Simon and the Colonel-Sahib discuss what happened next.

In the face of the new German advance, the French had moved back to protect Paris, but an American Army with Marine brigades attached took over the French positions and refused—quite colorfully, according to Simon—to retreat.

In and around Belleau Wood, the Marines fought for nearly the entire bloody month of June, giving and losing ground until in the end they held the wood. It was the stuff of legends, and this man had been with the 5th Marines, in the thick of it.

As I stitched up the wound, I asked, "Is it true the Germans called you Devil Dogs for your tenacity?"

He smiled tightly. "Ma'am, I don't speak any German. And probably just as well."

And then he was gone with the dusk, after only a few hours of rest.

I wrote to the Colonel-Sahib, telling him about the encounter, and it was my mother who replied.

Darling,

Your father is away again. I've put your letter on his desk where he will see it first thing. I know he will be interested in the young Marine. Which reminds me, there was a small paragraph on the last page of the latest Times. It seems that a soldier is missing, and Scotland Yard has appealed to the public to help find him. There was of course no mention of what he might have done. The plea was worded to leave the impression that he might have fallen ill or come to grief in his weakened state. Simon, meanwhile, has looked up the Major you'd inquired about. He asked me to tell you that he had had no luck there. He also looked for information on Mr. Lessup, and it appears the man's career has been quite ordinary, something to do with trench design.

Which brought me back to my original question to Inspector Jester: was the murder of Lessup personal or related to the war? It appeared now to be personal.

The letter went on to give me all the news of home, and I slept well that night, comforted to know that Somerset, at least, was still my rock. My place of safety through all the chaos and uncertainty of war.

It was several days later when another letter came, this one written well before my mother's but taking longer to reach me.

It was from Simon, and quite brief.

I met a friend at Sandhurst who mentioned he'd met the Nevilles in the early days of the war. Miss

Neville's father had opened his London house to officers, after his son had joined the Army. This continued until August 1916, when his son was killed on the Somme. He himself died shortly afterward. The London house has been closed ever since. There's still black crepe on the door knocker. It has never been taken down. I went to see for myself if it was still there. Neither Miss Neville nor her stepmother has come down to London since that time. I have that on good authority. However, Miss Neville sometimes visits friends from her school days. My friend couldn't be sure, but he rather thought she'd attended Aldersgate. I went in search of Diana, but Mrs. Hennessey tells me she's in France.

And Diana had also been sent to Aldersgate, a distinguished school for young ladies near St. Albans. She and Miss Neville must be close enough in age to remember each other.

But where was Diana?

I couldn't very well ask around. But I did have one possible resource. I let it be known to the next Australian patient I encountered that I had a message for Sergeant Lassiter.

He was the cocky Australian I'd treated on occasion—the last being a badly infected shrapnel wound in his palm—and over time he'd become a friend. He seemed to know half the soldiers serving in France, and he had helped me more than once to find someone whose whereabouts I badly needed to discover. In fact, once he'd nearly been taken up for desertion on my behalf. A very fine soldier by all reports and popular with everyone who knew him.

It was a New Zealander who brought me word that Sergeant Lassiter had received my message, and a Scot who slipped me a scrap of paper early one evening as I was on my way to find a cup of much needed tea. We'd been busy since before dawn and it was now after seven.

"Begging your pardon, Sister," the Scot asked, "do you ken the cocoaburro bird?"

In his Scots accent I almost didn't recognize the kookaburra, a bird of Sergeant Lassiter's native land. He always used its odd, laughing call to alert me to his presence. In this case, it was intended to discover, without asking names, the right recipient of the note.

"Yes—yes, I do, Corporal," I said at once. He passed me the scrap of paper and with a nod, went on his way, his kilt swinging with that ground-covering stride common to men of the Highlands.

I put the message in my pocket, for we were not to correspond with the men we treated, and I wasn't sure what Sergeant Lassiter might have written. Explaining about Diana and Aldersgate School and Miss Neville would be difficult.

Sister Baker, just coming from the dwindling line of patients and on her way to where we kept our supplies, called to me. "Who is your handsome beau?"

She meant it as a jest. But I was careful, hoping she hadn't noticed what he'd given me.

"Alas, he was looking for one of his officers. He didn't stay to chat."

A buxom girl from Rutland with fair hair and freckles, she laughed. "Alas, indeed. I sometimes think the only way to get their attention is to dig a bit of metal out of them."

Sister Baker hurried on, intent on her errand, and I quickly drank my cup of tea before going back on duty. We finished the last of the line of wounded just after nightfall, and I sat down on an overturned pail to catch my breath. And then the shelling began, the first ranging shots falling perilously close to us. There were no ambulances now to take away the last of the wounded, but we moved them back as quickly as we could. Men from one of the reserve trenches came to help us, and that speeded up the operation. By that time, the German shells were finding their mark, and a new line of wounded soon demanded our attention.

I had had only the sketchiest breakfast and half a sandwich for lunch. By midnight, I was achingly tired and very hungry—hungry enough now to feel a little light-headed. The incessant shelling didn't help, but I held on grimly until I was relieved, a little after two in the morning, by two new Sisters brought up by the ambulances that were taking our wounded back.

I fell on my cot too exhausted to think. Then far too soon an orderly was calling to me, and I had to find the strength to get up again.

But he had also just brought me a tin of hot soup and a chunk of bread that had also come up with the ambulances, and with the food a large mug of hot tea.

It was bliss. I broke up some of my bread into the soup—my mother would have been horrified—and enjoyed every mouthful. The rest I ate with my tea, wishing it were a sweet bun from the bakery in the village at home, those we had in such plenty before the war and the rationing.

And that for some reason reminded me of the message still in my pocket.

It was a little bloodstained now, spatters from when I'd staunched the bleeding in a badly mangled thigh.

Sergeant Lassiter hadn't used a name.

She's closer to the Ypres Road.

And then he'd given me the number of the aid station.

She might as well be on the moon, for I was on the Somme.

The Germans were fighting ferociously. And it seemed they had shells to spare, the way they pounded at the British and French lines, looking for—praying for?—a break somewhere that would enable them to push farther south, as they had done in 1914, when they had caught the French off guard. They'd nearly had Paris then, and it had been at risk more than once since. In June, they might have had Paris again, if it hadn't been for the American Army and the gallant Marines.

We went about our duties without respite, trying to ignore rumors of peace, seeing the evidence of our own eyes in the stretchers brought to us. And the dread Spanish influenza was still with us, killing cruelly, taking an enormous toll.

Pulling back at one point, we came upon a small encampment of refugees caught by the shift in the fighting. Men and women who had tried desperately to hold on to their own bit of land, farms that had been in the same families for centuries. Most had fled long ago, south of the Seine, well away from the fighting.

These people had heard the rumors of peace, they too had believed them—or wanted to—and somehow they had made their way forward in the hope of reclaiming what was theirs as soon as the guns fell silent.

One woman was heavily pregnant and pale with the onset of labor. Three children clung to her, while her husband begged us to do something. There were seven other families, and one of the men had begun to cough in a way that worried me. The onset of influenza? Or tuberculosis? He hung well back, keeping out of the light we were using to set up the aid station again.

I hadn't delivered a baby since the days of my training. But I brought the woman in to lie down on one of the cots, fishing in my kit for some of the biscuits my mother had sent back with me. I'd been hoarding them, slowly savoring a touch of home, but now I gave them to the children, who stared at them as if they had never seen such things before, then gobbled them down hungrily as the father led them away. I realized all of them were hungry and tired and footsore, and I thought they must surely regret their impetuous decision to come north again.

The baby was slow to come. Ordinarily a second or third child came quickly, sometimes before its time. I remembered one woman from Hampstead Heath who complained that her first child had taken two days to make an appearance, while she nearly had the second one in the omnibus that had brought her to the hospital.

And then the problem was clear. This was going to be a breech birth, where the baby's head, usually the first part to appear, is in the wrong position and the legs or buttocks try to make their way through the birth canal.

I felt a frisson of fear. We weren't set up for a Cesarean. The chances were the mother would die, leaving three—possibly four, if the baby survived—children alone with the father to care for them. And there was no time, no ambulance available to take her back to a hospital equipped to help her. It had been nearly four years since I'd watched Dr. Morton gently and firmly reposition a baby for a normal delivery.

The woman, sweating and in great pain, looked up at me piteously. She had seen my face, she was afraid she was going to die.

I smiled at her, then said, in halting French, uncertain of the words, "The child is twisted, Madame. It will take a little work to right him. It will be painful, but it must be done." And it must be done at once before the child was in a position where a Cesarean was the only choice.

I set to work, praying that I wouldn't rupture the walls of the womb or twist the umbilical cord around the baby's neck, gently but firmly turning him while the mother cried out in pain. But I had nothing to give her. Nothing at all.

And then I had the baby's head, facedown, in the correct place, and I shouted, "Now, Madame, push, I beg of you!"

She did, and suddenly, as if it was what the child had intended all along, the head came smoothly into my waiting hands, and shortly after that it slid out of the mother's body with ease. "A girl, Madame!"

I realized that she was a very small infant. There had been little food for the mother, and she had probably given most of what she had to her children. Just as well, I thought, making it easier for me to shift the baby. But she cried lustily as I wrapped her warmly after tying off and clipping the cord, and I laid her in her mother's arms. The woman was crying with joy, now, the pain forgotten as I finished what had to be done. The father came forward timidly, to see the child, and I left them to it, going to clean myself up.

Later, when she had rested a little, I told the mother that she must return south. "If you don't, you'll lose this baby and perhaps your own life if infection sets in and there is not enough milk. Promise me."

I think they were frightened enough to listen, for afterward I heard an altercation with the other members of the little group. And then I saw the father, three children, and the exhausted mother carrying the baby moving away, back down the long road they'd managed to come up. He'd found a barrow for her—or taken it away from the others—and I watched them until they had disappeared into the night.

Sister Baker called to me, and I went to do my share of treating the wounded, but I was tired and sick at heart.

The long line of Crawford men who had fought for King and Country, and the long line of Crawford women who had stood by them through so many wars, kept me going through the hours ahead, although I couldn't remember if my great-great-grandmother had ever delivered a baby in the midst of a battle. When I fell onto my cot, I slept, mercifully without dreams.

Our aid station was merged with another two days later, and I went back with the ambulances, for we had two cases of bleeding that needed someone in attendance.

There, I was sent again to the influenza hospital.

A line of ambulances came in a few days later, and I heard a familiar voice long before I could see the speaker.

It was Diana. She had come with the ambulances and was seeing to the disposition of her patients, while

Matron did what she could to accommodate wounded who were also suffering from influenza.

It was chaos for half an hour as we arranged and rearranged our wards, and it wasn't until a little after eight that I could look for her. By that time the convoy of ambulances had already set out again for the Ypres Road. I'd missed my opportunity. Disappointed, I stepped over to the canteen for a cup of tea and a sandwich or bowl of soup.

To my surprise, Diana came in ten minutes later. Somehow she managed to look fresh and cool, well in command, despite the tumult of the convoy's arrival.

She spotted me, and hurried across the room to greet me.

"Darling Bess!" she exclaimed, giving me a hug. "I thought you might be back in London on leave."

"I was in the north, but the situation has changed, and I was reassigned here."

She shuddered. "This epidemic has taken such a toll. I'm transporting wounded men back to England tomorrow, and we don't know whether the clinics they're going to are fully staffed. So many are down with this flu. It changes daily—sometimes hourly. But I don't need to tell you that." Then she smiled ruefully. "We're passing through Dover. But they are trying to move the wounded to the trains as quickly as possible now, to keep them as far from any contagion as they can. I doubt I'll be allowed to go up to the castle."

And no time to spend with her fiancé. I knew how much she looked forward to those snatched moments together, for their leaves so seldom coincided. They were to be married as soon as the war ended.

She went to find tea and two sandwiches, then came back to where I was sitting. Attacking her food, she said, "I'm famished. Tell me your news while I eat."

I could hardly describe what had happened with Sergeant Wilkins. Nothing about those days on the road with Simon, hunting for the least link to him. Or how uncertain I'd been about my future in the Service.

I rattled on, mentioning Mrs. Hennessey and talking about a letter I'd had from Mary, anything I could think of.

"And the wonderful Simon?"

I laughed. Diana had always flirted with him outrageously. "Busy as ever. He and my father. I think they're trying to win the war single-handedly."

"Of course they are. They ran the regiment between them. What's a little war?"

Shifting the subject as she finished her sandwiches, I said, "There's another reason I'm happy to see you. Simon thought you might be able to tell us something about one of your old school chums. Barbara Neville."

Her eyebrows flew up. "Don't tell me she has her sights set on our Simon?"

He wasn't *our Simon,* but I knew what she meant, and I bit my tongue.

"She had a dreadful reputation as a flirt, you know. Her father despaired of her after she came out because she even turned down the Viscount who'd asked for her hand. Well, he was much older, of course. And do you remember Freddy Allerton? He proposed again and again, but she would have none of it. There was even a young officer, Lieutenant something or other. Those are just the ones I've heard whispers about. When her father died so suddenly, right on the heels of her brother being killed in France, she shut up the house in London and went back to Windward. At first she was in deep mourning, of course, but she's a great heiress now, and still unmarried. No one quite understands why she hasn't returned to London."

I pictured the haughty, brisk woman I'd encountered in Upper Dysoe. It was hard to imagine her doing what was expected of her.

"But then Barbara isn't like the rest of us," Diana went on thoughtfully. "She was very independent even at school. I remember a dreadful row with the French Mistress. Anyone else would have been sent down at once. But Barbara was summoned to the Head, and there was a conference with her father. Nothing else happened. All of us expected to see Mademoiselle Lavoisier dismissed on the spot. But Barbara apologized very prettily, and there was an end to it." She considered, her head to one side. "She couldn't have known, of course, that her father would die so young. He was barely into his fifties."

"Was she waiting for love? Is that why she turned down so many suitors?"

"More likely she was waiting for someone she could manage," Diana said, laughing.

Like the wounded Major she'd taken in. "Can you recall the name of that Lieutenant?" I asked. He could well have reached the rank of Major by now, with the massive losses on the Western Front.

"I don't know that I ever knew it." Frowning, she examined her memory. "It was something French, I think. Or sounded French, possibly. She seemed to like him better than her other suitors, or else she was just trying to annoy her father. Helena Kingsley made some remark about it. That it was just as well the French Mistress hadn't been dismissed, or Barbara would have nothing to say to the man."

We went on to speak of men we knew in common, some well, others wounded or dead.

"I think the greatest cost of this war is in lost friends," she added sadly. "All the young men I danced and dallied with, played tennis with or went to the theater with are gone. I try to imagine London, once the war is over, and I just can't. It will be dreadfully empty without anyone we know. Worse still to watch them hobble in on crutches or sit listlessly in wheeled chairs in some sunny room of a clinic, and remember how they used to be." Her eyes filled with tears, but she brushed them away angrily. "I can't stay, Bess, I've to meet my transport to Calais."

I knew what she felt, what she was trying to cope with. I myself had gone into nursing to save men, only to stand by helplessly while so many died. I managed not to think about it when I was busy in the wards or at a forward aid station, where there was no time to dwell on past or future. But at night it was harder to forget, and sometimes I worked until I knew I would collapse and sleep without dreams, the only antidote to lying awake and remembering the faces of men I'd come to know.

We talked briefly about her wedding plans, which seemed to cheer her up no end, and laughed over the problems of anyone making a cake that would be presentable, what with shortages of almost everything.

"Instead of gifts," she said, "perhaps we should ask everyone to bring his or her own dinner."

Finishing the last of her tea, she collected her dishes, and we took them back on our way out.

"That will hold me until I reach England, I hope. Any messages for anyone? Anything for your parents or Simon?"

"Tell Mrs. Hennessey that I'm well and busy as ever, and my parents that I send my love."

"And Simon?"

"Tell him if you manage to recall the name of that Lieutenant. It's important. And I shan't have to worry about censors reading it."

With that she was gone. And then the lorry carrying her to Calais stopped and she leaned out her window to shout to me.

I could barely make out the words. But I waved to her, and blew a kiss.

It had sounded like Evering.

I couldn't recall coming across anyone by that name, but then sometimes I didn't know the identity of the patient just brought to us.

I did wish she had begged the lorry driver to reverse a little way, so that I could be clear about the name, but I was sure she would also pass it along to Simon.

After all, it was far more important for her to tell Simon than to tell me. And I had to be content with that as the rear lamp of the lorry vanished around a bend in the road.

Chapter Twelve

I found myself thinking about the Major from time to time.

Who was he? Sitting there on a bench in the gardens of that lovely Tudor house, he seemed to be a part of the household. Yet Mrs. Neville had ordered him in such a familiar way to take the reluctant goat back where it belonged. Almost as if she were speaking to one of the footmen. That fleeting resemblance to Sergeant Wilkins had grown dimmer with time, and I still couldn't say with any certainty whether I should have spoken to Scotland Yard.

The problem was, the Army didn't look kindly on men being cared for in places they hadn't inspected or given official blessing to. If nothing else, it was the perfect opportunity to malinger, far from the watchful eye of doctors and nurses and orderlies. Indeed, there wasn't a doctor in any of the Dysoes, and I smiled to think what the Medical Corps would make of Maddie.

And yet Maddie had been as good as many of the tired, harassed doctors I'd dealt with in France. He understood the limitations of his failing eyesight, and he took no unnecessary risks.

I wondered how Mr. Warren had progressed, if he'd survived the probing, if he still had full use of that arm and shoulder, and if he had returned to his mill.

But as with so many patients, I seldom saw the final outcome of a case.

As I fed or bathed recovering patients, I did find myself asking them if they knew of a Major Evering. Everyone shook his head. The name wasn't one they knew.

The letter from Simon that arrived before dawn one morning, carried by a messenger on a motorcycle, reached me as I was looking forward to my bed after a long night with patients who were about to turn the corner in their suffering, either to die or to survive. Often sitting beside them, holding their hands, and speaking to them as a friend was enough to make that infinitely delicate difference between life and death, unpredictable by any medical science.

I opened it in my little room, leaning to read it by the light of a lamp whose wick was in dire need of trimming. But who had time or energy for such things?

Bess,

I spoke to Diana. She arrived safely in Dover, thence to London, where she telephoned me in a spare moment to give me the name we were after. I've gone through the rolls, and I've found twenty-three men by the name of Everard. Two are in the Royal Navy, and I've stricken them from my list. Another in the Flying Corps was killed over Passchendaele. This death has been confirmed. Another is a prisoner of the Germans, present whereabouts unknown. Information also confirmed. That leaves us with nineteen men. Seven of them are in the ranks, giving us twelve.

A Major Everard was reported missing at Passchendaele, a Captain Everard is serving in Egypt, and there's another Captain Everard on the Somme. Brothers, according to the records. Diana could have been mistaken about the name.

Everard. I'd thought Diana had said Evering. But it didn't matter. She'd have given Simon the right name.

So much for that. I could only hope now that Scotland Yard's newspaper appeal would be more successful than we'd been in finding Sergeant Wilkins.

The next morning, I was working with Corporal Minton, whose temperature had risen alarmingly during the night. We'd given him something to bring down his fever, tried bathing him in cool water, putting cool compresses on his forehead and wrists, but nothing helped. I'd been bending over him, and as I straightened with the basin in my hands, intending to fetch more cold water, all at once he reared up from his pillows, flailing wildly as he cried out to someone. His arm caught me across the throat and I went flying, the basin as well. Twisting to keep from falling on the patient in the next bed, I hit the floor rather hard, water splashing everywhere. The tin basin went rolling across the floor. One of the Sisters who'd been working with me tried to force Corporal Minton back down against his pillows while the other bent over me to ask if I was all right. The breath had been knocked out of me, but I nodded. As I moved, a pain went shooting through my right wrist, where it had struck the iron leg of the cot.

"Never mind me, help Sister Norton," I gasped as an orderly, hearing the commotion, came running. It required the two Sisters and the orderly to hold down the corporal. He lay there, wild-eyed, thrashing and fighting to free himself. And then he lapsed into unconsciousness, his flushed face a rictus of pain.

I managed to get up from the floor without using that wrist, collected the basin, and hurried out for more cold water. My hand and arm were very painful, but we worked for another hour before we were able to bring the fever down. Even so, his life was hanging in the balance. By that time my hand and forearm were red and swollen where I'd struck the bed, and heavy bruising was starting to appear.

I went to change to a dry uniform, spent another hour working with another patient, and finally reported to Matron. I could no longer hold anything in that right hand.

She sent me off to see Dr. Browning. He tested the wrist and smiled. "Nothing broken, I'm happy to say. But that's a very deep bruise, Sister. I'll tape it for you, and you'll need a sling for a while. You're not to lift anything heavy. No pitchers, bedpans, or making up cots for you. Give that wrist a rest, and it will be right as rain in a few days."

"I'm needed," I began, but he shook his head.

"No one is indispensable, Sister. Do as you're told." He sent me to soak the wrist in cold water, then bound it himself. I had no choice but to follow orders. Since it was the right wrist I couldn't even help Matron with the records she kept so meticulously. I sat and read to patients who were recovering, and made myself useful however I could, but the wrist was still very painful after several days.

I'd come back to my quarters one morning to find a letter waiting on my little writing table. It was from Mrs. Hennessey, and there was another letter inside.

> *Diana was so pleased to see you, and tells me you're all right, my dear. I've heard from Mary as well. I've had to have words with the butcher, for the piece of meat he gave me last week had gone off. What we're to eat if this war doesn't end soon, I don't know.*

She went on giving me all the news, and then added,

> *There's a letter here for you. Nothing on the envelope to tell me who might have written it. I've enclosed it here, in the event it's important.*

I finished her letter and then opened the second one. I didn't recognize the handwriting, and it began rather formally.

Sister Crawford,

I think something is wrong. I received a letter from someone named Maddie in the village of Upper Dysoe in Warwickshire. From the name, I must assume it's a woman who has written, but why should she write to me? She tells me that a man has asked repeatedly for me, but I don't know anyone there. She implores me to come, but how did she know where to direct her letter? I can only think it must have something to do with a certain person we both remember. I'm afraid to reply, because I've been in enough trouble over what happened in London, and yet I can't bring myself to turn the letter over to the Army. Please, will you tell me what to do? I can't take this to Matron.

It was signed *Sister Hammond*, and she included Maddie's note.

She was the Sister in Shrewsbury who had helped Sergeant Wilkins in his masquerade. I reread both messages.

I sat there on my cot, wondering what to do.

How had Maddie known where to direct his letter, if it hadn't been Sergeant Wilkins who told him? And what trouble was he in?

Was he really the Major we'd seen? Or had he been found somewhere and brought to Maddie for healing?

I had no idea. All I could think of was to write to Simon and ask him to do something.

But as it happened, I was in England before my letter reached Simon.

Matron called me into her officer later in the morning to tell me that she was sending me to England with a convoy.

It was the usual convoy of wounded, with a dozen or so men from this hospital, recovering from influenza but not yet well enough to return to duty. It was a debilitating disease, and some patients took weeks to regain their strength. I myself had experienced the exhaustion and lethargy that followed a severe case. I remembered how my father and Simon had taken turns carrying me to a chair or out to sit on the balcony of the Grand Hotel in Eastbourne to breathe the sea air.

And Matron needed beds. Any man who could be sent to England would have to go.

"You'll be in charge, there will be people to help you. And I shan't have to spare a Sister who is able-bodied. We need every pair of hands we can find."

"I'm so sorry—" I began, but Matron smiled, the lines of weariness in her face all too visible in the morning light.

"You have nothing to apologize for, Sister. But I would have that wrist looked at while in London, if I were you. It has been slow to heal."

We reached London with our full complement of wounded and recovering victims of the influenza epidemic. The crossing had been rough, for it was that time of year, but the transport had been large enough to mitigate some of the suffering. Belowdecks we were spared the worst.

The train to London through the dark countryside was slow, trundling along the tracks as troop trains went hurtling past, a blur of bright windows and pale faces. It was not quite dawn when we pulled into Victoria Station. Orderlies and women serving hot tea and sweet buns met us, and the task of unloading began. I could only supervise, making certain that the tags on the wounded were properly read and that the men were dispersed to the lorries that would take them to their final destination. Three, I saw, were going to the hospital outside Shrewsbury.

I quite seriously considered asking if I could ride north with them, but after I arrived, what then? I'd have no way of getting about, much less making the journey south to Upper Dysoe. Omnibuses could never have made their way around the tight bends of that hilly countryside. What's more, I couldn't drive.

I made my way through the train for a last inspection. Nothing had been left behind. My own kit was waiting for me on the platform. An orderly had already come through to collect bloodstained dressings, and three women were busy scrubbing floors in two of the carriages where wounds had bled.

Who did I know that I could talk into taking me to Shrewsbury?

My mother, for one. But I didn't want to worry her by explaining why I was still searching for Sergeant Wilkins. And my father was far too imposing a figure, never mind his rank. If Sergeant Wilkins was in the Dysoes, one look at the Colonel-Sahib and he would vanish again, certain the Army had found him.

That left Simon, and I had no idea where he might be.

I found a cab to take me to Mrs. Hennessey's and slipped in the door and up the stairs without waking her. I'd have given much for a cup of tea. There hadn't been time to take one of the mugs the women volunteers were passing out.

I changed into my nightdress, soaked my wrist for twenty minutes, then crawled into bed. A weak sun was already probing at the windowpanes in my room. I closed my eyes to shut out the light, and that was the last I remembered for several hours.

I woke with a start as I often did when I'd just returned to England. The different surroundings required a little getting used to, as well as the far more comfortable bed, and the quiet was almost unnerving. No guns, no men moaning in pain, no Sisters passing by in a swish of starched uniforms, low-voiced as they conferred.

I got out of bed and went to my window, looking out at the soft rain that was beginning to fall. Drawing on my robe, I walked into the sitting room, my bare feet quickly telling me that the floor was definitely chilly. I went to the cupboard to see if any of my flatmates had left tea, a tin of milk, or any honey in the jar I'd brought back from Somerset. The packet of tea was empty, there was no milk, and only a little honey was left. With a sigh of disappointment I shut the cupboard doors and turned away.

Movement outside the window caught my eye, and I glanced out in the hope that Mrs. Hennessey might be setting out to market. If so, I could go down in a bit and ask her to make me a cup.

Instead I saw Simon stepping out of his motorcar and walking toward the door.

I could hardly go down in my nightdress and robe, barefooted. I hurried back to my bedroom and threw on clothes as quickly as I could, fighting to draw on my stockings with only one good hand.

I could hear the door knocker as I finished dressing and hastily pinned up my hair, shoving it tidily under my cap.

I didn't hear Mrs. Hennessey's voice speaking to Simon, I didn't hear the sound of his voice echoing up the stairwell as he spoke to her.

Had she indeed gone to market? What if he believed no one was in the house, and left?

I flung open my door, racing for the head of the stairs. "Simon? I'm coming, please wait," I called as I went down them as fast as I dared.

But the knocker was silent, and I knew he'd given up, was already on his way back to his motorcar.

I threw myself at the house door, went through it into the rain, and saw him already in the motorcar and about to drive away.

Dashing after him, calling to him, I watched him drive off. All the while praying that he'd look into the little mirror and notice me standing there waving like a madwoman. The man who brought the milk stared openly at me as he passed, and at the foot of the street, Constable Williams turned to see what all the fuss was about.

He must have recognized me because he stepped into the street and flagged down Simon's motorcar, pointing back toward Mrs. Hennessey's house.

After a moment, with the constable's help to hold up traffic, Simon reversed, and then he was coming back up the street toward me.

By this time I'd moved into the shelter of the doorway, shivering in the damp, chill air. My wrist was throbbing, and I tried to remember where I'd dropped my sling last night.

Drawing up beside me, Simon put down his window and said, "Go back and fetch your coat. I'll take you to lunch, although it's fairly early still."

"I'll settle for breakfast, if you please," I replied, and still out of breath I went back up the stairs to retrieve my coat and sling, then close the flat door, which was standing wide.

Coming back down again more sedately, I met Mrs. Hennessey just coming in from doing her marketing.

"Bess, my dear," she exclaimed, setting down her market basket and coming to give me a damp embrace. "Did you know Sergeant-Major Brandon was just outside? I told him you weren't at home."

"Yes, I saw him drive up," I replied.

"Then hurry along. Here—take my umbrella. I didn't carry it with me, and look what has happened." She removed the umbrella from the stand by the door, handing it to me. "My dear, what's happened to your arm? Are you in any pain?" Looking around for my kit, she added, "Are you off to Somerset? You'll be needing help, surely." She reached out to tuck a strand of hair under my cap, settling it more securely, then straightened my apron and helped me into my coat. "There, that's much better."

"It's a bruise, thankfully. Sometimes it aches, but it should be better soon. I don't know what I'll be doing," I told her truthfully. "I have a little leave. It will depend on where my parents are just now. Simon will tell me, I'm sure."

"I'm so glad nothing is broken. Well, off with you." She opened the door for me and I dashed out to the motorcar, tossing the umbrella into the rear seat. Waving to Simon, she watched us out of sight.

"How did you know I'd just come in with the morning convoy?" I asked Simon.

"I didn't. I just got to London myself, and I stopped at the flat, on the off chance you were there." He gestured to my sling. "What have you done?"

"Well, I'm very glad you did stop. And it's a bruise, it will be better soon."

He eyed me suspiciously. "Truthfully?"

"Let's have our breakfast first," I said mildly. "Then we can talk."

Two hours later, I collected my kit from my room, told Mrs. Hennessey good-bye, and rejoined Simon in the motorcar.

He was still convinced I should see a doctor, after I'd nearly dropped my teacup trying to use my left hand.

We'd spent most of breakfast considering what we should do about Sister Hammond's letter. Simon hadn't received my own letter, and so my news was fresh.

"Even if you have ten days' leave, I don't think there's any point in going to Shrewsbury," he'd said, setting down his cup. "Time is short, and therefore the best move is to go directly to Upper Dysoe and see what this man Maddie has to say."

"It could be a wild-goose chase."

"Or a trap."

"Hardly that. Why should anyone wish to harm Sister Hammond?"

"Think about it. She was part of the small conspiracy that allowed Wilkins to go to London under false pretenses."

"But what would he gain by killing her? Now? It would only draw more attention to him if she disappeared or was found dead. There would be a renewed hue and cry for the sergeant as well."

"We won't know until we speak to Maddie. It's no use speculating."

He was right. But as the miles passed, I couldn't help but do just that.

I couldn't have guessed the truth if it had taken a month to make the journey north.

When we reached Maddie's little cottage, we discovered that he wasn't in.

It was Simon's suggestion that we drive on and come back later. The motorcar was quite conspicuous here in the village. A number of people had stared as we passed.

It was still lightly raining, and so we decided that we'd wait at the ruined barn where we'd spent the night on our first visit here. This might even be the direction Maddie would come on his way back to Upper Dysoe. To our surprise, it was nothing more than a blackened pile of lumber and rubble.

It had burned. The stone walls were scarred by fire, the roof gone, the high grasses all around little more than black stubble. The scorched trunk of the tree where the doves had roosted at the far end of the barn was wet with rain but miraculously was still standing.

Taking out Mrs. Hennessey's umbrella, we got out to walk over to what was left, and Simon commented, "It seems like a waste of time and labor. The barn was barely standing as it was."

"We saw evidence that someone had been living here, or at least using the barn in foul weather. Perhaps Miss Neville didn't care for that."

"It's possible, of course." He put out a hand to help me over several tumbled stones, and we went a little way down the rutted lane where the sheep had disappeared. It was overrun by grass and wildflowers, and we turned back. If there had been a farmhouse here at one time, it had suffered the same fate as the barn, because we didn't see any chimneys in the distance. The land was fit for grazing sheep and little more. We could see where they'd worn a rough track through the thicket of weeds.

As we were coming back to the road, we heard a goat calling to us.

And there it was, tethered in the same place, or nearly so, where we'd collected it to return it to Windward at Mrs. Neville's direction.

I laughed. "Mrs. Neville won't be best pleased."

"I'm damned if I'll tie it to the motorcar again," Simon responded.

Passing the umbrella to Simon, I climbed up the slight incline to peer into the undergrowth and brambles that partially concealed the goat from view, and it was indeed the same animal, the markings distinctive. Its strange yellow eyes glared balefully at me, and I beat a hasty retreat.

"I wonder if someone does this just to annoy Mrs. Neville," I asked.

"Very likely. Her views on Agriculture being the salvation of mankind would drive you mad in a very short time. I doubt if she'd brook much in the way of argument."

We went on to the motorcar and drove back the way we'd come.

This time the door was standing open in Maddie's cottage, and Simon rapped on the wood rather than walking straight in.

"Who is it?" Maddie called. "I'll be there in a moment."

Shortly afterward he appeared in the doorway, looking first at us in quickly concealed surprise, and then at the sling that cushioned my wrist.

He said, "What brings you back again, Sister?"

"I was wondering how Mr. Warren had fared. If he recovered or if infection had cost him his arm."

"He's quite recovered, although the arm is a little stiff. I've shown him how to strengthen it with exercises, and by the time winter sets in, it should be back to normal." As he spoke, he pulled the door wide and politely invited us in. But I could tell that he was not happy to see us. "I was about to put the kettle on. Would you care for a cup of tea?"

We said yes, equally politely, and as Maddie swung the blackened iron kettle in over the fire in the hearth,

Simon asked, "Did you ever discover who had shot the miller?"

"I doubt it matters," he said carefully. "Warren is happy enough with the arrangements made to see him through his recovery. I doubt he's interested in pressing charges."

"All the same, Warren could have been killed," Simon went on. "Someone going about shooting people is dangerous."

"It's an Upper Dysoe matter," Maddie said after a moment. "I shouldn't worry about it." He set out cups for us and I noticed that they were a rather fine china, and the spoons, though old, were silver, tarnished a little from being kept in a drawer in the cupboard. "What brings you back to us? Surely it isn't only your concern for Mr. Warren's welfare."

"Sister Hammond," I began slowly, "a friend of mine as well as a colleague, received a letter from you recently, asking her to come here as soon as possible. She was very worried, because she thought that someone she knew might be desperately ill. Or desperately in trouble. And as she had no means of reaching Upper Dysoe on her own, she asked me to come here in her place. The odd thing is, we ourselves were here looking for someone not that long ago. It could be that they are the same man. It's even possible that the Major knows where we can find him."

Maddie didn't reply at once. He dealt with the tea quietly and efficiently, and then while the pot was steeping, he looked across at me.

"I'm afraid I don't know anyone by that name. Sister Hammond, did you say?"

"She's serving at a hospital for wounded soldiers, outside Shrewsbury. *Someone* knew how to find her."

"And did she say why she'd been summoned here?"

"Only that someone had been asking for her. She thought the writer must be a woman, because the letter was signed *Maddie*." From my pocket I took the letters Mrs. Hennessey had forwarded to me. "Is this your handwriting? Or do you know whose it might be?"

He politely read the letter, folded it again and handed it back to me.

"This isn't my writing. For that matter, how could I possibly know anyone in a Shrewsbury hospital?"

He was avoiding answering me. He probably didn't know Sister Hammond. But someone must have known her.

I asked, "Why should someone else use your name? I assure you, the letter is genuine. The question is, who wrote it—and why? And if this man needs help, why won't you let us take him to Sister Hammond?"

He set the pot on the little table at my elbow, looked again at the sling and my puffy fingers where the swelling hadn't completely gone down, then poured the steaming tea into the delicate cups himself.

"I expect if someone didn't want to sign such a letter, the writer might have chosen the name of any number of other people. Madeleine isn't an uncommon name." He put honey in his tea, and stirred it with the silver spoon. "Not everything is what it seems."

It occurred to me that although I'd helped him in a very difficult bit of surgery, Maddie knew very little about me and even less about Simon. We were strangers asking questions that perhaps he didn't care to answer.

"I can bring Sister Hammond to you," I said. "If you wish it." I didn't know quite how, but I was willing to try.

"You could bring anyone here and call them by whatever name you liked." He smiled at me. "Have you considered that someone might have played a trick on your friend? Not a very nice one, to be sure. Still, there must be dozens of men in her care. And dozens of others who have left that hospital and moved on, back to France or invalided out of the Army altogether. Who knows what sort of feelings one of them has harbored."

He would have been a master at chess. Nothing in his face gave anything away. But then depending on his past, he might have had many years of experience hiding what he was thinking.

I was feeling hurt and angry. I'd come to his aid when he needed it. And in return, he'd refused to come to mine. I said, "Odd that a former patient serving in France would have thought to use your name and this village in his letter. Unless of course you're hiding something." I rose. There was no reason to prolong our stay. "Thank you for the tea."

A shadow passed over his face. "I'm an old man," he countered. "I have met many people in my lifetime. If they choose to use my name, I can't prevent it."

As we walked to the door, Simon turned. "Perhaps you will carry a message to the man who knew Sister Hammond. Tell him we came to help, and you sent us away."

We left him standing there, and went out to the motorcar. While Simon saw to the crank, I tried to think what to do next. Call on Sister Hammond? Or find a way to speak to the elusive Major?

In the end we drove on to Shrewsbury, and there we waited for more than an hour until Sister Hammond came off duty.

She greeted us apprehensively. She hadn't met Simon before, and this tall man in uniform was an unknown quantity.

I tried to set her mind at ease by introducing him as a friend, but her experiences with the Army and the

Nursing Service because of Sergeant Wilkins had left their mark.

"Did you receive my letter? I shouldn't have sent it, but I was worried, you see," she began anxiously. "I didn't quite know what I should do about it. I've heard nothing more from this woman Maddie. Perhaps it was all a mistake, and I read more into the message than I should have done."

We hadn't said anything—yet—to her about stopping in Upper Dysoe. Nor had I told her that Maddie was a man.

The rain had moved on. We were walking on the grounds, enjoying a warm evening and moonlight pointing our way. The gardens had lost their color without the sun. Now the late season pinks and whites and blues were varying shades of gray, deepening to black.

"You thought it was from Sergeant Wilkins. This letter." Simon hadn't phrased it as a question.

Sister Hammond turned to him. "I didn't know what to think. This person Maddie hadn't given me a name. But who else could it be? I didn't want any more trouble. Sergeant Wilkins had seemed so trustworthy, so open and honest. And look what happened? I never expected—and so when the letter came, I was frightened I'd be drawn back into his problems. I was even afraid to tell anyone else that it had come."

She left unsaid the fact that she must have felt something for the sergeant, and possibly still did. In spite of everything. She didn't want to be the one to turn him in, knowing he would very likely be shot for desertion. If he wasn't hanged for murder.

"Have you ever had such—er—difficulties with a patient before this?" I asked. "You *assumed* this person was referring to Sergeant Wilkins. But could it have been someone else, someone you'd treated in the past?"

"I've thought about that too," she told me, her voice on the edge of tears. "But there's no one. The men in this house are from the ranks," she went on with an uneasy glance at Simon. "We aren't encouraged to get to know any of them personally. But of course we do. We write letters to their families and read them their letters as well, if they're too ill. You know as well as I do that when you sit by a man in delirium, you learn things about him that no one else knows."

Beside me in the moonlight Simon stirred abruptly, but said nothing.

I'd sat by him when he was off his head with delirium. He'd relived old battles, but there may have been other confidences another Sister had heard. In fact, he'd questioned me afterward about what he'd said while feverish.

"And you form attachments, you can't help it," Sister Hammond went on. "You're warned against this in training, but it's only human to *feel*." She was trying to justify the reason she'd believed in Sergeant Wilkins.

"But have you heard from any of your other patients after they've been released? From Lovering Hall or elsewhere?"

"Only the usual. A note of gratitude from a wife or mother, sometimes from the patient as well. The officers write more often to thank the staff than the ranks do. I expect that's only natural."

"You've worked in a clinic or hospital that cares for officers?" Simon asked her.

"Well, yes, earlier in the war. Before I was sent here. Shrewsbury is closer to my home in Ludlow than Dorset. I can go there when I'm given leave."

Thirty miles or so compared to around one hundred and fifty. It made sense.

"Were there any officers who would think of you in a time of distress?" I asked.

"I don't know," Sister Hammond replied. "The hospital in Dorset dealt with severe head injuries. There were men who couldn't remember anything about their lives before the war. They woke up in hospital and couldn't even tell you how they'd been wounded, much less their names or where they came from." She started to cry. "It's too much. I'd just been kind, I'd just tried to help. And it nearly got me relieved of my duties. Matron is still watching everything I do, looking for a reason to pounce. I'm just so very *tired*."

We walked down to the small lake at the bottom of the garden. The moon silvered the surface, and as we moved around to the far side, the lights of the house were reflected like so many candles floating on the pewter face of the water.

Simon touched my shoulder briefly as we stood there, looking back at the tall windows that gave on to the terrace and the gardens below it. A lovely scene,

And then someone screamed, shattering the quiet.

Sister Hammond said, "That's Bobby Taylor. He has nightmares sometimes. We're used to it now. Some of the officers had nightmares too. Fragments of memory that tormented them in their sleep. They couldn't recall them afterward, no matter how hard they tried."

Or wouldn't, I thought, having had experience with such cases myself.

"And you did your best for them. Perhaps there's someone whose memories are coming back now, and he needs help coping with them."

"Do you think Maddie could be his wife?" she asked eagerly. "That would explain everything. I can't go to him, of course, I'm needed here. But I could write and make suggestions, couldn't I? I know there are clinics and hospitals—even doctors—who can help."

It was a way out for her. But I had to discourage her.

"Until you know, I wouldn't do that," I told her. "Write, I mean. Unless she gives you more information, a name, something you can take to Matron for advice. You don't want to find yourself in trouble again because you jumped to conclusions."

"No, that's true. But I feel better already." In the moonlight I could see her tentative smile. "I'll wait."

"Was there any officer in particular who might turn to you in dire distress?"

"I can't think of anyone." But she'd answered too quickly.

I waited until we were halfway to the house before asking, "Are you sure there's no one? Simon, here, has friends he can call on to find out what's being done for this man. It would take some of the burden from your shoulders."

She was silent for a time. We'd nearly reached the path that led to the drive when she said, "Of course there's Harry. Captain Cartwright, that is. We were all so fond of him, and we were overjoyed when we discovered his identity. And quite by chance, you know. Another officer, a new patient, recognized him at once, in spite of his bandages. He couldn't be sent back to France, but when he was to be released, we found a cousin to care for him. I'd hate to think he was having recurring problems. Or perhaps his memory is beginning to come back, and I'm sure that's frightening at first." I could see her sudden frown in the light spilling out of the lower windows. "I don't think his cousin's name was Maddie. She lives in Bakewell. Derbyshire. I don't suppose—do you think he might have wandered off and found his way to this woman Maddie, and she's writing for him?"

Sister Hammond was a hopeless romantic.

"I think it's better for Simon to find out, don't you? It could be a trick by Sergeant Wilkins to lure you somewhere and force you to help him escape. After all, the Army will be checking all the ports. And he has to do something to save himself."

That brought her back to reality. "I hadn't considered that. Now I'm even more confused than ever."

"You mustn't be. Leave this with us, Sister. We can get to the bottom of it quickly enough by looking to see whether Captain Cartwright is still with his cousin. For all we know, he's been returned to hospital in Dorset or somewhere else."

"Of course, you're right. I'm being stupid again. It's just that I like helping people, I can't hold my tongue when a word or a kindness might lift someone's spirits or make the difference between recovering and being an invalid. Matron tells me to be more objective, but I went into nursing because I *care*."

"The best of reasons," I agreed. "But if you hear again from Maddie—or you decide the letter might be from someone else entirely—let me know. Or speak to Matron if you can't reach me. Please. Two heads are better than one."

It was an old cliché, but it was the right thing to say to Sister Hammond.

She took that to heart, and shyly thanked me for my understanding.

We watched her until she had gone back indoors and disappeared down the long hall.

I said to Simon with a sigh, "We got nowhere. On the other hand, if we kept Sister Hammond from making a grave mistake, it was worth the time and trouble."

"She means well. But the road to hell is paved with good intentions," he responded.

It was too late to drive on, and so after a brief stop for petrol, we found an hotel in Shrewsbury, one with a view of the abbey ruins.

I sat up late, pulling a chair to the window, watching the moon reach its zenith, then start to sink toward the west. I wished I could put my finger on the problem that was vexing us. But Maddie was holding his tongue, and Sister Hammond couldn't be relied on to handle whatever it was sensibly.

Someone was walking down the dark street below the hotel. I realized all at once that it was Simon.

For some reason he'd been unable to sleep as well.

Chapter Thirteen

I had no real excuse to go in search of Captain Cartwright.

He most certainly couldn't be Sergeant Wilkins, and I couldn't see that he'd have anything useful to tell us about the man, even if the sergeant had served under him. But I *could* strike off the letter to Sister Hammond, if I learned that he'd sent it. But how had he come to know Maddie, if he lived in Derbyshire?

Still, short of knocking at the door of that lovely house tucked into the fold of a hill and demanding to speak to the Major, to make certain he wasn't Sergeant Wilkins after all, we'd run into a blank wall.

Was it a hoax? Sister Hammond's letter from Upper Dysoe? If so it was a cruel one. But again, who had known where to find her?

The next morning over breakfast, to my astonishment it was Simon who suggested we drive to Bakewell.

"You won't be satisfied until you see Cartwright for yourself. We must keep an eye to your leave. There's that to consider. I'm all right, just now."

"I could go to Inspector Stephens, at the Yard. It would be easy for him to get to the bottom of it. But Sister Hammond will be questioned again. And they'll come to speak to Maddie. The Cartwrights as well. I know what it's like, being under suspicion." I hesitated. "What if Sergeant Wilkins wrote that letter. Begging for her help. Why would Maddie protect him?"

"He just might. Depending on what tale Wilkins spun him." He asked the woman serving us to remove his empty plate. "There's another problem. If Sister Hammond receives a second letter, and it appears to be more desperate than the first, she might well find a way to reach Upper Dysoe. Or at the very least try. God knows what she'll find herself caught up in."

"Well, then, Bakewell, it is," I agreed. "Simon, I didn't expect Maddie to lie. I was quite angry with him at the time. A word from him and all of this could have been over."

"It's odd that everything we'd discovered—the bay horse's whereabouts, the long-distance hauling lorry, and now the letter to Sister Hammond—all lead us to

Upper Dysoe in one way or another. It's possible that Wilkins is somewhere nearby. And if his wound is troubling him, he'd seek out someone like Maddie, not a doctor who might report him."

We set out for Bakewell. It was interesting to see that by the time we'd reached the little town of Bidding-ton we'd lost those unique thimblelike hills, finding ourselves in more rolling countryside. Simon drove in silence for some time. Then he said, "That cluster of hills where the Dysoes are has had an uninterest-ing history. I looked it up, you know. That's to say, the Dysoes and Windward escaped most of the horrors of war from the time of the Conqueror onward. Isolated, difficult terrain, perfect setting for an ambush. No great abbeys, no castles, nothing to loot or burn, just a handful of small hamlets connected by a single wind-ing road. Much like Cheddar Gorge in a way. Only one way in or out."

"Which makes it an ideal place for a wanted man to hide," I pointed out. "There aren't any newspapers to carry stories about Sergeant Wilkins's flight, if ever the story makes it into print. And even if someone heard about his desertion on market day in Biddington, they'd hardly think of looking in the Dysoes. A stranger would stand out."

"Unless he doesn't appear to be a stranger. Like the Major."

"Which reminds me," I said, "are you certain Diana told you the Lieutenant's name was Everard? Not Evering?"

"The connection was clear. Even so, I asked her to spell it."

But perhaps Diana only thought she'd remembered the Lieutenant's name.

It was a long drive. We'd had an early start, but it was well after dark when we pulled up in front of the Rutland Arms Hotel.

There was no one behind the desk in Reception, but there was a small silver bell, which Simon rang.

Shortly afterward, a middle-aged man came out from the back and asked if we were looking for directions or accommodations.

Simon arranged for two rooms and went to see to the motorcar while the man at Reception carried my kit up the long elegant staircase to a very pretty room. He drew the curtains for me and asked if I'd care for tea, late as it was. I accepted gratefully. When he came back with the tray, Simon was going down the passage to his own room. He suggested meeting at eight the next morning for breakfast, and I agreed.

Tea was just the thing, and I slept well. When I went down in the morning, through the open door I could see the most wonderful view out toward what must be peaks of the Dales beyond. The small dining room was nearly empty when I came in, and Simon joined me shortly thereafter.

He'd already spoken to the morning desk clerk. The Cartwrights lived on the estate of Chatsworth House.

"I didn't expect it to be that easy," I replied, selecting a slice of toast and trying not to think how nice it would be with butter.

"It wasn't, actually. The clerk was reluctant to tell me. Miss Cartwright, the cousin, moved away from Bakewell after the Captain came to live with her. She took an older, smaller house on the Chatsworth estate, one that apparently had belonged to her father. It was empty, and she felt it was safer."

"Safer?" I asked warily.

"It appears that Captain Cartwright wasn't as well as Sister Hammond led us to believe. Or else he regressed in his cousin's care. Whatever the reason, he had a tendency to wander, and it made others in town uneasy. Miss Cartwright closed up the house and took her cousin with her. Apparently someone on the estate took pity on them and let them live there for her father's sake."

"Oh, dear."

"Precisely."

We finished our breakfast and went out to the motorcar. It was a pleasant drive toward the Chatsworth estate, and we took one of the farm gates into the property. I'd never realized how vast a holding it was. We covered what seemed like several miles, looping over the rolling, hilly landscape, glimpsing the great house in the far distance, half hidden by trees, and finally discovering a stone cottage set in a fold of the land, a small barn and other outbuildings behind it.

A weathered sign just in front read CARTWRIGHT.

We drew up and walked to the door. At Simon's suggestion, I was the one to use the knocker.

No one came at first, but I had the feeling the house wasn't empty. And so I persisted, knocking again and then a third time.

Finally a woman who looked to be about thirty came to the door. She had dark red hair and a very pretty face, but there were circles under her eyes and a thinness about her that came from worry.

"I've told you before," she said, speaking to my uniform rather than to me, "I have had no news. I don't know where he could be."

"Miss Cartwright? I'm so sorry. My name is Crawford, Bess Crawford. I'm not here officially. We were in Bakewell, staying at the Rutland Arms. Sister Hammond, who was the nurse in charge of your cousin in the Dorset hospital, asked us to stop and say hello. She still remembers him."

She was looking over my shoulder, staring at the motorcar and then at Simon. "We? Who is *he*?"

"Sergeant-Major Brandon. A friend. He's—er—taking me back to London."

I thought she would not ask us in. But after a moment she opened the door wider. "Come inside then. I've got to talk to someone. And Sister Hammond was very kind to my cousin."

Simon and I followed Miss Cartwright into the front room of the cottage. It was comfortable, the furniture chosen well for its dimensions, neither large nor heavy. She gestured to chairs by the cold hearth. The room seemed equally cold, and I had a feeling that Miss Cartwright was now wishing she'd turned us away.

I said gently, "Would you prefer that we leave? We had no intention of intruding."

"Harry isn't here," she said bluntly. "He hasn't been for five or six weeks. I went up to the house one day to thank them for the fruit the family had sent down, and when I came back, Harry wasn't here." She cleared her throat. "I sounded the alarm, of course, and we sent out search parties. The estate is a large one, as you may have gathered coming in. I didn't think Harry could have got very far. Not in that short length of time. But somehow he had. The search went beyond the bounds of the estate, and still no word of him. No one had seen him. I could only think that he'd hidden somewhere until nightfall, or perhaps found someone passing down the main road to give him a lift. It's farfetched, but there you are. What else were we to think?"

That he might have died somewhere and hadn't yet been found? I couldn't say so to this grieving woman. It would be too cruel.

"I'm so sorry," I said, meaning it in many senses of the word.

"Harry can't cope in a town he doesn't know. Where no one knows him. He can't always remember where he was going or why. People believe he's the worse for drink and send for the police. But he doesn't drink, you see. I keep hoping someone will see he's ill and take him to a doctor instead. I have no idea what identification he might have had in his pocket that day, or how much money. We didn't need either of them out here. He could be begging on the *street*." She reached for a handkerchief and blew her nose to hide her tears. "I'm catching a chill, I think," she said, angry with herself for her own weakness. "It's just—I think of him out there alone, lost, cold, hungry, nowhere to go, no one to turn to. And I feel so *guilty*."

"I don't see that it could be your fault," Simon told her.

"But it *is*. When everyone complained in Bakewell, I decided to take him away. That's why we came here. Where no one would be disturbed. I did try to keep him from wandering. I'd be sure he was asleep before I myself went to bed. And I'd be sure to be up before he woke. When I went to market I came home again as quickly as I could. And still he would slip away. Then someone would come to the door or would approach me while I was out searching for him, and tell me he'd frightened their custom away, coming into the shops, or that he'd frightened the children on their way to school, or he'd make their dog bark in the middle of the night, trying to come through their gate. It was never ending, the complaints. But I had to sleep sometime or have a bath or buy food—there was no one else to watch him. They told me he was so much better at the hospital there in Dorset, that he was ready to take up his old life. But he *wasn't*. He was still quite fragile, and I didn't have the *training* to help him or even help me care for him."

"I doubt if training would have mattered," I told her. "A hospital specializing in head injuries locks its doors, for that very reason."

Captain Cartwright sounded very much like the Major, who wandered away and shot at people and took goats out to the high road.

"And I locked mine," she was saying. "But he would find the key or break a window or wander off from the garden when I went in to fetch his tea or his lunch or a glass of water. I asked him what it was he wanted, where he wished to be, if not with me. But he couldn't tell me. He'd simply beg my pardon for worrying me and promise it wouldn't happen again. If I'd stayed in Bakewell, at least someone would have found him sooner or later, and brought him home or sent for me. Out here, there's nothing. No one but the estate people, and they're too busy to keep an eye out day and night. I'm a guest here, on sufferance. And so I tried to cope. For all I know they grew tired of bringing him back, and decided to let him go his way. I can't blame them."

"What is the Captain's background?" I asked. "Did he live somewhere else, is he trying to reach a home he remembers?"

"He grew up in Sheffield. But it wasn't a happy life there. His father was a cold-natured man, no warmth at all, and I think that's why Harry was eager to join the Army as soon as he could. He trained as an officer, and then the war came along. I can't think there's anything to draw him back to Sheffield, now his mother is dead. I'm his only relative."

"Could he walk far? Forty miles or more?"

"I doubt it. Not in a straight line, at any rate. He'd have a blackout, you see, and forget where it was he was going. Or where it was he'd come from."

"Most of the wounded are eager to return to France. To their comrades, their friends, the men who serve under them. It's something war does, it brings soldiers closer than brothers. Did your cousin talk about that?" Simon asked her.

"I don't know that Harry quite remembered the war. He never speaks of it. Never mentioned anyone he'd served with. It was as if the war no longer existed in his memory. Oddly enough, he did remember Sister Hammond. A time or two after I'd first brought him home, he called me by her name."

I took the letter to Sister Hammond from my apron pocket, and passed it to Miss Cartwright.

"Does this handwriting look familiar to you? Could it be your cousin's?"

She read it through, her face suddenly drawn, inward-looking. And I was prepared to hear her tell me she knew who had written it.

Yet she shook her head as she passed the letter back to me. "It isn't Harry's fist at all. Poor man, whoever he may be. I hope you find him and can help him."

I wondered then if Maddie had found Harry Cartwright in the ruined barn, trying to survive on a handful of fruit. If so, where was he now? Not in Maddie's cottage, for I'd been inside. Had he taken the Captain to the Nevilles? Not knowing his rank, had Maddie decided he was an officer and christened him a Major? And had Barbara Neville decided he'd be easier to manage than a fiancé who cared more for her dowry than for her? Mrs. Neville had told us the Major wasn't interested in her fortune. Perhaps he wasn't aware she was a heiress.

We would have to speak to someone in Dorset. They would know whether Captain Cartwright and the Major were one and the same.

Miss Cartwright was saying, "I wrote to the hospital. To Sister Hammond. Asking her if she could think where Harry might have gone. Sadly she didn't answer. I'd thought she liked him, that she would try to help me."

"She's been reassigned to a hospital in Shrewsbury," I said. "It's likely that she never got your letter. She told us that you'd taken Captain Cartwright, and she hoped he was happy, even possibly getting a little better."

"I should have refused to accept him. But I'm fond of Harry, I always have been. How could I turn him away, my own flesh and blood?"

Through the window just beyond where I was sitting, I could see the rolling, empty land, where the estate workers' cottages huddled together like a hamlet, and the nearest neighbor must be sheep. I could see them in the distance, heads down, grazing quietly.

"Do you have a photograph of your cousin?" I asked.

She looked vaguely around. "Somewhere. No, it must still be in the boxes I haven't unpacked. I never seemed to have the time, you see."

"Could you describe him?" Simon asked.

"Describe? Oh—yes. Fair, blue eyes. I take after my mother's side of the family. He's like his father's, straight, attractive features. Nice ears. Not as tall as the Sergeant-Major, but of good height."

"How would anyone know they'd found Cousin Harry?" I asked. "Is there anything that would distinguish him from other fair men?"

"His wounds, of course," she said, as if I were daft. "You can hardly see the scar on his head, the way his hair has grown out. You wouldn't know until you spoke to him that the damage was inside. But he was wounded in the leg as well. Machine gun, they told me. It won't ever be strong again. And as he went down, he took that bullet to the head. Of course there's a rather terrible scar on his left shoulder." She raised her hand, touching her own. "He got that on the Somme. The scar is raised, ugly, the skin twisted and pulled. I don't think it will ever fade."

Again, how many men would that description fit?

We left soon after that. There was nothing we could do or say to make the loss any easier for Miss Cartwright. I couldn't send her to Windward to see if the man there was her missing cousin. It would be unkind to her and unfair to the Neville family.

She stood at the door and watched us drive away, and I felt I'd failed her somehow. By coming I'd reopened wounds that were perhaps beginning to heal, and I'd given her no fresh hope.

We drove through the ornate gates of the estate and back to the road to Bakewell.

"What now?" Simon asked, wanting to know which direction to take as much as I myself did.

"I don't know. I've run out of choices."

"There's one we might try. Feel like bearding the lioness in her den? If you can call that Tudor manor house a den."

But what excuse could we possibly give?

"Perhaps we should have taken Miss Cartwright with us, to identify her cousin. Or not, as the case might be."

Simon pulled to the side of the road. "Do you think she would come?"

"Yes. But it could end badly for her. If this man is the sergeant and not her cousin. For that matter, if he's anyone's cousin but hers."

"Let her make that decision."

We turned back, passing through the gates of Chatsworth House once more and making our way to the Cartwright cottage.

Miss Cartwright was astonished to see us again. "Did you leave something behind?" she asked, frowning. "I didn't notice . . ." Her voice trailed away. "It's not gloves or a handkerchief, is it?" She lifted her hand, inviting us inside.

Simon smiled. "There's a matter we had to consider before broaching the subject to you."

I kept the story straightforward. That we'd been searching for someone from London who had gone missing, and failing to find him, we'd stumbled on this unknown man in Upper Dysoe. "For all we know, he could still be the man we're after—we've never seen him close to. He could be your cousin. Or someone else entirely. There's no way of telling. You've seen the letter. That's where it came from. There's the matter of rank as well. This man is a Major. At least we've been led to believe he is."

She'd leaned forward, afraid to miss a word. As I finished, she said, "If you think there's any possibility, of course I'll come with you. It's the first news I've had in such a very long time."

"But it isn't news," I gently admonished. "Please, you must be prepared for disappointment. As I have had to be, in my own search."

That gave her pause. "If I go with you—and it isn't Harry, if it's someone else—then I wouldn't be here if he found his way back. How would he manage, if I were gone for several days? Warwickshire is so far away. He might give up and leave." She began to shake her head. "The handwriting isn't Harry's. I would swear to that. If you believe this Major could have written it, then perhaps he did."

I couldn't press her, it was too slim a hope, and she had pinned all hers on Harry coming back to her here and finding her waiting.

We left a second time, and I felt thoroughly depressed. Guilty for dragging her into this muddle we were trying to resolve.

We spent the night in the town next but one to Biddington in cramped rooms above the pub. It was market day, and the little town was crowded.

The next morning, we drove through Upper Dysoe toward the burned-out ruin of the barn. I peered up into the overgrown thicket to look for the tethered goat, but there was no sign of it today.

Over breakfast Simon and I had decided that there would be nothing lost if we simply knocked at Windward's door and asked to speak to the Major. We could be refused, but I hardly expected them to set the dogs on us. Still, I could feel butterflies in my stomach as we drew nearer.

Just ahead were the gates to the house. As Simon turned in, the full glory of the facade greeted us, the morning sun bringing out the rich color of the brick.

Simon went down the drive and pulled up in front of the door.

We both glanced toward the bench under the tree. There was no one sitting there now.

He said, "Still game?" as I hesitated.

With a sigh, I waited until Simon held open my door for me, then alighted.

I pulled the chain for the bell and heard it echo dimly somewhere inside, then stood there, wondering what to say. And then the door swung wide.

"Maddie, he's taken a turn—" Mrs. Neville stopped short. "I'm sorry, we were expecting someone else. Ah. That infernal goat. You were the Sister who was here before, when we brought it home. Well, you'll have to do. Come with me."

"Sergeant-Major Brandon—" I began, gesturing to Simon just behind me.

"He can wait in the morning room. Come along. There's no time to dally." She nodded to a hovering maid, and Simon was taken off in a different direction.

I followed her through a wonderfully maintained Great Hall that soared over my head to the tall oriel window above. The stained-glass medallions were repeated on the floor at my feet where the sun had caught them. A staircase, ornately carved dark wood, possibly oak, loomed out of the shadows, and Mrs. Neville was already climbing it. I followed.

We went down a passage on the first floor, came to a room toward the end, and as I caught up with her, she thrust open the door.

A man lay in a large bed that was canopied and curtained, something, I thought to myself, Henry VIII might have slept in, when he was old and too heavy for an ordinary one.

He wore a white, old-fashioned nightshirt, which emphasized his paleness. Fair hair, overly long as if no one had cut it recently, spread out across the pillows under his head, and the fair mustache was in need of trimming. His eyes were shut, but I would have wagered that they were blue.

"How long has he been this ill?" I asked, moving a lamp closer to the bed so that I could see his face more clearly.

"For some days. My stepdaughter isn't here, she's gone away to Warwick. And I know nothing about treating the wounded."

Was it Sergeant Wilkins? I was nearly convinced that it was not, and then as the man feverishly turned his face this way and that, as if the lamplight troubled him, I found myself uncertain again.

If I could hear him speak, I thought . . .

But he was too feverish to answer when I spoke to him.

"What's his name?" I asked as I put my hand on his forehead. There was a basin of cool water by the bed, and I reached for the cloth beside it, dipping it into the basin and then wringing it nearly dry before placing it on the man's forehead.

"Major Findley," she said impatiently, as if that was of no importance. "It's the knee. It looks rather nasty. That's why I sent for Maddie. I didn't like to summon the doctor all the way from Warwick, if it would heal on its own. But this morning, it was so discolored, I was frightened for him."

At the word *discolored,* I had visions of gangrene setting in. I lifted the bedclothes and held the lamp closer to the leg. It was swollen, a dark red, and very angry-looking. There had been an old wound here, barely healed, and somehow it had reopened. Whether he'd fallen, caught it on something out in the wooded park, or even been kicked by that troublesome goat, I couldn't tell. But it looked to me as if initially, he'd been hit by machine-gun fire. I'd seen more knee wounds than I cared to remember.

"I'll need hot water, clean bandages, and anything that can be used as an antiseptic," I told Mrs. Neville, thinking of Maddie's well-stocked little cottage. "And would you ask Sergeant-Major Brandon to come up, please? I shall need his help."

She was about to refuse, then she thought better of it as the Major moved restlessly, groaning as the leg hurt from my examination, careful as I was.

I stood there by the bedside when she had gone, and I called the patient by the name of Sergeant Wilkins, then by Captain Cartwright. He never responded as far as I could tell. *But it could be the fever,* I thought, keeping him muddled and only partly conscious.

I was just about to put a hand on his left shoulder, to see if I could feel a ragged scar through the thin nightshirt, when the door opened and Simon stepped into the room, coming quickly across to the bed as soon as he was sure we were alone.

"Who is he?" he asked in a low voice, pitched for my ears, not for anyone listening at the door.

"I don't know," I said. "Sergeant Wilkins? Captain Cartwright. I need to see his shoulder. At least we might be able to eliminate the Captain."

"We might need Sister Hammond to be absolutely sure."

I'd hardly mentioned the name when something reached the Major in that dim, clouded world of fever.

He opened his eyes and reached out to catch my hand, grasping it with all his strength.

His eyes, bright with pain and fever, were very blue. Nearly the same color as I remembered Sergeant Wilkins's being.

"Sister?" he said in a voice barely above a whisper. "Please. Take me back to hospital. Please, I can't—I can't bear it any longer."

"Who are you?" I asked, bending over him. "Tell me your name."

"Sister?" he repeated. "I beg you."

Just then Maddie came into the room carrying a flat brown leather satchel or haversack. It had a long leather strap so that it could be carried over the shoulder or worn across the body, leaving his hands free. If he was surprised to see us, he didn't show it. Brushing me aside, he bent over the ill man.

"What have you done to that leg?" he demanded gruffly. "I've told you to stay off it, to protect it and keep it clean."

But the man in the bed called out to me again. "Sister? Please?"

Maddie said to me, "The bonnet of the motorcar is still warm. You haven't been here long, have you?"

"I've inspected the wound," I reported, as if Maddie were a doctor asking me to give him information about a patient. "And I've asked Mrs. Neville for hot water, clean bandages, and something to use as an antiseptic."

"That wound must be lanced," he said. "If it isn't drained, it will become gangrenous before morning."

"I haven't the tools," I began, but Maddie pointed to his satchel. Reaching into it, he pulled out a clean apron and handed it to me before putting on his own.

I removed my own apron, crossed the room, and set it across the back of a chair.

Maddie was rolling up his sleeves as Mrs. Neville and two maids came in. The housemaids were carrying what I'd asked for, their glances moving to the man on the bed almost warily, as if half afraid of him. Mrs. Neville, empty-handed, saw Maddie and said quickly, "Ah! They didn't tell me you'd come. Is there anything else you require?"

Maddie shook his head. "But ask one of the housemaids to stand outside the door, if you please. In the event I need something more."

She nodded and disappeared, taking the maids with her.

Pouring some of the hot water into an empty bowl, Maddie washed his hands thoroughly and dried them on one of the extra cloths. He nodded to me, and I did the same.

With Simon, silent and watchful, standing by, we set to work, putting a clean cloth beneath the knee, then washing it well with hot water and a strong soap.

The Major had closed his eyes, and I hoped he was not awake.

Maddie took his scalpel and quickly cut into the wound, letting it drain. The bloody fluid, laced with infection, was caught in the bowl we'd used to wash our hands, and removed as soon as the wound stopped weeping. I could smell the infection, but the odor of gangrene wasn't present. Maddie handed the bowl to Simon and then set about cleaning the wound a second time with soap and then sprinkling it with antiseptic powder. It had taken us nearly three quarters of an hour, but the wound was now as clean as we could make it.

I had a moment to glance at the Major's face. He was, mercifully, unconscious.

As we finished cleaning up the wound, then bandaging it afresh, I said to Maddie, "Who is this man? Is he the one who wrote to Sister Hammond? You must tell me. There's a woman in Derbyshire who thinks this man might be her missing cousin. It would be a comfort to her to know whether to hope or not. Harry Cartwright has been suffering from a head wound, and he's wandered away. He hasn't been seen for weeks."

Maddie turned to me, anger in his face as I began to wash my hands again.

"I don't know. I've been told his name, but whether it's his or not, I can't say. I have had another patient with a head wound. There was little I could do for him either. To try would be worse. At least the Major is here where he's well looked after. Miss Neville swears he's her fiancé, and I have accepted that."

"But it's possible—" I began, but Maddie rounded on me.

"I heal those I can. I don't pry. A wounded body is one thing, a wounded mind another. It's not as simple to save."

"He begged me to take him away—just now, before you came in. He said he couldn't stand it any longer."

"Was he speaking of his wound? Or his circumstances?" Maddie demanded.

"I don't know." There was nothing more I could say.

Simon spoke then. "The man we're after has committed cold-blooded murder. It's possible he could kill again. That's something to remember when you choose not to pry."

While he was distracting Maddie, I began to smooth the sheets on the bed, drawing them up to cover the patient. And without haste, I ran my fingertips over the left shoulder of the unconscious man.

It was as smooth as the flesh of my own shoulder. I did the same on the right side, in case Miss Cartwright had it wrong. But there were no ridges and lumps where a wound had torn the shoulder open and it had healed with difficulty.

"He shouldn't be disturbed. I won't allow it." Maddie glanced my way as he began to clear away the stained bandages and basins of water, preparing them for the housemaid to take downstairs. I was already bathing the Major's face in fresh water.

"Leave him now," he said. "I'll stay awhile, to look in on him in an hour."

It was dismissal. I began to remove the apron I'd been given, watching Maddie reach into his satchel once more to take out a powder that he mixed with a little water in a glass. Holding up the Major's head to prevent him from choking, Maddie got him to swallow the mixture. "That will keep him quiet. One of the housemaids must sit with him through the night. He shouldn't be left alone. And that wound must air." He arranged the bedclothes again to his satisfaction, then turned. "I understand your motives," he said slowly. "But you must understand this. We live here. The Nevilles and the Warrens, and everyone else in Upper Dysoe. Don't meddle."

With that he crossed to the door, gave his instructions to the waiting housemaid clearly and concisely, then asked her to repeat them. Nodding, he turned back to us.

"Thank you once more for your assistance. I think it best if we leave the patient to rest."

With that he ushered us out of the room. There was nothing more I could do but follow.

We walked down the ornate staircase together, and Maddie nodded to us before going off to find Mrs. Neville.

Simon started for the door. I was on the point of following him, when I looked down. I had taken off Maddie's apron, but I hadn't remembered to put on my own.

I turned quickly toward the stairs and began to run lightly up them.

"Bess, don't do this."

"It's my apron," I called over my shoulder.

I hurried down the passage. No one was in sight.

I put my hand on the knob and swung the door open.

Chapter Fourteen

Miss Neville was just drawing up a chair to the Major's bedside.

Whirling, she said angrily, "How many times must I tell you to knock?"

Breaking off, she stared at me.

"What are you doing in my house?" she demanded, her face flushing as her anger turned to fury. "Get out. Or I'll have you taken up for trespass."

I'd been told she was away. How had she arrived without our knowing it? Was it while Simon and I were with Maddie?

Of course it would be natural for her to come at once to the Major's room to look in on him. Someone must have told her Maddie had been sent for, that he was even then cleaning the wound.

I said, "I'm so sorry, Miss Neville. My apron." I pointed. But the apron wasn't where I'd set it. She'd moved it and taken that chair for her vigil.

All at once I remembered that the letter from Sister Hammond must still be in the apron's deep pocket. Had she noticed it there and taken it out to read? Had there been time?

As I caught it up, I pressed my hand against the pocket and felt the letter safely in place. But that still didn't tell me whether she'd read it or not.

As I stepped out into the passage, it occurred to me that her sudden flare of temper might well have been the realization that she'd nearly been caught with the letter in her hand.

She was still glaring angrily at me as I swung the door shut.

I hurried down the stairs. No one else was in the Great Hall, and I was glad. I let myself quietly out the door. Simon had already cranked the motorcar and was waiting for me.

The drive back to the gates seemed to be twice as long as it had when we'd come down it little over an hour before.

"Miss Neville was in the sick room when I went back. She wasn't especially happy to see me."

As we pulled away from the gates, Simon spoke. "You touched his shoulders. What did you feel?"

"Nothing," I said. "If there's a wound on either shoulder, it's healed well."

"Then this man isn't the missing Harry Cartwright?"

"Sadly, no. Or perhaps I should say, the odds are against it. I could wish he were, for his cousin's sake. Of course I couldn't see, I might have been pressing in the wrong places. But if the wound was as bad as Miss Cartwright described, I'd have felt something."

"It's been two years since the Somme."

"Still." I took a deep breath, glad to put Windward behind us.

"Was it Sergeant Wilkins? If it wasn't Cartwright."

"Yes, it could very well be. How long has it been since I've seen him? But England is full of fair men, Simon."

"His hands, then."

"I don't know. Yes. Maybe. If he's engaged to Miss Neville, why did he want me to take him back to hospital? Why had he written to Sister Hammond?"

"He was delirious, you can't judge him there."

"The words were so similar to those in the letter. And I think Maddie would have posted a letter for him, if the Major had asked. Simon, the letter was in my apron pocket. Miss Neville moved the apron when she took the chair over to the bed. She must have guessed it was mine. She might even have read the letter. She'd know his handwriting, surely."

"And what will she make of that, I wonder. I wouldn't wager on a happy marriage if she has."

"No, nor I. Especially if the Major fully recovers. And he very well could, given time."

I glanced across at Simon's profile, but it told me nothing. Simon Brandon could be inscrutable when he wished to be.

"You haven't told me your opinion. Have we found Sergeant Wilkins?"

"Maddie mentioned another patient with a head wound."

"Sister Hammond told us that Sergeant Wilkins didn't have one."

"At the mechanic's shop back in Shropshire we were told that the man asking for a lift to Kenilworth had a fresh head wound that looked rather nasty."

"That's right, I remember."

We drove straight through Upper Dysoe to the town where we'd stayed the night, just beyond Biddington. We stood there in the yard, trying to decide what to do.

I recalled something else. "Simon, did you hear? Mrs. Neville told me the Major's name was Findley."

"If I were in London, I'd look him up in the rolls."

"But we aren't," I replied absently, my mind elsewhere. "Simon. What if it wasn't Sergeant Wilkins who killed that man in Iron Bridge? Everyone assumes it must have been. The description is close enough to match. But that description is vague, isn't it. A man of such and such a height and build, such and such a coloring, no distinguishing marks or features. It would fit the Major—it would fit Harry Cartwright—and how many more men?"

"That's for Scotland Yard to determine. There was a witness, remember?"

"Yes, of course. All the same, I was drawn into this whole affair, an unwitting and unwilling accomplice, if you will. It was Scotland Yard that told us the murderer in Ironbridge was Sergeant Wilkins. A man *was* murdered there, the witness thought he resembled the photograph she'd seen of the sergeant before the audience with the King. But she had the briefest of looks at him. What if we've followed a killer? But not Sergeant Wilkins?"

Simon was exasperated. "Why are you so ready now to believe he's innocent?"

"I expect," I said slowly, "what worries me is that the sergeant has eluded the Army and the police. That's quite a feat. What if like poor Harry Cartwright, Sergeant Wilkins might be dead? No one has found either of them, and it could well be for the same reason. And if we can't, either, how will I clear my name? I need Sergeant Wilkins to be alive. Yet he might be at the bottom of the Thames. Or an unidentified corpse found in a field. What will I do then?"

"You mustn't give up hope, Bess," he said more gently. "It's not like you."

I tried to clear away the cobwebs. "Simon, I think the first order of business is to find a telephone and see if a Major Findley exists on the Army rolls. And what's become of him. In Biddington there's a nicer inn, we passed it just now. Leave me there to see what I can discover. Someone somewhere must have seen a strange man lurking about."

"I don't like leaving you alone, without any means of getting out of here if you needed to."

"There's no reason why I should need to leave here in a hurry. And it's probably just as well that I can't return to Upper Dysoe on my own. How long will it take you to find a telephone and reach the proper person in London? A few hours? A day?"

It took some persuasion, but in the end, Simon agreed to search for a telephone.

We had an early lunch in Biddington after Simon had inspected the inn there and seen my accommodations for himself. Shortly after one, he set out.

I watched his motorcar disappear in the direction of Stratford-on-Avon with a feeling of unease. It had seemed a very sensible thing to do when the two of us were discussing it. And quite another to realize how completely on my own I was. I felt quite conspicuous in my uniform while many of the other women in the town wore the drab clothing of a country at war, no bright new hats, no new styles, only what they could contrive to look a little different, enough to lift the spirits for one more day or week or year. It wasn't market day, but people were in the shops and on the street.

The feeling of unease soon passed as I strolled down the High Street, stopping first in the small post office to buy a few stamps, striking up a conversation with the postmistress, and from there to the pretty little stationer's shop, where I found a box of fine writing paper. At the milliner's I bought several ribbons and a small bunch of feathers for a hat. At the greengrocer's I purchased apples, and in the cheese shop a slab of cheese, from the baker's a half loaf of bread. And all the while I was gossiping.

It turned out to be rather easy, as Windward was the only grand house in Biddington's small world, and I had only to mention that a dear friend had been at school with Barbara Neville to begin a conversation.

Very few people here actually knew the Nevilles, but they most certainly knew of them. I heard stories about Barbara Neville's father and mother, listened to a harangue over her stepmother's peculiar view on the evils of the Industrial Revolution, and found myself in the midst of a circle of women wondering if it was true that she was soon to be married and whether there would now be parties and weekends at the house, or if she and her husband would choose to live in London. This was of some concern, as it could mean a drastic change in the running of Windward and therefore less money in the pockets of those who were purveyors of goods to the house. The general view was that her fiancé was quite mad and ought to be shut up in an asylum. Bits of information embroidered by rumor and envy.

The baker's wife raised her heavy eyebrows when talk turned to the Major. "A wild man," she told me. "I can't understand why she hasn't broken off her engagement. Imagine going around shooting at people."

"Why should he do such a thing?" I asked. "Surely not!"

"He's mad." She nodded. "Oh yes, quite mad, they say. He talks to goats and brings them into the house to sit at table. I have it on good authority. The miller's lad delivers our flour. He's often at Windward with theirs."

I wondered if Mr. Warren, the miller, knew that his lad told such tales.

It wasn't until I was sitting on a bench by the church, eating a ploughman's lunch of bread and cheese and apples, that I learned anything truly useful.

A man was scything the grass between gravestones, and when he stopped to rest, he nodded to me and asked what brought me to Biddington, if I'd brought someone home.

I explained that I was on leave and looking for my brother, who had walked away from the hospital where he was recovering.

"No strangers in Biddington that I've heard of," he assured me, leaning on the handle of his scythe. "I'd learn soon enough if there was. My wife cleans the church every week, and the committee ladies bringing in the flowers gossip freely."

Laughing, I asked if he'd heard all the talk about Barbara Neville's fiancé

"There's two schools of thought there," he said, casting a glance toward the Rectory to be sure he couldn't be seen chatting with me. "One says Miss Neville brought him home one day without a by your leave and announced she was going to nurse him back to health."

"And the other school?"

"That she found him wandering on a hillside, half mad and barely able to walk. And she took him in, claiming she knew him."

This was too close to the mark to ignore.

"Did she indeed?" I asked, offering him one of my apples. "What was he doing there?"

"Thankee, Sister. No one seems to know. And the servants are closemouthed, as you'd expect. But there must be some truth to it, because if she brought him back from London, no one saw her passing through Biddington."

"She might have driven in from Worcestershire." It was the direction we'd come from, and it would make some sense if Miss Neville were coming up from Dorset.

He shook his head. "It's what the gossip says."

"Have you ever seen him? Does he often come with her to Biddington?"

"No one has seen him. There was a story making the rounds that he was deformed and only walked out at night. Some claim they've seen him on the road in the evening, and they look the other way for fear he's burned or disfigured or some such."

He thanked me again for the apple and went back to work, whistling to himself as he moved between the graves.

Simon hadn't returned by late evening.

The next day I stayed close. I'd visited most of the shops and could think of no other way to approach people. But by late afternoon, tired of four walls, I went out again. Biddington was strung out along the road, like many villages and towns that had grown from a few huddled buildings to any size. Only a few lanes led off the High Street, and most were residential, cottages and bungalows in the direction of Upper Dysoe, and a scattering of cottage industries and a smithy toward the next village. I made a circuit, coming back by way of the churchyard. The grass cutter was nowhere to be seen.

Biddington's church to St. Martin was not very large. I walked up the path to the west door and stepped inside for a moment, looking around at the walls, where new memorials had been added to commemorate the dead who were buried in France. They were so new, the engraving sharp, the brass gleaming. I'd seen recent graves in the churchyard as well, raw mounds only beginning to grass over. The altar window was rich with greens and reds and even blues, and I thought it might have been endowed by a rich merchant, but the little visitor's booklet claimed it had been a gift of a Tudor-era Neville, in memory of his father, lost at Bosworth Field.

I walked out into the sunlight again and stood there, watching a woman pushing a pram along the road. I was reminded of the baby I'd delivered to the refugee woman, and I wondered if the little girl and her mother had survived.

Feeling a wave of sadness, I resolutely set out again. I was in a short street of small houses, hardly more than cottages. The door opened in one near the end of the street, and a young woman stepped out.

I knew her, I was sure of it, but at first I couldn't place her. She was coming toward me, and I smiled, still trying to remember who she was. Dark brown hair, hazel eyes, a long face . . .

Then it struck me. In a blue dress trimmed with cream and a small hat, she looked nothing like the trim housemaid who had brought hot water and clean bandages up to the Major's room.

What was her name? I don't think I'd heard it. But unless Miss Neville had told her staff about our incursion in the sickroom, no one knew I'd been sent away with a flea in my ear. I could at least try to speak to her.

She nodded to me as she came abreast. "Sister," she acknowledged shyly. She would have walked on, but I stopped, and so she was forced to pause as well.

"You were there when Maddie and I were treating the Major's leg," I said, using the tone of voice of a ward Sister inquiring about a patient. Professional without any personal overtones. "I'm afraid I can't remember your name. How is he today? Has the fever dropped?"

"It's Violet, Miss. As to the Major, I can't say," she went on. "Miss Neville was sitting with him in the morning, and this was my afternoon off. But I do believe he's less feverish than he was. And the powders Mr. Maddie left do keep him quiet. He was thrashing about quite a bit in the night after the wound was cleaned. It must have been hurting something fierce."

"I'm happy to hear he's improving." I turned to walk on, and she fell into step beside me. My interest having been established as purely medical, I went on. "What happened to his leg? It was an old wound close to the knee, I could see that, but recently reinfected."

"He keeps wandering off. The Major. A week past, he found the gates shut and locked. Trying to climb up and over them, he took a frightful fall. The new wound didn't appear to be that deep, but you never know, do you? All at once it became swollen and turned so dark a red, Mrs. Neville sent for Mr. Maddie, not waiting for the mistress to return."

"That explains it," I said, nodding. "Why it was so infected."

"He was off his head when Miss Neville first brought him home," Violet added confidingly. "And not from delirium. We'd find him in that old barn, the one that's burned down. Or someone would come across him lying on the road or away up the hill, too weak to go on. Then he took a fancy to that goat." She laughed. "Mrs. Neville claimed he was just taunting Miss Neville, but who's to say? I heard him going on to Miss Neville about the time he was a prisoner of the Germans. But *she* claims he was no such thing."

"Perhaps that's why he's always trying to escape," I said. "Because he thinks he was."

"It could well be," she said. "I'd never thought of that."

"Has Miss Neville known Major Findley very long?"

"That's the odd thing. We'd never heard her speak of him, then suddenly she brings him home and informs us they're engaged. Mrs. Neville says he's a nobody, that her stepdaughter could do far better. An earl or even a duke."

"When did he first come to Upper Dysoe?"

"It must be close on to six weeks, now."

Close to the time Sergeant Wilkins disappeared. In London.

We had reached the High Street, and she waved to the greengrocer's boy, who was just closing the back of the cart used for deliveries. I could see bundles and baskets of foodstuffs. The fragile fronds of carrots next to fat cabbages and the long pale shapes of parsnips.

"I'm sorry, Sister. He's to drop me at Windward," Violet said, bidding me a hasty farewell. Running lightly across the road, she hailed the boy, who could be no more than fifteen, and he helped her onto the cart's seat, talking animatedly to her as he took his own place.

She looked back at me, giving me a little smile that seemed to say, *What can one do?*, as if the boy's attentions made her feel a bit awkward.

I walked on to the inn, thinking about what Violet had told me.

Encountering Violet had been the second bit of luck I'd had since Simon had driven away.

Then I had another bit. I was just finishing my tea when the owner of the pub, a man named Oakham, was telling someone that he could borrow the mare for an hour at reasonable rates. But the man wasn't a rider and shook his head, asking if one of the shopkeepers might give him a lift to Lower Dysoe.

I waited until he'd thanked Mr. Oakham and left before approaching the bar.

"I'd like to take your mare out for an hour or so."

He looked me up and down. "I've no sidesaddle, Sister. Do you have riding clothes with you?"

"No, sorry, I don't. But I can manage, I think."

He was doubtful. Still, he took me around to the kitchen yard where the mare was in the stall that was at the near end of a small shed. He opened the half door and led her out.

She was a tall horse, a pretty, softly dappled gray with white mane and tail. She nuzzled my arm as I came forward to rub her nose.

"The Army didn't want her," Oakham was saying. "Not dark enough. And I can't say I wasn't glad. She's been gently reared, and I couldn't bear to think of her going off to war."

"Yes, I understand," I said, thinking of all the dead horses I'd seen in France. The mare nodded, as if in agreement.

Mr. Oakham fetched a saddle and bridle, then set about putting them on.

"Know horses, do you?"

"I've ridden since I was a child," I told him.

"Well, then, you'll have no trouble. Her name's Molly, and she has no bad habits. Wait here."

He went back inside the pub and soon reappeared with a worn but good pair of riding boots. "My late wife's," he said. "She wouldn't mind if you used them."

"That's very kind of you."

I went back inside, to my room, and changed into the boots. They fit very well, and I was glad of them.

Downstairs once more, I led the mare to the block and mounted in a flurry of skirts. But I managed to sit the horse with sufficient decorum to ride on. Mr. Oakham watched me out of sight, making certain I could handle Molly. We were soon trotting sedately down the road to Upper Dysoe.

Maddie was in his cottage when I arrived. I called to him, and after a moment he came out his door and stood there, looking up at me.

"That's Oakham's mare," he said, as if accusing me of stealing her.

"Yes, I've borrowed her for the afternoon. I'm staying on in Biddington for a while."

"What do you want with me?" His glance strayed to my right arm. I'd left off the sling after helping him with the infected leg, and I found I could even manage Molly's reins with only a little pain to remind me to be careful.

"I was concerned about Major Findley," I said, as if I'd never spoken to Violet. "If cleaning the wound had been enough."

"His fever is down," he said, almost reluctant to give me news. I couldn't help but wonder if Miss Neville had said anything about my interfering again. "And there's no sign of new infection."

"I'm glad."

"What keeps you in Biddington?" he asked, as if against his better judgment.

"I'm not sure," I replied, giving some thought to what I wanted to say. "We came here by accident the first time, you know. When the miller was shot. Looking for someone who had disappeared. A soldier. But we lost him near Upper Dysoe. And then after I'd returned to France, Sister Hammond wrote to me about the letter she'd received. Purportedly from you. It seemed to be an odd coincidence."

"We've discussed this before. I don't know this woman."

"I'm sure she didn't know *you,* I told you she thought Maddie was short for Madeleine. At any rate, that pleading letter has stayed with me. Someone was begging for help, and I still haven't found him. I can't ask you to break a promise. But if I could just hear that he's in good hands, I could go back to London." It was a different approach. I wondered if it would work.

"It will do you no good to linger. I can't tell you what I don't know." His gaze went beyond me, watching a young woman coming out of one of the shops farther down the street.

"Do you think it was Major Findley? I'm unde-cided—is he the man Sergeant-Major Brandon and I have been searching for? Wouldn't it be best for everyone if we could reconcile this problem once and for all? *Someone* wrote to Sister Hammond. *Someone* used your name and this address. How many people do you think even know where to find Upper Dysoe? It's hardly a crossroads of Empire."

He said nothing.

Remembering suddenly, I said, "You told me that you had another patient suffering from a head wound."

Maddie regarded me. I couldn't quite read his expression but I thought I'd caught him off guard. After a moment he said, "We have grown accustomed to war wounds. We have forgot that horses can still kick a farmer in the head or a child can still fall out of an apple tree." He sighed. "If you wish to know more about Major Findley, speak to him. Or failing that, to Miss Neville."

And that was, after all, good advice. But carrying it out was another matter.

I thanked him, turned the mare's head, and rode through Upper Dysoe toward Windward.

Soon after I passed the burned-out barn, I caught up with the young woman I'd seen earlier, doing her marketing. She looked up and smiled. I thought I must present quite a sight, my skirts tucked around me. Molly, lovely lady that she was, moved well, making it easy for me to keep them wrapped around my borrowed boots. And that reminded me that she was also tall, and I'd need help getting back into the saddle. I hadn't seen a mounting block by Windward's main door.

There wasn't one.

As I rang the bell, I tried to sort out what I was intending to say. I'd probably have only a matter of a few seconds to make my mission clear before the servant answering the door sent me about my business.

I didn't recognize the maid who answered my summons. As in so many grand houses, Windward's footmen and even butlers must have gone to war or off to do war work.

Older and quite prim, she politely asked my business.

Inviting me to step inside, she went away to see if Miss Neville would receive me.

It was several minutes before I was shown to a narrow room that opened out onto a garden. The door was standing wide, and it was quiet enough that I could hear the buzz of insects in a shrub just outside.

Miss Neville was trimming cut flowers. Beside her on the stone shelf was a large, elegant green-and-white vase.

She went on about her work as the housemaid withdrew. "I thought I was rid of you," she said, without looking up.

"I'm so sorry, Miss Neville," I said, keeping my voice level. "There's been a misunderstanding, one I'd like to clear up if I may."

At that she wheeled and stared at me as if I had grown two heads. I didn't think Miss Neville was accustomed to anyone who spoke to her as an equal.

I stared back. She was hardly as frightening as some of the Matrons I'd known.

"Indeed. What is your name, Sister?"

"Crawford."

"I shall remember that when I report you to your superiors for insolence."

If she'd meant to rattle me, she failed.

"I came to Upper Dysoe in search of a wounded man who had—er—been released too soon from the hospital where he was being treated. We failed to find him. I had seen Major Findley sitting on that bench under the tree on the front lawns, and he looked so much like the man we're been seeking that I was worried. I must apologize for my next question. If you had found him ill and wandering in his mind, had taken him in and cared for him until you could discover who he was, I could well have the answers you must also be looking for." That last wasn't quite the truth, but she couldn't prove it wasn't.

"Why should you dare to assume that a guest in this house was some lost soul missing from a hospital?" She was suddenly angrier than she ought to be, and I couldn't quite understand why.

"Because the last sighting we had of this patient was not so very far from here. And for several reasons, he could be considered dangerous. That's why the man called Maddie allowed me to help him treat the Major."

That gave her pause.

"A dangerous man? And you've misplaced him?"

"Baldly put, yes."

"I can assure you that he is not Major Findley. I brought him here from Dorset, because he didn't appear to be recovering quickly enough in that hospital filled with screaming men and a staff too exhausted to care for half of them."

"And yet there is no doctor available closer than Biddington. Unless of course you consult Maddie. The Medical Corps frowns on patients being cared for in less than ideal circumstances."

"Are you presuming to tell me that I was derelict in bringing the Major here?"

"Indeed not. It was a kindness. But you can see why I might have mistaken him for *our* missing patient. Under the circumstances."

She put down the scissors she was still holding in one hand, ready to shorten the stem she held in the other.

"You have a point," she said, although I thought it was a grudging concession.

As if the little room was suddenly claustrophobic, she gestured for me to follow her, and we stepped out into the very pretty cutting garden.

"What do you mean by dangerous?" she asked when we were out of hearing of anyone in the house.

I had no intention of mentioning murder. "In delirium, men sometimes believe they're back in France. They will lash out violently, even to the point of laying hands on the Sisters or orderlies." I held up my arm as a case in point. The bruises had faded nicely to a pea green mixed with yellow. "The same can be true of severe head wounds. If you don't know what to expect, it can be quite frightening."

Miss Neville frowned again. I wondered what was on her mind. Something most certainly was. Was she worried about Major Findley? I suddenly remembered what I'd been told about his wandering, and the problem with the goat. They had loomed large when I considered the possibility that the Major could be Sergeant Wilkins. She had seen both as an annoyance. But he had a head wound—and he'd been delirious from the infection in his knee. Was she thinking of her own safety? Someone at the hospital ought to have warned her about the risks of caring for this man on her own, fiancé or not.

She was silent, almost as if she would rather pace than stroll quietly as we moved up one path and down another. It was a full minute before she spoke again. I couldn't help but wonder if she were weighing the risks of a husband who might turn on her, rather than being ruled by her.

"Will the Major's leg heal properly? More to the point, will he be able to walk again?"

"I don't think anyone could answer that just now. If it heals properly, if there's no additional infection, if he learns to exercise it correctly, that is, without doing additional damage. He could well need to be seen by a specialist."

"There's Maddie. He's cared for everyone in the three villages—the servants here—the tenants on the estate."

"He's quite good," I agreed, not sure what to call him. Was he a doctor? Had he finished training? He must have had some experience somewhere. His hands were too sure, his knowledge too extensive. She was a wealthy woman. Why wasn't she seeing the best men on Harley Street? "But we've learned so much about wounds since the war began."

"Yes, yes, I'm sure." We had reached the gate at the far end of the garden and we turned back. "If he hadn't been such a fool as to try that wall," she said then, suddenly irritated, "none of this would have happened."

"Perhaps," I suggested, "he didn't realize what the wall represented. It was one thing to you—surrounding the estate, keeping unwanted strangers out. To him it could have triggered a very different memory."

She brushed that away as being of no importance. Something else was worrying her or she'd never have allowed me to stay this long. Was it because I was a stranger? Or a nursing Sister? Sometimes people spoke to the medical profession in almost the same fashion as confessing to a priest. With illness or wounds came other worries.

Then it occurred to me that she might indeed be thinking of the future, about marrying an invalid rather than a man who would look after the estate and her wealth and this house as she would want them to be handled. I'd seen very little of the Major. I didn't know what sort of person he was, what sort of gifts he might bring to a marriage. But I was fairly sure *she* knew precisely what she wanted.

Stopping abruptly, she seemed to realize I was still there.

"Will you find your missing patient?" she asked, surprising me. I hadn't expected her to care one way or another.

"I expect we will. Eventually."

"Where is the Sergeant-Major?"

Surprised again—because she'd remembered Simon—I said, "He has gone to Stratford on a military matter."

We walked on to the door to the flower room and this time she went inside.

"Thank you for explaining matters to me," she said, dismissing me. "Can you find your way out?"

"Yes, I believe so."

"Good day, Sister Crawford." She picked up the scissors and began to trim the flowers again. They had wilted only a little during our walk and would soon perk up in water. As I made my way through the quiet and empty Great Hall and let myself out the door, I briefly considered risking a run up the stairs to the Major's room and, if he was awake, speaking to him.

Would this wealthy, strong-minded woman actually consider taking in a stranger found on a hillside and pass him off as her fiancé? Even to protect her fortune and her estate? I was beginning to think it was impossible. On the other hand, I could see that the Major might well have written to Sister Hammond, if he'd been one of her patients, and begged to be returned to hospital, if he had had a change of heart about marrying Barbara Neville. Except when I'd seen her preparing to sit by his sickbed, she'd never given me a reason to think she was madly in love. From her questions just now, she might even have been regretting her choice.

Where then was Sergeant Wilkins?

I had stepped out the door and pulled it shut behind me. Molly was standing quietly, waiting for me. I was just wondering how I was going to mount her when a boy of about sixteen came around the corner of the house, pushing a barrow filled with the oddments of gardening.

I smiled. "Could I ask your help in getting back on my horse?" I said.

He looked around, as if uncertain whether I was speaking to him or not, then came forward.

"That's Mr. Oakham's Molly," he said, putting a hand on her flank as he walked past her.

"Yes, I'd borrowed her to call on Miss Neville."

He cast a doubtful eye over my skirts.

"She's rather tall, isn't she? But I can manage, once I've had a leg up."

He was still looking at me. He was nearly my height. "You tend wounded men?"

"Yes."

"What's it like to be wounded, Sister?"

I realized that he was thinking about himself. If the war lasted much longer, he'd be called up. Another year? Boys large for their age often managed to enlist at seventeen.

"It's very painful. If you survive the wound, if you're treated in a timely fashion, you'll be likely to live. But the scar will always be there, to remind you."

"I broke my leg once. Falling from a tree. It hurt like the very devil."

"Then you understand what I'm saying."

"Is there a lot of blood? There wasn't any when I fell. Except where I hit my chin on a branch coming down."

"There can be a great deal of blood," I answered truthfully. "After a while you get used to seeing men bleed, men with awful wounds. Nobody likes it, but there you are. It's war, and terrible things happen."

He nodded. "I reckon I can handle it."

"A brave man always can," I assured him, trying not to frighten him, but unwilling to lie. He needed to know the answer to his questions. But I felt a sweeping sadness at the thought.

He came forward, linked his hands together, and gave me a boost into the saddle, then stepped back. I was just wrapping my skirts around my borrowed boots when Violet, the maid I'd spoken to in Biddington, opened the door to the house and stopped short, seeing the boy beside me.

She glared at him, and he hastily returned to his barrow, trundling it toward the far side of the house. Violet watched him go.

When he was out of hearing, she reached into her pocket and brought out a folded sheet of paper.

"I was hoping to catch you. The Major told me you'd dropped this in his room while looking after his leg."

I almost replied that I hadn't visited the Major this time. Biting my tongue, I smiled. "Thank you, Violet. And please thank the Major for being so thoughtful."

I'd just shoved the paper into my pocket, as if it had indeed fallen out, when the older housemaid, the one who'd let me in and taken me to Miss Neville, came to the door.

"Why are you standing here, Violet? You're supposed—" She stopped short as the door swung wide enough for her to see me astride Molly. Her mouth thinned in disapproval of my riding without a sidesaddle, but she said, "Did you require something more, Sister?"

"Violet was kind enough to make sure I could mount again," I said. "There's no block here."

"Indeed, Sister."

During this exchange Violet had slipped back inside.

I nodded to her, turned Molly's head toward the gate, and trotted sedately away.

The folded sheet of paper felt like hot iron in my pocket.

I didn't know how the Major had learned I was in the house. Had someone told him? I wasn't even sure he remembered I'd helped Maddie lance that leg.

Then who had sent me this note?

Chapter Fifteen

I waited until I was well clear of the house before drawing out the sheet of paper. Pulling Molly to a walk, I unfolded the page.

The writing was a scrawl, barely legible.

For God's sake, get me out of here.

I sat there, reading it a second time.

Was it Major Findley who had written to Sister Hammond? I'd already begun to wonder, but here was proof before my eyes. There couldn't be two people writing to her. But why hadn't she recalled this patient when she told me about Captain Cartwright?

It was possible that the Major remembered Sister Hammond because she had been kind, even though she'd been assigned to another ward. Or in his muddled state, her name might have been the only one he could recall.

Folding up the sheet of paper again, I restored it to my pocket.

What was I to do about Major Findley?

I felt a surge of pity.

Was he confused, unable to remember where he was, or why? A prisoner in a strange house and looking for rescue? It would explain his odd behavior and his attempts to escape. It was even possible, saddest of all, that the Major might not even remember the woman he was pledged to marry.

On the other hand, I had never actually talked to the man. I couldn't say with any certainty whether he was halfway to madness or just troubled.

While I didn't particularly care for Miss Neville, I felt a surge of sympathy for her as well. It couldn't be easy to know the man one had decided to marry was willing to risk life and limb to flee.

Sympathy notwithstanding, I could do nothing.

I gave the mare the office to move on, and she broke into that comfortable trot once more.

We were drawing even with the burned-out ruins of the old barn. I heard something and thought the goat must have got free again, coming back to where it had been tethered to feast on the brambles and wild shrubs. I pulled up the mare and peered into the bushes, debating with myself what to do if I saw it. Return to Windward and report the fugitive or let the household discover for themselves that it had gone missing again? Certainly no harm would come to it, even if I left it. Someone was bound to notice it gone sooner or later.

I rose in my stirrups for a better look, and the borrowed boots slipped a little. Before I could settle onto the saddle once more, the mare reared and then bucked. Surprised, completely caught off guard, I was thrown.

It wasn't the first time I'd been tossed from my saddle. My first thought as I went flying over her head was to land well, so as not to break my neck or reinjure that wrist. The next as I collided with the road was, how was I to mount her again?

I hit harder than I expected. There was the heavy *thump* as my right shoulder went down into one of those deep ruts that marked most roads, and I let go of the reins involuntarily as pain erupted down my arm. And then my head struck something immovable that left me temporarily dazed.

As if from a great distance, I heard the mare set out at a gallop down the road toward Upper Dysoe before the darkness came down.

It lasted only a matter of seconds. I was nearly sure of that. But I lay where I'd fallen until the waves of darkness receded and I could look up at the sky and see white clouds billowing overheard in the summer heat.

Taking careful stock, I tested the fingers of my right hand. They moved easily, although there was some pain in my arm and shoulder. Not the pain of a break, I told myself, but it wouldn't be very long before an ugly bruise appeared.

Drat! I'd just got over the injury to my wrist.

I went on to lift my right forearm, and that went well. Next, I touched my face. A lump, rising fast near my hairline, was sensitive to the touch, but there was no blood on my fingers when I looked.

It was time to sit up before a carter came down the road and found me sprawled ignominiously in the middle of it.

I was a little dizzy at first, but that passed very quickly, and I managed to get to my feet without any trouble. Dusting down my sleeves and skirts was awkward with my left hand, but I didn't want to press my luck with the right.

Turning, I saw that there was a round stone embedded in the hardened mud of the rut, just about where my head had landed. Not large enough to do serious damage, but large enough to make its presence felt.

I stood there for a moment, to be certain that I was all right, then as I turned toward Upper Dysoe, and the pub, my hip told me I'd landed on it as well.

I smiled ruefully. I hadn't taken a tumble like that since—India? And then I'd come down squarely on the sunbaked sand, only knocking the wind out of myself.

Simon had leapt off his horse and knelt beside me, calling my name as I gasped for breath, then picked me up and carried me from the horse lines to the house where the Colonel Sahib and my mother were living at the time. Before the pair of us could alarm the servants, I got my breath back and he put me down, holding on to my shoulders until he was sure I was all right. And then he'd told me furiously not to do that again.

Well, in fact, I had not.

I walked the knot out of my hip, but my arm was a little stiff by the time the pub came into sight. I took stock of myself, this time to be certain that my cap and my apron and skirts were tidy. The borrowed boots were rubbing my heel as I opened the door and went into the pub, hoping to find someone there who could take me back to Biddington.

Just then I heard someone shouting my name, and I turned and went out again.

It was Tulley, and his face was red with fury.

This time it wasn't Simon who lectured me, it was Tulley.

Molly, it appeared, hadn't galloped all the way to Biddington. A frequent enough visitor to Upper Dysoe to feel right at home there, she had trotted around to the pub yard. There someone had seen her without a rider and gone in to tell Tulley, who went out to investigate. He must have thought I'd simply dismounted, without calling anyone to unsaddle her and rub her down.

I stood there, listening to him, thinking that he was more concerned about the wayward horse than he was about a woman who'd just been violently thrown. By this time the lump on my forehead was sizable and painful. I was about to cut him short and tell him that it was I who had come to harm, not the precious mare, when something he was shouting got through to me.

"I *what?*" I demanded. "I never touched her with a whip. I didn't have a whip with me. What's more I had no need of one."

"Come and see for yourself," he retorted and reached out to take my arm—unfortunately the right one—and I cried out.

Just at that moment, Simon drove into the pub yard.

The motorcar skidded to a stop in a spray of dust and small stones and bits of hay. He was out of it almost before it had stopped rocking.

"Take your hands off her," he all but snarled at the man pulling my arm to drag me away.

Tulley stepped back, startled, as Simon Brandon bore down on him.

He must have seen the quail egg on my forehead and the state of my clothes, and jumped to conclusions.

I quickly stepped into Simon's path and put out a hand to stop him before he could reach Tulley.

"It isn't what you think, Simon," I said hurriedly. "It's all right. I hit my head when I was thrown from Molly—the mare I borrowed from Mr. Oakham in Biddington." I pointed to my riding boots, dusty from walking back. "As you can see. Tulley has just accused me of taking a whip to the mare. But I hadn't. We were about to go and find out what he's talking about."

I wasn't sure whether Simon was satisfied or not. But he stopped and said grimly, "Then let's have a look at this mare."

A much subdued Tulley led the way around the pub to the shed in the back. Molly was standing in front of it, her saddle already removed, while the reins dragged in the dust of the yard.

I put my hand on the mare's neck, patting it gently before running it down her side toward her left flank, where Tulley was pointing.

There was a cut in Molly's hide, narrow, bleeding a very little, not serious enough to harm her but quite noticeable. And it did look as if I'd used a whip. I flicked a fly from the raw wound and said, "I didn't do this. I give you my word. Take her to Maddie to clean it."

Tulley was about to argue, but one look at Simon's scowl, and he bit back what he was going to say, instead nodding curtly. He collected the reins and walked away, his back stiff with suppressed resentment.

Simon watched him go, then turned to me. "Now tell me what happened."

I did. Simon listened to me, his gaze holding mine as I talked.

"What made the mare rear, then buck?"

"I don't know—I really didn't think about it at the time. Now? A horsefly? A bee's sting? But that's not what the cut looks like, does it, Simon?"

"Come with me."

We went back to the motorcar, and I got in while Simon bent to turn the crank.

Driving back the way I'd walked just a few minutes before, I went over what had happened. I'd been sitting on the horse, looking at the brambles and undergrowth for the goat, then I had turned toward the ruins, hadn't I?

Simon stopped the motorcar well short of the barn ruins, and we got down.

"Show me where you fell."

That was easier said than done; the road was so furrowed from traffic in rainy weather that one rut looked very much like the other. Bending over to see better made my shoulder and head hurt, but I persevered.

"Ah—that round stone." I straightened and tried to judge both sides of the road, getting my bearings. "I think that's the one my head struck. If it isn't, then it's near enough like it to be twins."

"Stay there."

Simon walked past me about the length of the horse and knelt to study the dusty track that here in the Dysoes was called a road.

He spent a good ten minutes scouring the place, then moved on another foot or so.

As far as I could tell, no one had come along this road since I'd reached the pub. But what was Simon looking for? Then I realized what he suspected. That someone had deliberately startled Molly, causing her to rear and buck.

The question was, how had it been done without my seeing someone?

I joined him, scanning the road surface. And we had no luck at all.

"Simon, we can't find it."

He stood up, looking toward the barn. "If someone threw something at the mare from that side of the wall, it had to be heavy enough to fly to the middle of the road. We must keep looking."

I walked back to the motorcar, then started forward once more. Perhaps I'd been wrong about the round stone.

And then I saw it. A bit of wood from the roof that must have escaped the fire. There was a broken nail protruding from it

"Simon, here!" I called, and he came at once. "Why would someone deliberately hurt my horse?"

He took the bit of wood and examined it, then hefted it in his hand. Satisfied, he turned and went toward the side of the barn. "Mark the place where you think you fell," he called, and I hurried to stand by the spot.

"I'll hit you," he said. "Move away."

"You need the flank of the horse to aim for," I said, refusing to budge.

He took his aim, then hurled the bit of wood toward me. It sailed through the air in an arc, and then losing momentum, it began to come down, landing just at my feet.

"Was it meant for me—or the horse?" I asked now, as he came back to join me.

"You said you'd stopped and were looking for the goat. You might have turned and ridden toward the barn next. Whoever it was, he couldn't take the chance. There's no place to hide, come to that. At least not enough concealment left to escape detection. He decided to startle the mare into bolting and take your mind off the ruins. Only his aim wasn't as good as mine."

"Then why did I find it so far from where I fell?"

He picked up the bit of wood and held it out. "The nail dug into the mare's flank. Enough to make her buck, and then it fell off as she raced back to the pub. That wasn't a deep cut, remember? Tulley wouldn't have accused you of using the whip if it had been deeper."

I tried to remember what I could from the moment the mare reared.

"I think you're right. She went up on her hind legs at first, startled—then bucked to dislodge whatever had stung her. Only it wasn't a fly. It was that nail. Poor Molly, she didn't deserve to be treated so shabbily."

"I don't think he intended to hurt the mare. Still, we'd never have thought to come back here if it hadn't been for that telltale cut." Simon went back to search the barn, but there was very little to see. A few bent stems of blackened stubble and that was all. "He must have heard the mare coming and took shelter here until you'd passed."

"It couldn't have been the Major," I said, and told him about my visit as we walked back to the motorcar. "He would have had his work cut out for him to nip down those stairs, much less walk this far."

"I thought you were staying in Biddington. When I didn't find you there, I came at once to Upper Dysoe."

And found me being threatened by Tulley. No wonder his anger had exploded into near violence.

We rode in silence back to Upper Dysoe, where Simon mounted Molly and I drove the rest of the way to Biddington, which did little for my still aching shoulder, but I said nothing about that.

It was necessary to explain the wound on Molly's flank to her suspicious owner, but after viewing the small cut, he shook his head. "The Broughton lads," he said. "They're always up to some mischief or other. The constable will have a word with them."

"I don't think it was the Broughtons," I began, not wanting to get them into trouble. "This was on the far side of Upper Dysoe."

Frowning, he said, "I've not known them to wander that far. Still, father's at the Front, mother can't manage them. There's a first time for everything."

"Do you know if there are any strangers about? Here in Biddington or in Upper Dysoe?" Simon asked.

"Now that you mention it, one of the miller's sons—young Matt—was telling people he saw a drunken soldier lying by the verge of the road this side of Lower Dysoe. Disheveled and dirty, he was. Matt was uncertain what to do. He took the sacks of flour on to the general store in Lower Dysoe, then came back to do what he could for the soldier. But the man had gone. He told his pa, but when they went back, they couldn't find any sign of him. Warren sent word to the constable here in Biddington, who thought the man might be a deserter, but the Army didn't have anyone from this area on their list. Warren wanted to believe he'd fallen on hard times, no work and no hope of finding any. He'd have taken him in and seen him right. He has boys of his own. One will be of an age to enlist soon. I reckon that worries the miller of nights."

I was reminded of the gardener's boy, asking me about the war.

"When was this?" A wounded man could appear to be drunk. Or an exhausted and hungry one.

Mr. Oakham scratched his chin. "Let me see. It was after the Goldsmith twins were born. We wet their heads in the pub that very night, best we could with the little beer I could manage to find." Nodding, he gave Simon the date.

It was five days after the murder at Ironbridge.

Could Sergeant Wilkins have got as far as Lower Dysoe by that time? It was possible. Just. With a lift from the lorry driver. Much would depend on how far he'd come before he'd lost the bay.

Simon and I exchanged glances.

Unless, of course, I suddenly remembered, it was the Major on one of his brief forays away from the house.

I didn't want to believe it was the Major.

Simon thanked Mr. Oakham, and we went back to the motorcar.

"What do you think?"

"I'd like it to be Sergeant Wilkins." But I told him about the Major's wanderings all the same.

"Let's have a talk with Warren's son. This could very well explain why someone wanted to startle the mare. If you nearly came upon Wilkins, Bess, he'd not want you to find him. You're the only one in these parts who could recognize him."

We went to the mill. Warren was sitting on a three-legged stool, supervising the sacking of flour. Clouds of white dust rose high on the still air as the flour was shoveled into bags by two boys of about fourteen and fifteen who looked enough like him to be his sons.

He nodded to us, and then recognized me. "Sister," he said, trying to stand. It was awkwardly done with his shoulder still taped.

"No, please don't get up," I said quickly, not wanting him to fall on my account. "I just wanted to see how you were faring."

"Maddie tells me it's healing well enough. Deep wounds take their time, he says. And I'm to learn to spare it when I do start to work in the mill again. The muscles will have knit, he says, but they won't be strong so soon."

"And he's right," I agreed. "It was a close-run thing."

"Aye. 'Don't tempt the Lord,'" he said, mimicking Maddie's quiet tone of voice. "And I haven't. You can see the lads doing most of the work."

"Speaking of your sons," Simon asked, "which one is Matt?"

"The taller of the two. Matt? Take a minute and come down here."

Matt willingly left the sacking to his brother and came down to his father. He was liberally coated in white flour dust, save for his lively gray eyes. Nearly as tall as his father, he had shoulders already widening into manhood. Another year, and he'd be enlisting.

"Yes, Pa?"

Simon spoke instead. "You were the one who found the drunken soldier along the roadside near Lower Dysoe?"

"I did indeed, Sergeant-Major. I felt that sorry for him, and I'd have helped him then and there but for the flour in the cart. There was no room for him. When I came back, he was gone. I did look."

"Did you tell anyone in Lower Dysoe what you'd seen?"

"I thought about it. But the shop owner in Lower Dysoe, Mr. Dedham, was in a hurry, and I didn't like to annoy him. Short-tempered, Mr. Dedham is. Pa can tell you." He looked to his father, who nodded. "So it was left to me to do something. I would have said he was too far gone in drink to move, and I couldn't have been away more than twenty minutes at most."

"What was the man's rank?" Simon continued. "Could it have been Major Findley?"

"I never thought about the Major," Matt answered, surprised. "This man wasn't an officer, but I was so worried for him I didn't look for his rank. I expected to come directly back, didn't I? This 'un was the worse for wear. Disheveled, like, and one side of his uniform was covered in burrs and twigs. As if he'd rolled down Dice Hill."

A niggling question occurred to me. Had Major Findley, whoever he was, begun his Army career as a private soldier? It would be too farfetched unless Miss Neville had given him his present rank. Bad enough to marry a man without title or standing. She would draw the line below the rank of officer. New uniforms could be ordered from a military tailor in London. They must have become accustomed to supplying proper gear to wounded men.

But Matt wasn't to be swayed in his opinion that the soldier he'd seen was not the Major.

"What do you think became of him?" Simon asked.

"I can't say. He didn't look to me as if he could drag himself off the road. But then I don't know how long he'd been there. He could have come to his senses." There was doubt in his voice. "What's more, when I bent over him to see if he was alive, he didn't smell of beer."

"Do you think some other Good Samaritan had come along and found him?"

Matt faced Simon squarely. "I was hoping so," he said. "I didn't care to leave him there. But what was I to do?" He glanced at his father, as if asking for reassurance. "My cousin's in France," he added in explanation for his concern. "I'd have wanted to help him."

"You did the right thing," Simon told him. "If I can find this man, I'd see that he gets medical care. The question is, how long had he been living rough?"

"Not around here," the elder Warren put in. "Someone would have stumbled across signs. What appears to be empty countryside to you is as familiar to us as our own hands. Lads roam the hills, a man will walk off a mood across them, and someone has an eye to where the sheep are. That's how we managed to find the Major when he took one of his spells."

Yet someone had been lying there on the road outside Lower Dysoe. And he had to have come from somewhere. He'd had to have gone somewhere. He hadn't simply disappeared.

And that reminded me of something else.

"When the Major was lost, did he ever say anything to you when you found him?"

"Say anything?" Warren considered the question. "He was always a quiet 'un. I doubt I've heard him put three words together. But Hancock, the greengrocer here in Upper Dysoe, told me he wept the first time he was found. Hancock reckoned it was the relief."

But *was* it relief? Or agonizing disappointment that his escape hadn't succeeded?

"Is there a priest in the Dysoes?" I asked. "I haven't seen a church."

"The vicar comes over from Biddington if he's sent for," Warren answered. "Before the war we talked about a church here in Upper Dysoe, but Mrs. Neville discouraged it. And the Bishop as well. A waste of money that could be put to better use, he said. We'd never have a congregation of a size to pay for the building of it." He grinned. "*Mrs.* Neville, now, she said the Lord wouldn't approve of taking perfectly good farmland for His house. Better to put it to the plow and feed the hungry."

We were going nowhere with our questions, and the Warrens were eager to return to their work.

Simon thanked them, and we left.

As we drove back toward Biddington, on impulse I said, "Please? Can we stop here? I'd like to speak to the greengrocer. Hancock?"

"About Findley?"

"Yes. There's something wrong in that house, Simon. There's a second note, I've told you."

"We aren't here to save Findley, Bess."

"I know. But this time the message came to me. I can't ignore it."

"Time's growing short. If we're to have any hope of finding Wilkins, we must concentrate on that."

"I'd just feel much better knowing what happened the first time Findley left that house."

With a sigh of frustration, Simon found a widening in the road where he could turn the motorcar. We drove back into Upper Dysoe and walked into the shop, next but one to the baker's. A young woman was inspecting the rows of parsnips, cabbages, carrots and onions, peppers and beets, setting them to rights after the day's marketgoers had picked them over.

She looked up, and when we asked for Mr. Hancock, we were told he was in the back of the shop. And we found him there, lifting an assortment of gourds out of a basket.

He was a tall, thin man, with tufts of graying hair for eyebrows. He started to say something, realized we were custom and not his assistant, and rose to his feet as if he were unfolding.

Glancing toward the young woman in the front of the shop, he asked if he could assist us.

I tried to capture that radiant smile of Diana's, the one that opened all doors to her. It wasn't very successful. I'm not Diana.

"I've acted as nurse for Maddie when he treated Major Findley. We're concerned about his knee, and whether he will attempt to wander again. Please, could you tell me how you found him the first time he—er—left the house unattended?"

Hancock frowned. "It was odd, I can tell you that. He'd walked as far as he could, then crawled until he gave out. We'd been told he was off his head sometimes, from the war. When I came up to him, he lay so still I thought he might have fallen and knocked himself senseless. I knelt beside him and spoke his name. It was all of a minute before he lifted his face from his arms and looked at me. I could see he'd been weeping. I asked if he was all right, telling him I was there to take him home, if he could manage to walk just a little way with me. 'How far to Dorset?' he said. 'Could I walk that far if I tried?' I thought he was making light of the distance. 'Not today, sir,' I said to him. 'Another day, perhaps.' We managed to reach the road, where I had my cart waiting. Then he asked me if I'd post a letter, if he could bring it to me. I said, 'If you ask one of the servants, sir, they'll see to it.' He just looked at me, and that was that."

The first attempt to contact Sister Hammond? Even then it had had to be forwarded from Dorset. Had he given up hope? And who posted it for him? Violet? I didn't think so. Mrs. Neville? She clearly didn't approve of the Major, and she might well help him leave that house.

"Poor man," I said aloud, thinking how desperate he must be. "And what did Miss Neville have to say when he was safely returned to her?"

"She was angry with him. And more than a little frightened that he wouldn't be found, I should think. I don't like to speak ill of my betters, Sister, but it was all she could do not to roar at him. And then she calmed herself down enough to ask if he had hurt himself, if she should send for Maddie."

"How did you manage to find him?" Simon asked.

"That was odd too. I thought I saw him coming over one of the Knobs. The hills that close us in. I left the cart there and then, climbing up to cut his track. But he wasn't there. I had to walk another quarter mile before I found him."

"Are you certain it was the Major you saw coming over the hill?"

"Who else could it be? There was only one man lost that day."

But another man at a distance might pass as the Major.

We thanked him and left.

Simon, speaking softly so that his voice wouldn't carry as we walked out of the greengrocer's shop, said, "I've never seen you smile like that before."

"My best imitation of Diana," I answered ruefully.

"Dear God." He grinned in spite of himself.

"I haven't asked you what you learned in Stratford. Or wherever it was you managed to find a telephone."

Simon shook his head. "It was a complicated business. That's why it took so long. Apparently Major Findley was reported killed in action. Much later, that was amended to missing. Four months ago, he was discovered in a clinic in Dorset that treated severe head wounds. He had no idea who he was. But another officer who came there recognized him and gave him a name again. With that information the doctors were able to help him more in two months than they had in all the weeks before that. His memory was sketchy at first, and then it began to build on each new discovery. This according to Dorset. I telephoned them after I'd spoken to the War Office."

"Then what happened to him?"

"The officer who recognized him must have told friends in London, and one day Miss Neville appeared on the hospital doorstep, so to speak, and convinced the doctors that a few weeks in familiar surroundings might do wonders for recovery. The Major was of two minds, but the staff convinced him to agree."

"And so Major Findley is who he says he is—or more to the point, who Miss Neville says he is."

"That's right. My guess is that he got here to Upper Dysoe and changed his mind. Perhaps Miss Neville tried to convince him that they'd been close before the war, and he couldn't remember, didn't believe her, or had a change of heart."

"Then we're left with the soldier Matt saw. And the one that confused Mr. Hancock."

"I'm afraid so."

"I'd very much like to ask Major Findley. The question is, will Miss Neville allow it?"

"I'll brave her displeasure if you will."

But when we arrived at the house, the gates were open, and when we used the heavy knocker, it was Violet who came to the door.

I asked for Miss Neville. Violet informed me that the mistress had gone riding. I asked for Mrs. Neville, but she had gone to sit with a tenant's ill wife.

"It's actually the Major I've come to see," I told the housemaid, indicating my kit, which I'd taken with me when I left the motorcar. There wasn't much in it to attend a wounded man, but Violet wasn't to know that.

"This way, Miss."

She showed us up the stairs, although I knew the way, and then left us to enter the Major's room alone. "He no longer needs a sitter in the morning," she said in explanation. "The fever's gone."

"Very good news," I responded, nodding.

Simon stayed by the door as I approached the bed. The Major had fallen asleep. I called softly, "Sergeant

Wilkins?" And then when he didn't answer, I changed that to "Major Findley?" And still he didn't answer.

But as soon as I touched his arm, his eyes flew wide and he stared at me, and then the expression in them changed from recognition to suspicion, as if he'd never seen me before. His brows twitching together, he finally said, "You came with Maddie." It was a statement not a question. "I thought at first you were someone else."

"Did you?" I asked with a friendly smile as I stepped away from the bed. "Who were you expecting?"

He cleared his throat, trying to sit up. I added pillows behind his back, to make it easier. "Sorry, I must have been asleep." He gestured to the powders beside the bed. "They're fairly strong."

As I listened to his voice, I had to accept the evidence of my own ears. Unless he was very clever at disguising it, this man couldn't possibly be Sergeant Wilkins. Not that I had doubted Simon or what he'd learned. It was just the final proof.

"I've come to ask how you're feeling," I began.

"Better, more's the pity," he answered sourly. "You should have let me die."

"I hardly think you were in danger of dying," I said briskly. "But you might have lost that leg."

He didn't answer me, glancing instead across the room toward Simon. "Have you come for me, Sergeant-Major?"

"No, sir. I've been seconded by the Colonel to accompany Sister Crawford," he answered smartly.

"More's the pity."

I didn't know how much time we had, and so I got to the point rather quickly. "I'm sorry to disturb you, Major, but we've misplaced one of our patients. Do you remember the first time when you were—er—lost? Mr. Hancock, the greengrocer in Upper Dysoe, found you on the hillside and helped you reach his cart on the road below."

"Yes," he snapped, as if he preferred not to think about that day. "Why are you reminding me of it?"

"I thought perhaps you might have seen another soldier in the hills that day. Perhaps on the skyline? In the distance? I don't believe you crossed paths."

His quick response was no. But I read the truth in his eyes before he looked away. There *had* been someone else.

"Did you think afterward that it was a hallucination? But at the time, you might have believed for an instant that you were back in France." It was possible, of course, that he believed the other man was escaping as well, and didn't want to betray him. Had they spoken? I would give much to know. But I didn't think the Major would tell me. His next words proved me right.

"No. There was no one to see, I tell you. I was alone."

"He's ill, Major. If you've seen him, it would be a kindness to help us find him."

He turned back to me. "Why?"

I couldn't tell him the truth, not about London and the King, about the Iron Bridge and the murder. "He's violent. He's already hurt someone."

"How did he get away? Knock down one of the orderlies? Reach the road and beg a lift while the hospital was in an uproar? Or did he have help?"

"He must have done," I said, wanting him to go on talking about this man he hadn't seen. "He wasn't well enough to go far on his own."

He lay back then, lifting an arm up across his face, shutting me out. "As I should have done," he said under his breath.

I looked for a way to engage his interest. "Your cases are quite different, Major. He wanted to find someone, and he refused to wait until he was fully healed. You, on the other hand, know precisely why it is you want to return to Dorset."

"Dorset?" He laughed harshly. "I'd go to hell if it would help."

Still standing by the door, Simon warned, "We haven't much time."

Nodding to Simon to let him know I'd heard, I asked the Major, "What's wrong, Major Findley?"

"You wouldn't believe me if I told you," he said, suddenly tired.

I could hear someone walking down the passage. Simon was right, we must go. But I risked one more question.

"Will you let me help you?"

"I don't trust anyone. Not any longer."

"But you sent a message to me, the last time I was here. By Violet. The upstairs maid."

"No. Never. I swear it." His voice was firm now, as if he'd heard the footsteps as well.

"I'm so sorry. I'd hoped that you could see your way clear to help this missing soldier." I walked to the door, then hesitated, hoping he might decide to call me back.

He didn't. He was listening to hear where the footsteps had gone. And so Simon and I went out into the passage, shutting the door. We made our way down the stairs, and no one stopped us as we left the house.

We drove sedately back through the gates, and turned toward Upper Dysoe.

"So much for saving Major Findley," Simon said, lightly.

"Or discovering that he is Sergeant Wilkins," I answered wryly.

"But now you want to know who this fellow was that Matt Warren saw lying on the road. You must realize that he could be miles from here now."

"Or he crawled off the road and found a safe place to die."

"Perhaps that's the kinder ending."

I said, "Maddie mentioned something about a second patient with a head wound. But when I asked him directly about that, he implied it was not a war wound. That could be true of Sergeant Wilkins. His head injury wasn't related to the war."

"Bess."

"Do you suppose someone here in the Dysoes has taken in the sergeant? He could have concocted some sort of tale, it needn't be true. That he'd been wounded and demobbed and had nowhere to go. It wouldn't be the first time he lied to someone."

"Bess," he said again, this time in a different voice.

I took a deep breath. "I know. I know. But, Simon, who tried to frighten the mare, Molly? It couldn't have been Major Findley, and somehow I can't imagine Miss Neville lying in wait for me."

He laughed against his will.

"We aren't even sure that Sergeant Wilkins stole the bay horse in Ironbridge. It could have been someone courting a girl in the next village who decided to ride rather than walk. Imagine his horror when the bay got free and disappeared."

"Perhaps the horse jumped the fence on its own, possessed by the desire to explore," I retorted.

"What, the love of its life sold as a cart horse to someone in Lower Dysoe?"

I smiled. "There's no constable in any of the Dysoe villages. The closest one is in Biddington. He keeps the peace, but I doubt he knows the village secrets. And there's no Rector. But Maddie knows all the secrets," I said.

"But he keeps them, Bess. He must, or people would refuse to turn to him in times of need. It's his livelihood as well as his duty."

"I wonder who Maddie is. And whether that's his first or his last name. He's got secrets too. Where did he train? Did he qualify as a doctor? Was he stricken from the lists for something that went wrong? Is that why he's willing to live in this backwater? People must pay him in kind, save for the Nevilles, who can afford his services. And perhaps a few other families."

"He never reported to the police that Warren had been shot. And no one has turned him in for not reporting it. Not even you."

"As you say, he must keep his secrets. And I had other reasons for not insisting on the police being involved. We were looking for a wanted man."

Simon was quiet for a moment. Then he said, "Bess. We've all assumed the Major shot Warren. But why would he have done such a thing?"

"I don't know. Miss Neville paid for Warren's care and for help at the mill until he was well enough to work again. That's a tacit admission of guilt."

"Yes, but look at it this way. Everyone *assumed* that it was Findley. It's known that sometimes he takes his revolver out and shoots at something. He's a man with a troubled mind, and perhaps this is his way of coping with his demons. But he had no reason to shoot the miller, did he? And most certainly Warren wasn't walking in the far corners of the grounds. God knows Windward must be large enough to accommodate shooting parties. Findley could have found a quiet corner for his marksmanship."

I could see where he was taking this.

"Why would anyone else want to shoot Mr. Warren?" I paused, thinking it through as Simon had done. "It wasn't Mr. Warren who stumbled on the soldier by the roadside. But it was the Warren *cart* that went past the man that day. Perhaps that's all someone saw, the cart, not who was driving it. Matt is nearly as tall as his father. Someone half dazed with hunger and exhaustion and pain could be forgiven for thinking he'd seen the miller and not the miller's son. But where did he get the revolver? That's an officer's weapon."

"Which might have served to save Warren's life. Most men in the ranks wouldn't be able to hit their mark with a revolver. In the melee of battle, even a novice could kill someone."

But Simon could hit his mark with a revolver. I'd seen him. "Revolvers don't grow on trees," I said. "Sergeant Wilkins hanged that man on Iron Bridge. If he'd had a revolver, why not simply shoot him?" I answered my own question. "The report would have echoed across the river and up the hillsides. He wouldn't have risked it."

"Exactly. But here, where the Major already has a reputation of sorts, everyone assumed he'd fired that shot. If Warren had died, it would be the Major the police would question. And if he was confused, couldn't defend himself, he'd soon be taken up for murder."

I felt cold. "We need to ask the miller what he saw when he was shot."

"A very good idea."

Mr. Warren was sitting in the small bare room where he kept his accounts. There was a deal table stained in places by ink spills, a pair of chairs, and to one side a small cabinet half filled with ledgers of various sizes. Other papers filled cubbyholes above the cabinet.

"You can't be worrying about my shoulder, again," the man said as Matt ushered us in.

I took the chair in front of the table. "In a round-about way, perhaps. Did you see who shot you?"

His mouth tightened, and I thought for a moment he didn't intend to answer. Then he said, "I don't want trouble. I gave my word to Miss Neville's steward. She paid for my care and brought in extra hands to help while I'm unable to do the work. Besides, the Major is not accountable for what was done. He's wounded, and all."

"I don't wish to cause trouble for you or for Major Findley. The problem is, I'm not sure it was Major Findley who shot you."

And that was the wrong approach to take, I could see it at once. Miss Neville had been generous. To admit that it wasn't Major Findley after all would mean losing her help. And Mr. Warren still needed that help.

I added hastily, "This is between the three of us, Mr. Warren. I have no wish to make this public knowledge. For my sake as well as yours. It was another wounded man who brought Sergeant-Major Brandon and me to Upper Dysoe. I wouldn't care to make trouble for him either."

"The soldier on the road my son saw? That's why you came to ask about him?"

"Yes, it could have been the same person. You see, we don't really know. If you could say unequivocally that it was the Major who shot you, that you saw him, then we must look elsewhere. If you aren't sure, then I'm obligated to go on looking for this man somewhere here in the Dysoes."

I could see in Mr. Warren's quick glance toward Simon, standing just behind my chair, that the miller had assumed, like everyone else, that it *was* Major Findley. Getting him to admit to anything else was going to be difficult.

He said as if in answer to my thought, "It was bound to be Major Findley."

"But that means you didn't see who it was," I responded quickly.

"The man was wandering about shooting at anything that moved."

"Yes, I'm sure he was. And the stories about that got rather out of hand. What took you to that distant part of the estate? That's the question. You make your deliveries to the kitchens at Windward. You had no business wandering about the grounds. Unless of course you fancied a pheasant for the pot?"

"I'm no poacher. Besides, it wasn't on the grounds. It was not far from that barn, the one that's burned down since."

That was all I could draw from him.

I turned to Simon, who said, "Mr. Warren, have you considered? It was Matt, in your cart, who saw the drunken soldier. It's possible that the man with the revolver thought it was you—and tried to kill you. If he realizes his mistake, he might come after your son."

"Here, what sort of person is it you're after?" he asked, alarmed. "Is he shell-shocked? Is that it?"

"He's capable of killing," I said. "That's the problem, you see. We want to find him before someone else is hurt."

Mr. Warren pushed his chair back and began to pace. "You aren't telling me this folderol just to frighten me, are you?"

"I'm afraid not." It was Simon who answered. "Why do you think I'm accompanying Sister Crawford instead of an orderly?"

He stopped pacing, looking out the door toward the mill. "There was someone in the old barn. It's where the Major went sometimes. Miss Neville doesn't like it when he wanders, and I slowed the horse, thinking to be sure it was him, not one of the local lads skipping lessons, before sending word to her. And then he fired, whoever he was. If it hadn't been for the horse taking me home, I'd have been lying there in the road until someone discovered me. I'd never heard of the Major coming as far as the road to do his shooting. But there's a first time for everything. He's known to wander. But he was never armed then."

"And you never saw a face—a uniform?"

"He must have been inside the barn, in the shadows cast by the fallen roof. Just a shape in the darkness. I was about to call to him. Then something hit my shoulder hard, nearly knocking me over into the cart, just as I heard the shot. It didn't hurt at first. Then it felt as if my arm had been taken off. It was bleeding something fierce, and I couldn't seem to draw a breath." He flinched at the memory. "I couldn't think clearly, but I was as sure as I was alive that it had to have been the Major."

It could well have been.

I stood, ready to thank him and take my leave.

And then he said, half to himself, half to us, "He wasn't wearing his officer's cap." Looking up, he added, "I slowed the horse because I was trying to see who it was in the barn. A shadow, as I told you. But the reason I wasn't certain, that I was thinking it might not be the Major, is that I'd never seen him without his cap. It covered the bandages over his head, where the hair was still growing out. As if he doesn't want anyone to notice. And there was no cap on that shadow. Why would he take that cap off in the barn? Did he think he was indoors?"

Only a slim lead—but I was grateful for it.

"Are you certain?" I asked. "I promise you, I won't say a word to Miss Neville."

"I am," he said, gazing from Simon to me. "I'd not thought about it since it happened. It wasn't something that mattered, was it? But now it makes sense."

It most certainly did. And the Major's head wasn't bandaged now. His hair had grown over the wound.

Simon asked, "Where would this man find a revolver?"

"I don't know. There's only the Major I know of, with a revolver."

The Dysoes, I thought, being such small villages, little more than hamlets, weren't likely to have produced many officers.

And then Mr. Warren said, "Of course there's Mrs. Chatham. Her husband died at Mons. He was a career soldier. A Captain."

The revolver could have come back with the Captain's belongings. Boxed up by someone in his unit and sent back behind the lines to be returned to the dead man's survivors as soon as possible. And if the Captain had purchased his own revolver, as some officers did, it would belong to his family like any other possession.

"Where can we find Mrs. Chatham?" I asked.

"Chatham Hall. That's in Lower Dysoe. Up the lane that comes into the main road just by the old tithe barn wall. The house had belonged to her husband's parents, and she came back to live there in 1916."

Mons had been one of the first battles of the war and it had been fought by the British Army regulars. A fierce, last-ditch effort to keep part of the German Army from taking the coast road. Many a brave man died there.

We thanked the miller and walked back to the motorcar.

"How do you ask a widow if she knows where her late husband's revolver is?" Simon asked as we settled ourselves in the motorcar.

"The question really is, how could someone just passing through Lower Dysoe discover that she possessed one?"

"There's that," Simon agreed. "Do you think in his erratic wandering, the Major left the revolver in the old barn? It could have been used, and then returned to where it was found. Who would notice, unless Findley was accustomed to checking how many shots were left?"

"It's possible, of course," I said as Simon drove out of the miller's yard to the main road. "But can we trust his memory?"

Clouds were gathering to the west, dark and ominous, and a wind was rising. Ahead of us, just past the gates to Windward, I saw a well-dressed young woman walking briskly toward Middle Dysoe, a market basket in either hand. They appeared to be heavy. As we came nearer, I remembered having seen her in Upper Dysoe a few times.

"We ought to offer her a lift," I said, watching the clouds racing toward us. "She'll be caught in the storm."

Simon slowed, and I spoke to her.

She hesitated, then cast a worried eye toward the storm. "It's kind of you to ask," she said.

Simon put on the brake and came around to help her set the baskets in the rear seat. He was just closing the door when we heard the first low rumbles of thunder.

We'd hardly reached Middle Dysoe when rain came down in hard driving drops that struck the windscreen and splattered. The rounded hills that surrounded us echoed the thunder, making it difficult to tell how near it was. But the lightning flashed across the windscreen with a brightness that made me blink.

"Where can we set you down?" I asked over the roar of the rain. In that same instant, lightning flashed blue and thunder followed hard on its heels. "Or perhaps it would be better to wait until the worst has passed." Wind rocked the motorcar, whipping at the words.

Our passenger looked out at the sky. "It's very bad, isn't it? Perhaps a few minutes . . ." She let her words trail off.

Looking out as the rain swept through Middle Dysoe, moving in a curtain down the High Street, I couldn't help but think the village had an air of timelessness about it. As if we could have come here a hundred—two hundred—years ago and it would have looked much the same. And a hundred years from now, it would have hardly changed at all.

We had pulled to the side of the High Street, and I saw that the shop next to us was a small bakery that was no doubt one of Mr. Warren's many customers. There were half-empty trays in the window, and by this time of day most of the loaves would have been sold. There was one lonely round loaf next to a half dozen fruit tarts, and even as I watched, a hand moved into the window from inside the shop and took away three of the tarts.

I'd tried to make conversation, but our passenger appeared to be shy, for she answered questions with a quiet *yes* or *no,* when she could. We'd fallen silent, listening to the rain change from thumps to a steady drumbeat, and finally to a simple patter.

Simon turned. "If you'll tell me where you live . . . ?"

"Oh, that won't be necessary. I must stop in the bakery for a moment. I'll be all right from here."

"We'll be happy to wait," I offered, but she shook her head, blushing a little as Simon came to help her out and hand the baskets to her one by one. She thanked him, and quickly ducked into the bakery before he could hold the door, wedging her baskets ahead of her.

Simon returned to the wheel and we drove on. "As we come into Lower Dysoe, watch for the lane where Mrs. Chatham lives."

I almost missed it, for it turned at a sharp angle, half hidden by that old section of wall, just as Mr. Warren had told us. The stone was rampantly covered in wisteria, the green leaves and tendrils reaching up into the air where a roof had once been.

We took the lane past a handful of cottages, and came upon a low wall that enclosed a wood. Across the way was another, higher wall that I thought might be part of Windward land. Very soon we could see a small manor house tucked away to our right, in a dip of the hill. It was built of the same mellow rose brick as Windward, but that was the only similarity.

Simon pulled up the brake. It was still raining, and the lead roof gleamed dully in the gray light. I could hear the thunder behind us now, moving toward Upper Dysoe and Biddington.

"It must have been a dower house of the original estate," I said. "Or the home of a less distinguished relative."

And yet the house was serene, welcoming, as if one only needed to knock at the door to be admitted. But the gates were firmly closed, shutting us out. "Locked," Simon noted.

The name of the house, Chatham Hall, was carved into one of the marble blocks set into the stone gateposts.

"I can see why Mrs. Chatham chose to come back here, rather than live in London. It's a lovely setting," I said.

"It is."

"I can't imagine how anyone could possibly walk into the grounds, steal into that house, find a single revolver, and slip out again without arousing suspicion."

"Certainly there's been no gossip about a break-in."

"Then we're back to the possibility that the Major left the revolver in the barn. But that's rather a coincidence, don't you think? The miller, the forgotten weapon, and the man who intended to use it, happening to be in the same place at the same moment. The only other possibility is that someone living in this house had access to the revolver and took it out to use it." I peered out at the gates. "We could walk up to the house."

"Hardly the most auspicious way to arrive, muddy and damp, asking inconvenient questions," Simon commented. He released the brake and drove past the gates, following the low wall for a little way. But there appeared to be no other entrance. Reversing, he drove back the way we'd come and continued down the lane toward the main road. "We'll have to find an excuse to call."

We had just reached the wisteria-clad wall at the junction with the main road when someone came hurrying around the corner and stopped short at the sight of our motorcar.

It was the young woman we'd left in Middle Dysoe, in the baker's shop.

Chapter Sixteen

S he still held a heavy marketing basket in each hand, and her hair had begun to straggle out from under her sodden hat. The shoulders of her coat were wet and so were her shoes.

We stared at each other for a stunned moment.

I put down the window and said, "I'm so sorry. We could have brought you here. But you said Middle Dysoe . . ." It was the best opening I could think of. We *had* offered.

She stood there, her mouth still open, trying to think of something to say. Finally she blurted, "I—I stopped to look in on a sick friend."

I doubted very much that there was a sick friend, any more than there had been a pressing need to stop in the little bakery.

Simon had put on the brake and was already out of the motorcar. "Let me set these in the rear," he said solicitously. "You are already wet through." She wanted to protest but didn't know quite how to refuse Simon.

She blinked once or twice, as if her mind was still muddled. Then she said, "I don't like to ask favors when I can't possibly return them."

"You're not in our debt," Simon replied easily and helped her climb into the rear seat.

She was still faintly protesting as Simon headed back down the lane. "Tell me where to go. One of the cottages?"

Our passenger was too well dressed to belong to one of those, but I knew that Simon was trying to put her at her ease.

"No, the house—farther along." I could tell from the direction of her voice that she was sitting stiffly on the edge of the seat. "Why were you on this lane? Not many people come up it."

"We'd driven farther than we'd intended. I was looking for a wide enough space to turn the motorcar." He and I had silently agreed to lie rather than tell her what we were doing. At least for now.

"Oh," she said, as if she'd not been thinking of such a simple explanation. But what could be worrying about our presence here?

"Just there," she said, pointing over my shoulder. "The gates."

Simon obligingly nodded, and then pulled into the space before them.

"Oh," she said again. "Someone's locked the gates." She seemed uncertain what to do now, as if we had somehow overwhelmed her by giving her a lift.

Or as if she had a secret she was afraid she might accidentally reveal?

Her secret—or someone else's?

Simon got out and went to look. The gates were latched, but not locked. I'd have sworn he was right earlier, that they had been locked. He swung them wide and then came back to drive the motorcar through.

"I'll close them when we drive out," he said over his shoulder to the woman.

She didn't reply. I glanced over my own shoulder to smile at her, and watched as she made an effort to give me an answering smile. It wavered, then vanished.

The arched doorframe was set off by stone facings, and the windows were old and elegant, many of them mullioned, the others plain glass inset with shields and emblems. The ornate knocker, brass in the shape of a lion, was heavily draped with the black crepe of mourning.

Almost as soon as we'd come to a full stop, before Simon could step out and help her, she'd opened her door and was trying to pull the heavy baskets toward her across the rear seat. He lifted them for her and started toward the door, but she was there before him, thanking him profusely and telling him that she could manage now.

It was clear that she wouldn't open the door to the house until he had rejoined me in the motorcar and we'd started around the loop in the drive that led to the gates.

"She's gone inside," he said, finally looking back. "It wasn't another red herring."

Simon got out and closed the gate, latching it as promised, and then when he was once more settled behind the wheel, he said, "Those were very heavy baskets. Was she doing the marketing for that entire household?"

"And why walk all the way to Upper Dysoe? Simon, I've seen her before, I told you. In Upper Dysoe several times. I'm sure of it. And I think Maddie must know who she is. I remember once when he was speaking to me that he turned to watch her as she came out of a shop. Perhaps she doesn't want to be seen here in her own village buying more than usual?"

"If she lives in that house, and her clothes suggest it, added to the fact that she walked in the main door, not a servants' entrance, why not take a carriage or use a dogcart?" Simon asked.

"Perhaps she didn't want anyone to know how far she had to walk?"

Of course none of this confirmed that Sergeant Wilkins was inside that house. But the soldier Matt had seen was lying just outside this village. Circumstantial evidence still. But it was intriguing.

We drove into Lower Dysoe and looked at the handful of shops as we passed. There was nothing here to match the shops in Upper Dysoe. When we came to the end of the hamlet, we found a farm track that led into the estate where we'd just left the woman. Simon turned in and we drove a little way into the grounds, stopping short of the outbuildings of what must be the home farm or a tenant's house. As we were reversing, a dog began to bark at the motorcar, and I looked back to see the little spaniel we'd nearly run down one day when it got free from its owner. She'd had quite a fright. I remembered the look of horror on her face. Was that why she'd left the little dog at home after that?

There was a rainbow in the sky as we drove into Upper Dysoe. The storm had moved on eastward, and the sun was trying to break through in the west, now and again picking out the sparkle of raindrops on trees or turning puddles on the road into bright mirrors of light.

Simon continued into Biddington, and at the inn where I'd stayed, he also took a room.

We'd missed our lunch, and so we went down for an early dinner. I found Simon already there, talking to the man behind the bar. I waited for him to join me, and together we went into the small dining room.

"What did you learn?" I asked, when we'd given our order.

Simon smiled. "Mrs. Chatham is a war widow, as we know. She's brought her younger sister to live in the house with her. Her name is Phyllis Percy, and she sounds very much like the young woman in question. Most of the staff went off to war while the house was closed. Mrs. Chatham insisted on opening it anyway. There are three tenant houses on the property. One is occupied by an older couple whose son is at sea on a frigate. The other is quite small, a grace-and-favor cottage where the former nanny lives. She suffers from rheumatism, and her meals are brought to her from the main house. The third cottage is empty. It's some distance from the other two, on the far side of the road we explored. It's where the head groom, later chauffeur, lived. He was killed in France."

"The man at the bar was an endless source of information," I said, surprised.

"It seems he spent his boyhood in Lower Dysoe and still has an aunt who lives there."

"Lucky for us," I said, smiling. "Do you think it's true? What he told you?"

"He has no reason to lie. He also told me that Miss Percy often takes the little spaniel for a walk. It must be lonely and rather dull in that house. Mrs. Chatham never entertains and seldom goes out. She sits in her room, mourning her husband, taking most of her meals there."

"Then why bring her sister to the house?"

"To keep it running smoothly, I should think. If Mrs. Chatham intended to retreat into the past."

Still, Phyllis Percy would not be required to do the work herself. Only to supervise the household through the housekeeper, decide on what was to be prepared for meals, and keep an eye on the outside staff, whatever gardeners, grooms, and their helpers remained in wartime. A young woman would find she had time on her hands, but that wouldn't explain the daily walk to Upper Dysoe and back.

Our meal arrived, and we ate in silence for a time. I always found the silences comfortable when I was with Simon.

Then a thought occurred to me as I considered what must be the patterns of Phyllis Percy's life.

"She must be hiding something. She doesn't do her marketing in the village. She doesn't send the cook or housekeeper to do it for her. She doesn't order the pony cart or carriage to take her to Upper Dysoe. And when we brought her home she waited until we were leaving before opening the door and going inside. Almost as if she was afraid someone might be standing on the other side of it, waiting for her. Yet she'd allowed us to drive to the entrance, so she isn't watched. No one seems to mind if she disappears for several hours to go into Upper Dysoe."

"And no one opened the door, exclaiming over how wet she was, ready to take the baskets from her. That was a rather vicious storm and she'd been out in it."

The lightning had been fearsome. Surely someone would have worried about her? One of the maids or my mother would have met me on the drive, scolding me for risking a chill.

I said slowly, "She's rather like Sister Hammond, isn't she? The sort of person it would be easy to take advantage of."

"Has this been going on for some time? Or has she recently begun to walk to Upper Dysoe?" Simon asked.

"Maddie might know. I remember him watching her. And I'm sure she hasn't conceived a sudden passion for the Upper Dysoe greengrocer."

Simon laughed. "Not at all likely."

"If her sister keeps to her rooms, wrapped in grief, it would depend on where the loyalty of the staff lies as to how much Miss Percy could get away with."

As we finished our dinner, I said, "There's money in that house. I can't imagine that the sister, however blinded by grief, would allow Phyllis to take up with a mere sergeant, much less one under some sort of cloud. After all, he's not on leave, he isn't in a clinic, and he's not at the Front. The most likely interpretation must be that he's a deserter."

"Unless of course Miss Percy has concocted a tale that makes her the heroine of a romantic mésalliance."

"Romeo and Juliet, star-crossed and unhappy?" I smiled. But then I realized that there might be a kernel of truth in all this speculation. "Miss Percy would have to convince the servants as well as her sister."

"I think," Simon replied, "that we need to learn more about Mrs. Chatham. But not here. I've asked enough questions for one day. It will seem odd if I begin to pry into matters that go beyond general gossip."

"Who then?"

"That's the problem, isn't it? We really don't have an entrée anywhere that would allow us to ask personal questions. We aren't invited to dine or to attend an evening party. We're the outsiders. But I think there's a way to get to the bottom of one of our problems." He rose and escorted me to the stairs. "Wait here. I'll be back in a few minutes."

He strode off toward the nether regions of the inn, and if I hadn't known better, I'd have thought he was on his way to the kitchen.

Five minutes later he was back, bearing a rather greasy packet, which he took directly out to the motorcar.

"Are you up for an adventure?" he asked as I started to follow him.

Mystified, I said, "Of course."

"Let's go upstairs. I'll call for you a little after ten. Don't wear your cap or your apron. Too much white."

I led the way up to the first-floor passage, thinking hard.

"We're going to do a little late-night reconnaissance," I said.

"Bess." He raised his eyebrows in mock disbelief. "Would I lead you into trouble?"

I laughed. "Of course you would, if you didn't wish to leave me here alone in this inn."

Yet I'd spent several nights by myself in this inn while he was in Stratford.

It was nearly fifteen minutes past ten o'clock when Simon tapped very lightly at my door. I'd heard the case clock in the hall below strike the hour.

I wore my regulation coat over my uniform. It was rather chilly after the storm had passed, and so this didn't seem unusual. Simon wore a dark jumper over his shirt, and dark trousers.

We went quietly down the stairs and out to his motorcar. He turned the crank, and we rolled out into the road.

It was dark here in this hilly part of the country, and the stars hadn't appeared because of the light cloud cover left over from the storm. But as the wind picked up, it was quickly dissipating. Our headlamps slashed through the night, illuminating the road ahead of us with an almost blinding glare. Simon drove carefully, watchful for sheep and other denizens of the night.

Twisting and turning through the rounded hills, we passed through Upper Dysoe first. The houses were dark, no one on the streets. The only light I saw was in the low, thatched cottage belonging to Maddie, and I wondered if he was treating a patient. We reached the ruined barn, and I could have sworn that I'd caught a whiff of cigarette smoke. Surely it was just the wind stirring up the ashes from the fire?

The gates of Windward appeared on our left. The house too was dark, looming like a misshapen shadow tucked into its shallow bowl, its beauty hidden.

Middle Dysoe was shrouded in blackness, the huddled shapes of houses and shops silent and shuttered, dark, although a dog barked from a tanner's yard. And then we reached Lower Dysoe. Our headlamps skimmed the broken wall with its covering of vines. They fluttered as we passed, as if ruffled by an invisible hand.

We didn't stop in Lower Dysoe, and I knew then precisely what Simon was planning.

We hadn't spoken during the drive, concentrating on the road, still muddy from the storm, pools of water masking the deeper ruts and splashing up against our tires.

Now I said quietly, "I see why dark clothes were necessary, if we're walking back to the farm lane."

"Not we. I'm the only one going in. I can't leave this motorcar in plain sight. It would draw attention if anyone looked out and saw it. Nor do I want to leave it unattended."

He pulled to the verge just beyond the next bend. Behind us the village appeared to have vanished.

"I won't stay here," I whispered fiercely. "If you're going to walk into the grounds of that house, I want to be with you. I want to see for myself what's there."

"One person can travel more swiftly that two. And more quietly. What's more, one person has a better chance of escaping undetected."

It was true. And Simon seemed to have no trouble seeing in the dark. He could move like the wind, avoiding obstacles—and people—with ease. Not only that, he kept his head in tight places. The Colonel Sahib had frequently used him to reconnoiter in dangerous situations.

Trying to bridle my frustration, I said, "Yes, all right. Go on."

He flashed me a grin just as he cut the headlamps. "I know, Bess. I'm sorry."

And then he was gone, only to return seconds later to fetch the packet from the floor in the rear.

I knew now what that packet was—meat scraps from the kitchen for the spaniel or any other dog he encountered. But if the spaniel belonged to Phyllis Percy, it would sleep with her. If that was so, then no amount of raw meat could stop it from barking. I could only pray that her room didn't overlook the rear of the house.

I watched Simon out of sight, then settled back, grateful for my coat. But a few minutes later, my feet were beginning to feel the cold too.

Getting out, I walked a bit to warm them. Once as I paced, I went to the side of the hill to peer around it, but the road through Lower Dysoe was just as empty and quiet as when we passed through.

I got back behind the wheel, my mind trying to follow Simon. But I didn't know the way. We'd just driven a little distance into the farm track, well short of the cottages. I could only use my imagination.

Restless and chilled again, I got out of the motorcar a second time and walked a bit, standing close to the bend, listening to the night sounds. Even in my dark clothes, I stayed well out of sight of anyone on the road or looking out a window. The high autumn grass was a perfect cover.

Back to the motorcar again.

And then in the distance I heard a dog bark drowsily, as if its sleep had been disturbed.

The sound had come from the town, not the estate. I was fairly sure of it.

Was it Simon, on his way back? I hesitated to crank the motorcar, but if he needed to move out of here in a hurry, I should to be prepared.

I hurried to my vantage point, looking toward the village.

And this time someone was coming down the road. Limping a little. Keeping to the deeper shadows. He'd just reached the wisteria-covered wall.

Simon? Finding himself in a tight corner and having to circle round?

I watched for a moment longer. No, whoever it was, his stride wasn't as long as Simon's. Nor was he as tall. At first I thought he would turn down the lane, one of the cottagers coming home late. But he didn't.

A few yards closer. I could see now that he was in uniform.

I froze.

It couldn't be the Major.

A soldier on leave? Walking from the nearest railway station?

Or Sergeant Wilkins? If so, where had he been— and where was he going?

If he was simply passing through the village, he'd stumble on the motorcar. What's more, he'd recognize it. And me. I'd have to move it. Now.

I stood there a few seconds longer, all but holding my breath, hoping that whoever it was, he wouldn't turn down the farm lane. Simon would be boxed in.

He passed the handful of shops, taking his time, moving as if he were tired. And he was being careful. Very careful. A night bird called, and his head swung instantly in that direction. For a moment he stopped, listening.

The last shop before the track was a tobacconist cum men's wear. Half the size of one in Biddington.

I stayed where I was, debating what to do. There was no earthly way to warn Simon. Even if I dared to sound the motorcar's horn, he could blunder right into whoever this was.

The man halted just before he reached the tobacconist. Looking back the way he'd come, he scanned the street. Then he looked in my direction. Satisfied, he settled into the shadows of a doorway—was it the tea shop?—and waited.

I was certain he'd stared longer than necessary toward where I was concealed, peering through the high grass. Even with cat's eyes, he couldn't see me there. But if he had cat's hearing, could he hear my heart pounding?

Now what should I do about Simon? Was this man intending to stay where he was for the better part of the night? Was he intending to break into one of the shops? Waiting for someone? Or just taking shelter from the chill of the wind?

It felt like half an hour had passed before he moved again. Stepping out of the shadow of the doorway, he walked silently but swiftly toward the farm lane and almost at once was swallowed up in the deeper shadows of the trees.

Had he been making certain he wasn't being followed before going on to one of the tenant cottages and to his bed? But who could he have thought was following him? Surely not Simon!

Or had he decided to move around the far side of the hill where I was crouched, and slip up behind me? Was that what he was doing even now?

I felt a shudder down my spine, as if I could feel him coming toward me in the dark.

I refused to believe it.

All the same, I went quickly to the boot and took a spanner from the tool kit. I had no other weapon, but that would do.

Then I waited behind the motorcar, counting to one hundred. If he'd come around the hill, he'd see the motorcar before he saw me. And that would draw his attention. Two could play at cat and mouse.

But he didn't appear. I gave him another five minutes, and there was still no sign of him.

He could be a third of the way down the farm track now. Running straight into Simon. Simon, unsuspecting, unprepared for a threat from the rear.

Simon hadn't survived countless campaigns without learning how to protect himself from the expected—or the unexpected. I knew I shouldn't worry.

But as time went on, I did worry. I couldn't see the hands on my little watch, pinned to my uniform inside my coat. But I had a fair idea that it must be well after midnight. Overhead the clouds had moved on, the wind was dropping, and the ambient light of the stars would soon make it brighter than it was now. And Simon had been gone for a very long time.

Still carrying the spanner, I walked quietly around the shoulder of my hill toward the village, where the track turned off the main road. Trees had been planted to form a park in this relatively treeless country, concealing the farm buildings from the house, and vice versa. I edged my way from trunk to trunk.

The night was still as silent as it had been from the moment Simon left the motorcar. No dogs barking, save for the one the soldier must have roused.

I strained to hear.

And suddenly I had the feeling that a quiet game of hide-and-seek was going on in these woods. I'd lived on unsafe frontiers, I'd served nearly four years close by the trenches in France. My position had almost been overrun by the Germans. That sense of imminent danger, of something about to happen, was so strong I took a few more steps into the trees. And then a few strides.

For all I knew, whoever had walked down that track had a revolver with him. And Simon was not armed.

At that moment I heard someone call, "Who's there? Come out where I can see you." The voice carried but not clearly enough for me to know whose it was.

A light—a torch—flashed through the trees. It couldn't reach me, but I instinctively stepped into the shelter of the nearest trunk.

"Come out and identify yourself. I've a shotgun here. I'll use it if I must."

Had someone in a cottage been roused by the same sense of danger and come to investigate?

Someone was shuffling about in the thick layer of fallen leaves underfoot.

I was too close to the track; if whoever held that torch came down this way, I could be spotted. But where had the soldier gone? And where was Simon?

The thought had hardly passed through my mind when a hand went across my face, covering my mouth, and I was being lifted bodily sideways, moving laterally toward a towering tree with a divided trunk, wide enough to hide both of us. I'd begun to struggle almost at once, kicking out with my heels and was just about to bite the palm across my lips when Simon whispered, "Bess!"

At once I ceased my efforts to free myself and he dropped his hand but not his arm around my waist.

I'd forgot the spanner. I lifted it and pressed it into his free hand.

The torch light swept the woods two or three times, then suddenly stopped. "Patches? What the devil are you doing out here? Come on, back to bed, you naughty cat. It's the middle of the bloody *night*."

The light moved away, was cut off, and after a moment I heard a door shut.

I stirred, but Simon held me close, not setting me free.

We stayed where we were for what seemed like a quarter of an hour. I could feel his breathing, slow and strong. And then finally Simon released me.

Gripping my hand, he led me through the wood, taking his time, avoiding the open track, choosing his path, always keeping trees between us and the cottages. When the tree line thinned at the edge of the estate, he stopped again, waiting, listening. Satisfied that we were alone, he pressed my fingers to warn me that we were close to the wall, then helped me over it. Again we stopped and listened. At length we walked on to the motorcar, and while Simon turned the crank, I took my seat.

We drove off, away from Lower Dysoe without turning on the massive headlamps, neither of us speaking.

We'd gone two miles, perhaps even three, when Simon stopped.

"What were you planning to do, Sister Crawford?" he asked, retrieving the spanner from under his feet and tossing it onto the rear seat. "Break his skull with this? And then bandage it tidily?"

"If need be," I said calmly. "You were in trouble and unarmed. What happened?"

"There was no warning of course—but let me start at the beginning. I moved off the track before I came to the first of the cottages. Someone had built a fire on the hearth, and I could smell the woodsmoke. The second cottage was dark as well, but when I stood outside one of the windows, I could hear someone snoring. By a roundabout way I made it as far as the third cottage without any problem. It took longer than I anticipated, because I had to be careful of the kitchen gardens. I didn't want to leave footprints there to be discovered later. When I reached the cottage at last, it was dark, quiet. Nothing to indicate whether it was occupied or not. I did put my hand on the chimney, but it was cold. I took a risk, trying the door. It opened, and I listened, but there was a mustiness about the air, as if the cottage had been closed up for some time. I didn't step in, I didn't know what I'd find. I shut the door and moved well clear of the cottage before starting back."

He shifted in his seat. "Just then I had a feeling that I was being watched. I couldn't say why."

There it was, that sixth sense.

"Go on."

"My first thought was, you'd grown tired of waiting. But the feeling went deeper than that. I heard something in the direction of the house and almost at the same time there was a brief flash of light. I could see the kitchen door from where I was standing. It was almost as if someone had opened it, realized the light was spilling into the yard, and shut it quickly. That's probably true, because it opened a second time, and the lamp had been turned down. I could just see someone step out of the door and start down the path. I expected him to go to the cottage, but once he was well away from the kitchen gardens, he turned and walked around the house, toward the front drive. I followed, and he continued down the drive to the gates. Only instead of opening them, he scrambled over the wall. My last glimpse of him was on the lane, walking toward the road."

"But I saw him—" I began.

"When?" Simon asked quickly.

"I don't know. You'd been gone quite some time, and I was trying to warm my feet by walking about a little. I found a place where I could watch the village street without being seen, and suddenly there he was, at the far end, by the old wall. I'd swear he hadn't come out of the lane." I described what the man had done. "My first worry was that he'd seen me. That's when I took out the spanner. But he'd disappeared down the farm track, and for all I knew, the two of you were going to meet in the dark."

"Why did he walk in a circle?" Simon asked, almost to himself. "That's odd."

"For the exercise? Or had he seen you by the cottages and decided to come around and cut you off?"

"I'm sure he didn't. He would have searched there and then, for one thing. I think he uses the kitchen door because it's quieter. I never expected him to come back the other way, I can tell you that. He wasn't strolling, he was moving with a purpose. Nevertheless, I had no warning he'd returned. I hadn't followed him out into the lane, you see. I decided it was best to return the way I'd come in. And there he was, in the clearing around the cottages. Barely visible, but I saw him before he saw me. He looked tired, something in the way he was standing. Just then the blasted cat found me, sniffing out the meat I was carrying. I'd expected the spaniel or another dog. She was weaving in and out around my feet, and he must have caught the movement. I managed to give her a few of the scraps just as he started looking for me. We began to shadow each other, and that went on for some time. The cat finished her food and went to him, expecting more. I thought that satisfied him because he went on to the last cottage and stepped inside."

"Then he must be living there."

"But he didn't shut the door, you see. I listened for that. Having closed it myself, I knew the sound. He just stood in the dark of the open door. Just then a light came on in the first cottage. He walked toward it, and I thought he might be asking for help finding me. But he'd picked up the cat and set her down by the cottage door. He must have startled her, because I think she scratched him. I heard a muffled oath. That brought whoever was awake in the first cottage outside with a torch."

"Yes, I saw it, probing the trees. He called to whoever was out there to step forward and identify himself."

"I expected the other man to do just that. I was busy emptying the rest of the scraps where I'd been standing, and then I set out in the general direction of the track, but staying among the trees well clear of it. Thank God the cat's owner found her and took her inside and shut the door. That kept the other man pinned where he was a little longer and gave us the chance to get clear. You know the rest."

"But, Simon, did he know for certain that you were there? Or was he just starting at shadows?"

"I'm not sure. I rather think he was only half convinced that he'd seen the cat, not an intruder. He was taking no chances."

"Why didn't he raise the alarm, when he had the chance?"

"While I'm very happy he didn't, it puzzled me as well."

"Did he think you were the police? The Army? Or a passerby looking to find something he could sell for a few pence?"

"God knows."

We sat there without speaking.

It had been a close call. I didn't think Sergeant Wilkins, wounded and still not fit, was a match for Simon physically. But there was still the revolver. The question was, at what point would he have used it? Would he have dared to shoot and claim he'd stopped a thief? But of course that would have brought in the police. He couldn't afford that.

My feet were really cold now, not just chilly. Simon must have realized that, for he took off the brake and began to turn the motorcar. "You can see now why I didn't want you with me." Then he smiled as he flicked on the headlamps. "Still, you had the spanner."

A spanner was no match for a revolver.

He must have been thinking the same thing, because his smile faded and he kept his gaze on the road.

Chapter Seventeen

I thought I would lie awake until first light, cold as I was, the lump on my forehead throbbing. But once I was in my bed and the coverlet drawn up to my chin, my eyes didn't stay open for very long.

My last thought, as I drifted off, was amusement at the night clerk's expression when Simon and I slipped into the inn and started for the stairs.

Simon nodded to him and said simply, "Owls."

The poor man was still gazing after us in bewilderment as we reached the top of the stairs and turned toward our rooms.

The next morning we walked up and down the High Street, where there was no danger of being overheard, and planned what to do next.

"It could be Miss Percy's lover, escaped from the Army," I said. "We can't prove it's Sergeant Wilkins.

We could try to waylay Phyllis Percy. She walks to Upper Dysoe nearly every day. We might be able to persuade her to tell us who this man is. If he walks in and out of the house that freely, she must know who he is. Unless," I added as the thought occurred to me, "he belongs to one of the servants. A son, brother."

"If that were true, she could send someone else to do the marketing."

And so we set out for Upper Dysoe, in search of Miss Percy.

We'd only reached the burned-out barn when Mrs. Neville all but stepped out in front of our motorcar and commanded us to stop.

"I'm surprised to find you still here, Sister Crawford," she said, coming around to my side of the motorcar. "Still, it's a bit of luck and I won't concern myself with why. Maddie has just refused to have a word with my stepdaughter. It's really most annoying. He's not *actually* a doctor, is he? A charlatan at best, however good he is. The problem is, she pays him. In pounds. And I suppose he's reluctant to lose a good living. One can eat only so many hens, I daresay, or so many eggs or cabbages. And one can't barter them for lamp oil or medical supplies."

Completely at a loss, I said, "Good morning, Mrs. Neville. Is the Major running a fever again?"

"No, no, nothing of that sort. Maddie brought him crutches, and he's trying them out. A foolish mistake, if you want my opinion. The poor man will break his neck. Now, if you'll allow me, I'll explain on our way to the house."

She reached for my door, and I had no choice but to step down and move to the rear seat while she took my place.

Simon said nothing. I knew he didn't care for her overbearing manner or the way she treated the Colonel Sahib's daughter like a servant. But I was curious enough not to mind. I didn't take my measure of myself from Mrs. Neville.

"Now then, young man," she said to Simon as she settled in, indicating that we could continue on our way.

I smothered a smile. Simon was too well mannered to tell her he would do nothing of the sort, but I caught what he was saying under his breath in Urdu.

She ignored him, turning a little to tell me over her shoulder, "You seem like a sensible young woman, and your uniform tells me that you've had more than your share of experience dealing with wounded men."

Not knowing where she was going with this, I simply nodded.

"Here's the problem, in my view," she began, settling back, now that she knew she had my full attention.

"My stepdaughter is a very wealthy young woman with a social position to maintain. Her father tried to see her happily settled, but she'd have nothing to do with it. And yes, I do know the war has taken a terrible toll of eligible men. In my opinion, now that she's finally decided to marry, she's made the worst possible choice. The Major has no title, no fortune, and no position. He was a *solicitor* before the war. No doubt a charming and eligible young man to many. But not a suitable partner for a Neville."

"I expect she loves him," I suggested.

"What has love to do with it?" she demanded. "A young woman marries as her father dictates."

Simon moved sharply and then was still.

"Not in every case," I said. Mrs. Neville clearly had strong opinions about a good many things.

"Where there is a large fortune and immense property involved, it's an arrangement between two families, not a match made at a dance party."

"Was your own marriage arranged?" I asked.

"Of course it was. My father was a baronet and my dowry was substantial."

"What is it you wish me to do?"

"Explain to my stepdaughter, if you please, that a wounded man with a damaged mind isn't going to heal properly, no matter how much she insists it's possible.

I have the strongest feeling that he will never be any better than he is now, confused, intransigent, angry at the world."

It was a fair assessment of the Major, as far as I could judge. For now. What the future held was another matter.

And then Mrs. Neville added, "You know why she's done this, don't you? To spite *me*. Her father left her in my care, and she's done everything in her power to thwart me."

Daughters and stepmothers didn't always get along.

"I'm not qualified to judge how well he'll heal. I doubt anyone is. So many things matter. With the right encouragement, who knows what he could achieve?"

She didn't want to hear this.

"Nonsense. Her father would be appalled. Whether she likes it or not, she must do what's best for her and for the family. Heiresses know this from birth."

But Barbara Neville never expected to be the heir to Windward or her father's fortune. If her brother hadn't been killed, who could say what her future might have been.

It wasn't just the head wound. To put it simply, the Major wasn't suitable.

This woman who believed that modern progress was anathema and land had only one use, to support an agricultural population returning to the ways of their forebears, had no liberal views on marriage. I wondered if she also believed in drowning witches or burning heretics at the stake.

"I haven't actually examined the Major," I said, taking a different tack. "How can I possibly judge his case when I've seen him only once or twice?"

She turned to look at me again. "Don't be difficult, my dear. I need your help. You're in the Nursing Service, it's your duty to cope with the wounded."

After weeks of training and years of experience as a battlefield nurse, I had learned many things, come to understand more, and acknowledged my limitations. That was a far cry from offering medical opinions about a man's future.

We had reached the gates. They stood open, and Simon drove straight through. As we swept around the circle and came to a halt by the broad curve of the steps, I tried to stop this matter a last time.

"Mrs. Neville, I'm aware of how trying this must be for you. But I really must insist—"

She waited until Simon had helped her alight from the motorcar, then turned to me as I also got down. "I have friends in London, Sister Crawford, some of whom are connected with Queen Alexandra's Imperial Military Nursing Service. What's more, my cousin is a high-ranking officer in the British Army. Shall I write to them and tell them that you were less than helpful in my time of need?"

Simon stepped forward, brows drawn in anger, but I put my hand on his arm to stop him.

"That's blackmail," I replied quietly, "not a request for assistance in a serious matter in which I am not trained to offer an opinion."

Before she could respond, the door behind her opened and Barbara Neville stopped short on her own threshold. Looking first at Simon, then at her step-mother, she turned to me.

"I was told you'd left Upper Dysoe."

Mrs. Neville said, not allowing me to answer, "Barbara. I've brought Sister Crawford here to talk some sense into you."

"Indeed?" Her fair eyebrows went up, and I expect Queen Mary couldn't have looked more imperious than the woman before me. "And why should you think Sister Crawford is qualified to advise me?"

Mrs. Neville opened her mouth to answer, but Barbara Neville turned to look over her shoulder, inside the house.

"This is not the place to discuss my affairs. Come inside."

We followed her into the dim, cool hall and down a passage to our left. Miss Neville opened a door halfway along and stood aside to let us enter. It was a large, beautifully decorated library. Shelves of books ranged round the central walls, there was a large fireplace with Dutch tiles in the surrounds, and long windows gave out onto a view of gardens. The ceiling was magnificent, intertwined garlands and musical instruments cascading into corners, a Tudor rose taking pride of place in the center.

There was a table in the center of the room, a globe next to it, and several chairs were arranged in front of the cold hearth. We sat down, save for Simon, who stood by the mantel, as if showing he was not a part of what was happening, and yet he was still the commanding presence in the room.

Barbara Neville studied him for a moment, and he held her gaze. Turning away, she said to me, "Explain yourself."

"Mrs. Neville insists that I inform you of the problems involving marriage with a man whose wounds are—" I cast about for the right words. "Whose wounds are of such a nature that it might be years before he's well enough to make a decision as important as marriage. She's insisted in such a way that I had no—"

The door swung open and the Major came in, clumsily using crutches. His face was pale, his blue eyes clear but dark with pain. He swayed as he attempted to swing the door closed, and Simon stepped forward as we all watched in dismay.

He managed to keep his balance and moved toward the only vacant chair. I thought to myself that Maddie must have given him crutches against his better judgment.

"If you wish to discuss me, Barbara, I should at least be present." He folded his crutches together and passed them to Simon.

"Thank you, Sergeant-Major," he said, then turned to me. "You were saying?"

"I was saying that Mrs. Neville fails to understand that I've never examined you properly, and I haven't seen your hospital records. I'm in no position to offer a clear picture of your prospects."

Mrs. Neville opened her mouth to speak, then thought better of it.

"Nor are you," Major Findley agreed. "The leg is much better, by the way. As you can see."

"I would have insisted on a longer period of bed rest."

"So has Maddie. But I'll go mad sitting in that room with nothing to do but think."

Barbara was on the point of taking charge of the conversation again, but he forestalled her. "If this is about me, I should set the rules. You will leave the room, Barbara, Mrs. Neville. And give Sister Crawford an opportunity to decide whether her patient is sane or half mad."

An argument broke out at once. I glanced at Simon and he shook his head very slightly. *Let it play out*, he seemed to be saying.

It was fierce, vituperative. All the underlying dislike between stepmother and stepdaughter came out into the open, while Major Findley insisted that if he was to be judged, he must have it his way.

And then as suddenly as it had begun, it was over. Mrs. Neville rose and stalked from the room like an insulted tigress. Barbara turned to the Major and said, "I will not allow it."

"You will, or I shall declare here, before these witnesses, that I have no intention of marrying you now or ever, and I will instruct Sister Crawford to use her authority to have me returned at once to Dorset."

Barbara Neville looked as if she'd just been slapped. Her face flamed and then went pale almost at once. She cast an odd look at the man she must have thought she knew well, and without speaking got up and walked steadily out of the room, shutting the door behind her.

Silence fell. I really had no idea what to say to the Major. He eased his bad leg, stretching it out before him, grimacing at the pain.

"You ought to be in your bed," I told him. This close, looking at him in the sunlight pouring through the long windows, listening to his voice, no longer tight with pain, I wondered how I could ever have suspected he might be Sergeant Wilkins. And yet—there was something about the two men that made me wonder, even now.

I thought it must be a strong sense of purpose. Something driving them to the exclusion of everything else.

The Major took a deep breath. "When I first came here," he said, keeping his voice low in case there were ears pressed to the library door, "I hated it. I hated her."

"Why?" It was Simon who spoke.

"Because I couldn't keep two thoughts swimming together. My head felt as if it would burst, hurt like hel—the very devil, and there were parts of my past that were completely blank. Even after I was told my name, it meant very little to me. I didn't know if I was married, promised to someone, or a widower. I didn't know if I could practice law again, or must find a way to support myself. I remembered France, the war, some of the men under me, but not my own father and mother. There were blackouts, confusion, tremendous bouts of anger. At one point a doctor informed me I'd very likely wind up in an institution. Another told me that if I put my mind to it in a quiet setting, I might, with time, heal. I was depressed enough to look for ways to kill myself, but they were very careful, at the hospital. Sister Hammond told me one day that I was selfish and uncaring, that because I hadn't come back from France whole, I wanted to find the courage to die rather than the courage to live. And she told me too that it took far more courage to live. I think I needed to hear those things. I looked around and saw men far worse off than I. It was shocking to realize I'd been such a fool."

He glanced up at Simon, as if seeking agreement, then turned back to me.

"It was at this stage that Barbara appeared at the hospital. I don't know how she'd found me, and I couldn't have told you why she would have wanted to. She would sit and talk to me. Day after day. And gradually I began to remember her. I can't tell you how miraculous it was to piece a little of the past together. We'd met a few times at various parties before the war. I liked her, I enjoyed her company. We were paired several times for doubles at tennis. She's a strong player and we usually won. She was a good dancer and so was I. It never went beyond that. I was no fool, she wasn't likely to marry a solicitor from a small town. When the war came, of course, I was glad to be fancy free. It was safer. Still, I thought about her more than once while I was in France."

He stared at the cold hearth for a time, struggling to collect his thoughts. "She came more frequently. I was afraid she pitied me and sought my company as an act of charity. A good deed for the wounded hero. It began to rankle. Then she broached the subject of my coming here to finish healing. The doctors—overawed by her, in my view—tried to persuade me to accept. It was clear I wouldn't be going back to France before the fighting was over. They were probably just as happy to give my bed to someone else. I refused. They asked if I had anywhere else to go, and I told them I did not. Finally they suggested a trial period of a month or two, and to stop them from badgering me, I agreed."

He shifted his leg again, then glanced toward the closed door. "And they were right, the peace and quiet helped. I could sleep at night, I began to read a little, and some of the dizziness was fading. There were still gaps in my memory, still some confusion, but on the whole I could see the doctors had been right. I hadn't been here three weeks when I overheard a conversation between two of the maids. They were saying that I was Barbara's fiancé, here to recover before the wedding, and they were debating whether they would take on a man in my condition. I grant you, I was taking medicines for my head and I wasn't always the brightest penny in the purse, but it had never occurred to me that I was anything more than a good deed to Barbara. When I broached the subject, she told me she hoped that more might come of our friendship, given time. But I was looking straight at her when she said this, and there was nothing in her face or in her eyes that gave me to believe she'd fallen in love with me. Soon after that Mrs. Neville made it clear that I was to be the reason Barbara wasn't going to marry anyone else. The damaged suitor she couldn't honorably turn her back on."

Trying to conceal my shock, I said, "And so you wrote those letters to Sister Hammond. Did you smuggle them out?"

"She was the only Sister whose name I could recall. There's a boy who works in the gardens. He was brought in sometimes to help lift me from the bed to a chair or back again. I paid him to post the letters for me. I couldn't give this address. I used Maddie's instead. But she never answered. That's when I tried to escape."

"But she did," I told him. "Only not in the way you'd expected. You hadn't signed them, you see. And so we thought you were someone else in need of rescue."

There was alarm in his face now. "Don't tell me Barbara's got another officer here—in the event I won't go through with whatever it is she wants?"

"Sadly, this is a man who is also wanted by the police."

I explained that Sister Hammond had transferred to Shropshire, where a private soldier had gone missing. "You may have seen him," I said. "One of the days when you managed to escape. He was also trying to get away. Walking across the hills. I'd asked before. Do you remember?"

Major Findley frowned. "Sometimes I can't remember things. When you cleaned my leg, I thought I was back in the hospital. I couldn't understand why Maddie was there as well. When my head was clearer, I realized that I'd been wrong. That I'd seen you here the day the goat was brought in. I gave one of the maids a note for you."

"Why did you shoot Mr. Warren?" I asked. "You'd been roaming the grounds, firing your revolver. You'd tied the goat out by the old barn. Why turn to murder?"

"I never shot anyone!" he said, taken aback. "Yes, I'd fired at trees, yes, I took the goat out. And tried to escape. Anything I could think of to get out of here. I wanted Barbara to believe I was hopelessly mad and send me back to Dorset. But I never shot anyone, I don't even know who this man Warren is."

"The miller," Simon put in. "He was on the road just beyond the gates. Someone fired at him from the old barn."

"My God, I wanted to leave, not to find myself in the hands of the hangman. I only used the revolver well out of the way of hitting anyone. I swear to you."

"Perhaps you thought you were back in France," I suggested.

"I was never shell-shocked." He leaned forward and parted his thick hair. "Do you see? It was a head wound."

I could see the line of the scar, still raised and red. I believed him. The shock in his face was real. And he was right, killing Mr. Warren would see him in prison.

I said before I could stop myself, "Do you care for her? At all? I must know if I'm to do anything to help you."

His face changed. "I could. Given the chance. But not like this. Not as a prisoner here. I hardly see her. I think she knows how I feel. And still she won't let me go."

"Is she in love with you?"

"How could she be? I'm a convenience, like a new carpet sweeper or motorcar." He saw my expression. "If she marries a man who isn't right in his head, she won't lose this house, her fortune, anything. She'll control him, and through him, her money."

"On the other hand, if you weren't right in your head—and it got worse—you could take the opportunity for a little revenge, and shut *her* up here. Who would stop you?"

"Dear God, that never occurred to me." He rubbed his forehead, taking in the possibility I'd outlined. "I just wanted to leave here, I'm not interested in revenge."

"Do you have any family, Major? Anyone we could call to come and take you with them?"

"My parents are dead. My only brother died when he was twelve."

There was a knock at the door and before any of us could speak, it opened and Barbara Neville came in.

"You've had enough time to evaluate his condition." Instead of taking the chair she'd occupied before, she walked past Simon and stood on the far side of the hearth.

"I've made my decision," I said, carefully choosing my words. "I think the Major should return to Dorset for further treatment. Or if there are no beds for him there, they will find another suitable place."

I was watching her face as I spoke. Her jaw had tightened, and she reminded me of someone expecting a blow.

"That's ridiculous."

"Have you considered," I asked, "that the brain is unmapped territory. With time, Major Findley could become violent, even vicious. You might find it nearly impossible to manage him."

There was alarm in her gaze now. "That's ridiculous!" she snapped.

"Is it?" Simon asked. "You have no experience of war wounds."

Before she could turn on him, I rose.

"I think this is something the two of you would prefer to discuss in private."

The Major and Miss Neville interrupted me in a rush, their voices clashing.

The Major said, "You don't intend to leave me here—for the love of God—"

While Miss Neville was saying, "You have no idea what you're doing. It's my house, I'll decide—"

I held up my hands for peace. They stopped at once.

I said, "You can't hold him prisoner, Miss Neville. If you want to keep him here, you must see that he's properly examined. And then you will have to consult his wishes."

The uproar began all over again. The door opened and Mrs. Neville stepped in, adding her own voice to the argument.

Barbara Neville to my astonishment was now in tears, although I couldn't tell whether they were fury or grief.

There was nothing more I could do. I glanced at Simon, and the two of us moved toward the door. No one stopped us. I'd delivered my verdict, and now I was no longer important to any of them.

We walked down the passage and through the high-ceilinged hall, had nearly gained the motorcar when Barbara Neville came rushing after us.

Her face was streaked with tears.

"You think you know. You think you understand. But you're wrong, you've meddled, and now it's hopeless." With that she turned on her heel and went inside, slamming the door hard behind her.

It rattled the tall windows above us.

Amazed, I stood there, staring after her.

"I think she loves him. She must. After all."

"She has a clever way of showing it," Simon replied as he bent to turn the crank. "There's something you haven't thought of. If anything happens to her, who will inherit that house and the Neville fortune? She may not want to marry, but she must have a child. A legitimate heir. On that previous visit, when she asked you how healthy Findley was likely to be, after injuring that leg so badly, she was probably trying to discover whether he could give her a child."

It was something to consider. Barbara Neville, like so many women of her class, had less freedom than I did.

He got in beside me, and we drove toward the gates.

"They ought to be closed," I said, putting my hand on the handle, preparing to open my door.

"If they want the gates closed, they can come out and shut them themselves," he said, not pausing for me to get down.

We had nearly reached the tumble-down ruins of the barn. I said, "Simon. What about Phyllis Percy?"

We had forgot her.

"Have we missed her, do you think?"

"I can't believe we have."

"Then we should drive as far as Lower Dysoe. In the event she got a late start on her marketing."

We were halfway to Lower Dysoe when I spotted Miss Percy coming toward us, a market basket in both hands. Why was she so willing to walk such a distance each day?

She was smiling shyly as we approached, not encouraging us to stop and chat, but acknowledging the fact that we'd rescued her during the storm.

Simon slowed. "Can we give you a lift?" he asked.

"Thank you, no. I'm on my way to Middle Dysoe. It's just ahead."

I didn't think she was. The shops there were little better than the village at her back.

I opened my door, and she looked toward me, alarm in her face. "I need to stretch my limbs," I said. "Do you mind if I walk a little way with you? The Sergeant-Major has business in Lower Dysoe. He'll collect me when he's finished there."

She couldn't say no. I was already getting down, and the roadside was free to anyone who cared to walk along it.

I waved cheerily to Simon, who let in the clutch and drove away.

"My name is Crawford. Bess Crawford," I said. "I don't recall whether or not we introduced ourselves the first time." When she made no effort to tell me her name, I went on as if that didn't matter. "Could I carry one of those for you?" I gestured toward the baskets.

"No—thank you—that's not necessary," she said politely but surprisingly firmly.

"Of course. They must be empty now."

We went a little way in silence. "Why do you walk such a distance to Upper Dysoe? I've seen you there, I think. Surely Mrs. Chatham has a pony cart or even a carriage."

"I like—I enjoy walking."

"You must. It's miles each way. It must feel longer, with the market baskets full."

"What do you want?" she said then, afraid to look at me. "Why are you asking so many questions?"

"I've been searching for someone," I said gently. "I'm sure he doesn't want to be found. I'm sure he's happy where he is. But he belongs in hospital." I wasn't sure how much she knew about Sergeant Wilkins, how much or how little of the truth he'd told her.

"I'm afraid my sister and I lead very quiet lives. We seldom go out, we seldom entertain guests. She's in deep mourning. You must have seen the crepe on our door."

"Yes, of course, I'm so sorry," I said. "But you haven't answered my question."

Color rose in her cheeks. I hated pressing her, and I felt a surge of guilt. But did she know that the man she was concealing might be a murderer?

She couldn't have heard about the killing in Ironbridge. Not this far south, and I wasn't sure if it had been in any of the London papers.

"The only ill person I know of is Miss Neville's fiancé, Major Findley. Perhaps you've received faulty information."

"Perhaps you're right. But rumor has it that he's presently living in the empty cottage on your sister's property."

She whirled to face me, one of her market baskets colliding with my leg as she did. But she didn't apologize. Instead I read fear in her eyes, and a mounting anger.

"Someone has lied to you," she told me.

"Miss Percy, is it your sister who is keeping this wounded soldier hidden? Or is it you?"

She walked away from me, then, moving briskly, her head down, and I was nearly sure she was crying.

I didn't follow her. I had done all I could. I had no authority to question her, or to force her to answer truthfully.

I could contact Scotland Yard and tell them what we suspected. But what if it wasn't Sergeant Wilkins? Only a deserter who had found sanctuary and a kind heart? For that matter it could be this young woman's sweetheart, hoping that no one would search for him here.

I waited where I was for Simon to come back for me. When at last the motorcar appeared in the distance, I glanced up the road. Phyllis Percy was still walking briskly, her face turned away from the road, her shoulders hunched, as if she had heard the motorcar coming and dreaded the possibility that we would stop her again and ask questions she didn't want to answer.

Simon knew at once that I'd had no luck. "You can't blame yourself," he said quietly. "Wilkins is a dangerous man. He's killed once, and Warren's wounding could also be his work. Phyllis Percy isn't safe. She knows too much. If she becomes a problem rather than a protector, he will do whatever he has to do."

He turned the motorcar, driving in the opposite direction, back toward Little Dysoe.

"Where are we going?"

"Give her time to reach Middle Dysoe. She'll feel safer there."

I repeated our conversation for Simon's benefit, and he listened carefully.

"She's hiding something," he agreed when I'd finished. "She may have fallen in love with him. She's young. Alone. He may appear a romantic figure to her, in trouble and in need of her help."

I sighed. "She and Barbara Neville aren't so very different, are they?"

"That's true, in a way."

We'd traveled well beyond Little Dysoe, now. These strange rounded hills with the road snaking around them were beginning to flatten.

Simon was already slowing, preparing to go back the way we'd come.

He was looking over his shoulder to be sure the road was clear while I was looking at the hillsides, wishing Major Findley had told us what he'd seen while he was trying to get away from Windward.

And there, just cresting the last hill but one, pausing to stare toward us, was a man in uniform. I could see only his head and shoulders. He'd stopped before he'd come into full view.

"Simon—" I exclaimed, reaching out to catch his arm. *"Look."*

The motorcar was broadside in the road. In the distance I could hear a horse-drawn cart coming toward us at a fast clip. Simon leaned across me to look in the direction I'd indicated. And as he did, the figure didn't turn but simply backed away, his shoulders and then his head disappearing from our sight.

"Damn," Simon muttered under his breath, and then smartly maneuvered the motorcar so that it had cleared the road just as the cart was upon us.

It was a farm cart bringing vegetables to market, dark green cabbages, golden yellow gourds, deep red beets, and a scattering of carrots and parsnips. I had just time enough to note what it was carrying before we were safely out of the horses' path. As it was, they snorted and pulled to the far side of the road. The farmer, sitting high above his crops, glared at us and told us to watch what we were doing.

By the time the cart had moved beyond us, the figure up on the hillside was nowhere to be seen.

"Can we catch him up?" I asked.

"I doubt it. He knows the countryside by now. And we don't."

All the same we moved out behind the slower farm cart, all the while scouring the hills now on Simon's side of the road. To no avail.

I asked, "He has a safe enough place to stay. A sanctuary. Why is he out walking the hills? If he wants to strengthen that leg, he should do it at night, when he's less likely to be seen." I put out a hand. "Yes, that's what he must have been doing last night. He's seen us, now, Simon. He's put a face to us, this motorcar. Whether he recognized me at this distance I don't know."

"It's been an odd business from the start. Let's hope it isn't a blind end, like Cartwright and Findley."

We had reached Lower Dysoe, and the farm cart pulled over in front of one of the shops. Simon passed him and then said, "Do you fancy stopping and speaking to Mrs. Chatham? We know her sister is out of the house."

"On what pretext?" I asked.

"The truth. Or part of it. That you're a Nursing Sister looking for a straying patient. Tell her that Major Findley had spotted the man."

"And we're hoping not to involve the police, because he's been in trouble before."

He turned down the lane and drove on to the gates of Chatham Hall.

They were open, and we passed through without any difficulty. I could smell the wafting woodsmoke from where the gardeners must be burning the debris of summer, trimmings, fallen branches, and leaves. It carried the scent of autumn.

Simon stopped by the door, then asked, "Ready?"

"Yes," I said, nodding. "It has to be done, doesn't it?"

Without waiting for his answer, I walked up the broad steps and lifted the knocker. With its knotted bouquet of crepe, it rang dully. After a while, an older woman came to the door and looked beyond me toward Simon's motorcar. I wondered if she had seen it when we'd brought Miss Percy home after the rain. Then her attention came back to me, and she said, "How may I help you, Sister?"

"I'm so sorry to disturb you," I said, indicating the crepe around the knocker. "But it's very important that I speak to Mrs. Chatham."

"I'm afraid she doesn't see visitors. And Miss Percy isn't in."

I scoured my brain for a way around this problem, and finally said, "I've come from Lovering Hall just outside Shrewsbury. Perhaps you know of it?"

She shook her head. "I'm sorry, Sister, I've never been as far as Shrewsbury. Only to Ludlow. If you're seeking a contribution to a fund for wounded men, I can't help you. Mrs. Chatham attends to all matters of charity."

"No, this isn't a charity call," I told her. It hadn't occurred to me that she might think I was soliciting on behalf of wounded soldiers and their care. "I'm looking for one of our patients. He wandered off, you see. I know it's a long way from Shrewsbury, but I wondered if you had seen him, if perhaps he'd come begging."

"Beggars generally go to the kitchen quarters, Miss," she responded primly, as if it were not within the scope of her duties to attend to the needs of a beggar.

"Yes, I know. The question is, has any of the household seen this soldier? He could be desperate for food," I added. And remembering something from the past, I added, "Perhaps a chicken or two missing? Or some vegetables from the kitchen garden?"

"We're too far from the main road, Sister, and not easily found. I'd ask at the cottages closer to the village, if I was you. I'm sorry I can't help you."

It occurred to me that she was taking me quite literally—a beggar rather than a soldier in trouble. I said before she could shut the door, "I saw such a man on the skyline today, crossing one of the hills just beyond Lower Dysoe. I was hoping it might be the man we've been seeking." In for a penny, in for a pound. "I met Miss Percy earlier. She felt I must be mistaken, that the soldier we saw might well be the man presently staying with you—"

Her mouth tightened, and her eyes were hard as they looked me up and down. "I'm sure Miss Percy never suggested any such thing. I don't know who you are, Miss, but I'll ask you to leave now." She swung the door shut almost in my face, and I heard the bolt slot home.

I turned and went down the steps to the motorcar.

"So much for our agreed approach."

Simon had heard most of the conversation, I didn't need to repeat it. As he let in the clutch and drove the rest of the way around the circle to where the drive began, he said, "Something is wrong in that house."

"Whatever it is," I said, looking back at Chatham Hall as we turned into the lane, "they aren't likely to confide in us."

"Let Inspector Stephens sort it out."

"Perhaps we're going at this backward. There could be a perfectly good explanation here. That man might be Mrs. Chatham's husband. She might not be a widow after all, but if he's been severely wounded, with no expectation of recovering, he might have chosen to let the world believe he's dead."

"It's possible." Simon glanced at me. "Is it likely?"

"We'll leave for London tomorrow," I said. "I wonder if Major Findley will decide to go with us."

"It's best to leave well enough alone there, Bess."

We fell silent. I was bound to report the conditions under which a patient was living, whether in a private home or a clinic. And while the Major had not been mistreated—in fact I was sure he'd been looked after properly in many respects—a doctor would have something to say about his endangering life and limb trying to escape. As for Maddie, Miss Neville had had no qualms about consulting him, because he could be trusted to hold his tongue. He knew who buttered his bread.

Did he owe that same allegiance to Mrs. Chatham?

I said, "I should like to speak to Maddie again."

"He won't tell you what you want to know."

"He might, given the new direction of our interest."

"Worth a try."

But he wasn't in when we went to his cottage. A passerby, seeing us there, called, "He's been summoned to a farm. Nora Fletcher's baby is on its way."

Babies took their time.

Thanking him, we returned to the motorcar.

"You must be hungry. Shall I bespeak sandwiches and a bottle of wine from The Shepherd's Crook? We could picnic."

I smiled. "Yes, I'd like that." I knew better than to suggest we simply have our meal in the common room. Simon wouldn't have allowed it.

"I'll leave the motorcar here and walk down to the pub."

Simon was gone for more than half an hour. I got out and walked about a bit, hoping that Maddie would come back sooner rather than later. But there was no sign of him.

Pacing the scruffy yard in front of the cottage, I turned to walk back the other way. And as I did, I saw Miss Percy coming out of the greengrocer's.

Her market baskets were full. I wondered again why the kitchen garden at the house wasn't sufficient to meet the needs of the occupants. From what I'd seen, there was only a small staff, which meant that rooms must be shut off, perhaps an entire wing, and cleaned infrequently. Even without entertaining or receiving guests, the work of caring for a house that size was never ending. The dusting and polishing, the sweeping, cleaning the grates and the hearths, seeing to the laundry and ironing, changing beds—the list was long, and the kitchen staff would have to see that everyone was fed. There would be no idle hands. Who then would have the time to plant and care for a garden, when there was money to buy what was needed? Indoor servants could hardly be asked to take on that duty as well.

What's more, who would have time to care for a wounded soldier?

Miss Percy started my way, then stopped short when she recognized me. I realized that she must have a pressing need to speak to Maddie, because she took a deep breath and resolutely came straight toward his cottage.

I said as soon as she was in earshot, "I'm sorry. Maddie is out. I've been waiting for him myself."

"Oh." She looked toward the cottage. "My sister's migraine—she doesn't have any more of her powders." I could guess what she was thinking, that it would mean either waiting and being caught out in the dusk, or walking all the way back in the dark, in the hope of finding him in later.

I wondered if the powders were for Mrs. Chatham, or the man Simon had seen stepping out the kitchen door late at night.

"Don't you have horses?" I asked.

"The Army took them all. It was early in the war, the house was closed up then. There was no need to keep one back."

Which explained why Simon hadn't mentioned seeing or hearing them in the outbuildings.

"Would you like me to ask Maddie for the powders? He must know what you need. We could drive them over to Lower Dysoe then. If it would help."

She shook her head vehemently. "No, I couldn't possibly put you out on my account. I'm sure it can wait one more day." She had set her baskets down and now leaned over to lift them again.

"Shall I tell Maddie, if I see him, that you will come tomorrow?"

"Yes—no. I can't be sure when I'll be coming in."

Before she could turn and walk away, I said, "I am so sorry I badgered you with questions. It—it's because I've been anxious about finding our missing patient. He can't manage on his own, and it's possible he may've been hurt trying to steal a horse. I don't want to bring the Army into this problem if I can help it."

"We're a household of women," she said wearily, as if no longer able to hide her feelings. "If we'd seen this man, we'd have reported him, wouldn't we? To Maddie, to the police in Biddington, to the vicar there."

"And if he couldn't be handed over to the police?" I asked gently. "If that would mean jail or worse, what then?"

She lifted her chin. "Fortunately we haven't been faced with such a decision."

And she walked away, without her powders.

Chapter Eighteen

Not ten minutes later I saw Simon returning with a wicker basket in one hand.

As we drove out of Upper Dysoe, I told him about my brief conversation with Phyllis Percy.

"Yes, I saw her walking past the pub. I asked Tulley about her. He seemed to know less than the barkeep in Biddington. All he could tell me was that the house had been closed up when Chatham went to France. His wife chose to stay in London where she had a better chance of seeing him during his leaves. By the time she came back to Warwickshire, there was only a skeleton staff. Able-bodied men in France, younger women doing some sort of war work. One former maid is driving an omnibus in London. She was a friend of Violet's."

We'd driven out of Upper Dysoe, looking for a picnic site. Simon slowed a little when we came abreast of the barn. Since the fire it offered very little in the way of charm.

"We've never been any distance down the lane past the barn," he said. "It's where the sheep go when they cross the road. Shall we explore?"

"Why not?" We'd tried once before, but the grass had been too high and there had been no sign of any house. But where the sheep grazed, there must be a quiet meadow.

We turned off the road, bumped and bounced past the barn and then forded our way through the high grass that brushed against the sides of the motorcar. It was much easier than attempting to walk through it. No one had driven down this track in years, and even the ruts had begun to fill in a little, helped by the passage of many hooves. We crossed a stream on a low bridge that rattled alarmingly, and then rounded the hill. Spread out before us was a small meadow, what appeared to be a lambing pen, though it had suffered from disuse, and on the next rise, a shepherd's hut. Isolated and quite pretty, with a small flock of sheep that lifted their heads to stare at us. Where the lane broadened, we came to a halt.

"The sheep are downwind," Simon told me with a grin. He took the rug out of the boot, and spread it over the dry stalks of daisies and other wildflowers.

I joined him on my side of the basket, and he added, "It's not a Fortnum's hamper."

I laughed as I lifted the cloth and peered inside the basket. In place of the wine was a jug of water and two tin cups.

There were pork pies, thick slices of local cheese, and a half dozen boiled eggs. A pair of dark red apples sat on top.

"No bread," Simon informed me as I took out one of the pewter plates and began to help myself. "Apparently the noon diners ate the lot."

"This is such a lovely spot," I said. "And quite hidden. You'd never guess it was here."

"Actually, if my sense of direction is right, the flour mill is just over there, behind the trees. The mill wheel must be fed by the stream we crossed."

I turned to look, but even the rooflines were lost in the trees that followed the stream. "Grazing, running water. I'm not surprised the sheep come here."

We ate our meal, watched by the inquisitive ewes. Some of them had black faces, others had white. Finally losing interest when it was apparent we weren't sharing with them, they went back to grazing.

I took my apple and walked closer to them as I bit into it. They moved aside a little but didn't seem to fear me. Already growing their winter coat, they were rounded and fat, unlike the skinny, shivering ewes after spring shearing.

Continuing to the shepherd's hut, I peered in the only window. Turning quickly, I called to Simon.

He rose and came directly to me, leaning past me to look in the window too.

"Someone has been living here," I said. "Look, there's a coverlet on the bed, and there on the shelf, in that dented tin bowl are apples very like the one in my hand. I see the remains of a meal on the table too." A shallow enameled basin served as a plate. In it was a rind of bacon with a heel of bread.

Simon walked past me and opened the door. On a shelf was a bit of cheese wrapped in a cloth, and there were several tins of food as well. A battered teapot sat next to a tin of tea, and another bowl held fresh eggs. Someone had raided a henhouse. An old oil lamp with a cracked shade sat on a low stool. The oil was cloudy, the wick untrimmed. But I thought it still worked.

"A shepherd?" I asked.

"I don't think so. Whoever comes here lives frugally, at a guess making the best of what he found here or scavenged elsewhere."

"But someone would notice if he came into the shops—he'd be marked down as a stranger almost at once. And there would be gossip about him. Which means he must go quite a distance to buy what he needs."

"The Major?" Simon suggested. "Was this his hideaway?"

I frowned, considering the possibility. "I think he spent time in the old barn, but could he have made it this far? After all, we turned back once. How would he have found it?"

"There was the man walking over the hills. The one the greengrocer saw. If he lives in Chatham Hall, why has this hut seen recent use?" He pointed to the bacon.

I had finished my apple and was about to toss the core aside when I thought better of it. Except for the bent stalks of grass, there was nothing to show that we'd been here, in this secluded place.

"Here's a better explanation. We saw that someone had been using the old barn. What if the Major had frightened him off, and he retreated to this place? And he's kept it because he's not certain how far he can depend on Phyllis Percy's kindness." I paused. "Do you think he'd harm her? Or trust her to keep his secret?"

"I've never seen a shepherd with those sheep," Simon commented thoughtfully. "They seem to roam at will this time of year."

"Where could they go?" I agreed. "There's almost no traffic on this road, and the people who do use it would be aware of the flock."

He turned to look around. "The lambing pen, this hut, even the barn. My guess is that they haven't been kept up since before the war. A new pen must have been built elsewhere. A more convenient one." He pulled the door closed. "When winter comes, this hut will be too cold to live in without a fire."

"And that's why he's staying at Chatham Hall. But he hasn't given up the hut."

We walked back to the remains of our picnic, carefully packing up the lunch basket, leaving behind not so much as an eggshell to be found. I drank the last of the water in the jug, shook out the cups, and added them as well, along with our apple cores. Simon shook out the rug and folded it, restoring it to the boot.

We drove back the way we came, both of us hoping we hadn't flattened the grass too noticeably. But if he came here after dark, he might not see it.

"Shall we come back tonight?" Simon asked.

I smiled. "You've been reading my mind."

Passing through Upper Dysoe on our way to Biddington, we saw Maddie just coming back from somewhere, his satchel over his shoulder. We didn't stop.

"How will you manage it?"

"The flour mill is closed at dusk. We'll take the motorcar that far, and then I'll go the rest of the way on foot. I'll try to find a way from there to the hut, around the flank of that hill. The problem will be the sheep. But I saw the lay of the land, I can find a place where I can watch the hut without being seen." He looked across at me, half serious, half teasing. "You must promise me you won't come after me this time. Whatever happens."

"It's too exposed," I agreed.

And we left it at that.

As soon as it was quite dark, Simon and I set out for the mill. It was hours earlier than our previous foray, but we found the mill shut up and no one around. Still, he pulled the motorcar into the deepest shadows he could find. "Here," he said, and I felt something drop into my lap. It was the little pistol he'd given me from time to time to protect myself. "It was in my valise. Try not to kill anyone. But shoot to kill if you must."

He took the rug from the boot and put it to hand if I got cold, for the temperature was once again falling. And then he disappeared into the night, in the direction of the hut.

I waited fifteen minutes, in case he came back again for some reason.

And then I got out of the motorcar and tried to find my bearings.

There was the road, of course. The only sensible way through these hills. But the mill sat down a lane on a dammed-up stream, and if Simon was right, it was the one we'd crossed on that rickety bridge on our way to the hut. If Simon could ford it, he'd soon be in the rather triangular-shaped meadow where the sheep grazed and we'd had our picnic.

There was no reason I couldn't find my own way to the stream, far enough that I'd be able to see if a lamp was burning in the shepherd's hut. It wouldn't be—couldn't be—visible from the mill or the ruins of the barn or the road. Someone would have gone to investigate long before this.

My eyes were accustomed to the dark now. And my shoes were sturdy. All the same, I reached into the boot and found Simon's torch, in case I needed it.

Keeping to the shadows, I made my way to the bottom of the mill yard where high grass began. I wished I knew just where Simon had gone through it, to save some time, but it had been too dark to be sure. I plowed into the grass, moving slowly so as not to make any noise. I soon came to a low stone wall. I couldn't tell how far it ran in either direction, but I thought it must mark the boundary between the Warren property and Neville land. It was just high enough to stop the sheep from wandering over to the mill and falling into the millpond.

Clambering over it, I knocked a stone off the top and it tumbled down the far side. I froze as I heard a sneeze. And then there was movement immediately to my left. I fumbled in my pocket for the little pistol. Then I realized that whatever it was, it was going away from me, not toward me, as if some of the sheep had been sheltering against the wall, out of the rising wind.

I could just make out half a dozen shapes ahead of me. Something or someone sneezed again, and my heart thudded.

Somewhere in the depths of my memory, I recalled that sheep sneeze when they're wary or nervous. Was that true?

I stood still, waiting for them to settle again. It occurred to me then that whoever used the hut had a very fine ring of sentries in these sheep. They must be used to his coming and going now. But if anyone else came through—a different smell, perhaps—they would be the first to realize it.

After a time they seemed to have found a new bed and I moved forward, watching that I didn't step on an outstretched hoof or stumble over a huddled body.

A dozen steps later, I came to the stream. It was madness to try to cross it in the dark but I could follow to my left and surely find a vantage point.

Just then I saw the black bulk of the hut—and there was a square of light from the window. A dim glow, as if the lamp wick had been turned well down, so that whoever was inside could see what needed to be seen and no more.

I crouched down beside a clump of briars, and my heart nearly stopped when something jerked almost under my skirts and went haring off back the way I'd come. A small rabbit? I didn't know, only that I'd come so close to crying out that I wanted to sit down and steady myself. But there was no place to sit.

I stayed where I was until my ankles and knees were complaining. The light didn't move, and the door to the hut remained closed.

Carefully standing up so that my blood could circulate a little, I waited.

Sometime later, the lamp went out. There had been a brief silhouette thrown against the window, and then darkness.

After a moment or two, the door must have quietly opened. The next thing I heard was the snap of a twig in the high grass. It sounded terribly loud in the stillness.

I had no idea where he was going. To the barn? To the road? Or had he discovered that Simon was somewhere out there in the night?

I turned and made my careful way back along the stream, searching for the wall. I found it, cut through the high grass easily enough—and somehow lost my bearings before I reached the mill yard. Instead I found myself within sight of the barn ruins.

And I very nearly blundered right into him.

It wasn't Simon, I would have sworn to that.

He'd stopped in the shadows near the barn wall, and I thought he might be trying to be sure the road was empty.

An owl that had been hunting in the ruins flew up and climbed sharply. It must have startled him—I'd caught my breath myself—because I heard him clear his throat, as if to cover his instant of panic.

He began to walk on, out to the road, turning in the direction of Lower Dysoe, moving at the steady ground-covering pace of a soldier on a night march. He limped a little, but he was making reasonable time.

I waited until he was far enough away, intending to find my way to the mill yard before Simon came back.

Out of the corner of my eye I saw movement. Someone came over the wall near the gates to Windward, dropping silently into the heavy grass growing along its base. He crouched there, then slowly straightened, turning to look my way.

Simon? But what was he doing across the road? Had he nearly been caught and tried to lead whoever it was away from where I was waiting with the motorcar?

I looked, but the figure I'd seen by the barn was out of sight now, already around the bend in the road.

I wasn't sure Simon had seen me, but I thought it likely that he'd sensed me there, beyond the barn. He didn't signal to me to come across the road, and so I stayed where I was, waiting.

He started down the road away from me, keeping carefully to the shadows, moving cautiously, as if he were on night patrol, following our quarry.

I watched him out of sight.

Did he intend for me to bring up the motorcar? Or stay where I was? It would make more sense to catch him up in the motorcar.

After no more than half a dozen steps, I changed my mind. I had the pistol now. Simon was unarmed.

Swinging around, I crossed the road and began to walk in the same direction.

The night was quiet. I would be able to hear a lorry or a cart coming toward me or from behind me. But I took no chances, staying to the shadows wherever possible. Walking at a steady pace, I took care not to run up on Simon if he'd had to stop and wait for the man ahead of us to move on.

I'd reached the outskirts of Middle Dysoe. I was wary now. This was a hazard I'd not considered. I stopped and looked for Simon. But of course I couldn't see him. If I could, then one glance over his shoulder and our quarry would also be able to.

I waited where I was, counting to one hundred. I'd reached ninety when I heard a dog bark in a window above the general store. Someone called to it to be quiet. I began to move again, and then was nearly undone when someone opened a cottage door and threw out a basin of water, shutting the door again as a woman's voice called from another room. As I paused in the doorway of a bungalow, I heard a sleepy child's voice singing a nursery song off key, a woman's voice joining in.

It must be nearing ten o'clock, dinner over, the children put to bed, and a man stepping out for a last pipe or cigarette. Somewhere behind me I could smell tobacco. I took my time, moving on. Once out in the open road again it was growing quite cool, and I was grateful for my coat. Overhead the stars were crisp and clear, Orion shining brightly.

I hadn't seen Simon for some time. I had no idea how far ahead of me he was, but it was certain he hadn't turned around and started back. I was beginning to worry. Should I have brought the motorcar after all?

Before very long I spotted the broken wall with its covering of wisteria. I stopped well short of it.

Had our quarry chosen to go through the front gates of Chatham Hall or the farm track on the other side of Lower Dysoe?

I felt too exposed standing here on the road, but I was reluctant to move around behind the wall and into a nest of spiders. After a few minutes I hurried around the corner and up the lane, past the several cottages, to the wall surrounding Chatham Hall.

There was a thick-trunked tree just beyond the wall, and I decided that it provided as good a vantage point as any. I could see the road from there and anyone coming or going from the Hall. I swung myself over the wall just as I heard the gates of Chatham Hall swing closed, the distinctive *snap* as the heavy latch touched the heavy plate.

After some minutes a figure came toward me down the lane, moving slowly, limping a little, as if footsore. It wasn't Simon.

I clutched my tree trunk and held my breath, waiting for whoever it was to pass. Was he taking his evening stroll around the estate, after walking all the way from the shepherd's hut?

He went on past me, reached the junction with the main road, and turned toward Middle Dysoe.

Why did he come this far on foot, only to go back? It made no sense.

I waited, expecting to see Simon following him. But there was no sign of him. I looked down the lane toward the Hall gates, but it was empty.

Now I began to worry in earnest. What had become of Simon? And what should I do? Go to look for him? But I had no feeling where I'd lost him. The only thing I could think to do was keep an eye on our quarry. At least I might find Simon if I did that.

I stepped out from behind my tree, and with a last glance down toward the gates, started forward. When I came to where the lane reached the road, I peered up and down it. In the distance someone coughed. He was still heading for Middle Dysoe then.

Keeping my distance, I walked on, my ears straining to hear anything that could tell me what lay ahead. It was one thing to trail Simon, quite another to be so close to our quarry. A light cloud cover had shut out the starlight now, and several times I lost sight of him, only to pick him up again in the distance as he moved along the road.

When we reached the outskirts of Middle Dysoe I glimpsed the figure ahead of me as he paused. I realized suddenly that he must be gazing at the buildings on either side of the street, searching for something. Or someone?

I don't know what alerted me. But I knew all at once that he was about to turn around and walk back the way we'd just come.

There was no cover to be had. Frantically looking behind me, I could see nothing but the road running toward the base of the next hill. I was well and truly caught.

I could climb . . .

And so I did, going up the nearest hill like a monkey, and then dropping flat. I was on the side of it, not really at the front. I lay there, my face in my arms, praying that my petticoats didn't show like a beacon against the darkness of the hillside. And I kept the little pistol in my hand.

I could hear him walking toward me, and I shut my eyes. But he went past me without looking up. I waited for some time after he'd rounded the next bend, then clambered down, brushing at my coat and skirts as I reached the level of the road.

I set out after him, wondering what had possessed him to come this far and then turn back. Had he forgot something? Had he seen me and was he even now looking for me?

It didn't matter. I walked all the way back to Lower Dysoe, and rounded the last hill just in time to see him turn down the lane toward the gates. I followed as closely as I dared, taking refuge once more behind my tree trunk. In the distance I heard the low sound of the gate opening. Moving diagonally toward the house, I searched for a vantage point where I had a clear view of the main door. This time I'd make very sure he was inside.

But it didn't open. Instead a side door swung wide, light spilling out brightly across the lawn. He stepped inside and the door closed behind him. The light was cut off.

I stayed there a good ten minutes or more, but he never reappeared.

As I started back toward Middle Dysoe, I tried to think. Where had Simon gone? Was he waiting by the empty cottage on the grounds, unaware that the man had used the main gates instead?

Well. Simon was no fool, he'd stay where he was until he was satisfied that he'd done all he could.

And so I began the long cold walk back to Upper Dysoe and Mr. Warren's mill, where the motorcar was waiting. This time, I'd drive the distance.

I made it without incident, got into the motorcar, and after a bit, pulled up the rug.

The night grew colder, and I shoved the torch beneath the rug, turned it on with my hand shielding it, and looked at the watch pinned to my dress.

It was going on midnight.

Had something happened to Simon?

I felt uneasy, as if sitting here was the last thing I should be doing. But unlike the cavalry, I could hardly go charging in to save the day.

I tried to tell myself all was well, and the harder I tried, the more I knew it was not.

I got down from the motorcar and went around to turn the crank.

And Simon's voice said softly, "Wait."

I straightened up, looking for him, and then he materialized out of the shadows, a darker shadow moving toward me.

"Going back to Biddington without me?" he asked, keeping his voice low, but I could hear the amusement in it.

"I thought by this time you might need rescuing."

"Once or twice I wished for the pistol I'd left with you," he said grimly.

"What happened?"

"Not here. Not yet." We stood by the motorcar for several minutes. And then Simon turned the crank himself, and with the headlamps off we rolled down the lane's slight incline toward the main road.

"I wanted to be sure I hadn't been followed in my turn," he said as we passed through Upper Dysoe. "I lost him after he turned in past the barn, and I stayed concealed for a good half hour until I was sure he wasn't standing in the shadows, waiting me out."

"Which barn?" I asked, confused.

"The one that burned. He came back there."

"Did he?" I was surprised. "When? What on earth for?"

"I'd give much to have an answer to that myself."

I remembered the powders that Phyllis Percy had been so eager to replace, the ones she claimed her sister had used up. Was it for the man hidden in that house? Was he in pain, and he walked through the night because he couldn't bear it otherwise? Did he find it hard to sleep or fear crying out in his dreams? At the hut, only the sheep would be frightened.

Simon pulled up outside the hotel. "It was worth following him tonight. Still, careful as I was, he must have known I was there. He stayed in the shadows, close by the cottage wall, but appeared to be reluctant to go in, where he could be cornered. Patient devil. Rather than compromise the house, he finally left."

"Simon—he left by the front gate and returned the same way. I saw a side door open and admit him."

Even in the darkness I could feel his gaze on me.

"You—what did you do? Follow us?"

"I know you told me to stay by the motorcar, but I wanted to know, Simon. I was sure I'd be safe enough. You were between us. But that's when I watched him leave the grounds and come back again. Standing near the kitchen gardens you probably couldn't see that door open or shut. I saw him walk *in*."

I could almost feel his fury, sitting there beside him in the narrow confines of the motorcar.

"You promised me—"

"I didn't promise. You never asked me to promise, Simon. I did what I thought best. And no harm came of it." Except where I'd had to climb that hill and lie flat.

"Damn it, Wilkins knows you—you could have been in trouble."

"But I wasn't. I wasn't, Simon. I was sitting in the motorcar when you came back to the mill."

We'd turned to face each other. I was looking for a way to divert his anger, for I was too tired and cold to argue with him.

And that was when it struck me. All my fatigue vanished with the horrifying possibility.

Chapter Nineteen

"Simon. Do you think—what if we've been following two *different* people? Not one, as we'd believed? Because I was sure you were just ahead of me. I thought you'd been following this man from the hut to see where he went."

He stared at me. "That's not possible. Findley is still on crutches."

"No, think about it. What if one man is hiding, just as we thought, with Mrs. Chatham and her sister? And what if Sergeant Wilkins came here because that man is his next victim? It would explain why Miss Percy is so protective. If it became general knowledge that he was at Chatham Hall, he'd have been in worse danger. As it is, the sergeant has been moving heaven and earth to find him. He may even have thought at first that Major Findley was his target."

"Good God," he said, and I watched as his weariness vanished as swiftly as mine had done. He considered all the ramifications, taking his time. And then he nodded. "We've been thrown off the track by the Major. He was here, he was wounded, he sent those pleas to Sister Hammond. But she never considered it might be Findley, did she? She was afraid it was either Wilkins or Captain Cartwright who'd written."

"That's because she believed Major Findley was safe with Miss Neville, who probably had led the doctors in Dorset to believe she was taking him to London. And perhaps she did just that, then decided he was too difficult to be cared for in town."

"Tell me exactly what you did."

I started where I'd nearly blundered into our quarry by the burned-out barn. "And when you came out of the shadows by Windward's gates, I decided to see where the chase would lead."

"But I wasn't anywhere near Windward's gates. Bess, I followed him from the hilltops. I thought he might be too clever and double back. I've done much the same thing along the Northwest Frontier, where the terrain was much rougher. All I had to do was be certain I didn't stand out on the skyline."

"I followed two men. The one from the old barn and the one from the gates. Didn't you see us?"

"I was generally ahead of him well before Middle Dysoe. There was just one man. Bess, are you sure?"

Whoever was by the gates had stayed well back. As had I. If Simon had been too far ahead to see us, who was the second person, if not Wilkins and whoever was living at Chatham Hall?

"I saw two men walking toward Middle Dysoe. If you were up on the hills, how do *you* account for them?"

After a moment, Simon nodded. "I can't." And then he added, "It appears you've been right all along. This was the place to search."

"Lessup, the man who was killed at Ironbridge, had returned home on extended leave. Wherever he was posted before, I expect Sergeant Wilkins couldn't reach him. And the same could be true of whoever it is in Chatham Hall. He can be reached now. Don't you see? And what about Miss Percy and her sister, if Wilkins corners the other man? How much danger are they in? The servants sleep at the top of the house, they won't hear anything until the next morning, unless he's forced to use the revolver."

We sat there, staring up at the facade of the inn. Simon was frowning. "We must find a telephone, Bess. I need to ask the Colonel to look into Wilkins's military records. And Lessup's as well. He has the seniority to open them, even if they're secret. There must be more to what lies between them than we know. Then we should telephone Scotland Yard."

"Where will we find a telephone at this hour of the night? Stratford?"

"It's very late, Bess. Go to bed, and we'll deal with this in the morning."

"You won't decide to go back and search for Wilkins?"

"I promise." I handed him the rug and left him there. But once in my room I went to the window and looked out.

Simon was just crossing the yard to the inn door. I drew my curtains and undressed in the dark, wondering if I could even shut my eyes, much less sleep.

A watery sun greeted me the next morning. The water in my pitcher was cold, but I bathed anyway before dressing. I'd just wound my hair into a knot at the back of my neck, so that it would fit nicely under my cap, when there was a knock at my door and Simon called my name.

He stood there with a jug of hot water in one hand, and with the other he balanced a tray with my breakfast on it under a napkin.

"You're dressed," he said, surprised. "But that's good, we can leave in an hour."

424 • CHARLES TODD

I was ready well before the hour, and Simon escorted me down to the motorcar, setting my kit in the back before settling the bill.

"Where are we going?"

"I asked the man at the desk. There's a telephone in Warwick. It's at an hotel there. From what he tells me, it's more accessible than the one I used in Stratford. Shall we give it a try? I brought our luggage in the event we have to stay the night. I have no idea where your father might be."

The Warwick Arms was such a contrast to Biddington that I had to smile when we stepped through the door into Reception. Well-dressed guests were just leaving the dining room, and I thought perhaps there had been a wedding party.

There was indeed a telephone, we were told by the rather haughty man behind the reception desk. But it was for the use of guests.

We had to tell the clerk that it was urgent military business that had brought us here before he pointed us toward a passage behind the stairs. The spacious telephone closet had velvet seats on either side of the small table that held the instrument. In the cubby beneath the telephone were hotel stationery and a fountain pen.

"Will you call or shall I?" I asked.

"Your mother would be happy to hear your voice. And if your father isn't there, she won't be worried."

I put through the call and waited for it to ring in Somerset. After a moment or two Iris primly answered.

"Hallo, Iris. Bess here. Is my mother at home, by any chance?"

"No, Miss, she's traveled to Gloucester only this morning. She'll be that sorry to miss you. But your father is here, and about to leave for London. Shall I fetch him?"

"Yes, please."

I waited, and finally my father's deep voice came over the line. "Bess? Are you in London? I'm on my way in less than half an hour. Shall I meet you at the flat?"

"I'm in Warwick, I'm afraid. But all is well. Simon is with me, and there's a puzzle we can't solve on our own. We thought perhaps you could help."

"What took you to Warwick?"

"There isn't time to explain, and we aren't very private here. I'm perfectly fine and hope to be in London shortly. Speak to Simon."

Just at that moment a group of people, chatting together down the passage, staring curiously at us as they walked by.

Simon said, "Hallo, sir." He glanced at me with a wry smile as he answered something my father was saying. "She's safe and very much herself, sir." And then he went on in Hindi, outlining what we needed to know about Sergeant Jason Wilkins. "Anything in his background that might explain why he killed one man and could very well be stalking the next. And why he might have it in for Henry Lessup, his first victim. There's bound to be a connection. It might help me understand what's happening."

There was a pause as my father asked a question. And then a longer exchange began. I listened to Simon's side of the conversation, trying to piece together what was being said on both sides.

At last Simon put up the receiver. "It will take some time. I expect we'll be here for the better part of the day."

We left the motorcar where it was and five minutes later found a tea shop where we could sit in a quiet corner. The drizzling rain that we'd met on the outskirts of town moved on, and we walked for some time, admiring the castle and taking shelter in St. Mary's from a heavier shower. That was followed by a cold wind. I thought about France and the mud and cold rain, and men blowing on their fingers in the dark, waiting for the first sign of dawn and the next push. We stopped in another tea shop for tea to warm us. The windows were steamed over in the cold air and it was quite cozy inside, the tables spread with white cloths embroidered with strawberry blossoms. All the while Simon kept an eye on the time. A little after four o'clock we returned to the hotel. Someone else was in the telephone closet, and we waited with what patience we could muster for the man to finish his conversation.

"A penny for your thoughts." Simon dropped a penny in my hand.

I smiled. "They aren't worth a farthing. I was thinking about the witness in Ironbridge. The young pregnant woman. She was walking home across the bridge and passed a murderer. I wondered if he'd taken pity on her. Or if it was just the fact that he didn't know where to find her afterward. After he'd killed Henry Lessup."

"We'll be in time, Bess. I shouldn't worry."

But I did.

And then the telephone closet was ours.

I waited tensely while Simon put through the call.

We had to try twice more, because the telephone at the other end was engaged. I was inordinately relieved when my father answered. I watched Simon's face and realized that the Colonel Sahib hadn't found anything useful.

He turned to me. "Do you have any other suggestions? It seems that until now, Wilkins has had an exemplary career. Good man, no marks on his record, nothing that would indicate an unresolved problem."

I tried to think. We knew so much—and so little—about this man.

"His family. A sweetheart, a broken engagement?"

Simon relayed the answer. "His pay went to his mother as long as she was alive and then was sent to his bank."

"Yes, I'd forgot, his brother died earlier in the war. All right, what about Lessup?"

Simon turned back to the telephone. After a moment, he said to me, "His brother was killed. But not in France, oddly enough. In the Hoo Peninsula."

I stared at him. The Hoo Peninsula.

I could hear the young woman's voice, recounting what she'd seen on the bridge the evening of the murder. And what the killer had said to Henry Lessup when they'd met in the center of the bridge.

Well, well, there you are. I've come about Who.

Not *Who*. Hoo. I've come about *Hoo*.

It was a flat marshy finger of land that jutted out into the sea between the estuary of the River Medway in Kent and the lower Thames. There were a handful of small villages there, mostly on what was considered higher ground. Best known for its bird colonies and for the hulks of wrecks strewn about the shoreline, it had had a long history, back to Roman times and even before.

I reached out and caught Simon's arm.

"What was he doing there?" I asked urgently, and Simon questioned my father. Then he passed on the Colonel Sahib's reply.

"Training exercises. They were secret. I haven't been involved with those. But the Colonel knew about them. Apparently they have been shut down this close to the end."

It made no sense.

Simon turned back to the telephone. I could hear my father explaining something at length.

Simon thanked him, and asked if he wished to speak to me again. I sent my love to him and to my mother, and put up the telephone.

"Wait until we're outside," he said, and we walked out of the hotel in silence, to where we'd left the motor-car. It was well past teatime, the streets all but empty as the wind gusted through them. I could feel it swirling about my shoulders as Simon quietly explained my father's response to the questions about Hoo.

"Your father has given us what we need. I don't know how much Scotland Yard has been told. Bare bones, most likely. But here's the truth. Lessup had spent the war working with recruits out on the Hoo Peninsula.

A great deal to do with trenches, ours as well as the German ones. And all quite secret. There was an accident one morning and a number of men were wounded, several men killed. Among them, Wilkins's brother. There was an investigation into the deaths, even some talk of a court-martial for Lessup, but this would have made too much information public."

"Dear God. Do you think Wilkins believes these two men are responsible for his brother's death?"

"If he does, the question is, how did he find out? The Army wouldn't have told him the details. Or given him Lessup's name. But coupled with the photograph Jester's witness brought in, and the name of the victim, Scotland Yard must have begun to ask questions. Your father couldn't find who the other man is. He's afraid it might be the officer who decided not to pursue a court-martial. Effectively clearing Lessup of charges. Or the corporal who took the official blame and was reduced in rank for carelessness. He'll continue looking."

Lessup. An officer. A private.

Did Sergeant Wilkins intend to kill all *three*?

"I wish we knew more about him. The one living with Mrs. Chatham and her sister. I wish we could have linked him to the Hoo. But it doesn't matter, does it, as long as Sergeant Wilkins believes *he* knows? Even if he's wrong."

"At least when we speak to Mrs. Chatham, we'll have more than supposition to go on. She deserves to be warned. We can't wait for Scotland Yard to act."

We sat in silence for a long moment. It was the break we'd been searching for. And we'd found it because we'd discovered there were two men.

"Bess, shall we have dinner at a decent restaurant before driving back to Lower Dysoe?"

"I'm not hungry, Simon. I have the strongest feeling that there isn't much time left."

After a brief stop for petrol, a packet of sandwiches to take with us, and a thermos of tea, we set out for Biddington. The wind had dropped with sunset, but the air whistling around the motorcar was distinctly cold. I longed for the rug in the boot, for the tiny heater was struggling to warm my feet much less my shoulders. But I didn't want to stop for that or any other reason.

I said, "Sergeant Wilkins didn't waste much time finding his first victim and dispatching him in Ironbridge. Why has he taken so long with this man?"

"He may not be sure he's the right one. And the man in Chatham Hall hasn't been as accessible as Lessup. He's cautious."

"The man who came out of the Hall's kitchen door and the man you saw standing in the doorway of the empty cottage. Were they the same?"

"I thought at the time they must be. Now—now I'm not so sure."

"And which man were you following from the shepherd's hut? Which one was waiting by the gates to Windward?" I asked.

"At a guess? I'd say it was Wilkins in the hut. The man at the gate must have come from Chatham Hall. But how did he know he was being stalked? Had he seen Wilkins somewhere? Or had Phyllis Percy put him on his guard after you began to ask questions? It's even possible Lessup's sister wrote to him, warning him to be careful."

The sister Inspector Jester refused to let me speak to. We had been left in the dark from the beginning. The wonder was that Scotland Yard hadn't found Sergeant Wilkins and taken him into custody long since. Why hadn't the Yard come to Lower Dysoe before now?

Simon kept his eyes on the road, making what time he could. The rain had left puddles in the ruts, and we splashed through them. Once a badger ambled out from the grass along the verge and stared blindly at our powerful headlamps. We managed to avoid him somehow.

Thinking about it, I said, "A man with something to hide could easily start to worry. The thing is, training accidents do happen. I know that as well as you do. Why was this one so appalling that it calls for revenge?"

"I think because so many men were involved, and the inquiry into it reached a stage that court-martial was considered. Whatever went wrong, the Army tried to cover it up, because what was being done on Hoo was already secret. To a grieving brother, the official account must have appeared to be a tissue of lies. And it probably was. But for very different reasons. If Wilkins was having nightmares about his brother's death and brooding over it while in hospital, he could have convinced himself that revenge was expected of him."

After a while Simon and I shared the sandwiches and I passed him a cup of tea from the thermos. Mine was warming my fingers nicely as I held it in both hands, and I sipped it slowly.

Finally the lights of Biddington loomed out of the darkness. First a cottage or two, and then the village seemed to rush at us, shops and pubs and houses and the square-towered church near the High Street.

Our rooms were still available at the inn, and after Simon had seen to that, we decided, late as it was, we should still speak with Mrs. Chatham and her sister. I felt a wash of relief that Simon agreed with me. That niggling feeling of being too late hadn't gone away.

We set out again, following the road to Upper Dysoe, and we were just passing the turning to the miller's yard when I stopped Simon. "This is the time of night when the man in the hut is on the prowl. Be careful."

He switched off the lights and slowed to a crawl. Now we could just see the road ahead. To our right was the old barn, to our left the distant gates of Windward.

"There!" Simon whispered, pulling up the brake.

At first I couldn't see anything. Peering through the windscreen, I finally caught the barest hint of movement where Windward's wall cast its long shadow. Just then a figure appeared at the bend in the road where there was no concealment, hurrying to leave the open as quickly as possible.

"We might have bumped right into him," I said, still whispering, although no one but Simon could hear me.

We gave him five minutes and then went in pursuit. Simon kept well back, and I was beginning to fear we might lose him. The cold wind forgotten, I bit my lip anxiously, my gaze on the road, watching for any sign that we'd overtaken him even while I wanted to urge Simon to close the gap.

We were no more than a hundred yards from the lane leading to Chatham Hall when Simon pulled to the verge. "Better to walk from here. Are you game? Or would you rather wait in the motorcar?"

"I'll go. If you lose him, I can return and drive on to Chatham Hall while you search. We still need to warn those two women."

We got down, starting toward Lower Dysoe. Soon enough we saw the wall ahead of us, and by silent agreement we stopped there to look for Sergeant Wilkins. We could see no one down the lane toward the Hall, and no one ahead of us on the street. He'd disappeared.

And that was worrying.

"I'll go back to the motorcar," I said in a whisper.

"Do you have your pistol?" Simon asked softly.

I took it from my pocket and put it into his outstretched hand. His fingers were warm, mine icy. I had forgot my gloves. They were in my kit in Biddington.

I was about to turn back when a figure detached itself from a deep-set doorway near the end of the village. And almost at once, it stepped swiftly, back into the shadows.

"He's seen us," I said. "Still, we've found him."

"Stay where you are."

Someone was emerging from the farm lane that led to the tenant cottages.

Beside me, Simon quietly retrieved the pistol from his pocket. It was no good at long range, but he could move fast if he needed to.

The figure from the lane came toward us. He was taking his time, searching the shop fronts and alleys between shops and cottages.

Without warning the man who was in the doorway stepped out. He'd have been seen sooner or later, but he chose the element of surprise, forcing the other man to stop in his tracks.

They stared at each other. We weren't close enough to tell whether they were speaking or not.

I stood on tiptoe to whisper in Simon's ear. "He spoke to the man on the bridge. They talked *first*."

Simon broke into a run, with me at his heels.

But before we could reach the two men standing in the middle of the road, the one from the farm lane moved, his arm swinging up fast.

I cried out, "*No*," certain that he was about to shoot. "Please, no."

Instead he struck the other man, putting his shoulder into the blow, and his victim dropped like a stone at his feet. Turning on his heel, he raced for the shelter of the trees and the farm track.

It had happened so fast. Simon got there first, kneeling over the fallen man. He looked up at me as I reached them.

"He's unconscious. There's a pulse."

"There's blood on his chin," I said, pointing to a dark, wet patch just below the corner of his mouth.

"I'll stay here. Go fetch the motorcar," Simon told me. "Hurry."

I set off at a trot, very glad that the motorcar was closer, but I was out of breath by the time I'd reached it. Bending to turn the crank, I prayed it would fire on the first try.

Driving as fast as I dared, I reached Lower Dysoe to find Simon holding a small crowd of men at bay, talking to them. He looked up, clearly relieved as I came into view, and as I stopped, pulling up the brake, he was saying, "You can see she's all right."

They turned to stare at me. I could tell they were local men, and they had stuffed their nightshirts into their trousers, hair still tousled from sleep, to rush to the scene.

"We heard a woman cry out," a square-set man in his forties said. "Was it you?"

"Yes." I didn't know what Simon had been telling them, but I hazarded a guess. "We saw this man here being set upon, and came to his rescue."

"And what were the two of you doing walking through the village at this hour?" another man demanded.

"I told you," Simon said, his voice weary, as if he'd repeated the same story over and over again. "We've been searching for my brother. If you don't believe me, ask Mrs. Chatham. Or Miss Neville. They will vouch for us."

I wasn't all that certain about either of them.

"Who was it set upon him?" someone asked. "There's no one else here."

"I don't know, I tell you. He disappeared. It could be any one of you." That brought a growl of protest. "Or someone bent on robbery. He came from there." Simon turned to point to the farm lane into Chatham Hall.

We could be here most of the night, arguing. There was no constable in Lower Dysoe to settle matters.

The man on the ground was moaning, coming round. I said, in Matron's firmest voice, "He needs a doctor. Sergeant-Major, lift him into the motorcar, if you will, and we'll take him to Maddie."

That gave them something to think about.

Two men stepped forward to help Simon put our victim on the rear seat of the motorcar, while the others stood back, watching, still of two minds.

I covered him with the rug Simon handed to me and came around to my seat. Simon thanked the men who'd assisted him and walked around to his door.

Then, as a parting shot, he told them, "If I were you, I'd make sure none of the shops have been broken into." The suggestion worked.

That sent several men running to look, one switching on a torch to examine a door.

We turned the motorcar in the muddy street and drove sedately out of the village, only picking up speed when we were well out of sight. Simon stopped just short of Middle Dysoe, pulled to the side of the road, and got out. I heard him in the boot, searching for something. He came back with rope in his hand and opened the rear door.

Our passenger was still dazed, but he roused as Simon leaned in and tied his hands together, looping the rest of the rope around the man's ankles. I could see the whites of his eyes as he watched.

"A precaution," Simon told him briskly. "Until we know what we've got."

He said nothing, just lay back against the seat as if he felt sick.

"Who are you? Why did you and that other man argue?" I asked, trying to get a better look at him. But it was hopeless, the shadows in the motorcar too deep, and the man, whoever he was, refusing to open his eyes again.

I said to Simon, "Bring the torch, will you?"

But our prisoner cried out, and Simon answered, "We'll be at Maddie's soon enough."

We drove on to Upper Dysoe, and it was Simon who knocked on Maddie's door.

I'd expected him to be asleep, but a light shone in the window, and when he came to the door almost at once, fully dressed, I saw that he'd been sitting at the table he used for his surgeries, reading. The book lay open, the lamp beside it, and a pair of spectacles marked his place on the page. I had a feeling that he often stayed up late, unable to sleep.

He said at once, his voice carrying, "What's the trouble? What do you need?"

"We have a head wound," Simon told him, and came back to help our prisoner, first freeing his ankles.

The man moved reluctantly from the rear of the motorcar, stumbled, resisted Simon's arm for a moment, and then leaned heavily against him, as if his head was spinning.

I was just behind them, and I closed the door, shutting out the night. Maddie was removing the lamp to a tall stool on the far side of the table, folding his spectacles, and setting them with the book on a shelf by his bed. He placed a clean sheet over the tabletop and went to the dry sink where there was a pitcher and basin to wash his hands. Meanwhile Simon was lowering our patient onto the table, removing the rope and neatly coiling it.

"A precaution, to keep him from hurting himself," Simon said blandly.

I moved to one side for a better view. As Simon stepped away from the table, I gasped, feeling shock ripple through me.

Chapter Twenty

I hardly recognized the man lying on the sheet. As Maddie lifted his head to place a pillow beneath it, I stared.

He had closed his eyes, as if to shut out what was happening to him. I could see the bloody knot and scrape on his chin, and my first thought was that it hadn't been made by a fist, but by a heavy stone held in a hand.

Although he was fairly clean shaven, his hair was poorly cut, as if he'd tried to do it with a knife. He wasn't in uniform, wearing instead a heavy jumper over a flannel shirt and dark brown corduroy trousers, both of them well worn. What struck me was how thin he was, as if he had had very little to eat for a very long time. Dark smudges below his eyes told of pain and weariness.

I realized all at once that he was gazing at me. He tried for defiance, failed, and simply shut his eyes again.

It was Sergeant Wilkins. We had found him at last. And, thank God, before he could kill again.

A wave of relief swept me, and I felt vindicated for the days and nights spent away from my family and all that was so dear to me. For keeping Simon beside me, and accepting his help in my determination to find this man.

Maddie was bending over him, testing the jaw, frowning as he reached for a wad of cotton wool and deftly bathed the still weeping scrape.

Simon, watching him, was silent.

"There's a bit of dirt and grit here," Maddie said, showing us the cotton wool. "Was it a stone that struck this man?"

It was an echo of my own thought. I told him about the confrontation and the blow that had knocked the sergeant down. "I don't know what was said between them, but it ended then and there. The other man simply walked away."

"It's a wonder the jaw isn't broken," he went on. He didn't ask what we were doing in Lower Dysoe at that hour.

Maddie's question brought the scene vividly back to me. I hadn't seen Wilkins's attacker stoop to pick up a stone. He couldn't have known that Wilkins was there waiting. Yet he'd come prepared for trouble. A stone against a revolver.

But why had he left the house at all? To protect the women living there?

And where was the revolver? What had become of it? Looking down at the sergeant, I couldn't see anything as bulky as a weapon hidden in his clothing. Simon must also have looked for it while he was tying the man up, but he hadn't mentioned it. I turned and went out to the motorcar, thinking he'd managed to hide it there. I couldn't find it. But then he'd hanged Lessup. He hadn't wanted to give him an easy death. Was he planning to do the same with this victim? There were enough trees in the park . . .

I came back in, and as Maddie worked, I said, "Sergeant Wilkins? Can you hear me?"

He didn't answer.

Maddie glanced up at me as he finished cleaning the wound and reached for antiseptic powder and a dressing. Then he bent over his patient and lifted an eyelid. "Was he unconscious for very long?"

It was Simon who answered, "Yes, I was beginning to worry."

"Rightly so. He's concussed."

I could see for myself the onset of bruising. Dark red for now, but black and blue soon enough. It had been a heavy blow, even without the stone.

As Maddie finished cleaning the wound and prepared to dress it, enough of my shock and euphoria had subsided that I began to ask myself what we were to do with this man, now that we had him.

We weren't the police. We'd brought him to Maddie for treatment, but we couldn't hold him prisoner. Take him to the nearest constable? All the way to Inspector Stephens in London or Inspector Jester in Ironbridge? Hand him over to the Army? If so, Simon could take him in charge. No, not the Army, he must have a trial where he could defend himself, if he could muster any defense for murder. And clear my name once and for all.

But there was still what remained of the night. Was the sergeant fit to be taken anywhere?

That left me with the constable in Biddington. But what facilities were there for a prisoner who was hurt?

Simon was standing at the foot of the table, between the patient and the door as I worked with Maddie. Now he met my glance, and I knew he was also considering the problem of what to do with the sergeant.

I said to Maddie, "We must turn this man over to the police as soon as possible. Will he be able to travel as far as Biddington? I'd send for Scotland Yard, but there's no telephone closer than Warwick or Stratford."

Maddie's hands were busy, and he didn't look up. "I thought *he* was the victim here."

"Yes, that's true. The problem is, he's also wanted for murder."

Maddie's hands were still for a moment. Then he replied, "I know nothing about this murder. How do you?"

"He's the man I've been looking for. We've been searching for. I've told you."

"The police have not been here. The constable in Biddington hasn't told me this man is being sought." His gaze was flat.

"I know, it's a long story, it's been kept out of the newspapers."

I was intending to plead my case, and instead I stopped. It wouldn't do any good to argue. I had only to look into his eyes to realize he'd made up his mind. And I remembered too that Maddie had refused to bring in the Biddington constable when the miller, Warren, was shot. I'd thought at the time it was to protect Miss Neville. She paid in coin, not kind, and he probably needed that income. But this had nothing to do with the Nevilles. Looking back I saw that he'd refused to help me discover who'd written those messages to Sister Hammond, he wouldn't tell me who else had head wounds, he wouldn't give me the Major's name—the list went on.

Yes, I was a stranger, he had no reason to trust me, but I thought it went beyond that, to Maddie's decision to bury himself here in Upper Dysoe.

He was willing to use his extensive medical knowledge and skills to heal people, but that's as far as it went. He refused to become involved in their lives. To turn Major Findley or Sergeant Wilkins over to the police, whatever they'd done, was to accept responsibility for them.

What had so divorced him from the world that even duty was anathema to him? What had he done, what could he be hiding from, not just in a tiny cottage in this out-of-the-way hamlet, but literally in his own mind?

I couldn't solve the enigma of Maddie. And there was still the question of what to do with the sergeant.

In spite of Maddie's reluctance to talk to me, there were some questions I needed to ask, whether he'd answer me or not. "Have you seen this man before?" I kept my tone of voice light, curious, not probing. "He's been in the vicinity of Upper Dysoe for some time, I think."

Maddie shook his head. "He hasn't sought my help." He was working with the sergeant's leg now, poking and probing. The man's eyes were closed, and I couldn't judge how much of our conversation he'd heard. "I don't know how he's been able to walk. Look at this."

I did. The leg had healed, but improperly, newly knitted muscles forced to work too soon. The scar itself was inflamed, a ragged line of puffed red flesh. He would need weeks in hospital before he could stand trial. How on earth had he been able to walk miles in such unbearable pain? It must have taken every bit of his will and determination just to overcome the weariness of struggling day in and day out.

"Do you by any chance know the man who is staying with Mrs. Chatham and her sister?" I went on. "It was he who struck down the sergeant, here."

Sergeant Wilkins moved abruptly, distracting Maddie, who was trying to clean around the leg scar and urged him to be still.

So much for questions.

Washing my hands, I went to stand by Simon. He gestured, and I stepped outside where we couldn't be overheard.

"We should start for London tonight, if he can travel. Meanwhile, I'm going to the hut. His uniform may be there, and anything else he will need." He handed me the pistol. "If you need to use it, wound him. I want to talk to him."

So did I.

I put the pistol in my pocket as Simon set out for the hut, leaving the motorcar in the yard.

Maddie had finished putting the dressing on the sergeant's chin and done what he could about the leg. He came outside, leaving his patient for a moment, and crossed to where I was standing.

"You brought this man to me in ropes. Will you tie him up again when he leaves? If he is nauseated with this concussion, you must be sure he isn't left to choke on his own vomit."

"We will have to restrain him. He's a soldier who walked away from a London hotel and has been missing for quite a while. There's every reason to believe he's already killed one man. I think tonight he intended to kill another. Scotland Yard has been hunting him. We were just lucky enough to find him." I hesitated. Then I added, "I'm on leave now. But he's the reason I couldn't return to France for a time. It was thought I was his accomplice. My reputation has suffered. Unfairly so."

"You thought the Major was the man you sought," he pointed out. "Perhaps you are wrong again."

"I don't think so. Once I spoke to the Major, once I could see him for myself, I knew my error. This time I'm right. The Major has been unhappy at Windward, and Miss Neville refuses to listen, and so he was begging Sister Hammond to help him escape what he views as his prison, however handsome it may be. That complicated my search for Sergeant Wilkins."

And then Maddie surprised me. "I have known Miss Neville and her father for a very long time. They were too much alike, always at loggerheads. Strong-minded, stubborn, unwilling to listen to reason if it didn't march with what they wished to do. It brings pain and suffering in its wake, this insistence on going one's own way."

I glanced over my shoulder to be sure Sergeant Wilkins was resting quietly. He appeared to be asleep, one arm flung across his eyes, as if to shut out the light. Or the present. Then I said, "Are you telling me that the Major doesn't belong at Windward?"

"Possibly. She wants a pliable husband. He wants a wife, not a prison warder. No one has spoken of love. Do you intend to report his recent wounds to the Army? Miss Neville will be seen as negligent."

Was he asking me to do what he himself could not? Or simply speaking to me as doctor to Sister?

"I don't know. Regardless of what you may think, I didn't come here to meddle." Changing the subject, I said, "When we caught up with Sergeant Wilkins tonight we were on our way to Chatham Hall. We believed the sergeant intended to kill the man staying there. We won't be able to go there now. Would you please tell them that there is no danger? That we've caught this man?"

Maddie frowned. "It's a long way for me to travel on foot. I'll find a way to see that this message is delivered."

The miller's son? I stood there, looking in the direction of the mill and the hut beyond, thinking how much Sergeant Wilkins had disrupted the lives of people in three villages. And neither Simon nor I had intended to do any harm, but we had, because we came here with the intention of searching. I went back to watching the sergeant.

Maddie said, "Captain Chatham was not an extraordinary man. Kind and good and caring. That's all, nothing more. His widow has turned him into a saint. She sits in his room below his portrait and insists he was the bravest of the brave, nothing short of Sir Galahad. It's not healthy. For herself or Miss Percy—"

Maddie broke off, staring fixedly at something over my shoulder.

I turned to see what had distracted him.

The sky in that direction seemed oddly paler. I too stared, thinking that it was far too early for the sunrise this time of year, and besides, I wasn't facing east.

Abruptly the first flame shot high into the dark sky, then another leapt after it, and another.

Fire—

Maddie said, "My God. The mill is burning. I must find the Warrens straightaway. If you will stay with my patient?"

He was already heading for the road.

"No, wait," I called after him. "I don't believe it's the mill." But he was already on his way.

It was the hut, surely—and where was Simon? He wouldn't have fired it, there was no reason.

I spun around, heading for the cottage door. I dared not leave Wilkins alone. If he escaped us now, how would we ever find him again?

A shot rang out. *Revolver*, I thought madly—the Major shooting at shadows? Yet I knew it couldn't be him.

I came rushing through the door. Wilkins was on one elbow, staring at me, alarm in his eyes, even as he shook his head to clear it. "Who's firing? I've got to—" He frowned, losing his train of thought. "I need—*help me*," he managed to say.

"It's nothing," I said, catching up the rope that Simon had left coiled beneath the table.

Before he could guess what I was doing, I wrapped it around his hands, then around his body twice, binding him to the table and tying off the ends around one of the wooden legs, well out of his reach. Makeshift, but I didn't think in his present condition that he could free himself. And the table was too heavy to drag with him.

I could hear the frantic ringing of the fire bell at the pub as I raced for the door and cut across the yard, heading for the flour mill. The fastest way there from Maddie's cottage was through the shops and cottages across the road. My sense of direction was good enough to take me over low walls, past windows, through gardens—several dogs, roused from their sleep by the bell, barked at me, and one tried to follow me a short way—until I found the bridge over the stream that was overflow from the pond and the mill. From that point, I made my way around the mill, through deepest shadow. The night sky was red and gold, flames reflecting against the night haze, while the mill and the large adjacent shed seemed to be no more than black silhouettes.

Another shot. And it was much nearer.

I reached the corner of the shed, already debating whether to break out across the mill yard, leaving the shadows, and make a dash toward the rough grass that led on to the hut. But would I become a perfect target? I might even put Simon at greater risk trying to protect me.

I collided with a solid immovable wall, my breath coming out in a long hiss.

I hadn't seen anyone there, it was too dark. I hadn't expected anyone there.

Before I could recover, Simon whispered, "What the hell are you doing here?"

I didn't answer, just shoved the pistol into his hand. In his turn he passed a bulky, dusty sack to me, almost making me sneeze as I caught it in my arms.

Behind us in the village we could hear men shouting and running in this direction.

"They'll be here any minute. Go back, toward the bridge. Tell them the fire isn't here. He'll shoot the first person he sees. *Quickly.*"

I set down the sack and hurried back toward the bridge. Another shot, and I could swear it was by the shed. Where I'd just come from . . .

It was followed almost at once by the sound of the little pistol. I knew that sound, I knew too how short a range it had.

And someone cried out in pain.

Simon—or his attacker?

There was no time to find out. I reached the bridge and stopped the oncoming rush of men, buckets and axes in hand, bent on saving the mill.

Behind me the flames seemed to be dying down. With only the shepherd's hut to feed on, they had nowhere to go.

"It's the shepherd's hut," I called. "Down the lane past the old barn. But someone is shooting—you must be careful."

In the end, I think the only reason they heeded me was that they could see the silhouette of the mill and its outbuildings, with no sign of fire. But flour dust was quite volatile, and there was a brief argument, and questions about the revolver shots.

I heard men curse the Major, others saying he'd burned down the barn, hadn't he?

Someone shoved his way forward, demanding to know if the sheep were in any danger. But they weren't in the dell, I assured him, all the while wishing they would heed me and turn back, freeing me to find Simon.

The tail of the crocodile was already turning, heading for the road and the barn, and as the rest, still grumbling, threatening me with mayhem if anything happened to the mill, reluctantly followed, I didn't wait to hear any more. I got back to the shed where I'd last seen Simon, but he wasn't there.

It seemed to be darker now, the flames still crackling but no longer soaring high overhead, lighting the scene with that macabre glow.

In the distance I could hear a horse's hoofbeats, trotting at first and then going into full gallop.

With great care I rounded the shed, then ran across the miller's yard to the low wall and the stile.

Simon was coming back across it, and I asked, "Are you all right?"

"Yes. But I think I winged him."

"But who was it? And where is he now?"

"I don't know. He'd brought a horse. You must have heard him getting away."

I had.

And I could think of only two places—the pub and the Neville house—where horses could be found. There must be others of course, but those I knew of. What's more, Mrs. Chatham had none . . .

"What have you done with Wilkins?" Simon was asking. "Was it you who rang the fire bell?"

"That was Maddie," I answered.

"My God, he'll be gone."

"I don't think so. I tied Wilkins to the table."

Simon laughed helplessly. We hurried toward the mill. Behind us we could hear the first of the village men reaching the hut, shouting to each other in the distance.

"Duty first," I said, more than a little put out by his laughter. But that was the aftermath of worry.

We retrieved the sack I'd left by the shed, found the little bridge—it was quite dark by now—and made our way to the road.

We arrived to find Maddie untying the rope around Sergeant Wilkins, and the sergeant, paler than before, demanding to know what the shooting was all about.

"An arsonist," Simon told him shortly, and set the sack to one side. "Your uniform and other belongings," he added in explanation.

As he turned back, I saw blood on his sleeve, and I said, "You were hit."

"As a matter of fact, he missed his aim because I hurled the sack at him just before he fired. It isn't very deep." He turned to Maddie. "We must go. Will you keep him here?" He held out the little pistol. "It's urgent, or I wouldn't ask."

Maddie took the pistol without demur. I'd expected him to refuse to take it. What's more, he handled it easily.

I had the fleetingly thought that he must have been a military surgeon at some point. It all fit together too easily—his knowledge, his steadiness, and now that telltale familiarity with a weapon that wasn't the usual country shotgun.

Simon was already turning the crank, and we drove out of Maddie's yard with speed, avoiding questions from clusters of women asking what was happening.

"Why was the hut burned down?"

Simon kept his eyes on the road. "He must have seen me moving around inside and took me for Wilkins. He blocked the door and set the hut afire. The wood was old, weathered, it began to burn quickly. I kicked through the rear wall and got away. He saw me in the light from the flames and it was touch and go. I made it to the mill shed when—"

We had reached the old barn.

Men were already streaming back from the fire. There wasn't much that could be done to save the hut, and as long as the grasses hadn't caught, spreading the blaze, there was no need for this army of firefighters.

But they weren't heading to Upper Dysoe, as I'd expected them to. They were marching toward the gates to the Neville house. And they were angry.

The gates weren't locked. And so they shoved them wide and poured down the drive in a stream, buzzing like a swarm of bees as they encouraged one another.

Simon swore. "They're going after the Major." He turned in through the gates, and using his horn, he drove through the crowd heading for the door.

Someone was already there, pounding on the wood. Someone else found the door knocker and banged it against the plate.

It was several minutes before the door opened and a frightened housekeeper, a lamp in her trembling hand, demanded to know what this was about. Her hair had been hastily pinned up and she had missed a button on her dress and another on one sleeve.

Behind her, Miss Neville was just coming down the staircase, imperiously demanding what these men thought they were about.

The wait hadn't cooled their temper.

I had stepped out of the motorcar and pushed my way to the front, past the men in the opening.

"You!" she said, her anger rising as she spotted me in her doorway backed by an angry throng. "Are you behind this? Because if you are—"

I cut across her words. "Miss Neville, there was no way to stop them. There's been a fire in the village, and someone was firing wildly—a revolver. They think— they believe it must have been the Major's doing."

I felt Simon there to stand behind me.

The nearest group of men had calmed down a little, faced with Miss Neville in a temper. But those behind them were still clamoring for the Major.

"Of course it's not his doing," she snapped. I thought if she'd had a sword in her hand, she might have attacked the lot of us. "You know it couldn't possibly be."

"I'm sorry, Miss Neville," I began, just as I heard a door slam above us. "They won't listen to us." At that moment the Major appeared at the top of the stairs.

He began to make his painful way down the first flight, clutching the banister and grimacing with the effort of each step. In his hurry, he hadn't bothered with his crutches.

The men who'd reached the doorway fell back, staring.

"You men, stop this at once," he ordered, and it was a command, given in the same tones I'd heard my father use when he expected instant obedience.

To my astonishment, it worked now.

As he reached the bottom of the steps, I went to support him. Setting me aside, he made his way, furious, to stand beside Miss Neville. "Now what is this all about?"

It was the greengrocer, Hancock, who answered him. "I'm sorry, sir, but as you were the one using a revolver on the estate and were very likely the one who burned down the old barn—"

"And most likely who shot the miller, whatever he might say to the contrary—" someone else added loudly.

"—then when the hut was set afire just now, and someone was firing a revolver, you appeared to be the one behind it," Hancock finished.

Someone behind him shouted, "We've not sent for the constable in Biddington, but we will, if you can't explain yourself."

"I'm damned if I owe any of you an explanation," he said stiffly, "but for the sake of Miss Neville and her stepmother, I will ask you to come inside and see for yourselves if I had anything to do with tonight's events."

But no one stirred. Miss Neville turned, ignoring the cluster of frightened servants at the back of the hall, and set about lighting candles in the room, taking the lamp from the housekeeper's trembling hand and putting it safely down on a table near the door.

Major Findley stepped forward, intending to walk outside. The crowd fell back before him. Simon had taken my place at his side, and the Major stood for a moment in the doorway the villagers had hastily abandoned, and then kept going. Men quickly moved out of his way as he walked unsteadily but with determination past Simon's motorcar, so that everyone could see him. By this time, despite his fury, his face was pale and there was perspiration on his forehead as he struggled on.

An uneasy silence fell. The Major stopped, swaying a little, his mouth in a tight line. Simon was at his back, ready to help him.

No one in his right mind could have thought that this man could possibly have made it to the gate, much less as far as the burning hut.

Without a word, he turned and made his way back to the doorway. There he faced the men in the drive, pointing toward Upper Dysoe. "Go back to your beds. If you wish to send for the constable tomorrow morning, by all means do so. I shall be here." He almost stumbled as he tried to keep his balance, but Simon was there, lending him a shoulder.

I could almost describe it as slinking away. By twos and threes, the crowd was already making for the gates, quiet now, not even talking among themselves. In short order, the drive was cleared and the gates carefully shut behind the last man.

Simon waited until the last man was out of sight before helping the Major back inside. Miss Neville had a chair ready, and he sank down into it. Even in the candlelight he looked drained, exhausted. But he had done what he'd set out to do. Now he could admit to weakness without dishonor.

"I'm sorry," he said to Miss Neville, looking straight at her. "It's my fault they came here tonight. I had no idea . . ." His voice trailed off as he clenched his teeth against the pain.

"Thank you" was all she said in reply. Turning to Simon, she added, "Will you see him back to bed?" Then she rounded on the housekeeper and the other servants. I expected her to lash out at them for doing nothing to help her. Instead she said, "And thank you as well. Go to bed. There's nothing more any of us can do tonight."

"Should I wake up Cook to put the kettle on?" the housekeeper asked.

"No, that's not necessary. If the Major requires anything, it will be a brandy."

She waited until the housekeeper, still a little pale from the shock of finding angry men in her face as she opened the door, had gone on to the kitchen stairs.

"Tell me exactly what has happened?" she asked Simon, ignoring me.

"Someone set the shepherd's hut afire. The one up the lane, where the sheep sometimes graze. No harm done, save for the loss of the hut. But whoever it was kept firing a revolver. No harm done there, either, but the villagers were angry. They believed it was the Major. There was no way to stop them, and so we followed them here in the event you needed help." It was an expurgated version of the truth, but there was no need to tell her about Sergeant Wilkins.

"No harm done. I wonder?" She reached out and touched Simon's sleeve, where she could see blood. "I'm grateful to you."

"I could have told them I'd wounded the man with the revolver, that he couldn't have been Major Findley. But it was better this way. They won't be back."

The Major snapped angrily, "I should think not. I'll sit here all night if need be."

Simon smiled. "No, sir. I don't think it will be necessary. If you'll allow me?"

I thought the Major was going to refuse. But he nodded curtly and with Simon's help he got to his feet and started for the stairs. Then he hesitated.

"I'm sorry," he said to Miss Neville again. "I can't tell you how sorry I am."

I wondered if she knew that he was apologizing to her for more than just this night's mob.

Miss Neville said nothing, standing there watching them go. When they were halfway up the stairs, she pushed the chair back to the wall where it belonged.

"I'll be glad to see the last of you," she told me. "You bring trouble in your wake. Now tell me the truth. Who was responsible for that fire?"

"We don't know," I told her honestly. "Someone who had a horse. Perhaps from The Shepherd's Crook, perhaps one of yours. I don't think he'll go far. You'll find it in the morning."

"You're wrong. The miller has a horse, and there must be more than a dozen other people in these three villages who still have one. I doubt they had anything to do with the fire or the shooting. But you know who did, I think."

"He's staying at Chatham Hall. I can't tell you his name. He couldn't have known what had happened to the man who'd come here to kill him. We never expected he would follow that man to Upper Dysoe, to finish whatever is between them."

"You must summon the police. This is a danger- ous business. I don't care to be threatened as I was this evening."

"I shall have to send for Scotland Yard," I replied. "But first we need to make sure that this doesn't happen again. We were on our way to Chatham Hall to tell them it was over, when we saw those men coming here."

"Leave it to the police, I tell you."

But there was only a constable in Biddington.

"I wish we could. Unfortunately, it's more compli- cated than that." When she appeared to want to argue, I added, "It has something to do with the war."

Head on one side, she regarded me. "You're rather brave, if you're searching for a man who would shoot the Sergeant-Major and cared nothing for the sheep in the meadow. What if the grass had caught as well? My sheep, as a matter of fact." She glanced toward the stairs. "I'm astonished that the Major came so quickly to my aid. I could have handled those men myself, of course."

I thought it bravado on her part. The insistence that she was not dependent on anyone.

"He wanted to protect you," I said. I could hear Simon coming to the head of the stairs and silently begged him to hurry. "The Major could care for you, if you'd let him."

"Nonsense," she said sharply, but there was no force behind it.

"Please yourself," I told her. "I know what I see."

Simon ran lightly down the stairs, saying. "I gave him a little brandy from the decanter in his room. He should rest comfortably now."

"Thank you." Once more she studied Simon. I wondered if she found him attractive, or if she couldn't quite read him, and it annoyed her. Neither her expression nor her eyes gave her away.

We took our leave and she shut the door firmly behind us. Through the long windows above the door, we watched the lamplight stay where it was for a moment, and then move resolutely toward the stairs.

I saw to the gates as Simon turned the bonnet toward Lower Dysoe.

"I wonder if this man would have beaten Sergeant Wilkins to death if we hadn't come along. He was prepared to use the revolver tonight. I don't think he intended to die as easily as Henry Lessup. Which reminds me, where is the sergeant's revolver?"

"I was looking for it when the door was barred and the fire began. There was a loose floorboard that I didn't have a chance to raise. As for the man in Lower Dysoe, I don't think we'll ever know. When he set fire to the hut, he intended to finish it."

We were silent after that, tired and knowing the night was far from over if we were to drive on to London.

We'd just reached the wisteria-covered wall when I heard a horse coming fast from the direction of the lane.

Simon was already reaching for the brake.

The horse came thundering down the lane, turned toward Middle Dysoe, and swerved wildly as it came almost head-on toward the motorcar.

There was someone crouched on its back, low over the withers, and it was several seconds before I realized what I was seeing was a woman, not a man.

Chapter Twenty-one

"I think it's Miss Percy!"

"You're right." Simon turned the motorcar around and started after the horse. It didn't take us long to catch it up. Simon gave it a wide berth so that it wouldn't throw its rider.

I said as we pulled even with it, "Miss Percy? What's wrong? Where did you find this horse?"

She turned a tear-streaked face toward me. "Please, leave me alone," she pleaded. "I must get to Upper Dysoe as quickly as I can."

"Who needs a doctor? Can I help? I'm trained—"

The horse was shying from the motorcar, and Simon dropped back a little.

Phyllis Percy ignored me.

"Let her go," Simon told me, dropping farther back. "We'll only frighten that horse, and he looks as if he's been hard-ridden already."

"If she needs Maddie, we could bring him to her."

"She won't listen to reason."

"It must be serious then. Take me on to Chatham Hall. There may be something I can do until Maddie gets there. You'll have to go on to Upper Dysoe to be sure the sergeant isn't left alone."

He wasn't happy with that proposal, but we didn't have any idea what we'd find at Chatham Hall.

"I'll see you safe first, and then worry about Wilkins."

It was the best I could do.

We turned about, and he drove fast toward the village, then headed down the lane. Long before we'd reached the gates, I could see that they were standing wide and that the house was as brightly lit as if Mrs. Chatham were entertaining guests.

When I reached the door, I knocked twice before an elderly woman I'd seen on another occasion opened it to me and stared, frowning.

"You aren't Maddie," she accused me, as if I'd spirited Maddie away and taken his place.

"No. But I'm trained to deal with wounds," I said, indicating my uniform. "I'll be happy to help until Maddie can come."

She was about to turn me away when someone on the stairs behind her called, "Let her in, Mary."

And so for the first time I stepped into the foyer of this house, Simon just behind me.

"Who is *he*?" the woman on the stairs asked in alarm.

"He's a friend," I said. "We saw Miss Percy just now. She was on the road to Upper Dysoe. We felt you might need help sooner."

Mrs. Chatham was a petite woman, fair and fragile, but I could see the resemblance to her sister. Her face was pale against the heavy black of mourning she wore, even to the tiny scrap of black lace on her fair hair. *Like Queen Victoria*, I thought, remembering photographs of the Widow of Windsor.

"Then come—quickly."

She hurried back up the stairs, and I was hard-pressed to keep up with her. When I reached the top, Simon just behind me, she was just disappearing through a doorway down the passage to our right.

We followed her. It was a guest room, handsomely decorated and clearly in use. I could see clothes hanging in the armoire, hairbrushes on the top of the tall chest, a book open on the table that served as a desk. On the bed lay a man without a shirt, and beside the bed were pails of water and bloody cloths.

His eyes were closed. I thought he was probably in and out of consciousness, because there was a long crease wound along one side of his head, and it was bleeding copiously.

I glanced toward Simon. His aim had been truer than he'd thought. Here was the man he'd shot, the man who had tried to kill Sergeant Wilkins with that stone and who had then come to Upper Dysoe to finish what he'd begun by burning down the hut.

"We can't stop the bleeding," Mrs. Chatham was saying, wringing her hands and on the verge of tears. "I don't quite know what to do. I think he's dying."

Head wounds tended to bleed profusely. Yes, in time it could weaken the patient, but on the whole this man was very likely going to live to answer questions.

I took off my coat and set to work. I sent Mrs. Chatham away, asked Mary to bring me cold water, as cold as she could find, and more cloths. When they had gone, I leaned over the bed.

I hadn't thought to ask the man's name or who he was. Now I said, "Can you hear me? You're going to be all right. It's not a serious wound."

Simon hadn't spoken since we'd come up the stairs. Believing we were alone in the room, the man in the bed reared up, lunging toward me, his hands groping for my throat, his face twisted with anger. For an instant I was too surprised to fight back, but Simon was there, wrestling the wounded man back into his pillows.

"Try that again," Simon told him, "and I'll finish what I began there by the mill."

He shoved his hand under the man's pillow and pulled out a revolver. Spinning the chamber, he could see that there were several shots left. He dropped it in his pocket and stood back.

"Are you all right?" he asked me.

"Yes, startled, that's all. How did you know the revolver was there? That he'd brought it upstairs with him?"

"Because he wouldn't have left it behind. Not after what happened at the mill," Simon answered, anger still there in his voice. "He'd have been prepared to defend himself."

The man lay there. He had light brown hair, sun streaked, with hazel eyes, and they were blazing up at us.

"Who are you?" Simon asked harshly.

But he shut his eyes and said nothing more.

More careful now, I began to bathe the groove, and wished I had a little of the powder that Maddie used to stem the bleeding. Despite my best efforts, it wouldn't stop. I pressed the cloth against the side of the man's head to see if that would help.

Simon was leaning against the wall, within reach, his arms folded across his chest.

The room was silent, except for the sound of our breathing.

"Someone will have to sort this out. We can't," Simon told me in Urdu. "As soon as you have him stabilized, we'll find the Biddington constable and have him take both men into custody until Inspector Stephens arrives."

My patient's eyes flew open. He hadn't understood Simon, but he'd recognized the words *Biddington* and *constable*.

"Lie still," I said. "Or you'll pass out from blood loss."

He believed me, shutting his eyes again.

A few minutes later, Mary came back with another maid, both of them carrying pitchers of water and a basketful of clean cloths.

"Leave us now," I said briskly. "Keep watch for Miss Percy and Maddie." They had just reached the door, when I said, "Can you tell me the patient's name?"

But they looked at me, too frightened to answer, and hurriedly pulled the door closed behind them.

I turned to see my patient's gaze on the doorway.

"I expect they've been told to keep quiet," I said to Simon in English. "He doesn't look like a hardened criminal, does he? And yet he was prepared to shoot you and choke me to death."

"I'm not a criminal." The words came from the bed in a tired voice. "Just frightened. Someone has been trying to kill me. How did I know it wasn't you?"

"You could have gone to the police," I said.

"Oh, yes? Try finding a policeman here." He lapsed into silence again.

The blood was clotting now, although the wound was still wet. I left the bedside to sit in one of the chairs by the cold hearth. I wondered why the fire hadn't been lit—it was laid, ready for a match. The room was distinctly chilly.

Half an hour passed. I put my coat on again. Simon stayed where he was, keeping watch. I went to look at my patient from time to time, but I couldn't tell whether he was sleeping or simply lying there, waiting for us to leave.

Mrs. Chatham looked in on us, and then left just as quickly as she'd appeared at the door.

At length I heard the sound of horses outside.

Simon gestured to me, and I went quietly to the door, slipping down the stairs as noiselessly as I could.

But Mary had heard the horses as well. Carrying a lamp, she was at the door before I could cross to it.

Flinging it open, she called into the darkness, "Miss Percy? Oh thank heavens."

"Why is that motorcar here? Oh, God, Mary, did you let them *in*?" She came flying into the house, lifting her skirts a little to be sure she didn't trip. I heard Maddie's voice just behind her.

She caught sight of me, rushing at me, beating me with her fists and shouting, "I hate you, I hate you!"

Mary was calling to her. "Miss, he's all right, Mrs. Chatham says he's sleeping."

But she didn't heed anyone or anything. Breaking away from me, she ran up the stairs, disappearing down the passage as Maddie stepped into the foyer. He looked tired, old, as if the night had been more than he could face.

"Sister Crawford?" he said, surprised to see me. "The motorcar . . ." He didn't finish what he was about to say, turning slightly, as if to ask Mary to see to the horses.

To my astonishment, Sergeant Wilkins walked unsteadily through the door.

He was haggard, and I guessed his head must be splitting. Very like that of the man lying in the bedroom under Simon's eye.

"Why is *he* here?" I asked Maddie, although I couldn't imagine what else he could have done with the sergeant, given what must have been Miss Percy's frantic pleas for him to attend what she believed, given all the blood, was a man on the verge of dying.

"He couldn't ride, even though we could have taken Mr. Tulley's other horse. Mr. Warren has allowed us to borrow his cart." Maddie smiled slightly. "He was grateful for the effort to protect his mill."

It was Maddie who had rung the fire bell.

"Why didn't you simply tie him to the table, as I'd done?"

"He was persuasive," Maddie said. "And nauseated."

Not unexpected with concussion.

From the passage above, I could hear Phyllis screaming at Simon. Turning, I ran up the stairs. Behind me, Mary shut the door as Maddie started to climb after me. I glanced down to see Sergeant Wilkins standing there, staring after us, as if he was uncertain what he should do. Was he really so dazed still? Or was it an act? Like the nausea, perhaps?

He was a clever man. And the unattended miller's cart was still just outside the door. So was Simon's motorcar.

I stopped, leaning against the balustrade.

"You wanted to come here. You wanted to see if Simon Brandon had killed him for you. Isn't that what brought you here, when you can barely stand on your own two feet?"

It was severe and, in the view of the others who overheard me, uncalled for. I could feel their gaze swinging toward me, Maddie just below me on the stairs and the maid, still standing by the door. But I knew I had to do something to keep the sergeant from leaving while our backs were turned. It worked.

Sergeant Wilkins looked as if I'd slapped him.

Reluctantly he walked toward the stairs, casting a glance over his shoulder toward Mary. Then he started up the steps, stumbling again, as if he couldn't focus his eyes. Maddie waited for him, and together they followed me.

Drawing a breath of relief, I hurried on toward the room where I'd left Simon. Phyllis Percy was now sitting in the chair I'd used, head in her hands, crying. The man on the bed was trying to sit up. Simon, his face like a thundercloud, stood by the window.

I paused in the doorway. "Miss Percy?" I said, just as Mrs. Chatham came running down the passage from a room at the far end to see what the commotion was about.

"Phyllis? My dear, what's happened? He can't be dead. Surely not!"

She pushed past me into the room. Maddie had reached the top of the stairs now, his arm half supporting Sergeant Wilkins, who looked as if he were about to be sick. As Mrs. Chatham demanded answers, I saw Wilkins break away from Maddie's grip, and stand, swaying, in the middle of the passage.

"No," he said savagely. "I won't go in there. I refuse. Whatever you wish to say."

The man on the bed, hearing his voice, swung his feet to the floor and sat up. Too quickly, for he too looked ill now.

"Keep him out of here," he demanded, turning to Simon. "Keep him away. He'll kill me."

"Why should I?" Simon asked coldly. "You've been wanting to kill each other. You blocked the door of that hut and tried to burn him alive, then shot at him. It's his turn."

Both Mrs. Chatham and her sister cried out in alarm, taking him at his word. It was Miss Percy who bent over the bed, fiercely protective.

"You're lying," she exclaimed. "This is my fiancé. He's been lost for years. Hunted, hounded, and he's done nothing to deserve it."

"You're engaged?" I asked Miss Percy. She must have been very young when she accepted this man's proposal. Perhaps too young to see clearly. Perhaps trying for a little happiness while it seemed to be in their grasp.

Maddie moved past me into the room, carrying his worn leather satchel. He gently set Miss Percy aside and leaned over the patient. Straightening up, he turned to me. "The bleeding has stopped," he said, approvingly.

"He'll have a nasty headache, nothing more. Who was firing the revolver? Did the Major do this? Did he also set the fire?"

"It was this man," I said. "The Major couldn't have walked that far. It was also this man who struck the sergeant with a stone."

"Gentle God. Then I shouldn't have brought the sergeant with me."

"It's too late now." Sergeant Wilkins spoke from just behind me. I moved aside, and he stepped into room.

Chapter Twenty-two

The man on the bed stiffened.

"Hello, Jeremy," the sergeant said, his voice strained and weary. Then to Simon and me, he gestured. "My dead brother."

"Brother?" both Simon and I said nearly at the same time. We looked from one man to the other. I thought at first there was no resemblance between them. Sergeant Wilkins's hair was much lighter, his eyes a clear blue. And yet when I looked more closely, it was there in the structure of the face. In a photograph, where there was no certainty about the color of the hair or eyes, the similarities would have been striking. Forehead, nose, chin, even the shape of the cheekbones.

"Four men died during a training exercise out on the Hoo Peninsula," Sergeant Wilkins was saying.

"Another five or six were wounded. It was rather nasty, bodies everywhere. The sergeant in charge, the man responsible for the accident, was rattled, and he mixed up the names of the dead and the wounded. Jeremy was sent to hospital under another man's name. When he was well enough, he simply walked away. I didn't discover he was still alive until two months ago."

"But why did he want to kill you?" I asked. "And why were you stalking *him*? I don't understand."

Jeremy Wilkins pointed a shaking finger toward his brother. He seemed to be in great distress. "He's a killer. I knew if he found me I was a dead man. I want to live, I want to marry Phyllis. I've found her again, I don't want to lose her."

"Your brother is being sought by the police. Why not send for them?" Simon asked, moving from the window.

"I don't exist," he answered sharply. "I can't go to the police or anyone else. I had to do this myself. The war is finished. I can start a new life."

"I still don't know why he should wish to kill you," I retorted.

"If I'm dead, he can blame that killing in Ironbridge on me. Don't you see? He can claim he succeeded in catching me where everyone else has failed. He'll be a hero. Again."

"I should think you had a better reason for killing Henry Lessup than your brother did." I was very aware of Sergeant Wilkins standing close to me—within reach. If he wanted to escape, he could use me as a shield. Simon wouldn't shoot if I were in the way. I moved slightly, out of his reach.

"He was my older brother, he always tried to protect me. But now he's got to choose between me and himself."

"Ask him why," the sergeant said, his voice suddenly stronger, making me more wary still, "if I'm a killer, he struck the first blow. Then came after me to burn me alive."

Jeremy Wilkins reached out, pleading. "He's got it *wrong*. He was shooting at *me*." He touched the long groove in his scalp. "The war has changed him. I don't know who he is anymore." He looked around the room for support, trying to explain to Miss Percy and her sister. "Sergeant Lessup was the man responsible for what happened in that training exercise. Hoo is isolated, marshy, nearly surrounded by water. Ideal place to test trenches and trench warfare, trying to find the best way to end the stalemate in France. The Army took more than half the peninsula for it. Only, Lessup was eager to make training as real as possible. He told us it was for our own good. That we wouldn't be as nervous when we faced the real test, in France. He was ambitious, was Lessup. He wanted to be seen as the authority on trenches. There were good men there on Hoo. He wasn't one of them. He used live ammunition without warning us. It was a shambles, a bloody, stupid shambles."

"You're both deserters," Simon put in. He moved again, this time to the hearth, standing with his back to it. From there he had a field of fire taking in the entire room—and the doorway. I stepped farther away from the sergeant. "If the Army had its way, the two of you would be shot."

"Yes, well, I'd done my bit for King and Country, hadn't I?" Jeremy retorted bitterly. "I nearly lost my life. My foot is twisted, ugly. I walk with a limp, I always will. There are scars on my hip and my back as well. That's what machine-gun fire can do. I moved, just as the chaplain was giving me last rites. He called me Paul something, I didn't quite grasp it. I didn't have the strength to care. And that's when Jeremy Wilkins ceased to exist. It was the Army's mistake, not mine. When I was discharged from hospital, I had my orders for France. As Paul Addison. It was then I tried to find Phyllis. The house in London was closed—I didn't think to look here. And then one day when I was desperate, I came here, half afraid Mrs. Chatham wouldn't let me in. A ghost with no name. Besides, I don't think her late husband approved of me." He smiled at Mrs. Chatham. "I was wrong. When I fainted almost on your doorstep, you welcomed me. Phyllis couldn't believe I was alive. She laughed and cried for two days."

It was a well-told story. Phyllis Percy and Mrs. Chatham accepted it. They were hanging on every word. I found myself disliking Jeremy Wilkins.

Almost as if he'd read my thoughts, Sergeant Wilkins spoke from near the doorway.

"You were always one to know which way the wind blew, Jeremy. The only reason I might have killed Lessup was in revenge for what happened to you. Why should I want to do such a thing, once I learned you were very much alive and looking for him yourself?"

"You couldn't have known such a thing. It's impossible."

"Remember Corporal Benton? He was in the same ward when you were in hospital. He'd also known Paul Addison. He couldn't see you, he'd been gassed and his eyes were bandaged. But he could hear you. He didn't think your voice sounded like Addison's. And when you didn't rejoin your unit, he couldn't believe Addison would have deserted. But he kept his mouth shut, went back to France, and was wounded a second time. He thought at first I was you, when he came to

Shrewsbury. We sound enough alike, after all. When he realized his mistake, he told me about Paul Addison. He wanted to know if Addison was a cousin." Wilkins turned to Simon. "The Army won't give us a chance in hell. I don't want to hang. I'd rather be shot."

"You should have thought about that in London, before you dragged Sister Crawford into your plot."

"I didn't think—I wanted to believe she wouldn't be in any trouble. I had to find my brother. I went to warn Lessup, but he was already dead when I got there. I saw him hanging from the bridge. It was just before dawn. And I kept walking, all the way to Wolverhampton before I dared take a train."

"There's someone who can sort this out. My father. The Army will listen to him," I said. "We'll take both men to him."

"You will not take this man from my house," Mrs. Chatham said.

Phyllis, her face twisted by fright, asked, "Why did you have to come here? Why didn't you leave us alone? It's cruel, what you're doing. We're to be *married* at Christmas. The war will surely end before Christmas."

But we'd thought the war would end before Christmas in 1914, and we'd been wrong.

Jeremy Wilkins got out of bed and walked unsteadily toward Mrs. Chatham. His face was strained, his gaze never leaving her face. I could see, through his stocking, the twisted, damaged foot. "I'm ready to face anyone. I'm telling the truth. Just give me a chance to prove it, that's all I ask." He turned and lightly kissed Phyllis Percy. "I love you. Remember that, whatever happens to me."

It occurred to me suddenly that while he was speaking to Mrs. Chatham, Simon was well in range of Jeremy Wilkins's peripheral vision.

Without warning Jeremy Wilkins lunged halfway across the room, shoved me hard, in the direction of Mrs. Chatham, and I stumbled against the chair next to her, effectively blocking Simon's view.

Before I could recover, Jeremy Wilkins was out the door, racing for the stairs as fast as his bad foot would allow him. And Sergeant Wilkins was on his heels.

Picking myself up, I collided with Phyllis Percy as I ran to the door, shouting to Simon, "The miller's cart—your motorcar—they're both *there*."

She had taken a death grip on my apron, trying to prevent me from following. I heard it tear as I broke away, nearly tripping myself on the trailing edge. Simon was right behind me, and Maddie had come forward to take Miss Percy's arm. She turned on him, fighting him mercilessly.

Out in the passage, I heard the two men struggling at the top of the stairs, one of them shouting, "You can't want me to *hang*—"

Then they were falling. I reached the railing where the passage overlooked the hall just in time to see them strike the last few steps before landing hard on the bare wood floor below.

They lay there, tangled in each other's arms, not moving.

"Maddie!" I cried, and started down the stairs. Simon caught my arm and pulled me back.

"Wait here."

I could hear Phyllis Percy screaming as she ran after us, Maddie, older and slower, just behind her.

Simon had reached the two men, was kneeling beside them, putting out a hand to feel for a pulse. After a moment he called up to us, "I think they're both alive."

I caught Miss Percy's arm, letting Maddie go ahead of us.

"Wait," I said sternly to her. "You'll do more harm than good." But she didn't want to listen. Pulling me with her, her will stronger than her body, she went down the stairs after Maddie.

I let her go. Simon was there to deal with her.

I looked around, expecting to find Mrs. Chatham behind me as well. But she hadn't left the bedroom.

The Widow of Windsor, denying she had any part of the world her husband no longer inhabited. I thought it coldhearted.

Mary was coming out the kitchen door, drawn by the racket and Miss Percy's screams, while other servants pushed out past her to stare.

Maddie had managed to untangle the two brothers. He was lifting the eyelids of first one and then the other, then running his hands down their limbs and their bodies.

Phyllis Percy was kneeling beside Jeremy Wilkins, begging him to speak to her.

Looking over her head to where Simon waited, Maddie said, pointing to Sergeant Wilkins, "This one has a dislocated shoulder and a broken wrist. Just as well his shoulder took the brunt of the fall, and not his head. The other—Private Wilkins—has a broken leg. Badly broken, I'm afraid. There may be more injuries—internal ones. I can't be sure."

I called down to Mary. "Bedding, quickly. And pillows. We must make them comfortable where they are for now." Maddie wouldn't let them be moved until he was certain about the internal injuries.

He was already busy, with Simon's help, setting the shoulder while Sergeant Wilkins was unconscious. Then he looked at the wrist. "A nasty break." Turning to me, he called, "My satchel."

I hurried back to the bedroom. It was lying on the floor where he'd set it while examining Jeremy Wilkins.

Mrs. Chatham was still sitting where we'd left her. She looked at me, but didn't ask any questions.

I said, "Both men are still alive but badly hurt. We can't move them. I'm afraid they'll have to stay where they are."

"Yes, of course," she said, although I didn't think she cared either way.

Rising, she walked to the door, with me but apart from me. I stood back to allow her to go before me, thinking she would be going down to see to her unwelcome guests. Instead she turned toward the end of the passage, intending to shut herself away again.

And then she stopped, showing the first sign of compassion I'd seen in her.

"Phyllis loved him, and that was all that mattered to me. I was happy once, I know how it feels to be happy."

And then she was gone. She hadn't even asked if we knew yet which brother had been a murderer.

I hurried back to Maddie with his satchel. Mary had brought bedding and pillows, another maid took chairs from one of the nearby rooms and brought them to us. Delicate brocade, delicate chairs intended to be sat on quietly while sipping tea. I asked her to take them back and find more comfortable ones. We went to the attics and discovered cots, and with Simon's help brought them down along with tables to put beside them.

Phyllis Percy sat beside Jeremy Wilkins, holding his hand, whispering to him. Both men had come around but neither tried to speak.

By the time I had organized a sickroom here in the spacious hall, and we had carefully lifted both men to their respective cots, it was close to dawn, although the sun hadn't yet crept over the hills that marked the Dysoes.

Simon stood by the door. I thought he must be very tired by now, and I asked Mary to bring tea and whatever the kitchens could provide in the way of sandwiches.

He and I helped Maddie set Sergeant Wilkins's wrist, then simply splinted his brother's leg. We had no access to an X-ray. That would have to come once they were moved to hospital. Phyllis Percy collapsed from sheer exhaustion, and was taken to her room. I went up as well, found the key, and locked the door from the outside.

Simon went to Upper Dysoe to fetch the sergeant's belongings and to bring back someone to drive the miller's cart home. Then he went up to a room Mary prepared for him. I'd asked for another pair of cots so that Maddie and I could stay close by our patients.

It wasn't until late that same afternoon, after Jeremy Wilkins had been given something for his pain and was now lightly snoring, that his brother softly called my name. I got up, glanced at Maddie, who appeared to be asleep as well, and crossed to the sergeant's cot.

"What's going to happen now?"

"Sergeant-Major Brandon has sent one of Tulley's people to find the nearest railway station. He's to send a telegram to my father. Colonel Crawford."

"Yes, I remember. The King spoke of him. And when your father comes?"

"We must get you both to hospital. That wrist is very nasty, and so is your brother's leg. It's really a miracle that both of you survived your fall."

"And then?"

"We leave it to Scotland Yard to determine which of you is a killer."

"I'd wanted both of us to die, there on the stairs. Easier than hanging. And both of us *will* hang. One for murder, the other for desertion." He turned his face away for a moment, looking at nothing.

"How did you know your brother was here, at Chatham Hall?" I pulled a chair closer to the bed and sat down.

"I couldn't think of any other place to look. Jeremy couldn't go home. My parents are dead, the house occupied by others. The constable in our town is very much alive and would give him away at once. He never liked Jeremy. This was the perfect hideaway. Mrs. Chatham was in mourning, they never entertained. I went to the Chatham's London house first, you know. Expecting to slip back into the hotel before you came to fetch me. The house was closed, mourning crepe on the door. A neighbor's boot boy, on his way to the shops, told me Mrs. Chatham was in the country for the duration. That meant I had to go to Warwickshire. I couldn't go back to the hotel after all. I'm sorry. I never intended to land you in hot water. Was it very bad?"

"For a time, very much so," I told him truthfully. "It was the worst thing possible, to be accused, to be suspended from nursing. And then I was questioned by Scotland Yard about Henry Lessup's death. It was painful to be considered an accomplice to murder, however unwitting or unwilling."

He took a deep breath. "Corporal Benton knew Lessup had been put on extended leave. That meant that Jeremy could reach him, you see. I knew he'd try. He'd always been vindictive. He couldn't act as long as Lessup was a serving soldier. That's when I decided to disappear. But the Palace made other arrangements, which meant I'd be in London. The Monarch Hotel wasn't all that far from the Chatham house in London. If I was late getting back to the hotel, I could claim my friends insisted on taking me to breakfast. You'd have scolded me, but no harm done. Only it didn't quite work out that way, did it?"

"It would look very bad, in the newspapers. A hero disappearing—a mad search for you, and the dawning suspicion that you'd deserted. Didn't you think about that?"

"I did, but where could I have turned? Not to the Army. I even thought about asking you to speak to your father, but for all I knew, he'd think me mad and do nothing."

"Who killed Lessup?" I asked then.

"I won't stand up in a courtroom and testify against my own brother. Would you?"

And yet Jeremy Wilkins had said before witnesses that his brother was a murderer.

When I didn't answer, he said, "What does it matter? Scotland Yard can take their choice." He closed his eyes again and pretended to sleep.

I said quietly, my voice not carrying beyond the cot where the sergeant lay, "The accident that injured your brother was two years ago. I know he was in hospital for a time. Why didn't he look for Miss Percy after he was released? He didn't address that gap, did he? He left the impression it was only recently that he could search for her. Where has he been all this time?"

"Your guess is as good as mine. For that matter, I didn't know they were engaged. He liked her well enough, but she was only seventeen when he first met her." He sighed. "He's always been popular with women. She was lonely, she believed he was dead. I don't think she asked many questions."

But that didn't make Jeremy Wilkins a murderer. Except that when he'd appeared, exhausted, in pain, it was dreadfully close to the time Henry Lessup had been killed.

I studied the man in the bed. The cleverest thing he could do was refuse to accuse his brother.

On the other cot, Private Wilkins stirred, then was quiet again. But the light snoring had stopped. I glanced in his direction. His eyes were closed.

It occurred to me that I could play a trick of my own. Not as well planned as the one Sergeant Wilkins had played on me, but it would do.

I said, pitching my voice so that both men could hear me, and at the same time appearing to be speaking to the sergeant privately, "There was someone who saw the killer speak to Henry Lessup. This person overheard what they said to each other. And I know what it was. I was told, you see."

"Were you, by God." He waited.

"If you intend to tell Colonel Crawford that you murdered that man, you'll have to know the right answers. If you didn't kill him, then I'd be very careful if I were you, trusting anything your brother has to say about it. Oh, and I nearly forgot. I shouldn't tell you this, but Scotland Yard hinted that one of you dropped something on that bridge." I smiled. "That's why Sergeant-Major Brandon went to the hut to retrieve your uniform. We'll be looking at both tunics as soon as Colonel Crawford arrives."

I made to rise; then, almost as an afterthought, I said, "Why would Jeremy blame you last night for Lessup's death, when you'd risked your life to kill Lessup for him? He'll do it again, you know. He'll offer to testify against you, if it will save him from charges of desertion."

He said, his voice weary. "Why are you taunting me? Is it to pay me back for what I did to you?"

"That's something you'll have to worry about, isn't it?" I asked, and walked back to my cot.

It was a little after dark when Miss Percy discovered her door was locked, and banged on it for nearly a quarter of an hour. Mary took her dinner up to her, with

Simon to stand guard. Mrs. Chatham didn't appear, although she must surely have heard her sister calling to her to help, pleading with her to unlock the door.

Simon and I went for a walk in the garden, wrapped up against the chill wind, and I told him about my conversation with Sergeant Wilkins.

"You don't want him to be the murderer," Simon responded. "Even after what he did to you."

"I don't think that's true," I said, defending myself. "I watched Jeremy Wilkins's face there in the bedroom. He would happily have let his brother hang. While Jason did his best to kill them both and put an end it. I don't know what Miss Percy sees in that man. He let her walk nearly every day to Upper Dysoe. Alone."

"How many eligible young men has she met since her sister brought her here? He's attractive enough, she's lonely. She wanted to believe him. Besides, he's been pleasant to Mrs. Chatham and he's promised to make her sister happy."

I was happy once, I know how it feels to be happy. Mrs. Chatham's words.

"I won't see the end of this, Simon. I must leave soon for London."

"Trust your father to find a way."

And he arrived that night in the middle of a cold downpour, Inspector Stephens in the motorcar with him. The Inspector looked a little green, as if driving with the Colonel Sahib when he was in a hurry had not been the happiest of experiences.

They found both brothers sleeping under Maddie's watchful eye. We adjourned to the library, where Simon and I told them everything we'd done and what we thought we'd discovered.

My father listened impassively, occasionally casting a glance in the Inspector's direction. Stephens, braced with a small brandy, heard us out before asking a number of questions.

"There's the problem with the Army," I ended. "Both men are deserters, of course. Will the Army take precedence?"

My father glanced at me, as if he could read my mind. Then he cleared his throat. "I defer to Scotland Yard."

"Thank you, Colonel. I'd rather see a charge of murder and attempted murder brought. I'd like to question both men, as soon as possible. Just the Colonel and myself, if you don't mind."

Simon and I waited in the library while my father as witness accompanied the Inspector to speak to the two brothers. We said very little, neither of us wanting to speculate on the outcome of Inspector Stephens's inquiries. Neither of us felt like rejoicing.

We had done what we'd set out to do, that was all that mattered now.

When they returned to the library two hours later, Inspector Stephens said, "I have formally charged Private Jeremy Wilkins with the murder of Henry Lessup, and the attempted murders of Fred Warren, miller, and of Sergeant Jason Wilkins."

"How did you know? How could you tell?" I asked quickly.

"I brought out their tunics, telling them the same tale you'd told Wilkins. The maid fetched them for me, and the younger brother, Jeremy, was all afidget. I thought he was going to leap out of that bed and tear his tunic out of your father's hand. The older brother lay there with the resigned look of a man knowing the ax was about to fall and unable to stop it."

"But is it enough?" Simon asked. "Do you have real proof?"

"There's the young woman, of course, who saw the killer on the bridge, and the man in the garage, where the killer was waiting for the lorry. The man will remember sharing his beer. There's also the stationmaster in Wolverhampton, who can tell me which brother took the train and where." He paused. "And Mary, one of the maids, has confirmed that Jeremy Wilkins was found on the road, passed out. She was on her way to Middle Dysoe. He came to, and she brought him back to the house, when he told her that was where he was headed in the first place. The maid also remembers the rather nasty wound on his forehead. He explained he'd fallen from a borrowed horse. And that was why she found him on the road, not on the doorstep. She kept an eye out for that horse. She knew the household needed one. She even asked around Lower Dysoe, but no one had seen it. Of course they hadn't. It never got this far. Maddie can speak to the wound on Private Wilkins's head. With the Sergeant-Major's testimony, we've placed him at the hut. And both of you can describe how Sergeant Wilkins was attacked. The Warren wounding may be a little more difficult, but I'm sure Major Findley will be well enough to testify that he wasn't the shooter. Yes, I think we'll be all right."

"And the charges of desertion?" Simon asked.

"We will tell the Army that the sergeant has been helping us with our inquiries. Which in a way he has." Inspector Stevens turned to me. "I can't condone what was done in London. It embarrassed the Palace and left you in a very awkward position as well. If I had my way, I'd charge Sergeant Wilkins with obstruction for not calling in the Yard at once. But there you are. The war is all but finished, they tell me. Neither man will have recovered from his injuries in time to serve again." He paused. "The King is involved. We must tread with care."

Ambulances arrived not long afterward. One to take Sergeant Wilkins back to Shrewsbury, the other to take his brother to a private hospital under guard. I watched the brothers bid each other good-bye. It was strained, difficult on the sergeant's part. Still angry on Private Wilkins's side. He had expected his brother to stand by him, even in face of a charge of murder. Miss Percy was allowed to say farewell to Private Wilkins. She was in tears, promising to come to London as soon as possible to prove to the Yard they were wrong. She would see that he had the finest barrister in the country. No matter what it cost. She would appeal to the King.

Mrs. Chatham never appeared.

Simon and my father and I drove back to London. I was in my father's motorcar, while Simon drove his own. Inspector Stephens had gone with the ambulance carrying Jeremy Wilkins. Before leaving, the Inspector had had something to say about our search for Sergeant Wilkins, reminding me that it was the Yard's place, not mine.

I refrained from reminding him in turn that we'd been successful.

We dropped Maddie at his cottage in Upper Dysoe on our way to Biddington to retrieve my kit and Simon's.

As we turned toward Biddington, I said to my father, "Inspector Stephens is expecting Maddie to testify. He won't. I know him too well."

"I daresay he'll be willing." In the darkness I could see the certainty in my father's face. But I didn't think even the Colonel Sahib could sway Maddie.

He glanced across at me. "This is for your ears only, my dear. The man you call Maddie isn't what he appears to be. It was the Second Afghan War. 1878. Your grandfather's war. An Army surgeon by the name of Dr. Madison was serving in another regiment. Disease killed more men than battle did, and he worked tirelessly in appalling conditions, without regard for himself. God knows how many lives he saved. Your grandfather was wounded, as you know, and he'd have lost his arm if it hadn't been for Dr. Madison. There was talk of a VC, but nothing came of it. And then, worn out by what he'd been through, the doctor was invalided home. He left the Army as soon as he could, and shortly afterward disappeared. My father searched for him whenever he was in England and was finally convinced that he was dead."

"But how could you know this man was Maddie?"

"He always carried that leather satchel with the long strap. I noticed it at once. God knows my father described it to us often enough. And I asked him outright. I also made him a promise. He can remain anonymous. An elderly doctor tending the people of three small villages in the middle of nowhere? No one will recognize him as the hero of Kandahar. He'll return to Warwickshire, and who will be the wiser?"

"The newspapers—"

"Inspector Stephens sees him as he is today. I've made sure of that. Why should the newspapers know any better? If Miss Neville were involved, it might be very different. Mrs. Chatham and her sister are of little interest in the popular press. Besides, the government will wish to keep Hoo out of the newspapers. They'll not care for any additional sensationalism."

I had my doubts all the same.

Two days after we reached London I was boarding my transport to France.

As we sailed out of Portsmouth harbor, I waved good-bye to my parents, who, having seen so little of me, had been determined to enjoy every minute left of my leave.

Simon had been called away.

I had spent so much time in his company of late that I found myself missing him.

A letter from the Queen Alexandra's Imperial Military Nursing Service found me in France soon after I'd arrived at my first posting. It informed me that all questions about the performance of my duties in the matter of Sergeant Wilkins's activities had been permanently removed from my record. I carefully restored the letter to its envelope and tucked it in my kit. It had been a long journey, earning that restoration of my good name. It was possible that either the Army or Scotland Yard would have sorted out Sergeant Wilkins's guilt or innocence eventually. But I wasn't convinced of it.

Much later my mother sent me the cutting. Jeremy Wilkins had been convicted on all charges, even as he denied any role in the events. His brother had refused to testify against him. Miss Percy was not there in the courtroom when the verdict was handed down. In spite of her promises of support.

According to the newspaper cutting, Dr. Lawrence Madison had made an impression on judge and jurors alike with his clear, comprehensive account of events.

My father had kept *his* promise to Maddie. No mention was made of Dr. Madison's previous service. He'd been sick of war, and he'd found in the isolated world of the Dysoes a haven of peace. Villages that had escaped so many armies century after century hadn't managed to avoid the Great War completely. Major Findley, the Wilkins brothers, and how many others had brought the fighting closer than Maddie had ever dreamed.

Still later, my mother sent another cutting. It was the brief announcement of the engagement of Miss Barbara Alice Mary Neville to Major Arthur James Clifton Findley.

And I was back at the Front, where I belonged. For now.

About the Author

Charles Todd is the author of the Bess Crawford mysteries, the Inspector Ian Rutledge mysteries, and two stand-alone novels. A mother and son writing team, they live in Delaware and North Carolina, respectively.